Malpractice

Growing up in the enchanting west of Ireland gave Rory McCormac a love of nature and an individualistic outlook on life, while veterinary practice there and in Malta and Oman has 'unfurled new perspectives'. Despite his enthusiastic wanderlust, he still calls Connemara home. He is married, with two grown sons. *Malpractice* is his third novel featuring Frank Samson. It follows *Playing Dead* and *Outbreak*.

Also by Rory McCormac
Playing Dead
Outbreak

MALPRACTICE

Rory McCormac

ARROW

Published by Arrow Books in 2000

1 3 5 7 9 10 8 6 4 2

Copyright © Muiris O'Scanaill 2000

Muiris O'Scanaill has asserted his right under
the Copyright, Designs and Patents Act, 1988 to be
identified as the author of this work

First published in the United Kingdom in 2000 by Arrow Books

Arrow Books
The Random House Group Limited
20 Vauxhall Bridge Road, London, SW1V 2SA

Random House Australia (Pty) Limited
20 Alfred Street, Milsons Point, Sydney,
New South Wales 2061, Australia

Random House New Zealand Limited
18 Poland Road, Glenfield
Auckland 10, New Zealand

Random House (Pty) Limited
Endulini, 5a Jubilee Road, Parktown 2193, South Africa

The Random House Group Limited Reg. No. 954009

www.randomhouse.co.uk

A CIP catalogue record for this book is available from the British Library

Papers used by Random House are natural,
recyclable products made from wood grown in sustainable forests.
The manufacturing processes conform to the environmental
regulations of the country of origin

ISBN 0 09 960741 7

Typeset by Deltatype Ltd, Birkenhead, Merseyside

Printed and bound in Great Britain by
Cox & Wyman Ltd, Reading

For Ciarán

ACKNOWLEDGEMENTS

I'd like to acknowledge the contribution made by my wife Alex who constantly encouraged me and kept my nose firmly to the grindstone, and to my agent, Dinah Wiener, for all her help and advice. Thanks also to Peter and Paula Vine who thought it all worth it, and to my sons, Cormac and Ruairi, who lent me their names. I must also acknowledge the generous assistance of my friends in the field of human medicine: Doctor Elizabeth Clarke and Doctors Michael and Dominique Geary. And of course, I should like to thank the friends who have helped me along the way: Chris and Sally Holt, Roger and Gay Greene, Mike and Frances Tierney and Chris Moseley.

I

The building was a plain two-storey structure without character or ornament, its red-brick façade breached at street level by three tall windows and a door, all freshly painted a glossy white. Behind the four upstairs windows fluorescent tubes burned, despite the fact that it was bright afternoon on this side of the Venetian blinds. Offices. I stepped reluctantly from the Land Rover, locked the door and, when the traffic broke briefly, darted across the street.

To the left of the neo-Georgian door, a shiny half-circle of brass was fixed to the wall. It read: MARBHLANN CHATHAIR ÁTHA CHLIATH, in a vaulted arc and, underneath, straight across, the translation: DUBLIN CITY MORGUE. When I fingered the enamel bell button, the door clicked inwards to reveal a small porch, barely big enough to stand in. An inner door, a lattice of small, bubbled panes, cut off the rest of the building.

I rubbed my palms along the seams of my chinos and nervously cleared my throat as a figure approached from the other side, undefined and wavery, like a diver coming to the surface of a ruffled sea. The polished knob turned and the door, brushing noisily across the rough-fibre foot mat, swung in. An intense-looking young man in a starched lab coat gave me a keen look, professionally assessing my level of grief. 'Good afternoon,' he said. 'May I help you?'

'I've come to identify a . . . I'm supposed to meet an Inspector Curley here, at four thirty.'

He checked a notebook. 'So, you'll be . . . Mr Samson?'

I nodded, tried to say 'That's right', but only managed a gravelly laryngitic croak.

He motioned me through, showed me to a small, sparse waiting room and said: 'You can wait in here. It's only twenty past. If it's Inspector Curley, he'll be right on time, as usual.'

I cleared the throat. 'Thanks.'

'Do you need anything?'

'No, thank you. Nothing,' I assured him.

'A cousin, wasn't it?' he murmured, again consulting his book.

'Yes.'

'My sympathies,' he said automatically. He nodded and headed for the door. Evidently, cousins of corpses didn't come high on his list of bereaved needing special handling. Never too many hysterics over cousins.

I held the vague smile until he'd gone out, then picked up a newspaper from a chipped formica table and chose one of the three unmatched chairs which completed the small room's impersonal furnishings. I could feel myself shaking all over and was surprised that, externally, the tremors didn't show. My throat burned with nervous bile. On the way here I'd gone through wide mood swings, oscillating between despair and wild hope but now, inside this grim building with its silent atmosphere of finality, the indicator pointed in one direction only and it wasn't towards hope. I stared unseeingly at the front page – since this morning's phone call I hadn't been able to concentrate and the 200-mile drive from Carndonna in the far north of Donegal had passed in a blur.

There are cousins and there are cousins.

Despite Curley's blunt assertion that the identification process was a mere legal formality, I still harboured a faint hope that it wouldn't be Dave. I'd asked him how he could be so sure and he had replied with grim irony that they knew it was Dave because they knew Dave well – they'd been watching him for months. I'd asked him what he meant by that, but he had refused to elaborate, merely repeating that he would meet me at the morgue at 4.30. He'd apologised for the fact that I'd have to travel such a distance. Actually, it was no problem – I'd been planning to go to Dublin for the weekend anyway – but I didn't tell him that.

I tried again to concentrate on the paper, but my hands were now shaking so badly that the pages actually rustled.

Oh, sweet Jesus! It just couldn't be Dave. People didn't just die at our age. There had to be a mistake. I abandoned the paper and slumped forward on the armchair, elbows on knees, fingertips massaging my temples. Closing my eyes tight, I tried to visualise Dave lying dead. Had he been wounded? Was he disfigured? Had he been in a car crash? Would his face, so similar to mine, be marked, broken . . . I wished I'd asked the bloke in the white coat what had happened, how Dave had died and why the police were involved.

I tried again to summon a mental image of a strange, lifeless Dave but, although I could visualise him lying, pale and cold, on a marble slab, his chest kept rising and falling, up and down, with the regularity of a metronome. Please, God, let it not be Dave!

The doorbell rang again and I jumped. The shrill peal was followed at once by a tapping on the inner door and a voice calling loudly: 'Anybody home? Bill? Bill?' A moment later the man who had let me in led two men into the waiting room and made introductions. Inspector Curley turned out to be as bald as a brown trout, middle-aged, short, overweight and grumpy-looking. His sergeant, Flynn, was tall, consumptively thin and stooped – a classic vaudeville duo. Flynn even had the morose expression.

'Sorry about this, Mr Samson.' Curley shook hands briefly. 'I appreciate that it's a very unpleasant duty but, as I told you this morning, it's a formality we have to go through, a legal requirement. I assure you we'll be as quick as we can.' He looked around at the others, then back to me. Patting the pockets of his overcoat, he said with forced enthusiasm: 'Well, then . . . If everyone's ready?' I wanted to ask him what had happened, to prepare myself, but they were already filing out of the tiny room and I had no option but to follow.

Bill led us towards the rear of the building, smells redolent of carbolic and formaldehyde becoming stronger as we went, turning corners in an extremely crooked and pungent corridor until we came to large, white double doors. There he paused, hand spread on the door, ready to push. He looked questioningly at me, giving me a last chance to compose myself – he must have been through this routine a thousand times – and, when I nodded, briskly ushered us in. The knot in my gut, which had started with Curley's morning phone call, began to twist and writhe and coil, threshing within me like a wounded snake, and I thought I might be sick.

The room was lined with huge metal drawers and was tiled in white from the high ceiling to the floor, which sloped gently towards a shallow central gully; this in turn emptied into a covered drain. In the centre stood three enamel tables, some seven feet long and three wide. Two were empty but, on the one nearest us, a draped human form lay, so still and unlifelike that it might have been part of the table. I faltered for the brief second it took for my last, forlorn hope to ebb – even tented and petrified beneath the shroud, I knew it was Dave.

'Just a quick look,' Curley whispered, as if we were in church, and propelled me forward by the elbow to where Bill waited at the head end of the corpse, the sheet hem gathered in his hands. He gave me another querying look, I replied with a further nod and then, with great sensitivity, he exposed my cousin's face and neck. Because of the police interest, I had prepared myself for the most appalling signs of violence – a slashed-open throat, or multiple, livid stab holes, or blackened gunshot wounds with enormous exit craters, or mashed and bloodied features unrecognisable from some horrendous road accident – and I was oddly relieved to see that not a single mark disfigured Dave's face.

Peeping out from under the upper end of the sheet, I could see the beginning of what I took to be the pathologist's incision and, overcome by a sudden feeling that I had to check for myself, I took hold of the hem and, to the alarm of Bill, uncovered Dave's corpse to the navel. Apart from the large autopsy incision, the body was unmarked. I laid my hand gently on the icy forehead, said: 'It's Dave,' then, trailing my hand down over his shoulder and along his stiff-cold arm, I held his hand briefly. Then I turned away and headed, through the blur of my gathering tears, for the door.

Upstairs in one of the offices facing the street, I dumbly signed whatever they put before me, then asked where the bathroom was. On my way, it suddenly struck me that outside this overheated, stuffy building with its respectful atmosphere and hushed undertones of death, traffic was rushing by busily, tyres swishing on wet streets, little winds blowing leaves around in tiny circles. I decided that I needed normal life signs much more than I needed the bathroom, so I ran down the stairs and just kept going for the street.

Curley caught up with me on the pavement, where the torrent of traffic, in full spate between me and my Land Rover, had forced me to halt. 'Don't you even want to know *how* he died?' he panted, voice raised against the rush-hour city. He must have heard my rapid feet on the stairs – probably nobody had ever run in that depressing building before – or maybe he just happened to be looking out of the window when I made my urgent exit.

'Leave me alone,' I said wearily. As far as I was concerned, the details could wait. I was still a long way from coming to terms with the fact that Dave was actually dead and I didn't really need the extra grief. Especially from the police. Still . . . 'How?' I asked, turning to face him.

'OD. Heroin.'

I looked at him in disbelief. '*Dave? On heroin?* You're out of your mind!' I turned back towards the road but there was no way across, not until the lights changed. Heroin, my ass! Dave was one of those people who can't bear not being in full control of themselves. He was almost teetotal – a glass of wine at Christmas or champagne at a celebration. A three-packs-a-day man from his youth, he'd even managed to quit smoking a couple of years back, although he'd had to enlist the help of a hypnotist to kick the habit. To someone like that, heroin would be anathema. However, there didn't seem to be much point in elaborating on Dave's abstemiousness to Curley who was now, despite the fact that he was talking to my totally uncommunicative back, warming to his subject.

'I hate to disillusion you,' he said apologetically, 'but he was full of it. I can't remember the exact amount, but the doc said he had enough in him to kill a horse. Being a vet, you might know how much that would be?'

'I wouldn't. Horses don't take heroin.'

'Horse sense, aye? Heh, heh.' When that little joke fell flat, he went on, 'Found dead in his flat this morning, he was. Dead about six hours, the doc reckoned.'

'Who found him?'

'A girlfriend of his. A Rachel Donaldson. Do you know her?'

'Never heard of her. Were they living together?'

'No. She and your cousin were supposed to be going for a short holiday today and she began to worry when she couldn't get him on the phone this morning. Their flight was for the early afternoon so she drove over and knocked on the door. That was about nine o'clock. When there was no reply, she called the building superintendent and he opened the door.'

'And then she called you?'

'Well, not me personally, but that's what happened.'

'What does she have to say about it?'

'She had no idea that your cousin took drugs.'

'She's right. He didn't. Had she been with him last night?'

'No. She hasn't seen him for a week. She's a lecturer in geology and she was off on a field trip with a bunch of students. She didn't get home until about midnight and she went straight to bed.'

6

'She was with students till midnight. Does she have an alibi for the rest of the night?'

'Alibi?' He cocked his head sideways at me and frowned. 'Why should anyone need an alibi? It was an accident.'

I shook my head in denial, but didn't turn. 'If they found heroin, then, believe me, it was no accident. Someone gave it to him. Dave was a fitness freak and I can assure you he was not into heroin; nor any other form of substance abuse, either.'

'What?'

I repeated it, this time louder, but Curley just shouted 'What?' again, also louder.

I turned because it was important that he heard my opinion . . .

Curley was grinning at me – he'd heard me perfectly well; he just wanted me to turn. 'I must say that's what I thought at first, too. We were a bit surprised ourselves.'

'Why should *you* be surprised?' Smart bastard, Curley. Despite myself, he'd got me talking.

'I told you this morning. We've been watching him . . .'

'Then you ought to know that he wasn't on drugs,' I snapped.

'When did you last see him?' he parried.

'May eighteenth, about a quarter to midnight.'

That shook him a bit. 'But that's nearly a *year* ago, man! How can you be so precise?'

'May eighteenth is our birthday. We had dinner together – we always do on our birthday. We finished about half-eleven.' I thought back for a moment; it was, or used to be, an annual event; and now it never would be again, never, ever. 'We were born on the same day.' I sniffed, again feeling the tears on the way. 'Just seven hours apart. Twin cousins. We even *looked* alike.'

'I can see that.'

'I must have been five before I realised that we weren't brothers.'

Suddenly I was weeping. I laid my arm against a lamp-post, rested my head on it and sobbed quietly until I got it out of my system. When I raised my red, stinging eyes again, Curley was still there.

'C'mon,' he said gently, draping an arm over my back and nodding towards a pub a few yards along, 'I'll buy you a pint.' He beckoned to Flynn who was sitting, watchful, in their car.

Nothing was said until we were seated, three black pints of porter on the low table between us. '*Sláinte mhaith*,' Curley said and took a mighty draught from his glass. Raising my pint towards him, then Flynn, I sniffed in moist reply and followed suit.

'So, then.' Curley wiped the creamy froth from the length of his upper lip and squinted across at me through the smoke-smeared pub air. 'What can you tell us about your late cousin?'

'Apart from family stuff, not a lot. Since I started my locum business I've been moving about the country a fair deal, so we didn't see as much of each other as we used to.' I placed my glass back on its coaster.

'Do you know what he did for a living?'

I thought for a moment and found that, oddly enough, I didn't. At least, not in any detail. 'Not exactly. Some kind of middleman, I think. Putting sellers in contact with buyers, finding things that people wanted, that sort of thing . . . I don't know what you'd call it, precisely. A fixer, maybe? A facilitator?'

'Go on.'

'That's all I know. He wasn't on a salary – he made his money on commissions. He seemed to be doing fairly well.' I had a sudden memory. 'Last time we met – as I told you, on our birthday – he gave me a present of this fantastic state-of-the-art sound system.' I smiled ruefully. 'I felt lousy, because all I had for *him* was a mickey mouse ballpoint and propelling-pencil set which someone had given *me* for Christmas. Look . . . I've asked you already – do you mind telling me just *why* you were watching him?'

Both men took simultaneous draughts from their porter

glasses and exchanged glances. It was clear that they were playing for a few seconds' time to get their approaches right.

Then Curley began, 'I'm afraid, Mr Samson, that your cousin was *not* a middleman, at least not in the sense that *you* mean.' He lifted his pint again, watching me over the rim of the glass to see how I was taking it; then, setting the glass back down on its coaster, untouched, he continued: 'We have very strong reasons to believe, in fact we *know*, that he was a receiver of stolen goods, a buyer and seller of narcotics, a smuggler of anything he could sell for profit, a gun-runner, a dealer in armaments and a sanctions buster. He tried his hand at fraud, forgery, blackmail, robbing jewellery shops . . . He was very clever, but then, so are we – even if it sometimes takes us a while longer than we'd like – and we were closing in on him. It was just a matter of time before either we nailed him, or . . . he ended up dead. Life expectancy in his line of business is low, although they all think they can beat it.' He shook his head ruefully, philosophically. 'It's ironic that he should have died accidentally in the end,' he mused. 'I'd have bet my pension that Dave Ryder would have been murdered.'

My faculties were now thoroughly scattered, bludgeoned into disarray by Curley's litany – it seemed to cover the whole criminal spectrum bar genocide. In a numbed stupor I tried to fit in the charges with Dave's eternally sunny personality, but couldn't. Eventually I managed: 'Well if you actually *expected* him to be murdered, then how come you've ruled out murder so quickly?'

'The pathologist found no marks to indicate physical restraint and nothing in the body to suggest chemical restraint – no sleeping tablets or the like. They've got machines now, you know, that can check for hundreds of different substances at the same time and, in your cousin's case, the only wrong one that spiked was heroin. There was nothing to suggest that the heroin had been administered by anybody but himself. His prints, and only his, were on the syringe . . . As for suicide, there was no note and no evidence from our recent surveillance that he was depressed, worried . . .'

I interrupted him impatiently. 'I *know* it wasn't suicide. Not Dave . . . But I also know it wasn't an accident. Dave was no dope user. Believe me. I *knew* the guy.'

My companions exchanged glances again. 'With all due respect, Mr Samson, I don't see how you can claim that. I mean, *you* thought he was an honest agent . . .'

'That's different. That's a *totally* different thing. I'm talking about whether he used drugs or not. Christ, man, did you not notice the chest and arms on him? Built like bloody Tarzan, he was.'

Flynn spoke for the first time: 'True. If that man was on heroin, then I reckon the government ought to make it compulsory . . .' He tailed off as we both swung astonished stares towards him and, by wrinkling the bridge of his long nose, contrived to turn his nascent grin into a grimace, followed by a small cough and a large blush. Having accomplished which, he sought refuge in his pint glass.

Curley said to me: 'Nobody is suggesting that he was a *regular* user – he only had one needle hole in him, after all – but every user has to have a first time and it's easy to see how a first-timer could make a mistake. With heroin, even one mistake is more than you're allowed. It's not like riding a bike, you know. Where you can keep falling off for weeks before you get the hang of it,' he added pedantically, in case I wasn't following his drift.

Once again it was obvious that I wasn't going to get far by labouring Dave's abstemiousness and clean living record.

'Was his door locked from the inside?' I tried another angle. 'You know, chain across, etc.?' I knew the chain couldn't have been across because the supervisor had been able to get into the flat with his master key. Still, I thought I'd ask, if for no better reason than to change the subject.

'No chain, but then lots of people *don't* use their door chains – especially young men.'

'Don't you think that's extremely odd for a man in the dangerous business *you* claim Dave was in? Surely, more than almost anyone else, he'd have the most up-to-date security and alarm systems? And use them? Unfailingly. Maybe you're mistaken about him?'

Curley shrugged, reluctant to get into that again, and had a quaff.

'No sign of forced entry?' I asked after a considerate pause to let him swallow.

'Of course not,' he snapped a shade testily. 'If there had been, we wouldn't be treating it as an accident, now would we?'

'So if someone had been in the apartment with Dave, they'd just have to pull the door shut after them as they left and no one would be any the wiser?'

He shrugged again.

'Was Dave being followed last night?'

'Yes, but we lost him for about two hours . . .'

'Oh, great. Well done.'

'Look, we were just keeping an eye on him, to build up a picture of his haunts and contacts. A one-man tail is going to get lost many times in a busy city.'

'Fine,' I said in placating tones, as if everyone in the whole wide world knew that. 'Great!' I showed him a soothing palm. 'But you can't say then, can you,' I hauled him back to the point, my point, 'whether or not he came home last night with somebody?'

'Oh, yes, I can. When he lost him, our man went back to the apartment block. Your cousin arrived home just after midnight, alone. I realise that that in itself doesn't rule out anything,' he conceded generously, 'but our man saw no one that *we* knew go in. And many of your cousin's "friends" are known to us, *well* known to us. But then again, that block, as you probably know . . .'

'I've never been to Dave's apartment.'

'Whatever . . . Anyway, that block has four doors into the foyer – one from each side. The tail could only cover one, so he obviously picked the one nearest your cousin's parking space, the door he always used. So, you're right – someone *could* have gone in through one of the other three doors. The

11

night desk man says he saw nobody last night who didn't actually live there. None of the other residents saw any strangers either, but they all claimed that the night man is rarely at the desk after midnight. He's supposed to be there all night, fancy apartment block like that.' He paused a moment. 'Did you ever notice drugs or syringes and needles unaccountably missing from your car or surgery? Or did your cousin ever approach you about supplying him with drugs of any kind? Or even just *hint*?'

I exploded indignantly. 'He most certainly did not! First off, I use only veterinary drugs which, I imagine, do not exactly fetch millions on the streets. Nobody is going to get high on anything that I use . . . Besides, I don't actually own or carry any drugs at all. So, in fact, I have nothing to give, to Dave or to anyone else. I do locum work only, and all drugs, syringes, needles and the like are provided by whatever practice employs me.'

'You don't keep a supply at all? Even a small store – for emergencies?'

'If I'm not in practice, then how in the hell can I have emergencies?'

Curley, unimpressed by my smarmy reply, summarised: 'So, if you don't actually *carry* drugs, then your cousin would never have asked you for them and couldn't have stolen any from your car or home.'

'What the hell do you mean?' I demanded. 'Dave would never steal.' Then, feeling a little foolish, I added lamely, 'Well, not from me, anyhow.' I took a swig. So did they.

A few minutes later, during which I asked all the questions and Curley seemed to have all the answers, we finished our pints and I called to the barman for the same again. In unison, they stopped me – they didn't drink on duty. I glanced involuntarily at their empty glasses and Curley said: 'Sure that was only a pint, man. You wouldn't call *that* drinking!'

We left the bar together, with me promising to contact Curley if I had any helpful thoughts. He gave me a card, writing his home number on the back. I watched them drive off, then, suddenly overcome by a vast, gnawing loneliness, turned and went straight back in. By the end of my third pint I'd come to accept that what Curley had said about Dave just might have a grain of truth to it.

2

I sat at the bar, hunched over my new pint, hating myself for
having even listened to Curley's damned lies. Talk was
cheap, but where was the proof? If Curley was so goddam
cocksure, then why hadn't Dave been arrested and charged?
He'd made Dave sound like a one-man crime wave, so why
had he still been at large, a sitting duck for any lowlife with a
hankering to murder him? Curley should be the one being
asked the awkward questions, not me. I grew more and more
angry with myself as I began to think of whole lists of
questions that I hadn't thought to ask. I sat, getting slowly
drunk and thinking furiously.

Maybe Dave hadn't been arrested because the evidence
against him was not yet watertight. Perhaps his continued
freedom was a tactical matter – the police might, for instance,
have been waiting for the last pieces of evidence which would
enable them to round up a whole gang of crooks . . . By the
time I called for yet another pint, the list of Dave's crimes
was swirling endlessly through my head – stolen goods,
narcotics, smuggler, gun-runner, fraud, forgery . . . In the
end, try as I might to find something exonerating, I had to
admit that Curley's charges were possible – in fact, if Dave
had not been my closest and oldest friend I'd have had little
bother in accepting them. Actually, with hindsight, some of
his accusations even made sense of a few of the odd little
mannerisms and ways that Dave had been developing about
him for some time now – some years, come to think of it . . .

As a boat lifts free of the sucking mud on the incoming tide, my thoughts began to float buoyantly on a black swell of Guinness and, freed from the restrictions of logic and reason, moved backwards in time, ignoring chronology or order. Isolated incidents became almost as one as they merged and knitted, willy-nilly, into the image of this new Dave, Curley's Dave.

I remembered how he would always change the topic if anyone mentioned his work. He'd dismiss it with a grimace and claim that it was so boring that he had no intention of spoiling the night, the party, the meal, or whatever, by talking about it. The nearest he ever came was one evening when he and I met for a drink and I remarked that he was looking a bit down. Things, he said, were not too good at the moment 'at work'. When I asked him what work, he mumbled: 'Import–Export, Pharmaceuticals.' Which, I now supposed, was a euphemism that any drug dealer with attitude might employ.

Thoughtfully I sucked at my pint.

And what about all the expensive presents he gave me? These were always dismissed laughingly – like the recent Hi-Fi. 'If only you knew, Frank, how little that cost me, you'd be insulted. I swear! I bought a job lot of them for a song – they were supposed to be fire-damaged – but ninety per cent of them were perfect. Not as much as a *scratch* on them.' Fire-damaged sale was one explanation; another was that the goods were hot for another reason, which had nothing whatever to do with fire. Jeez, I hoped I wouldn't have to give that Hi-Fi back. It was only brilliant.

Then there was the sunny afternoon at the traffic lights at the top of Grafton Street. I looked across admiringly at the gleaming blue Jaguar convertible that had just slid in beside me and was amazed to see Dave behind the wheel. I tooted my horn and called to him to pull in at the Shelbourne for coffee. When I remarked enviously on the gorgeous car and joshingly suggested that he must be making an absolute fortune, Dave laughed, told me that business had never been so bad, that he was skint and that the car belonged to a friend. Later, returning to the cars, which we had parked nose to kerb along Stephen's Green, I noticed that the head of the Jaguar emblem on the bonnet was missing. I was horrified that it should happen when he was driving a friend's car, but Dave laughed it off, saying that it had happened weeks ago and that he kept meaning to order a new one, but somehow just never seemed to get around to it. Which left me wondering: if the emblem had lost its head since Dave had borrowed the car, then how could he be so offhand about replacing it? If, on the other hand, the emblem had already been broken when he had borrowed the car, then why should *Dave*, and not the owner, be concerned with getting a new one? I'd ended up concluding, as I returned Dave's airy salute when he flashed past, that the car was in fact his own and I explained his little white lie by attributing it to his sensitivity about our respective fortunes. I was going through very lean times that year, having just packed in well-paid regular employment to start my locum business. What a sweet, thoughtful, wonderful guy was my cousin!

Now, full of porter and pessimism, I wondered if maybe he was just trying to prevent me from seeing how well he was doing; maybe his conscience was at him, or maybe he just didn't want me wondering – if he was being uncharacteristi-cally reticent about something like the Jag, then it was a fair guess that it was a dodgy Jag, or at least a Jag acquired by dodgy means.

I quaffed some more and my thoughts turned even more maudlin, back to his death. In no circumstances could I accept that he would even *touch* heroin, and I would tell that cop what I thought of him and his stupid theory. Tomorrow. Or should I ring now? Aw fuckit, tomorrow'd do. Now, I'd have another pint. 'Barman!'

With the relentlessly slow and grinding thought processes of the half-drunk, I went back again over the facts, round and round: if Dave hadn't OD-ed by accident, then he had to have committed suicide or been murdered. Suicide was totally unthinkable – it just wasn't in his character; suicide by heroin was even more totally unthinkable. That left murder, but by this stage I was a little too drunk to go on. Three pints later, or possibly five, the barman sent me home in a taxi.

I fumbled the key into the hall door and staggered upstairs to an empty apartment. Claire was in Cairo, covering yet another session of interminable Middle East peace talks. In the silent flat I lay on the sofa, trying to sleep, but after a restless hour and several visits to the loo I gave up and headed for the drinks cupboard. At the last moment I swerved into the kitchen and went on black coffee. Some time in the small hours, although I still didn't feel like sleeping, I went back to bed and, eventually, by crawling over to Claire's side and burying my face in her pillow, managed to soothe my agitated brain just enough to permit the mists of sleep to waft in and mercifully damp it down.

Next morning, loaded with aspirin and more black coffee, I tackled the sombre business of arranging the funeral.

The undertaker in our home town had obviously been expecting my call, because as soon as I announced myself I was subjected to several minutes of fulsome praise for the 'sterling qualities of the deceased'. It came out in one long spiel, without an 'em' or an 'ah' and I reckoned that it had to have been rehearsed. I thanked him and asked him how he'd heard 'Father Boland prayed for him this morning at eight o'clock mass. And sure, anyway, isn't it in the papers?' Once the arrangements had been agreed, I phoned the newspapers to insert the death notices. Two of the papers asked me to hold on, could they put me through to their newsrooms? I said no, they couldn't, but as I had to leave my number for verification both newsrooms rang back anyway within minutes. I told them I wasn't there, that I was someone else altogether, just a friend who knew nothing about anything, and refused to give my address.

I called the nursing home which had housed Dave's father, my uncle Clem, for the past eight years. He suffered from Parkinson's disease *and* Alzheimer's, and had long ceased to recognise Dave, me, or anybody else for that matter. The doctors now doubted that Uncle Clem remembered even who *he* was. Still, I felt that someone at the home ought to be aware of the death of his only child, in case he ever got lucid again, even momentarily. Although, on reflection, if he did come briefly to his senses it would be a hell of a cross for him to have to carry back with him into his twitching, swirling, confused, solitary world. Perhaps they'd have enough sense not to tell him.

I rang the captain of the rugby side for which I usually turned out at number 8 and cried off for next day's game.

I phoned Claire's mother. She was, to say the least, a bit shocked when I told her Dave had been a cousin. 'I've just read about it in the papers, Frank. A . . . a distant cousin?' she suggested hopefully.

'No, actually. A *first* cousin. A very close one. Listen, Jane, I'm going to be busy with this for the next few days. If Claire calls, tell her what happened.' Claire and I often used Jane as a message service if we couldn't contact each other.

Pulling on a shirt and jeans, I went to the end of the road to buy a paper and ended up buying one of each. Dave hadn't made the front page in any of them but his life, whatever the truth of it was, had earned him a substantial obituary on the inside pages. I wondered why I'd bothered inserting the death notices at all, those discreet little notifications of demise to inform anyone who might be interested to know that so-and-so has popped his/her clogs. When the deceased is infamous, or even thought to be infamous, the newspapers inform the public for free; it's only those who don't help to boost circulation figures who have to pay.

None of the papers was saying anything definite – there were lots of cop-out phrases like 'under suspicious circumstances' and 'rumoured to have had contacts in Dublin's underworld' and 'Gardai keeping an open mind' . . . I took immediate and deep umbrage at that last phrase – Curley's mind had seemed anything but open to me, so I fished indignantly in my pocket and found the number he had given me yesterday in the pub beside the morgue.

Our brief, curt conversation left me with the distinct feeling that Curley's mind was not only closed, it was almost hermetically sealed and, what's more, he didn't really give a damn *how* the population of Dublin's ungodly got reduced, just so long as it did. I reiterated my conviction that Dave had been murdered and he said to leave it be – it was all being looked into. Grudgingly, but bereft of any fresh arguments, I hung up.

It suddenly dawned on me that I didn't own a suit and that I really ought to buy one, something dark, but not black. With mind full of double-breasted versus single, two–piece or three, with stripe or without, turn-ups or not, one vent or two, I reached the pavement and suddenly remembered I'd left the Land Rover parked across from the morgue. I went back up to the flat, rang for a taxi and sat looking out of the window until it arrived. It was lunchtime when it decanted me on to the pavement outside the morgue, so I went into the same pub again and ordered steak and kidney pie and a pint of milk.

'How's th'oul head?' asked the barman, punching a button on the microwave, and sliding a plastic mat and cutlery wrapped in a paper napkin along the counter towards me.

'Grand,' I said, lying through my much–brushed but still foul-tasting teeth. 'I'll have the milk straight away please.'

Sitting on the high stool, holding a jerky conversation with the barman every time he hustled busily by – a remark or a response, depending on whose turn it was – I began to wonder about Dave's possessions. If they *were* ill gotten would they now be confiscated by the state? Would the state have to *prove* they were ill gotten? Should I retain a lawyer? As his closest relative, apart from poor Uncle Clem and my mother – now cruising somewhere in the Caribbean with my father – shouldn't I be the one to take steps, if such were needed, to protect his belongings? Or at least to make sure that, regardless of his sins, he wasn't ripped off by the state? Did he still have the sexy Jag? He couldn't possibly have stolen *that* – it was *far* too recognisable . . .

On my way to buy the suit I found myself passing close to

Curley's station, so I went in. I thought, if I saw him face to face, I might be able to talk him into taking Dave's death a little more seriously. He kept me waiting about ten minutes, then called me in.

'But do you have any *new* reason for thinking it might be murder?' he asked with waning patience, after I had told him about my gut feeling being stronger than ever.

'No. I don't. Look, I'm willing to accept that Dave could have been all the things you said . . .'

'So, big deal, you read the morning papers, huh?'

'I came to that conclusion last night.'

He pulled a face and wobbled his head back and forth on his bull neck. 'So?'

'So I'm not just *blindly* defending him. He may have been all of those things you said, but what I'm saying is that he would never ever, not in a million years, take drugs. He might deal in them, but he would never take them. You have to believe that.'

'What am I going to do with you, at all, at all?' He shook his head slowly and looked at me in indulgent and exaggerated helplessness. 'Aye?'

'I'm telling you,' I repeated doggedly, 'there's not a chance in hell that he'd take drugs.'

'Look . . .' He opened a drawer and took out a box file with David Clement Ryder written on it, opened it and extracted a one-page typed report, a summary of the pathologist's findings. He scanned it quickly, placed his finger on the text and turned the sheet towards me. 'There. See?' He tapped the page several times with an impatient finger. 'Heroin.'

I reached for the paper and saw him hesitate a second before handing it across to me, as if he were afraid that criminal behaviour might run in the family. 'It's okay.' I smiled. 'I'm not going to eat it.' He smiled back and watched warily anyway.

The technical jargon boiled down to just two facts: Dave had died from an overdose of heroin and there were no marks, scratches, bruises or bumps on his body other than a needle mark in the crook of his left elbow, with an associated small subcutaneous haematoma, where the final beats of Dave's dying heart had pumped a few drops of blood out under the skin, discolouring it.

I handed the report back to Curley. 'It says he was unmarked except for that single, solitary, fresh needle hole and bruise in the crook of his left elbow.'

'That's right. Where he injected the stuff.'

'You mean, where *somebody* injected the stuff,' I corrected him. 'Dave was completely left-handed. He could barely turn a doorknob with his right.'

3

The morning of the funeral dawned, leaden and cold. As I drove towards the morgue, I hoped it wouldn't rain on my new suit and wondered why I hadn't thought of buying an overcoat, too. Or even just a black umbrella.

There were several hearses in the yard, each with its attendant little knot of mourners. When I walked in, Jo-Jo Ridgley came across, arm extended, and repeated, almost verbatim, the lengthy eulogy of yesterday, while he shook, pressed, kneaded and massaged my hand. 'A grand chap, he was. A gentleman. Like his father before him. *And* mother, God rest her,' he added quickly, obviously recalling that Dave and I were related through our mothers.

I nodded and smiled my acknowledgement as I repossessed the hand and hid it away in the crisp, linen-lined pocket of the trousers of my new suit. 'You must have had an early start, Jo-Jo?'

'Sure amn't I used to it. Still, we'd better get going. Will you get the wreaths from your car?'

'Wreaths? What wreaths?'

Jo-Jo looked shocked. How could a hearse drive through city and countryside without wreaths? People might think the coffin was *empty*. 'Never mind. There are lots of wreath shops around here. I'll send one of the lads out for a couple.'

'Good man. How much do you think they'll be?' I reached for my wallet.

He grabbed the hand again, this time in a restraining

fashion. 'We can talk about that again. I'll put them on the account,' he said magnanimously, as if he had just told me that the wreaths were on the house.

Dave's body had already been sealed in the coffin and I rested a hand on the wood and said my silent goodbyes. Seeing my own birth date on the silver plate gave me a nasty little turn and I stared a moment, eyes at half-focus, morbidly trying to conjure up what date would appear behind the hyphen when my time came.

We pushed the coffin on a trolley to the hearse, transferred it on to the smooth rollers in the back of the vehicle and slid it into place. Jo-Jo placed six little silvery pegs shaped like crosses around the coffin to prevent it from shifting, arranged the *six* wreaths which had materialised while we were in the morgue and closed the door. 'Will you want to stop?' he asked.

Funerals that had a long way to travel often made a prearranged stop for refreshments, but we hadn't that far to go – a little over an hour, including traffic. 'No. I don't think so,' I said.

'You're the boss.'

For the last five miles before our home town, cars began to join in behind us. Parked in every available space, in gateways, lay-bys and on the hard shoulder, all facing town, they swung in at the end of the line. Now that we had grown into a proper funeral, Jo-Jo slowed to an appropriate pace and, by the time we reached the church, we had a long carcade streaming along in our wake.

Outside the church a crowd had gathered, probably swollen by the fact that Dave's name had been in the papers; but it didn't have to be that – the Irish are inveterate and compulsive funeral-goers. Father Boland, the parish priest and a family friend since he was a young curate and Dave and I mere lads, received the remains, led the prayers and Dave's body was left to lie in the church overnight. The burial would take place next day after a solemn requiem mass. Outside again, I shook hands with everybody within range and although there was no formal receiving line – that would come tomorrow – most people seemed to find their way to me through the crush. I was embarrassed several times when people whose faces I had known since childhood came to have a special little comforting and personal chat and I couldn't even guess at their names. I just hoped that they would all put it down to 'the shock'. A cold, hissing drizzle began which, despite its potentially deleterious effects on the new suit, was really a blessing. No one wanted to hang about and it was all over in record time.

I ate an unaccustomedly subdued lunch with Father Boland, then headed back to Dublin. I'd promised Claire's parents I'd bring them down next day for the funeral proper and besides, I didn't really want to hang about the old home town for the whole evening, at least not in these circumstances. Too many memories. Too many innocent memories of childhood. Too many not-so-innocent memories of the present.

In the evening, Claire rang from Cairo. 'Hi, love. I didn't know whether you'd be at the flat yet or not. What time is it there?'

'Seven.'

'It's five past ten here. Cairo must be three hours and five minutes ahead of Dublin.' She laughed. Clearly she hadn't spoken to her mother. 'How did the match go?'

'I had to cry off,' I said and told her everything.

'Dave into all that?' Her incredulity came across the miles as a squeak.

'I couldn't believe it at first either, but now I'm not so sure. The cops say they've been watching him for months.'

'Gawd! You just never know, do you? Any ideas who might have done it?'

'No. And if the local rozzers have their way there won't be. As far as they're concerned, it's good riddance to bad rubbish. The head plod is trying to deny that it *was* murder, or at least he was until I pointed out that it would be virtually impossible for a hundred-per-cent left-hander to inject himself intravenously in the left arm. I don't think it's made much difference to him, though. He referred to hundreds of unsolved crimes involving what he called *decent* citizens. He said he'd have a go – but just how enthusiastic a go it will be remains to be seen.'

'It must be *awful* for you, love. I should be there.'

'I wish you were.'

'I'm sorry, Frank, but there's just no way . . . I'm glad the folks are going, though.'

Dave's death put a damper on the rest of the conversation, and soon Claire said goodbye and that she'd be thinking of me at three o'clock, Cairo time, tomorrow.

I didn't sleep too well that night either, even though this time I started off on Claire's side of the bed.

Evidently Jane O'Sullivan hadn't quite yet come to terms with the fact that her darling daughter was involved with a man who was closely related to a major criminal (alleged) and, for the first time since we'd met, conversation, as we sped along in their Audi, was desultory and disjointed. Usually Jane was a great chatterbox. Conor, Claire's father, never had much to say and was given to infrequent wise remarks, but even these were in short supply today.

It was a depressingly foul morning, with great sheets of rain slanting across the land; at times, the windscreen wipers were barely able to cope. After we'd turned off the motorway we got stuck behind a large truck and it was just not possible to overtake because the spray from its many wheels threw up a blinding wall of water across the oncoming lane. After some ten minutes the driver pulled into a lay-by to let the built-up traffic pass and we tried to make up time, but we ran into some very heavy flooding on the smaller approach roads and were the last to take our pews. I could sense the disapproval of the entire community as I followed the O'Sullivans into the main mourners' pew.

Dave's coffin, now completely hidden beneath a pyramid of wreaths, rested on a trestle at the end of the main aisle, and I had the silly thought that I hoped the undertaker hadn't decided to supply these, too, and put them on my bill. Just for atmosphere, like. I immediately felt guilty about having facetious thoughts at such a time and coughed, shuffled and concentrated on Father Boland's 'eulogy'. In fairness to him, he tackled the problem of Dave's reputed lifestyle head-on.

At lunch the previous day he had expressed some concern over how he was going to get over what the papers were saying. And the radio. And the TV. The emphasis in all the media had been on Dave's established connections with the Dublin drug barons; he had been described as being a close business associate and personal friend of one of these, now serving a long, and long-overdue, prison sentence and there were the photographs to prove it – thick as thieves on Greek islands, luxurious yachts, at the theatre, fancy restaurants, wallowing together in *la dolce vita* . . .

Father Boland, like me, had found it difficult to believe this of Dave, but on the other hand, all the media carried substantially the same allegations. Which left the good man in a bind: he couldn't very well ignore the thorny matter of Dave's personal Judgement Day, not after he'd been giving sinners unceasing stick every Sunday for yonks; and neither could he go for the usual comforting line about being sure that the dear departed was now nestling safely and snugly in the arms of God. Even less could he act the desperate defence counsel, demanding from the pulpit that the prosecuting attorney (in this case, God) had the burden of proving guilt beyond a reasonable doubt. It's tough on defendants when the prosecuting attorney Knows Everything and is also the Judge.

The previous Sunday's holy invective, he had told me the day before, had actually been *devoted* to drug pushers, for it had been reported that some shady characters had been hanging around the school gates, pushing 'special sweets'. He had gone for the theme: 'Woe to those who scandalise children, for it would be better for them if a millstone were tied around their necks and they be cast into the depths of the ocean.' And the congregation, its blood righteously up, had almost joined in with shouts of, 'Verily! Yea, Brother!'

'Frank,' he'd said earnestly, 'if I try to go softly, they'll storm the pulpit.'

So Father Boland addressed what the papers had been saying and, although he did make the point that only God knew the *absolute* truth, he himself had no option but to assume that there was truth in what he had read, to the great sadness of his heart, about one of the nicest young lads who had ever grown up in the parish. He rattled off a few anecdotes which showed Dave in a good light, just to prove how nice he had been as a kid, then blamed what had, allegedly, become of him in later years solely on the drugs-related life into which he had been seduced, nay sucked. He pointed at me, Dave's cousin, Dave's *twin* cousin, sitting there with his fiancée's parents, a paragon, a man to be admired, a man who had studied hard, who now worked hard, a man whom he was proud to call 'friend', a man who had been reared in the exact same manner as the dearly departed, with one major exception – he had *not*, my good people, been caught up in the sleazy world of the drugs culture. (I could feel my cheeks burning and was verily thankful that I was sitting in the front pew so that my blushes could not be seen.)

'Did I say *culture*, my dear people?' Father Boland suddenly thundered 'Forgive me. Culture is a good thing and that word should *never* be used in connection with drugs. There is nothing whatever "cultural" about drugs, in the same way as there is nothing whatever "clean" about "ethnic cleansing".'

He repeated once more that Dave, until the moment he had entered the drugs sewer, had been a fine boy and youth, and that brought him neatly back to the thugs and filthmongers at the school gate. The ceaseless need for vigilance and constant alertness of parents to changes in their children's temperament, habits, appearance, etc.

All in all, I thought Father Boland had played a blinder and there were appreciative noises from the congregation as they filed past the coffin and out into the lousy weather again.

Only those who absolutely had to (or *felt* they had to) braved the downpour to attend the actual burial and even some of those cried off after the first few sodden yards, most notably my mother's cousin, Aunt Moira, who hadn't missed a family funeral (or very few non-family ones either) since she was about four. That gave the nod to most of the other relatives and to her fellow funeralophiles and, as I followed the hearse out through the church gate, I could see most of the recent congregation heading up the road, in the opposite direction, in a barely controlled, genteel stampede, bound for the warmth and comfort of the local hotel, which had been booked to serve hot soup and sandwiches. The rest of us, huddled miserably under interlocked umbrellas like the remnants of a routed Roman testudo, followed the hearse to the nearby graveyard and gathered round in a small, sodden knot, making the responses to Father Boland's prayers for the immortal soul of Dave. I noticed everybody, including myself, being really emphatic about the prayers, as though we all knew that, this time, the prayers were truly up against it; we were, I suppose, just hoping against hope that they'd get through and tip the balance, do the business. God the Merciful was the main target this morning and we were all hoping that God the Just had the day off.

The grave was fully exposed to the rain, which now, with a new wind behind it, drilled malevolently between the headstones, like bullets, and my new-suit trousers clung clammily to my freezing calves as I stood and watched the mounting water in the grave undermine the loose soil of the sides, creating mudslides. At last the coffin was lowered on ropes, a rectangle of false grass hid the open grave mouth and, moments later, we too were moving briskly along the paths between the gravestones, tombs and mini-mausoleums, headed for the hotel.

I fetched hot whiskies for Conor and Jane – they had insisted on coming to the graveside 'because Claire would have' – but I hardly had time to talk to them as I spent the next hour having my hand pumped earnestly by the whole attendance as they muttered the sincere but hackneyed formulae of condolence. Many who had opted for the hotel rather than the cemetery salved their consciences by going that little bit extra, holding the hand that bit longer, being that little bit more effusive in their sympathies, mainly by just repeating the same phrase several times.

At last Aunt Moira hove into view and, taking me by the elbow, insisted we sit down. I steered her towards the O'Sullivans' table, which cramped her style, but only somewhat. She was so *worried* because she hadn't gone to the graveyard. What would poor Heather have thought of her if she were alive today? In fact, what did poor Heather, who was undoubtedly in heaven looking down on the whole sad scene, think of her, letting dear David, her (poor Heather's) only child, go to his tragically premature grave alone? I assured her that Dave had not been alone, a fact to which I, the O'Sullivans, Father Boland and all the other wet people she could see around the place, the ones with the steam rising off them, could attest. And besides, Heather would never have expected her to go out in such awful weather – we didn't want to be all back here again next week, burying *Aunt Moira*, now did we?

But there was no cheering her up. Moira was a gloomy, sombre soul; she was to our family what the hound was to the Baskervilles – if you saw Moira outside the confines of her large, gloomy house, then the chances were that somehow, somewhere, one of the tribe had just gone through that final door. Eventually, spotting some distant cousin whom I only vaguely recognised, she excused herself and left us with such alacrity that I wondered if perhaps the cousin hadn't some relative with a terminal, or at least life-threatening, illness.

I half expected Curley and Flynn to be there, but I supposed that only happened when a member of the family or a close friend was a suspect. In a 'gangland slaying' it seemed highly improbable that the hit man should feel an overwhelming compulsion to attend his victim's premature last rites. Besides, Curley had his precious 'decent' citizens to look after. Still, I thought, he might at least have sent Flynn.

I noticed one woman standing on her own beside the open roaring fire, steaming. I'd seen her at the grave but hadn't recognised her so I'd decided she was the wife of one of Dave's friends. But she didn't seem to be with anybody now, so I went across to her. 'Are you on your own? You don't even have a drink.'

'No. I'll be off in a few moments. I just felt I ought to come in and warm myself and dry out a bit before I head back to town. Awful day, wasn't it?'

'Could hardly be worse. I'm Frank Samson, David's cousin.'

'You look very alike. I'm Rachel Donaldson.'

'Oh! Forgive me. I'm not sure which of us should be sympathising with the other . . .'

'Don't worry, Mr Samson. I didn't really know David very well.'

'I see. But didn't the police say something about a holiday? That that was how you . . . eh . . . found him?'

'It's a group holiday.'

'Oh. More geology?'

'Yes. I've had a colleague stand in for the first two days. I'm flying out this evening.'

'Where to?'

'Morocco. The Atlas mountains.'

'I never realised that Dave was into geology,' I said, immediately regretting I'd said it. Probably he was more interested in Rachel Donaldson and I felt a sudden great sadness as I looked into the calm grey eyes set wide in her quietly beautiful, sensible face. I reckoned that here was a woman totally at peace with herself, a woman who, if she would have had him at all, might have led him back to a decent life. I felt suddenly tongue-tied and covered it by steering her across to where Claire's parents sat beside a radiator, and ordered soup and sandwiches for her. I felt an immediate kinship with Rachel Donaldson and, to this day, feel a sense of loss that that was the last time I ever saw her.

Excusing myself, I went to look for the Hartes and found them sitting quietly and sadly on their own at a corner table, a lot older-looking than the last time I'd seen them, some two years ago. I had hardly spoken to them yesterday outside the church, our meeting having consisted mainly of wordless consoling hugs and tears. Their eyes were red and raw. They had regarded David (as they always called him), and to a lesser extent me as the children they never had.

James and Julia Harte had come to live with Dave and Uncle Clem shortly after Aunt Heather's death, to run the large house. At first, they'd lived in the small lodge in the grounds, but that was only for a matter of months and I have no clear recollection of them ever being anywhere other than in the main house. When Clem fell sick they nursed him until he had to be hospitalised, then visited him every few weeks, telling him how the place was looking etc. and generally trying to cheer him up. They went on calling regularly until he no longer had a clue who they were or what they were talking about and, even now, although they were both several years his senior, visited him three or four times a year. Dave had been abroad for a few years, country hopping and, on his return to Ireland, had settled in Dublin. So the Hartes now lived on in the big old house on their own, keeping it immaculate and aired and heated.

There were ample funds for them to do so – my maternal grandfather had been a local big businessman, owning lots of land, quite a sizeable chunk of the town and various businesses. He'd sired three children, one son (the eldest) and two daughters, the younger of the two being my mother. The son had inherited most of the old man's estate and the remainder had been divided evenly between the girls. Within three months of his marriage the son, my late uncle Edward, had been killed in a water-skiing accident and when his rich widow remarried two years later she had left the area and gone to Australia with her new husband, a Brisbane lawyer; nobody had ever heard from her again. My mother and aunt, with their respective husbands, ran their businesses with varying degrees of success. Aunt Heather and Uncle Clem

31

were prudent and shrewd, and they prospered, whereas my parents were of a more Bohemian nature and never had much concern for worldly goods. They were still comfortably off when they sold their remaining business interests and 'Cartfield', our house, and bought a condominium in Florida, where they now live for ten months every year, coming back for July and August, and sometimes for a week or two at Christmas. The excuse for the move was my father's supposedly declining health and they now spend months of each year blowing every penny they have on one luxury cruise after another. They were at present somewhere in the Caribbean, their progress being marked by a series of conscience-prompted postcards.

My mother feels guilty about these extravagances, blowing my inheritance as she sees it, and when informing me of their next cruise, always manages to formulate some little conscience saver for herself. The present Caribbean binge, she had informed me, would not have been affordable were it not for the fact that it was an absolutely rock-bottom offer, the reason for this happy circumstance being that it was the beginning of the hurricane season and they'd be pretty damned lucky ever to get back *at all*! Several broken bones each were more or less a foregone conclusion. The previous cruise (of the Norwegian fjords) had been undertaken with the utmost trepidation because 'your father might catch his death of cold'. In the case of the Amazon cruise it had been the near certainty of death from malaria, poisoned darts from hostile natives and/or snakebite which had rendered the tour fraught with danger and Not Really a Thing to Be Envied at All.

So Dave's home remained open and lived in and maintained. Dave sometimes spent a night or two there, as did I, and when my parents were in Ireland they would use it as a base camp from which to launch their week-long forays for fishing, golfing, shopping, etc. In effect, the house had evolved into a kind of base for the whole family, although it actually belonged to Uncle Clem.

'Ah, Francis!' James said, struggling to stand up. (They

always called me Francis.) I put a hand on his shoulder to stop him and sat down opposite. Julia burst into fresh tears.

'Come on, Julia,' I urged quietly, covering her tiny, desiccated hand with mine. 'You shouldn't have gone to the cemetery,' I admonished them gently. 'Look at you both. You're soaking!'

'We just had to,' she replied simply. 'But we'll be going back to the house presently to change.' Then she broke down again.

'I know, I know,' I said, patting her hand some more.

'Poor David,' James said, slowly shaking his head. 'And all those horrible things they're saying about him . . .'

'I know, I know,' I said again, beckoning to a passing kinsman to bring two more hot whiskies, promptish. As chief mourner, I was allowed to be a bit imperious.

'What happened anyway, Francis?'

'Well, I think he was murdered, but don't spread it about, because it's not official yet. The police say he injected himself with too much heroin.'

'Is that a drug?' Julia asked.

'It is indeed, Julia. One of the worst. Probably *the* worst.'

'But *surely*, Francis, David would never take drugs?'

'That's what I think, too. That's mainly why I think he was murdered.'

We talked back and forth, covering the same ground over and over, until friends of theirs, their bridge partners, came to take them home. They left sadly and tearfully but thanking God that David had called to see them a few days earlier – they hadn't seen him for months before that. Now they had a fresh memory of him to treasure. I hugged them both and assured them that I would keep in touch.

In Clem's absence I was next of kin and protocol ordained that I should stay until the last maudlin mourner made his tipsy way towards home, but I didn't have the time. It wouldn't make the slightest difference to Dave how long I stayed and as for the diehards, they were perfectly able to get maudlin and tipsy on their own. So after another hour or so, pleading an urgent meeting for the O'Sullivans (untrue) and a long drive to the northernmost tip of the country for myself (true), I broke with convention, passed the mantle to Aunt Moira and left.

I didn't meet my temporary employer until late next morning as he'd already left on his rounds by the time I dragged myself into the office. When our paths finally did cross, about half-eleven, I was still groggy and feeling as if I'd been run through a turnip mangler. He, having come down with a heavy head cold, was feeling even worse. At seventy-four, Robert Sweeney had found the double shift hard going. I ordered him off home at once and told him not even to *think* of putting his nose round the surgery door again until he was fully fit. That took three days, which suited me fine – my mind was occupied for nearly all of my waking hours, thus saving me from the long periods of brooding which I had not been looking forward to.

Some locums you can't wait to see the back of and you promise yourself never ever to accept another job in that practice as long as you live. Unless, of course, you *really* need the money.

It may be the boss or the staff, the clients or the town, or just dreary countryside.

It might be losing a patient in the first few days – that's a real bummer. You could be absolutely blameless, but the word spreads like lightning and, when that happens, it sticks. By contrast, you could spend the rest of your time raising three-day-old carcases from the dead and you'd be wasting your time, publicity-wise – nobody ever hears about those; it's as if such owners are bound by an oath of silence.

As a locum, you're constantly on probation and you can't afford even one off day. In a settled practice everyone is allowed the odd lapse, a flare-up, a curt reply or two, to tick off a bothersome client – just so it doesn't happen too often –

but when you're looking after someone else's practice you've got to cure every case *and* go round all day with a smile fastened on your face, like a rictus.

Then there are the pet jobs, the ones you love no matter what. What makes a locum like this is as difficult to define as what makes one lousy. Robert Sweeney's was one of the nice ones.

When it came to the time for me to leave, he looked almost sad. 'Why do you hop about so much? Never found a nice place with nice people?'

'I have indeed, Robert,' I said. 'Lots. Maybe that's why I keep travelling – there seems to be an endless supply of them . . .'

'Well, then . . .'

'. . . but I'm not looking for somewhere permanent. At least not yet.'

'Pity. If you were, I'm sure we could find room for you here. Could probably even match the salary – well, nearly, anyway. You locums don't come cheap. You're not doing it purely for the money, are you?' he added suddenly.

'No.' I laughed. 'Although it helps.' I patted my breast pocket where I'd just put his cheque and held out my hand. 'I'd better be motoring, Robert. It's a fair old drive.'

He shook my hand, then held it. 'If you even *half* thought you might like to stop chasing your tail around the country and that here might not be the worst spot in the world, then don't leave it too long . . . I'm not getting any younger, you know.'

'You're like a two-year-old, Robert. And you know it.'

He smiled, happy I'd said it. 'I don't feel *too* bad, I suppose . . . for an ould fella. But that's neither here nor there. Just think about what I said, will you?'

'Okay, I will. But I honestly don't thi—'

He shushed me and let go of my hand. 'Just give it a thought. So long, Frank. Good luck.'

'See you next year.'

'If I'm still here.'

'If Carndonna's still here, you mean.'

He laughed again, backstepped a pace and saluted as I let out the clutch and drove out of the cobbled yard, through the archway and on to the main street.

A really nice man.

4

Like I said, good practices and bad, nice people, lousy town and vice versa. During the next months I saw my share of both. No practice had been bad enough for me to blacklist it for all time, but neither had there been one that would have tempted me to settle.

During those months, too, my contacts with Curley dried from a trickle to nothing. In the first weeks following the murder I'd badgered him mercilessly, phoning every other day, dropping in every time I was in Dublin. But the answer was always the same: they were still working on it, but getting nowhere. Growing thoroughly fed up with this, I'd taken to bothering politicians, but they'd all dutifully returned cloned reports from Curley. I'd even contacted Thomas F. Hilliard, the slippery ex-Minister for Agriculture, with whom I'd had some dealings and who owed me a big favour, but even he had been unable to have the investigation stepped up. That is, if he had even tried. To hear him tell it, he'd gone down on his knees to everyone from the cop on the beat to the Minister for Justice, but Thomas F.'s word meant absolutely nothing; it wasn't even worth the air it was breathed upon.

I hadn't contacted anyone for weeks now and, with strong twinges of guilt, I began to admit that I, too, was slowly giving up on Dave.

Perhaps it was the salutary lesson of Dave's death that had started it off, but recently, Claire and I had begun to think of

37

looking for a permanent base. Marriage and children had even been mentioned, but all that had to be postponed when Claire had been offered, and had accepted, the position of roving foreign correspondent for her paper, the *Daily Instructor*. She'd torn herself, and me, asunder over the decision, but after much soul-searching she'd accepted the job she had coveted for so long. So she now travelled a lot, sometimes with little or no notice, and these days often found me heading for the atlas after a brief, static-fractured phone call from some far-off trouble spot, or having to catch the evening news to find out just which international crisis had shattered whatever weekend plans we'd been presumptuous enough to make. My initial misgivings about her being away so often had, as Claire had assured me they would, turned out to be groundless. In fact, it was working out better than we could have hoped: we managed nearly as much shared time as ever at our apartment in Dublin and, with unexpectedly generous spare time between overseas trips, Claire was free to come and visit me whenever she was home, in whatever corner of the country I happened to be locuming at the time. I was thinking about her when I dropped from the fertile plain of the midlands into the shallow valley that cradled Monksford in its gentle slopes.

Monksford was a neat market town I'd often passed through but never actually stopped in, not even for fuel. Its public buildings and a couple of churches were arranged tidily about a grassy square set with white wooden benches and young trees caged in mesh-wire cylinders to stop the town dogs from pissing them out of existence. Like many a similar town it was festooned to the point of clutter with window boxes and hanging baskets overflowing with pansies, lobelia and cascading petunias. Its short streets and side roads ran, for the most part, between smallish, undistinguished dwelling houses, many of them done up in startling colours. Further on I found out why. Monksford fancied its chances in the upcoming annual National Tidy Towns Competition and its houses, freshly painted and decorated under the twin tyrannical thumbscrews of civic duty and peer pressure, sat in self-conscious rows, like reluctant and embarrassed contestants at some macabre, dowdy beauty pageant. Beside a large sign which warned tardy inhabitants that judgement day was a mere seventeen days away, I asked the way to the surgery of my employers for the next few weeks, Slattery and Partners.

There were three generations of Slatterys and two partners – Michael Stone, who was out on the farm rounds, and a Slattery cousin named Miriam who was on pregnancy leave.

Joe Slattery, the founder, was in his eighties and did few farm visits now; Joe's son, PJ, was in his early fifties, while PJ's son, JJ, was not long out of college. They were all short, thickset men who looked as if they could bend crowbars with their teeth. Even Joe. The other thing they shared was a worried frown fixed on their broad foreheads. At first I thought this was just the natural Slattery brow, Monksford's answer to the Hapsburg lip but, as I later found out, I was wrong: the furrows were from worry, nothing more.

I was introduced to Joe, who was poring over books in an inner office, to JJ, who was castrating a cat in the theatre and apologised for not shaking hands, and to the office staff of two ladies who were sitting chatting as we came in and sitting chatting as we went out again. They were Barbara, the practice manager, and Eve, the receptionist. Barbara gave me her hand and a large welcoming smile while Eve just nodded in my direction. The daybook lay open on the desk and I could see that there were only about ten calls, not nearly enough to keep a practice of this size going. I wondered why they needed me.

Introductions over, PJ took me on a tour of the premises. The practice house, of which he was justifiably proud – so much so that he took me out into the road so that I could get the overall view – was located at the junction of two quiet roads and was the most substantial house I'd seen so far in the town. Set well back from the street, behind heavy wrought-iron railings, it was a long, two-storeyed structure with thick walls and smallish, deepset windows. It had, until recently, had a thatched roof and was probably one of the oldest houses in town; it would have had associations with the local landlord family, whoever they'd been, before being acquired by either the emerging native merchant or professional classes. I doubted Joe was old enough to have been the one who'd taken over from the landlords; perhaps it had been his father.

There was a mature and well-tended front garden on either side of the flagstone walkway which ran from gate to door, and a recent shower had everything clean and gleaming. It was as if the house had been expecting the Tidy Town judges this morning and had gone to extra lengths to make itself look good.

Turning left as we reached the single step up to the hall door, we walked past three windows, hung a right at the gable and followed a well-worn gravelled footpath down by the side and through some trees, until we emerged through a small gate into a large backyard with cut-stone outbuildings. Two dusty cars, compact diesel hatchbacks, with consecutive registration plates and a couple of extra aerials each, were parked side by side, nose in to the back of the house, typical working vets' cars.

The vehicle entrance to the yard, a wide double gate, opened off to our left, on to the side road which turned off beside the Slatterys' property and headed gently up the western slope of the valley.

Evidently in no hurry, PJ showed me a stable block of six (empty) hospital boxes, a coach-house which had been converted into a modern and well-equipped large-animal operating theatre with a cushioned recovery room opening off it, a small but effective diagnostic laboratory in a little anteroom and, finally, a brick-built shed with sheep, goat and calf pens. There were also four paddocks, three small, one horse-sized, the fourth the same size as the three small ones together. 'That's it, apart from the kennels and cattery, which are on the other side of the house,' PJ brought the tour to a close.

'Very nice,' I said, impressed, but at the same time

wondering why there were no patients in the boxes and no clients' vehicles in the yard; at nine thirty on a Monday morning the place should have been humming.

JJ came through the back door and strolled towards us. If he'd finished morning ops already, I thought, then the cat castration must have been about the only one. It didn't look like they were overworked, that they needed to draft in hired help. Before JJ actually reached us a horsebox came through the gates and he veered off towards it. PJ waved to the driver and, leaving his son to deal with whatever was in the horsebox, steered me back inside the house.

My accommodation was to be the entire top floor of the practice house. When the last of Joe Slattery's six children had left the nest, he and his late wife had decided that the whole house was too big for just the two of them, so they'd turned the downstairs into offices, stores, consulting rooms and a small-animal operating theatre, and the upstairs into a very comfortable flat for themselves. At that point the practice had been the only one in town and the largest by far in the area. When Joe's wife died he lost interest in work and handed over to PJ. A year later he was finding the flat depressingly lonely on his own, so PJ and his wife, another Miriam, built a granny flat on to their new house for him where, surrounded by grandchildren, he was now as happy as could be.

When it became clear that Joe had no intention of ever getting seriously back into work again, Michael Stone had been taken on as an assistant. Michael had lived in the flat for almost four years, by which time he had become a partner in the practice and the fiancé of its then receptionist, Brenda. When they married, the previous year, they moved into their own house and the flat became, once again, empty. The family had thought of letting it but as this would have entailed the hassle of seeking planning permission and probably being refused ten times, building an outside stairway and other bothersome alterations, nothing had been done. I received this history from PJ while we sat over leisurely mugs of coffee at the kitchen table. He seemed to have all the time in the world and no interest whatever in putting his costly mercenary to work. Most vets try their damnedest to get more out of me than I do out of them but as far as PJ was concerned, my arrival might just as well have been a social call. Not only did he not have work for me, he himself seemed to have no work to do, either.

As I stood by the sink, rinsing out coffee mugs, I could see down into the yard. JJ and the driver of the horsebox were leading a lame bay towards one of the hospital boxes. Even from this distance I could see that the horse's right hock was swollen. As JJ opened the door the hinge squeaked loudly, further evidence of lack of use of the fine facilities. It squeaked again as they came out and closed it. 'Perhaps I'd better go down and see if JJ wants a hand with that horse,' I suggested, drying my hands on a dishcloth.

'No need,' PJ replied. 'He can manage.'

How can he say that when he doesn't even know what the problem is, I thought to myself as I came back to the table and glanced pointedly at my watch. 'So what should I do? Where do I start? Any more small-animal ops?'

'Nope.'

'Farm calls?'

'Michael is doing them.'

'So.' I shrugged. 'Where do I fit in?'

'Oh, we've a fair bit of TB testing to do in the next few weeks. Michael and JJ will do most of it – all of it, in fact – so you and I will handle the rest. Then I may have to go away for a few days and you'll come into your own. Don't worry, we'll keep you running about.' Although he tried to sound cheerful and confident, I had the distinct impression that he was lying, putting a brave face on a bad situation. Despite the fact that they were lashing out a sizeable sum on hiring me, I reckoned that the practice was, in fact, barely ticking over. The hospital boxes had not only been empty, they had looked unused, and as for the fancy large-animal theatre, there hadn't been the faintest whiff of surgical spirit, antiseptic, disinfectant, blood, or any of the other smells which linger for days, or even weeks sometimes, after surgeries.

When PJ left I went in search of his son and found him carrying a portable X-ray unit, a lead apron, lead gloves, and some X-ray cassettes towards the box with the lame horse in it. I took the apron and the cassettes from him and opened the squeaky door. JJ produced a 2cc syringe and a bottle of Domosedan from his pocket, and handed them to me. 'He's supposed to be a bit lively, this one. I was going to give him half a cc.'

I caught the big gelding by the halter and stroked his muzzle. 'So you're a handful then, are you? Well, we'll soon sort *that* out.' I let him go, flicked the purple plastic cap off the new vial and drew 0.5cc into the syringe. JJ was assembling the X-ray unit, taking the lead out over the half-door to plug it in to a power point with a waterproof cover on the wall outside. When he came back in I said: 'Can you give us a hand here, JJ' and, as he kept a steadying hold on the halter, I slid the needle into the horse's jugular vein and shot in the powerful sedative. Within seconds his head was hanging low and he had lost all interest in what was going on. To darken the stable so that we could more easily see the aiming crosswires in the machine's positioning light, we closed both halves of the door. The top half, I noticed, also squeaked.

We took various exposures of the swollen hock from different angles and at different settings and, leaving me to tidy up, JJ hurried off to the darkroom to develop them. I'd made coffee for us both by the time he reappeared holding the pictures.

The X-rays were top quality, but hocks, with their interlocking small bones, can be difficult to read, so we both studied them minutely before agreeing that there was no evidence of a fracture. JJ breathed a sigh of relief and immediately phoned through the good news to the owner. No breaks, no. Certain. The horse, whose name, according to the large X-ray envelope, was Fizzikle, would stay at the clinic and have complete box rest for the next week or so.

For the first few days he would have non-steroidal anti-inflammatory and analgesic injections, with morning and evening application of DMSO to the swollen hock; after that, progress would be gauged by continuous assessment.

While JJ was giving his guarded-to-favourable prognosis, I wandered into the outer office to check the daybook; there were two more calls and Michael Stone's initials had already been put against them. I counted down the list. Fourteen. And fourteen calls in a day didn't make it a busy practice. I turned back pages for the last week or so and the same grim story appeared day after day. Hell, Gino Callaghan, a one-man practice and a regular client of mine, did more than that on his own.

For the rest of the day I dabbled, looking for something to do. I went on a few revisits with PJ, had a pub lunch with JJ who was still a bachelor, but thinking of getting engaged, did a call or two with Michael Stone, a large, hairy, jovial character who was blusteringly rough with the farmers but gentle as a kitten with the animals. His conversation between farm visits consisted almost solely of fond reminiscings about his bachelor days in the flat above the surgery. He still missed it, he said, but sure what could he expect – he'd only been out of it for less than a year, since he and Brenda, another Slattery connection, had got married.

I ended my first working day in Monksford by standing in with JJ on evening surgery. Leaning unobtrusively against a cupboard, quiet as a student, speaking only when spoken to, I tried to sort out the confusing PJ/JJ business in my head and was pleased to smugness with myself when I came up with Pappy J and Junior J. For some reason the names came to me in an exaggerated American hillbilly accent. Yee-hah.

At about 1 a.m. I awoke with a start. I'd heard a noise through the open bedroom window and, even in my groggy state, I recognised it instantly – the squeaky hinge of the door of the loose box that housed our lame patient. My first thought was that Fizzikle had somehow damaged himself and that one of the Js, Pappy or Junior, had arrived to deal with the crisis. Being half asleep, it didn't occur to me to wonder who might have summoned them.

I scrambled from the bed, reached for my jeans and, even as I was pulling them on, hopped across to the window to see what was happening. The young moon, slung low in the sky, lit up most of the yard adequately, but the front of the stable block and the few yards directly before it were in deep shadow. Still coming awake, I took things in slowly. The only vehicle in the yard was mine, although the double gates on to the road were wide open. Perhaps JJ or PJ or Michael, or whoever it was, had parked out front and come through the office . . . but in that case why were there no lights on? I was struggling with these conundrums and my second shoe, when a faint moving light, a torch, presumably, became visible in the chink between the top and bottom halves of Fizzikle's door.

'Who's there?' I called out of the window and waited. No response. The torch moved again. I cleared my throat and tried once more, louder this time. 'Oy! Who's there?' There was still no response. Hardly surprising, I supposed – I was far away, there was a breeze and the stable doors were closed. At this point I still figured it was one of the vets, probably on his way back from a late call, just having a quiet look in on the new patient, checking.

I finished tying my shoelace, switched on the landing light and headed for the staircase. Downstairs, I switched on all the switches I came upon, turned the key in the back door and headed out into the night. As I pulled open the garden gate I heard the squeak of the door again, stopped and looked up. Now that my eyes had become more accustomed to the dark, I could make out two figures in the shadow in front of the stables. They were both inches taller than any of the Slatterys and inches smaller and thinner than Michael Stone. As I watched, I saw one silhouette stop and point towards the back of the house, now lit up like one of my parents' cruise liners in port. There was a brief flash of the torch being pointed in over the stable door and then the figures started to race for the back gates.

'Hey! Stop!' I shouted and began to run too, but they had too much of a headstart and, by the time I got to the gate, all I could see were rapidly diminishing tail-lights headed westwards up the hill. My immediate reaction was to telephone PJ but then I thought I ought first to check on Fizzikle.

Not knowing what to expect, but prepared for the worst, I switched on the light and looked over the half-door. To my relief, I saw that Fizzikle was standing. He had been tied on a very short rein to an iron ring set high in the wall, his nose almost touching it. He could just about peer nervously at me from the corner of one uneasy eye.

Talking soothingly, I untied him and removed the rope from his head collar. He went immediately to the water trough and while he was drinking I ran my hand over the powerfully muscled body, from ears to hooves, leaving the lame leg until last. Slowly and gently, and murmuring soothingly all the time, I slid my hand down towards the swollen hock. The big bay tensed and looked up from his drinking, but he let me touch the joint, his only dissenting action being a rapid swishing of his tail.

The hock felt greasy. This surprised me, as the evening's application of DMSO ought, I reckoned, to have dried well in by now. Puzzled, I moved directly under the light and examined the blob of reddish paste that had come away on my fingertips.

More because of its colour than anything else I guessed that it was a red blister, a strong vesicant used in the old days as a counter-irritant for damaged tendons and the like – long, long before my time. Old Joe Slattery would have used it in his day but, as I couldn't picture PJ or JJ resorting to it, I assumed that it had been smeared on by the recent visitors.

Having now drunk his fill, Fizzikle moved towards the back wall and, as his hooves rucked up the bedding straw, they uncovered a cellophane bandage wrapper and a plastic bag with 'Butterfly Kitchen Gloves – Size L' written on it. I knew enough about red blister to realise that it was not the sort of stuff to have on one's fingers so, leaving the bandage wrapper and the plastic bag on the manger for a moment, I stepped outside and washed my hands thoroughly under the outside tap.

Back inside, I put the wrappers into my jeans pocket, bent down and had another rummage in the straw, but all that turned up was a clasp for the bandage, two metal-toothed bits joined together by a half-inch of pinkish-grey knicker elastic.

I returned quickly to the surgery where I found a wooden spatula, a glass sample jar and a bottle of mild horse shampoo. With the spatula I scraped what I could of the suspect red substance off the hock and saved it in the sample jar. Leaving that to one side, I washed and rewashed the area around the damaged hock with warm soapy water until I was satisfied that I'd removed all the irritant. Then I dried it gently but thoroughly with soft towels.

Back again in the office, I called PJ, then went straight to the bookcases that housed the accumulated textbooks and references of three generations of veterinary students and practitioners. Within moments I found what I was looking for – an ancient book with 'Materia Medica' in faded gold lettering on its green–black spine. I took it to the desk, switched on the green–globed desk lamp and, turning the fragile yellowed pages with the greatest of care, soon came upon the section headed Blisters and Vesicants.

Red Blister was, I read, composed of one part of red iodide of mercury and eight parts of lard or lanolin. It was highly irritant and should not be handled with the bare hands, which explained the kitchen gloves wrapper; the visitors clearly knew what they were doing. In no circumstances, I read on, was a treated area to be covered by a bandage, as this would cause the skin to 'sweat' and, if the skin sweated for any length of time, it would become damaged and, soon after, the underlying tissues would become involved. Nasty stuff. Assuming that the people who had applied the blister knew all these details, the presence of the bandage wrapper was particularly ominous, pointing as it did to a very serious effort to damage the horse irreparably.

They hadn't managed to get the bandage on because I had suddenly popped up, but they'd nearly got lucky anyway: DMSO, dimethyl sulfoxide, which was being applied twice daily, carries almost any substance which mixes with it right in through the protective barrier of the skin. Had I not heard the squeaky door and spotted the red blister, then come morning, Fizzikle's hock, bandaged or not, would have been damaged beyond repair.

PJ arrived as I finished reading.

Hair askew, striped pyjama bottoms sticking out from under the cuffs of his working cords, shirt only half done up, he was nevertheless totally alert. I had the impression, as he let himself in through the front door, that he was worried but not terribly surprised, like a man who was used to bad news. I handed him a mug of coffee and told him the story. He examined the red substance in the sample jar and agreed with me that it probably was red blister – Joe would confirm it in the morning.

As we crossed the yard to check on the horse, I suggested he report the intrusion to the police. PJ shook his head, said he didn't want to 'bother' the Gardai, reckoning there wasn't much they could do at this hour of the night, especially as we couldn't give them a description of either men or vehicle. Together we checked Fizzikle again, going over him inch by inch, but we could find nothing amiss. The door squeaked closed and PJ fitted a strong padlock. 'That ought to keep the bastards out. For this night, anyway.'

Back in the office again, I asked him if he had any idea why someone should want to put red blister *and* a bandage on the horse. 'Who'd stand to benefit?'

'Whatever about benefit, I know who'd stand to lose,' he replied after a pause. 'Us. If that horse had been blistered and bandaged from now till eight in the morning, his hock would be a total mess. Even without the DMSO. And nobody would believe that it wasn't our fault. They'd think we'd used the wrong treatment and were trying to save our necks by making up a highly improbable story about midnight intruders.' There was bitterness in his voice and the frown was etched deeply into his brow.

I was about to ask why anybody should want to sabotage the practice, when he caught my hand and shook it sincerely. 'I have to thank you, Frank. You did a great job. I reckon you've earned your fee already. There's nothing more we can do here tonight. May as well try to get some more sleep. See you in the morning.' He went off out without a backward look and left me mulling over his remarks. Which was the 'great job' he had referred to – cleaning the blister off the leg or disturbing the two intruders? I had an odd feeling that it was the latter. In which case, was I here in this already overstaffed practice as yet another vet, or as some kind of glorified nightwatchman?

I slept a brittle sleep, listening all night for the tell-tale squeak of the stable door.

5

A few days later, with everything going reasonably well, Fizzikle improving almost by the hour and me getting a chance to do some work (though not a lot), I pulled up in the yard and headed for the office. Before I had even reached the building I could hear raised voices. As I came in the back, the door to PJ's office flew open and I heard him say angrily: '. . . *no way to speak to your father!*' Flushed and furious, JJ emerged, stuck his head back in and, equally angrily, retorted: 'Yeah? Well I was talking as a *colleague*, an equal, which, no doubt, is a concept far too difficult for *you* to understand. And I *still* say, if anything like that ever happens again, you check it with me first, you patronising, opinion-ated . . .' Stuck for a derogatory word to apply to fathers, he stormed out of the back door through which I'd just entered, seemingly unaware of the dumbstruck audience gaping at him. For once, Barbara and Eve, the garrulous practice lay staff, were dead quiet, their heads studiously bent over books. Seconds later, PJ's office door was slammed violently from within.

For an imprudent moment I considered knocking, then thought better of it, glanced at the list of calls – which hadn't grown any longer since I'd last looked – and headed for the stairs to my apartment. Outside, the sound of squealing tyres and a tortured engine marked JJ's enraged departure.

An hour or so later, as I sat at my kitchen table, eating a cheese sandwich and listening to the one o'clock news to see how Claire might be faring in Algiers, the door pushed open and JJ asked if he could come in.

'Sure,' I said, getting up to switch off the radio. The news was more than halfway through anyway. If Algeria hadn't come up by now, then it wasn't going to. 'Sit yourself down.' Moving absent-mindedly, he pushed the door closed, crossed to the table and, oblivious to the fact that my lunch was right in front of it, sat in the chair I'd just vacated. 'Fancy a sandwich?' I asked, moving my plate across to the other side. 'There's clammy squares of mousetrap cheese, softish tomato, or tuna.'

'No, thanks.' He sat a moment in scarcely controlled agitation. 'Although I wouldn't mind a coffee.' Springing up from the table so quickly that he almost knocked the chair backwards, he darted across the kitchen and put the kettle under the tap. 'You?'

I raised my pot of natural yoghurt. 'I'll stick with this, thanks.'

JJ made jerky small talk until he returned with his coffee to the table. 'Sorry about the big scene with the old man . . .' he began, then ran out of words.

I shrugged, waited, then spooned some yoghurt out of the pot. 'They happen.'

'Yeah, well . . .' He stopped again and rubbed at his brow. 'I feel lousy.'

'Why? Were you in the wrong?'

'Shit, no! He was as wrong as hell.'

'Then why should you feel lousy? He should be the one to feel lousy.'

'That'll be the day!' he snorted and rolled his eyes. 'Have you got kids, Frank?'

'No.'

'Well, no doubt when you have your first, there'll be some miserable old fart sitting outside the delivery room to teach you the first principle of fatherhood: "There are two sides to every story, the father's side and the wrong side."'

'Heh! I'll tell him to stuff it.' I spooned in more yoghurt,

51

watching his fidgeting fingers distractedly knead the table-cloth. It must have been the mother of father–son rows.

After another brooding pause, during which he downed most of his coffee, he looked at me. 'You know what it was about, of course, don't you?'

'Haven't a clue.'

'I thought we could be heard down in Main Street.'

'I came in the back door just as you came out of the office. I missed it. Story of my life.' I grinned, trying to ease things up a little.

'Oh. Well . . . A few days back there was a call to a cow with a turned–down horn that was beginning to grow into her face, just below the eye . . .'

'I remember. I saw it on the book.'

'Simple job, aye?' I nodded. 'The cow was a suckler so she was a wild one, right?' I nodded again. 'She was near calving, so I didn't want her struggling. Okay?' I nodded yet again. '*Because* she was near calving, I couldn't use xylazine to sedate her, could I?' I shook my head. 'She'd probably abort, no?' I nodded again; it was like going through a preflight check-up. 'So I gave her Bovised instead, then 15cc of local to numb the horn, waited a few minutes and cut the tip off the horn, just enough to stop it from growing in. Anything wrong so far? Tell me straight out if there is.'

'Sounds fine to me. Why do you think it was wrong?'

'I don't. If I'd thought it was wrong, then I wouldn't have done it that way. But the client comes storming into the office this morning, has a heated argument with my old man, shows him an eight-month foetus in a bag in the back of his pick-up, claims that the cow aborted and that it's my fault because I'd used *xylazine* to sedate her. Then, like a magician, he produces an empty xylazine bottle out of his pocket which, according to him, I'd left behind.'

'And you hadn't?'

'Of course not! For a start, I used Bovised, not xylazine. And anyway, I never leave *anything* on farms – not even used injection swabs. What's more, my bottle of xylazine is still in

52

the car. I've checked. So if mine is still in my car, then how could Patsy Melia have found it on his farm?'

'At the risk of being insultingly pedantic, JJ, could you have had two bottles in the car?'

'Who the hell carries *two* bottles of xylazine?'

'Suppose not.' He had a point. Xylazine is used for sedation or, in large doses, as a general anaesthetic, the dose rate being varied to produce the required degree, from mild to deep. The procedure is not often called for during the normal course of general practice. A single 25cc bottle contains enough for many animals, so, as JJ had said, most vets carry only one. Still, a very careful vet might consider the possibility of a breakage and carry a spare, while a very careless one (who couldn't remember whether or not there might be a bottle somewhere in the chaotic jumble of his car boot) might throw in another, just in case. Or a very ordinary vet might carry a second bottle if the first one was nearing its end. But it was not the time for hair-splitting. 'So, where's this mystery bottle now?' I asked. 'Has your father got it?'

'No. The guy kept it, as evidence, in case he decides to sue me. It's Exhibit fucking-well A, isn't it? Now all this is bad enough but wait till I tell you how my dear father handled it. He immediately believes your man's story, apologises on my behalf, offers my youth and inexperience as an excuse, assures the client it will never happen again and asks him to give me a break, to keep away from the lawyers as the practice will work something out with him.

'Then, as soon as I get back from morning rounds, he calls me in and gives me a right royal bollocking. I tried to tell him the client was pulling some sort of stunt, but would he listen? Would he hell! The rest you heard.'

'So where do you reckon this client got the bottle, then?'

'Who the hell knows? And what's to say that that particular foetus actually came from the cow I attended? He runs a couple of hundred sucklers up there. Any of the in-calves could have aborted. I think the old man should have admitted nothing until he'd spoken to me, and then insisted on going to the farm and checking it out.'

'Why don't you ask him to do it now?'

JJ snorted. 'Do you think he'd back down like that? No way. The customer is always right and I – or any of my siblings – will always be wrong. If he doesn't change that attitude there'll be trouble in this family soon. Big trouble. We're not goddam kids any longer.'

'Did your father make a note of the batch number on the bottle, or the expiry date? So that you could compare it with the xylazine in your stores, or against old invoices?'

'I don't know, but I doubt it. Like I said, with him the customer is always right and any action like that might be misconstrued as questioning the customer's word. And we just couldn't have that, now, could we? Oh no, siree! No fucking way!'

I had no desire to get involved in Slattery family problems, so I went off at a tangent. There were urgent steps to be taken if the irate client was to be dissuaded from spreading his tale of perceived woe to everyone he met. Big news like that would flow like fire along a dynamite fuse. 'Don't you think, JJ, that someone ought to go and talk with that client soon?' I asked. 'Like right now. This very minute . . .'

'Like who, for instance?' he asked after a pause. When I didn't reply, just looked steadily at him, he became indignant. 'Well, you needn't look at me like that! *I'm* not the one who got us into this fucking mess. Tell God the Father to go . . . He's the one who fucked up.'

When God the Father came back from lunch I was hanging around in the front office, waiting for him, but trying not to make it obvious.

'Busy day, Frank?' He paused briefly on his way to his office.

'I've had worse.'

'Any problems?'

'Not really. Although I wouldn't mind a word, if you're not too busy.'

'Sure. Come on in.'

When he learned what I wanted to talk about, a brief flash of displeasure appeared on his face, but was quickly smothered. 'Oh, that! I shouldn't worry. You know how youngsters are. They come out of college, think they know it all and then, when they make a little mistake, they'll do anything rather than admit it. I suppose it's only natural. It'll teach him a valuable lesson, though, aye?' When he got no response from me, he continued: 'Perhaps I spoke a bit harshly to him, but he'll get over it.' Still I remained silent so he tried a touch of humour. 'Well, at least I found out one thing: I'll have to get this office soundproofed.'

JJ was right. His father was a patronising, opinionated whatsit, grade one. 'Actually, I didn't overhear anything. JJ came and spoke to me.'

'Did he now? I see. Needed a shoulder to cry on, did he?'

'He needed a professional opinion from an outsider, with no axe to grind either way.'

'And what, pray, did you advise?' PJ, picking up from me the feeling that I was (inexplicably, unaccountably, incredibly) not on his side, began to turn smarmy.

'I told him that if someone had accused me of malpractice and I was *certain* that I hadn't done anything wrong, I'd follow it to the ends of the earth.'

'I see. So you don't think my son made a bloomer?'

'I'd put JJ at above average in both competence and conscientiousness. If he insists he didn't use xylazine then I think that, at the very least, he deserves the benefit of the doubt.'

'Okay. We'll have to agree to differ on that one. You see, I've actually seen the bottle.' He picked up a pen and pulled paper towards him, trying to indicate that the interview was over. Perhaps, as far as he was concerned, it was.

I, however, had more to say. 'Listen, PJ. Whatever there may be between you and your son is none of my business, but aren't you afraid that this client is going to talk about how young Slattery caused his cow to abort, and that the word will spread and that the practice could end up losing clients?'

For a moment I thought he was going to tell me that was

none of my business either – I could almost see the retort forming in his mouth – but instead, he sat back and smiled. 'Melia did threaten to sue, but I calmed him down. All the clients have great respect for me, you know. I'll see him all right, don't worry. And young JJ, too. So you can tell my seemingly self-proclaimed infallible son, whenever he turns up at your door again, that it's all taken care of, that he can relax. We all make mistakes.'

I could hardly believe my ears. PJ sat across from me, looking almost proud – the great statesman – and to hell with justice. He had allowed his son to be accused without a murmur in his defence; he had admitted JJ's guilt without checking his side of the story, he had then apologised on JJ's behalf, offering 'incompetence due to inexperience' in mitigation and, finally, he had 'solved' the problem by promising to deal sternly with the young incompetent to ensure that 'it wouldn't happen again'. Reparation for JJ's 'guilt' was the offering of a vague bribe that he would see the plaintiff 'all right'. Now he sat there, across from me, with a pleased pout on him, like he'd just pulled off the diplomatic coup of the century. With some considerable difficulty I returned to the more immediate problem. 'Fine. Let's say that the client, well pleased with his . . . ah . . .' (I searched my inner lexicon for a euphemism for 'pushover') . . . his ah . . . unexpectedly successful chat with you, undertook not to sue. Did he also guarantee not to talk about it?'

'To *talk* about it?'

'Yeah. To talk about it, PJ. Like in the pub? Or at the mart? Or even just to his neighbours, who are probably also clients of yours. You know what farmers are like. Talk, talk, talk. Bitch, bitch, bitch. Moan, moan, moan . . . I assume Melia undertook not to talk about it?'

'Eh . . . No.' Suddenly PJ didn't look so insufferably smug. 'No, actually, he didn't . . .'

'Well, didn't you *ask* him? Wasn't that the deal? His silence for your apology and promise to see him all right?' I sat, watching reality creep over him: despite his abject serving up of JJ's head on the platter of appeasement, he hadn't actually protected the practice at all. Stupid, pompous dickhead. I decided to try another tack. 'Did you get a good look at the empty bottle?'

'Listen, I've seen enough xylazine bottles in my time to recognise the genuine . . .'

'So have I, but did you examine the label? Did the client let you handle the bottle?'

More awkward silence. PJ cleared his throat. 'He didn't offer and I didn't like to ask. Under the circumstances, it would have been extremely . . . difficult . . . if he had refused. It was a delicate situation requiring very delicate handl—'

I cut across the craven, self-serving crap. 'So for all you know, that bottle might have expired ten years ago? Or it might be from a batch which was never even *delivered* to this practice?'

His only response to this was an uncomfortable shrug.

'Isn't that so?' I demanded, although quietly.

'Well, it's possible, I suppose.' He drew a theatrical sigh. 'But there's not much we can do about it now, is there?'

I smiled, determined to do my best to keep this friendly. 'Now there I must disagree with you. If I were you, I'd go straight out to this client, ask to see the cow, handle her to make sure that she actually *has* lost her calf and ask to see that bottle again. I'd write down all the details of that label, hightail it back here, and check it against your present stocks and past invoices. If they don't tally, then JJ and the practice are in the clear, and Melia will have no cause to bad-mouth you.'

'Look, Frank, I appreciate what you're saying, but even if I agreed fully with you, how can I suddenly change my attitude at this point and expect Patsy Melia not to become even more annoyed than he was? He'd be on to his lawyer before I'd left his farm. It would look as though I was going back on my word.'

The fault was entirely PJ's. He should never have given his 'word' in the first place. But, as it was now far too late to

57

undo that blunder, I could see his point. Having unequivo-
cally accepted Melia's story and irrevocably dumped the
sacrificial JJ up to his eyeballs in the slurry, he could hardly
turn up now, with a suddenly opened mind, not without
making a bad situation immeasurably worse.

So PJ couldn't go.

And JJ wouldn't go.

'What about Michael?' I asked. 'Could he soothe the
situation?'

'Michael! God, man, Michael, even on his best behaviour,
is about as soothing as sandpaper.'

'Could your father go, him being senior partner and all?'

'Hardly. He'd wonder why one of us wasn't handling it.'

And, I thought, ask questions and find that PJ had acted
like an idiot and caused the whole mess.

After a brief reflective silence, PJ looked at me and I
looked at PJ. When you thought about it, there was really
only one choice left. Me. I'd blindly and stupidly talked
myself into a minefield. More ridiculous still was the fact that
no matter what the outcome, it could have no possible effect
on my life or future . . .

Oh, good man yourself there, Frank. Smart move. Well
played.

6

Patsy Melia was a big farmer, in every sense of the word. During my pre-mission briefing, PJ had told me that he ran a two-hundred plus beef-cow suckler herd and had slatted fattening houses for rearing his weanlings to finishing. He also had up to a thousand ewes on a farm he had recently inherited from a bachelor uncle, a sub-species of *H. sapiens* which is not uncommon in rural Ireland. It is, however, a sub-species headed for extinction, mainly because, by definition, it does not breed, well not very often, anyway. But that's another story.

In the physical sense Melia stood an impressive six foot five. His haggard face was reddened from the elements, the tops of his ears raw and flaking, discoloured stumps of teeth showed fleetingly between pale cracked lips. His right eye had sustained some past injury that had left it milky white and semi-collapsed, like a dinged ping-pong ball. Bleached reddish hair clung in sparse clumps to his weatherbeaten pate, wisps of it waving and swaying in the light wind.

My first sight of him made me want to pretend that I was just a lost day tripper who wanted directions home. But, as usual, appearances were deceiving and the forbidding man in front of me turned out to be, if not quite one of nature's actual gentlemen, then certainly one of her more decent blokes. When I told him who I was and explained that I was here on JJ's behalf, he snorted. 'Coming to apologise, I suppose.'

'No, actually. Coming to try to find out what happened.'

'Does PJ know you're here?' he asked sharply.

'No,' I lied. There was no point in making this tougher. 'I told PJ what happened. This morning.'

'I know that. But JJ says there has to be a mistake.'

'He would, wouldn't he?'

I shrugged. 'Still, I think this should be thoroughly looked into. Even for your sake. I mean, if you were to go to court, you could lose your case if there hadn't been a proper veterinary investigation. Like a case of drunk-driving where the whole world can see that the guy is footless, but unless a doctor says so . . .'

'You can tell young Slattery from me that it won't go to court. That would be a rough start in life for the lad. It's not like I'd never made a mistake myself.'

'Well!' I said, slightly surprised and very much relieved. 'It's a decent man who'll admit that he's made mistakes. But that's the point: I reckon that JJ, too, just like yourself, would be man enough to own up to *his* mistakes. Do you know him well?'

Patsy scratched his head with gnarled fingers. 'He's been here several times and I must say I always found him to be a nice lad. Did some fair good jobs for me, too, so he did.'

'I can believe it. I've only known him for a few days really, but he strikes me as being a fairly conscientious and capable bloke. I've seen him do a few nice slick jobs too. So, as we both agree on that much, will you at least give me a few minutes of your time to see how the two of you, both honest men, could have got the same story so mixed up? I've spoken to JJ and now I'm speaking to you and I don't believe that either one of you is lying. So there must be some other explanation.'

He acknowledged the conundrum wordlessly, with elaborate movements of neck, head and face.

'Thanks,' I said. 'First, did JJ ask you if the cow was in calf or not?'

'He did. I remember that. But I'd already said she was when I rang in the call.'

'But he checked again anyway, right?'

'Right.'

'Sounds like a pretty conscientious approach to me. And this was *before* he injected her with anything?'

'Aye.'

'And you answered . . . ?'

'I told him she was over seven months gone.'

'You realise why he asked that question?' The huge man didn't volunteer an answer, so I answered for him. 'So that he could decide which sedative to use. I'd have asked the same question, too. To see if it was safe to give her xylazine. Don't you think it would be strange for a man to ask a question and then not know what to do with the answer? It would be totally pointless him asking in the first place.'

More silence from the giant.

I gave it a moment to sink in, then continued: 'Can you tell me if you saw JJ – I mean actually clearly remember seeing him – loading a syringe from that bottle you showed his father this morning?'

He thought for a moment before answering: 'Nope, I can't swear that I remember seeing him do that.'

'Well, he gave the cow two injections, right? One, in a small syringe, to quieten her down, and the other, in a large one, to numb the crooked horn. Did you notice what colour the drug in the *small* syringe was?'

Brow creased, he considered again. 'No, afraid not. I had my hands full trying to hold the cow for him. She's a bit of a lady, the same one.'

'You didn't notice if it was colourless or yellow?' Xylazine is clear, while Bovised is yellow.

'No, sorry. Like I said, I was busy.'

'Okay, no sweat. Can we check the cow, now?' I looked towards the barns and sheds a short distance off.

'Why?' he asked, immediately suspicious.

'I want a blood sample to rule out brucellosis and I'd also like to see that she's okay inside. You never know.' What I really wanted was to make sure the cow actually *had* aborted, but I could hardly tell him that in plainspeak.

Protesting that he had always had a brucellosis-free herd, he seemed about to refuse, but changed his mind. 'Okay, if that's what you want. But she's not here. She's on a piece of land I rent, about three miles away and, luckily, she's in a shed. If she was out we'd never get her in. She's a mad bitch, like I said. She's her mother's daughter and no mistake.'

'Why is she in the shed?' I asked, as we drove out of his gate.

'She hasn't passed the afterbirth. I'll keep her in until she does.'

That was one question already answered – if she had a retained placenta hanging from her, then she had to have given birth, by abortion or otherwise.

A dark string of foetal membrancs dragged like a second tail along the ground behind the cow as she galloped around under the spacious lean-to, time and again foiling our efforts to drive her into the narrow chute in one corner. At last we succeeded and I took the blood sample and put several antibiotic pessaries into the recently vacated uterus. The placenta was stuck tight inside – it often is when a cow miscarries. I moved up to check her head and JJ's work. The cut end of the horn was dry, bloodless and clean; the crater which the curving-in horn tip had gouged in her cheek had scabbed up nicely, too. There were no worries in that department. I remarked that JJ seemed to have done a very neat and competent job.

'I told you. I've never had any complaints about his work. Before.'

Too late I thought that we should have examined the yard under the lean-to for the tracks of strange boots. The saboteur must have had a hell of a job putting the cow into the chute on his own – Patsy and I had almost failed. If there had been tracks, then Patsy and I and the cow would have churned them well into the mud as she led us on our merry dance. Amateur! I scolded myself. Part-timer! Of course, I didn't mention it to Patsy Melia. It was bad enough *me* knowing I was an idiot. No need to spread it about.

'So where did you find that bottle, then?' I asked, giving the cow a final pat of dismissal.

'Just sitting on that window ledge there. Plain as day.'

The small, dirt-grimed window he pointed at was at the exit from the narrow chute, just where we stood, its sill slightly higher than my head height. 'You saw him put it there?'

'No. At least not that I remember.'

'Strange place for a short bloke to pick. He'd almost have to stand on tiptoe, I reckon.'

'Well, there's nowhere else around that he could leave it, no table, shelf . . .'

'He'd have put it in his pocket. That's where I put things. That's where most vets I know put things. Until they get back to the car.' Most vets only carry their heavy bag with them if they don't know what lies ahead. When you know exactly what the job is, you carry the few things you need with you. Why carry more? 'Isn't it a wonder JJ didn't spot it and take it with him? He tells me he never leaves empty bottles on farms. Did you not draw it to his attention?'

'Actually, I didn't notice it myself until the evening, about sixish.'

'Hmph! Maybe that was because it wasn't there in the morning. Odd that neither of you noticed it in the morning. It must have been plain to see up there. Like a sore thumb.'

'It was. It was the first thing I noticed when I came back, even though I was well flustered at the time, worrying about the cow.'

'Why were you worrying about the cow?'

'A bloke rang to tell me that she was lying down, unconscious.'

'A bloke! What bloke?'

'I don't know. He said he was a tourist just touring around. That he'd stepped into the field – he hoped I didn't mind – for a pee, saw the cow, unconscious, and phoned me.'

'A tourist?' I shook my head in slow disbelief. 'Well how about that, then? You live three miles away, Patsy, so how did the "tourist" know who owned the cow?'

'I figured maybe some local was passing on the road and he asked them . . .'

'Doesn't this whole story strike you as very odd?'

'Maybe now it does, but at the time I was just thankful for the news. Later on, though, I did think it odd – not so much that a tourist might call, but that he'd have seen the cow at all. If, as he said, he'd just hopped over the gate for a piss, what business would he have at the sheds here, three hundred yards away from the gate?'

'Perhaps he's the world's shyest tourist. Maybe he can only pee if there's a roof above him, in case passing aeroplanes or spy satellites might be able to see his willy? How about the cow? How'd you find her?'

Patsy was smiling gappily at my pissing-tourist sketch. Now he got serious again. 'She was up, but groggy. Staggering.'

'And how did she go afterwards? I presume you stayed with her?'

'God, yes. She got stronger and stronger. After an hour or so, she seemed fine.'

'What did you think was wrong with her? Had you seen other cows the same way?'

'Only cows after operations. She was just like one recovering from an anaesthetic. Improved at much the same rate and all.'

'That's what it sounds like to me, too. What time did your tourist ring?'

'Just before six. I came straight away.'

'And what time had JJ been?'

'Oh, early in the morning. Well before nine. He said it was his first call of the day.'

'Okay, let me tell you something, Patsy. I don't know what the hell is going on but even if JJ *had* given her xylazine, and a *huge* dose of it at that, the effect would have worn off in a few hours max. Did the cow go down after the injection in the morning?'

'No. She just got nice and quiet, like young Slattery said

she would. She was a wee bit wobbly, like as if she'd been on the booze, but you'd expect that.'

'So, it doesn't seem like he overdosed her, does it? Did you stay around to watch her?'

'I had some odd jobs that took a couple of hours.'

'I assume you checked her before you left?'

'And a few times before that, too.'

'How was she when you were leaving? Back to normal?'

'I wouldn't have left until she was.'

By this stage I felt that Patsy Melia must have given up any idea of JJ being responsible. 'So why do you think she was down and groggy again in the evening?' I asked, testing him.

'I really can't think. Sounds a bit dodgy to me, now. Maybe I didn't think before going to see PJ.'

'Maybe. I suppose the helpful tourist had left by the time you arrived?'

'There was no one here at all.'

'Did he have an accent?'

'Not that I noticed. He wasn't a foreigner, if that's what you mean.'

'Maybe he was the one who left the bottle there for you to find.'

Patsy made no reply to that. He wasn't quite ready to give in just yet.

Back at his home yard, I asked to see the bottle as I needed to check the label. Without the slightest hesitation he fetched it from the glove compartment of his pick-up, handed it to me and watched as I jotted down the relevant data. There was a notice round the bottom of the label, a warning in capital letters: CAUTION – NOT FOR USE IN PREGNANT ANIMALS. 'God,' I said, 'JJ would have had to be *blind* as well as professionally incompetent to have used this stuff.' Then I offered it back.

'Ah, hell,' he said, 'sure what do I want with it? You may as well keep it.'

'No, Patsy. You keep it. If it turns out that JJ did abort

your cow, then you deserve your day in court.' Having met him, I knew he wouldn't abuse the situation, so the gesture wasn't quite as grand as it seemed, or as chancy. 'One more thing,' I said, sitting into the Land Rover and reaching for my seat belt, 'as there is something very odd about all this, I think it would be fairest not to mention a word to anyone, not until we get to the bottom of it anyway. What do you reckon?'

'Aye, it would. Indeed it would. Don't worry. I've said nothing.'

'Well, that's damned fair-minded of you . . .'

'Arra, not really,' said Patsy. 'To be honest I just haven't seen anyone since.' He gave a short, barking laugh, showing off the bad teeth.

I laughed with him and, still grinning, let out the clutch and drove out of his yard.

7

Nothing is ever easy. The empty xylazine bottle turned out to be from the same batch as the second-last delivery to the Slattery practice, which also happened to be the same batch as the bottle that JJ had in his car. Damn!

'That proves nothing,' I said. 'They probably make a *million* bottles in each batch.'

JJ looked disappointed, angry and a little scared. His father just looked on.

At the outset there had been much flexing of the eyebrows between father and son but the sub-zero atmosphere soon began to thaw and JJ perked up visibly when I told them that, in my opinion, Patsy was beginning to think him innocent and had no intention of suing.

'Tourist, my arse!' he said, feeling more cocky now, his voice rasping with scorn.

'It's not unknown,' his father replied, almost civilly. 'We often get tourists calling in about sick animals.'

'This is different,' JJ said. 'The ones tourists call about are nearly always found injured on or beside the road.'

'Exactly where did Patsy *claim* to have found the bottle?' PJ asked, giving at least the impression of an open mind.

'On a window ledge next to the chute where they were working. But, as I said, he didn't find it until the evening.'

'That's odd for sure.' He yielded a little bit more and I wondered if he had, at last, decided to try fair-mindedness for a change – I later learned that Michael Stone had had a 'talk' with him while I was out on my mission of diplomacy and he, too, had been very much pro-JJ. Clearly the braves, even the temporary mercenary one, had, en masse, ganged up on the chief.

The talk soon became drily technical, which helped normalise relations even further.

Some narcotics can recycle in the body and cause re-narcosis, but none of us had ever seen, or even heard of, a cow re-narcotising on either xylazine or Bovised. Books and formularies were fetched and consulted; product information leaflets were pored over; pharmacopoeias were dusted off and read; JJ's pharmacology lecture notes were searched; various computer programmes were summoned up, but nowhere could we find case histories involving re-narcosis with either of the products in question. Eventually we decided that we could safely eliminate it as an explanation of why the cow had been down many hours after she had been seen to have recovered from her original dose, a dose so light that it had barely caused her to stagger, let alone go down. There was only one logical conclusion: someone had given the cow a *second* dose in the evening, a heavier dose, enough to put her off her feet and they had used a product which they knew would abort her – in other words, sabotage. Before going further, we checked out all our conclusions again as we were about to move on into speculative territory. We all agreed that the reasoning was sound and that it was safe for us to go on.

The saboteur had left an empty xylazine bottle where it just had to be noticed. He was taking no chances on Patsy Melia's deductive powers – if at first he missed the point, then he certainly wouldn't miss the bottle.

'It sounds like someone is deliberately trying to cause trouble for me,' JJ said miserably.

'Who would want to do that?' PJ snapped, seemingly annoyed that JJ should even suggest that he was, of himself, sufficiently important to warrant his very own, personal and private vendetta.

'Maybe', said JJ, 'the same people who tried to put the red blister on Phil Jones's horse?'

His father shrugged irritably. 'What possible connection could there be between Phil's horse and Patsy Melia's cow?'

'Whose cases were they, hey?' JJ demanded. 'Mine.' He tapped his chest belligerently. 'Both of them, mine.'

I stepped in quickly. 'That could be just coincidence, JJ. It's more likely that the practice is the target. Two cases of sabotage within a week.'

I watched them exhibit all the signs of people under stress – shaking heads, pushing fingers through hair, perplexed expressions ranging from helpless frustration to unfocused anger – and reckoned that there had to be something very wrong about this practice. I was no expert but I didn't need to be a financial wizard to know that Slattery and Partners could hardly generate enough income to feed one person, let alone the staff it carried.

Yet the practice was well equipped with state-of-the-art facilities, expensive apparatus that couldn't have been more than a year or two old. Presumably, then, in the quite recent past the practice had been thriving, so much so that it could afford this expensive refit. So why had it plunged so far so quickly?

'Tell me this,' I said, interrupting some low-grade argument which had broken out again. 'Would I be right in thinking that these are not the first two cases of sabotage? Have there been others? I'm thinking of fairly recently, say, mainly in the last year?'

'Why do you ask that?' Father and son exchanged meaningful glances.

I shrugged. 'Good equipment, excellent facilities, all expensive, and a small calls list . . . It doesn't tie in.' It was, of course, possible that the money had been spent in panic by an ailing practice hoping to buy its way out of trouble, but I didn't think so. There was too much good stuff about. 'The reason that I say a year is because most of the equipment can't be much older than that, so I figure it was bought when times were good – no?'

With a sigh, PJ began to explain how life in the partnership had been deteriorating, just as I had suggested, in the last year or so. Simple, straightforward cases had been going wrong for no apparent reason, clients had begun to move away and the partners were at each other's throats half the time, with accusations of stupidity, incompetence and carelessness being freely traded. 'So that may go some way towards explaining some of the short tempers and ... perhaps rather precipitate decisions you may have witnessed since you came.'

When I asked for examples, he listed a handful: a valuable stallion which had been having a course of intravenous injections had later developed a severe phlebitis and cellulitis at the injection site and a large part of the neck muscle had rotted away; a bitch had died of peritonitis six weeks after being spayed; two cows in the one yard had been treated for ketosis by PJ himself ('and, believe you me, I know ketosis when I see it') but, when neither had improved after two days, the client ('the ex-client', now) had called in another vet, who had cured them straight away. And on and on.

It was all fascinating stuff, but it left one huge question: why had they hired me? What was I supposed to do?

'I hope you'll excuse my bluntness, but I can't help wondering why you needed to take me on. You certainly don't need the manpower . . .' There was a very long silence and I couldn't figure why PJ was finding it such a difficult question to answer. Then it struck me. It seemed incredible but I reckoned that the practice had decided to hire me solely because, over the past couple of years, I had become unwittingly involved in a few widely publicised cases, scams of one sort or another which, mainly serendipitously, I had helped to unravel. Because of these, I'd acquired a bit of a reputation as a sort of troubleshooter or crime buster. As PJ still hadn't managed to come up with an answer, I asked him straight out.

'Yes, that's correct.' PJ looked shamefaced and embarrassed, and turned his eyes away from me.

'So, that's why you insisted on hiring a locum!' JJ angrily

challenged his father. He turned to me. 'I don't mind telling you, Frank, that I was totally against taking you on. Nothing personal, mind, but shit! – as you can see, we don't have enough work to keep *ourselves* going.' He rounded on his father again. 'Jeez! I'm supposed to be part of this practice too, you know. How about Michael? Did Michael know?' When his father didn't answer, JJ moved in again. 'Well, damn me but that beats everything. You didn't tell Michael either. You're not a partner, you're a bloody *dictator*!'

PJ held up his hands, pleading for peace, then began in a low voice: 'It was your grandfather's suggestion, JJ. At first he wanted a private detective. A few days later, after he'd read an article which mentioned Frank, nothing would do him but to get Frank. He didn't want anyone to know and he said he'd pay Frank's fee himself, so what could I do? He reckoned that Miriam's upcoming maternity leave would provide the perfect excuse to slip Frank into the practice unnoticed. Which it did.'

While JJ goggled wordlessly, PJ's revelations were making me do some serious rethinking. 'If that was the case,' I said quietly, 'then I think I should have been told so at the outset.'

'Too bloody right, you should,' said JJ, glaring again at his father.

PJ spent moments looking at his hands. 'Would you have taken on the job? If you had known?' he asked at last, glancing up at me.

'Probably not. I'm a vet, you know, not some kind of busybody sleuth, despite what you seem to think.'

'It's hard to think of you as "just a vet", Frank. What about *Catamaran*? And that anthrax business last year?'

'It's not the same thing. I was hired, genuinely hired, as a locum in both instances, by guys who were going on holiday. Neither I nor the vets who hired me had any inkling that there might be trouble in the offing. Coincidences both. Pure coincidence.'

'Agreed. But once the trouble began, you got the bit between your teeth and followed those cases through to the end, long after any ordinary man would have bowed out. They reckon that, if it hadn't been for you, those cases would never have been solved.'

I turned to JJ. 'See what I mean? Suddenly I'm Sherlock bloomin' Holmes!' Then, to his father. 'Who's "they"?'

'Any vet you talk to. They're still talking about it, ask anybody. What's more, the same "they" reckon you enjoyed the experiences, that you thrived on them.'

'Jesus! I was nearly killed both times. Literally!'

'I know. But you'd do it all over again, wouldn't you?'

I said nothing, determined not to be seduced by flattery. Secretly I had to admit that PJ was right. I could have left both cases to the experts, but in another way I couldn't. In the first place, I had had something to contribute – my veterinary knowledge – and in the second, I'd found myself totally caught up in the plots and ramifications, the developments and discoveries, the mad action and the quiet thinking, the surprises and the dangers, my life almost taken over by the excitement, like some adrenalin freak. Even now, with just the whiff of intrigue in the air, my blood was beginning to hum. 'I don't know . . .' I said, playing hard to get.

Spotting my hesitation, PJ pressed on. 'Look . . . Maybe there's no "crime" here at all. Perhaps it's just bad luck, or even bad veterinary. I'll tell you what . . . You can leave at any time, no notice required, but if someone is deliberately trying to kill this practice and you expose him, or them, then I guarantee you that Grandad will triple your fee and the practice will also pay you a large bonus . . . What do you say to that?'

'It's not the money,' I said. 'I just think I ought to have been given the choice. I should have been told.'

'Yes. You're right. I'm sorry.' PJ could afford to be humble, now that he knew he had me in the bag.

'Right. If Michael and JJ agree, I'll hang on and see what, if anything, happens. No promises, okay?'

'Done. No promises.'

'Are you happy with that, JJ?'

'I am. Now.'

So was I. Delighted, in fact, but I hid it well. I shook hands with both of them. 'Fine, then. That's settled. Now let's get down to business. Who stands to gain from your troubles?' I repeated the question I'd asked the night of the intruders in the yard.

'Other practices in the area, I suppose.'

'Are there many of those?'

'Four close by, but I suppose we touch on about ten altogether.'

'Are any of them losing clients the way you are?'

'Well, there's always some movement of clients between . . .'

'I'm aware of that. But have any of them had the heavy losses you've had during the past year?'

'Not that I know of.'

'Would you know? If they were?'

'I think so, yes. I'm sure we would.'

'Well, then, let's try it from the other end. Are any of them picking up more of your ex-clients than the others?'

'As far as we know, most of our disaffected clients – say sixty-five, seventy per cent? – have transferred to Val Crowther over in Breenstown, but that probably isn't as significant as it may seem, because he's very much the up-and-coming practice in the area and you'd expect them to gravitate towards him.' PJ looked at his son. 'We've thought of Crowther, you know, but it doesn't make sense. He's doing very well in his own right, so where's his motive? He's grown rapidly, year by year – started as a one-man show a little over five years ago and he's now got at least four vets working for him; nobody could expect to do better than that . . .'

'You wouldn't have thought so,' I agreed. 'But still . . . if this practice is losing clients at an unnatural rate and that practice is picking up most of them . . . ?'

'If he's that greedy for clients, then why isn't he working his ju-ju on the other practices around? Why us?'

'Maybe because your practice is the biggest one around?'

73

'Not for much longer at this rate,' JJ grumbled.

'If he could overtake you as the main practice in the area, then his rate of growth might become even faster.'

Neither of the Slatterys looked over-impressed with this theory. I went on: 'Well, we have to look at all the possibilities. Could there be a personal motive? Has Crowther got a grudge against any of you? Did you ever decline to employ him? Refuse him a reference?' PJ's head was shaking no as I ran through some possible scenarios. 'Did any of you ever attend a case of his and criticise his work? Have you ever opposed a proposal of his at a Clinical Society or Veterinary Union meeting? Anything like that, at all?'

'Not that I know of. Not knowingly, anyway. I've hardly ever spoken to the man. We're nodding acquaintances and that's all.'

'I've never even *seen* him,' said JJ.

'How about Michael? You said he's an abrasive character. Could he have had a run-in with him?'

'No. I'm almost one hundred per cent sure. He'd have told me. But I'll check with him anyway.'

'Well it can't just be greed,' I said. 'Apart from the fact that no other local practice is suffering your level of losses, Crowther's been in the area for five years and he was as quiet as a mouse for the first four. What could have suddenly turned him greedy a year ago?'

'I can't believe it could be him. It'd be too obvious. And besides, how could he, or anyone else for that matter, know where our calls even are, never mind be able to adversely influence the outcome of our treatments?'

'Well, we know that someone tried to screw up your treatments with Fizzikle and Melia's cow. They almost succeeded. Let's assume that they have succeeded with many others already.'

'Okay, but how did they know about Fizzikle or the cow in the first place?'

'That's the worry. Could it be coming from someone inside the practice?'

'Apart from Barbara we're all family and Barbara is closer than family. Lifelong friend.'

'How about the yardmen? How many are there, by the way?'

'Two. But they've been here since before JJ was born. Besides, they rarely, if ever, come into the office and certainly wouldn't go behind the counter.'

'How about Jimmy in the store?'

'The same. He's been here for years, too. He'd have no business looking at the call book either. If either Jimmy or the yardmen were seen reading the calls list, Barbara or Eve would spot them – there's always one of them about. But I'll ask them if you like – just to be sure.' He made a note on his scrap pad, beneath the one reminding himself to ask Michael if he'd ever had a run-in with Crowther.

'What I don't understand', said JJ, 'is why, if all these cases were sabotage, nobody has ever been caught actually interfering with the animals. Whoever it is must be damned clever.'

'I don't know if I'd agree with that,' I said. 'Whatever about the other cases, this time, with Melia's cow, he made lots of mistakes.'

'You think so?'

'Sure he did. His first mistake was actually picking this case. The cow was on an outfarm which, although ideal for sneaking about unseen, was a disaster insofar as he actually had to summon the owner by phone in order to get him even to *notice* the stricken animal. That brought in that outlandishly incredible tourist. What "innocent" tourist would be poking about at sheds such a long way from the road?

'Another mistake was leaving the empty xylazine bottle – for all he knew, the label details might not tally with any of yours and so his plant could have become the opposite, a complete giveaway. I assume that the bottle was directed straight at Melia who, if he read the label, couldn't fail to see the warning about pregnant animals.

'In which case it looks as if the saboteur was willing to risk tipping you off in his desire to stir up Melia and have him going around criticising you to all and sundry, spreading the bad news about the incompetent Slatterys. And perhaps he might even have made the right choice. You could deny all you liked and prove ten times over that the bottle wasn't yours, but nobody would believe you. Or very few.

'But his *biggest* mistake to my mind was the fact that he used xylazine at all to abort the cow. He could have got the same result with either prostaglandins or dexamethasone, neither of which would have sedated the cow in any way. That was the real giveaway because there's just no way that the cow, having recovered normally from the morning's shot, could be doped and down again *hours* later, regardless of what sedative you had used. He didn't need to signpost his plant so blatantly. He ought to have left it to Patsy Melia to make the connection, which he undoubtedly would have. It's human nature. Cause and effect. Vet did work on Tuesday morning, cow aborts Wednesday night.

'It's like the old story of the farmer who comes into the surgery one October morning and says: You remember that horse you castrated for me last April? Well he died last night. And the vet says to him: Did you know So-and-So from Main Street? Well he died last night, too, and I didn't castrate *him* last April.'

Being vets, of course they knew the old joke but, being vets, they laughed at it again anyway.

After going round the same circles for another hour, we finally broke up. The only really good thing that had come from the meeting was that by the time it ended the Js – Pappy and Junior – were once more on the same side.

8

The last time I'd seen Ellen Ollin, she'd been Ellen Hendricks and she'd been as crazy about me as I was about her.

We were in my flat in Landsdowne Road, in Dublin, in the dying hour of the day that I'd finished my fourth-year exams. We lay on my narrow bed, clinging to each other and storing up love and memories for our imminent three-month separation, the annual brutal slash into the weave of the life of provincial students. As my flatmates had already dispersed for the long summer break, I was pressing her to stay the night, but Ellen, ever practical, said she needed her sleep. It was all right for me, I'd finished my exams, but she still had one paper and a couple of vivas to go for her BA. A while later, roused by midnight's chimes, she pushed herself out of my sleepy embrace and kissed me a gentle goodnight. In the dusky gloom of street lights through flimsy curtains, she blew me a kiss from the door, admonished me in mock-stern tones to be good and left. And that was the last time I'd ever seen her.

Until now.

Now she stood, framed in another door and said: 'Hi, Frank. Remember me?'

I could only goggle like a halfwit.

She twitched me a nervous smile and her eyes darted momentarily away – at least she had the decency to look unsure of her reception. 'May I come in?'

'Why not?' I managed at last in a tone that held just the right amount of ambiguity, let her take it any way she liked. I half rose from behind the desk and offered my hand. When she took it I was relieved to note that I'd forgotten the feel of her. 'Won't you sit down?' I said, doing well so far.

She sat and I waited – she was the one who had come barging back into my life, let her start the ball rolling.

'So! How have you been?' She attempted a bright smile but it didn't quite come off.

'Never better. And you?'

She shrugged and had another go at the smile. 'Oh . . . Great. Fine.'

'Glad to hear it.' I was wondering why she'd come into the surgery. She wasn't surprised to see me, so she must have known I was here.

'I read about Dave in the papers, Frank. I'm sorry.'

'Yeah, it's been six months now.' I remembered how the three of us, Dave, Ellen and I, had been such a unit in those days. We went everywhere together, shared money, food; she even wore our shirts sometimes.

'I was shocked to hear what they said about him. It wasn't true, was it?'

It was my turn to shrug. 'If you're referring to his reportedly less than legal lifestyle then, sadly, I think it was true. If you mean did he die from a self-inflicted overdose of heroin, then no. He was murdered. With an overdose of heroin.'

'God! How awful! Have they found whoever did it?'

'No and, at the rate they're going, they probably never will.'

I waited again for her next comment, still wondering why she was here, but clearly decorum dictated that further platitudes were necessary before any explanation for the visit would be forthcoming. I mean, you leave a guy, swearing eternal love, then seven weeks and two days later, send him a letter telling him you've met someone else and that it's all off, finished, over, you're very, very, very, very sorry, you never meant it to happen, but there it is, I hope we can always be friends ... Sure, friends ...

'Well, I must say, *you're* looking well,' she said, having another stab at breaking the ice.

'So are you,' I said. She was, too. Very.

More uncomfortable silence, this time longer. Maybe she was finding the ice thicker than she'd bargained for. 'Is this awkward for you, Frank?' she asked suddenly, stuck, I suspected, for something to say.

'For *me*?' Just because I'd spent two weeks beseeching her on the phone until she had refused to take any more of my calls; just because I'd caught trains and buses three times to plead personally with her and each time had had to leave, the vain hopes of my journey in desolate ruins when she refused even to share the same town with me. She hadn't actually left until her watching friends reported that the coast was clear, that I'd taken the bus back out again. Just because I'd spent a whole year not wanting to live any more ...

'No.' I summoned up a puzzled expression, hamming complete incomprehension. 'Should it?'

She swallowed. 'I felt awful, Frank. You've no idea. Sometimes I still do. I never wanted anything to go wrong between us, but what we want or don't want often has very little to do with what actually happens.' Ellen, the philosopher. 'No hard feelings, then?'

'Hah!' I laughed lightly. 'Water under the bridge. One of life's little character moulding experiences ...' *Little*! I'd almost lost my reason, and when it did steady itself, I employed it solely in the fabrication of self-deluding theories to ease my torment. I'd heard he had money so I immediately began to cast serious doubts on her hitherto unbesmirchable character. The logic was simple: she couldn't love him as much as she loved me, therefore she had to be after his money. The judgement was equally simple: therefore she was a scheming gold-digger, little better than a whore. In light of these facts, the conclusion was, of course, foregone: open and shut case. Although I'd never given the matter much thought, I realised suddenly that, more than almost anything else in the whole wide world, I despised heartless, mercenary, gold-digging, opportunistic whores. *Especially* ones who slyly and cunningly hid these deplorable traits for over two years . . . Good bloody riddance to bad bloody rubbish, was all I could say, and ta ever so to the Guardian Angel for the lucky escape.

Then, when one of the lads mentioned one night in the pub some time in the following spring that he'd heard that Ellen had got married, I laughed hollowly and said to the company in general: 'Jays! The poor bloody sucker. Well, *he'll* soon learn . . .' There was general laughter and another of the lads smirked: 'Well, Frankie boy, you should know.'

'Too bloody right, I know,' I replied with a worldly-wise pantomimed shake of the head and a melodramatic raising of the eyeballs towards the smoke-browned ceiling, and we all laughed again. Then I finished my pint, manufactured a yawn, stretched pointedly, and said I was knackered and was off home. Instead, I drove out to the lakeshore in my mother's car and bawled my eyes out for an hour, howling like a lost soul into the utter dark.

'Did someone say you'd married?' I asked, trying to sound offhand.

'That's right.'

'Congratulations! Recently? I can't remember when I heard it . . .'

'Oh, it was *ages* ago. Not long after we . . . eh. Well, put it this way, I never went back to do my MA. I didn't see much point in it. Things had changed . . .' She shrugged. 'How about yourself? Are you married?'

'Not legally. Not on the register, like.'

'But you are in a relationship?'

'Oh yes,' I said, as if this were inevitable. Did she think I might still be waiting for her?

'I'm glad, Frank. Is she nice?'

'Well *I* think so anyway . . .' I almost added 'but then, can you ever *really* be sure?' but didn't – I wasn't going to manufacture some doubts about my beloved Claire just to score a petty put-down on my ex-loved one.

'Silly question. If she wasn't, you'd hardly be going out with her.'

Again, I thought, that could be open to argument, but again, I didn't say anything.

'What's her name?'

'Claire. Claire O'Sullivan. She's a reporter.'

'Oh, still the same one, then,' Ellen said and shut up at once.

'How did you know about Claire?' I asked in surprise.

Ellen blushed. 'Oh, I can't remember, really. I expect someone must have mentioned it to me. Eh . . . a mutual acquaintance, probably.'

'Which mutual acquaintance?'

'I don't know, Frank. I honestly can't remember . . .'

Bullshit, I thought, but dropped the cross-examination. After all, what did it matter now? Although it did seem odd that Ellen had been keeping a check on my progress through life, to the point where she remembered Claire's name.

'Would you like some coffee?' I asked.

'No, thanks. Actually, I wanted to have a talk with you. Professionally.'

At last, a reason. 'Professionally?' I raised my eyebrows. 'What about?'

'I don't know if you know it, but I live here now, just along the Dublin road, just before the next village . . . We run a stud farm, all Arabians.'

'Don't tell me you're a client of *this* practice!' I softened enough to smile ironically.

She looked uncomfortable. 'Well, we used to be but em . . . Not now. Not any longer.'

I pulled a face. 'So. Why do you think I can help, then?'

'We've been having some trouble lately. In fact, to tell you the truth, it's been one hell of a year so far. If it goes on like this . . .' She didn't finish.

'I'm sorry to hear that, Ellen, but like I said, if we don't do your work, what makes you think I can help?'

'Well you're a vet . . .'

'So are the others.'

'You're also someone I know and can trust.'

The infernal *gall* of the woman! How *dare* she even mention knowing and trusting to me! 'Ellen, you're asking me to do something unethical, which you know I can't do, unless I check with my colleagues here and inform your regular vet.'

'No. Don't do that,' she said quickly and I saw a faint lick of fear cross her eyes. I reckoned that PJ must have given her the full sarcastic treatment once she had ceased to be a client. She seemed about to add something, then changed her mind. 'Okay, let's forget about the professional bit. I also wanted to see you and chat about old times. Why don't you drop by for lunch?'

That took me aback, but I couldn't show it. 'Why not indeed? When?' Suave, that, Frank. Good one.

'Half-twelve, one, whatever's good for you.'

'You mean, *today*?'

'Please say yes,' she said in a slightly desperate tone.

I shrugged uncomfortably because I hate being crowded. 'Well, okay. I've got a few calls out your way anyway.'

'Thanks, Frank. I always could rely on you.' She seemed not to notice the sudden grim set to my mouth. 'What time do you think you'll be there?'

I glanced at my watch. 'As you said, half-twelve, one-ish. Okay?'

'Thank you, Frank,' she said, drawing a quick map. 'Thank you very much. I appreciate this.' She stood abruptly and walked to the door. As I rose from my chair, she turned, hand on the handle, and said with a secretive smile. 'Remember. Not a word to anyone.' She put a silencing finger to her lips, then she was gone. I had the strongest déjà vu. The last time I'd seen her she'd done almost the exact same things – she'd stood at the door, hand on handle, smiled secretively, said 'Be good' and blown me a kiss.

Then she'd vanished for years.

I finished my paperwork and went to the store to stock up on supplies.

PJ was there, signing out his requirements. 'Was that our ex-client, the delectable Mrs Ollin, I saw just now coming out of the office?'

'Yes.'

'I'm surprised to see *her* here,' he remarked, clearly not satisfied with my simple 'yes'. 'She have any problems?'

'No,' I lied without hesitation. 'It was a personal visit. We knew each other at college, so when she heard I was in town, she stopped by to say hello.'

'Oh, I see. Well, see you around then, Frank.'

'Ya. See you,' I said, livid with myself for lying, for jumping through Ellen's hoop so readily. Like a fucking trained poodle.

'Here y'are, Mr Samson,' said Jimmy, hoisting a wire supermarket basket on to the counter. He placed the stocks in a cardboard box for me, calling them out and ticking them off against my list as he went. 'Sign here,' he said, turning a thick ledger towards me.

Laurel House Stud Farm was a long, low, luxurious bungalow set just below the brow of a gentle hill. It was approached by a curving tarmacadam drive that ran between the freshly painted stud railings of neat paddocks, some of which had mares and foals grazing in them. I counted some twenty mares near the driveway and as many again in more distant paddocks. If it hadn't been for Ellen's talk of trouble, I would have guessed that Laurel House Stud Farm was a very nice and prosperous going concern. Of course, the brilliant autumn sunshine helped – everything looks better in the sun.

I was annoyed to find that my hands were shaking slightly. I wasn't looking forward to meeting her husband who, I assumed, was fully aware of the fact that I was the forlorn fool who had spent that whole summer trying desperately to win Ellen back from him and failing spectacularly. It was too much to hope that he didn't know – she'd probably sought refuge in his arms from my importunate wooing; she'd most likely gone to ground with him while I hung about her town like a lovelorn loon; he might actually have been with her when she answered some of my despairing, imploring phone calls. Of course, no mention would be made of those times, so I'd be stuck with trying to convince them, by demeanour alone, that no ember of panic-stricken, embarrassing love remained smouldering in my bosom and that I wasn't about to start making either a fool or a nuisance of myself all over again.

But he wasn't there. Ellen met me at the door and apologised for Laurence's absence – I hadn't heard his name before – and for a fleeting moment I wondered if her troubles mightn't be marital rather than professional. She wore no make-up and was dressed in Relaxed Domestic – faded jeans, plaid work shirt and battered slippers; four small kids surged and shifted about her like a restless sea around the legs of an oil rig. Apart from the crawling one in rompers, who was concentrating on eating carpet fluff mixed with the yield of a runny nose and ignored me totally, Ellen's offspring just gave me the long, silent once-over.

Lunch was chaotic. In the large, bright kitchen I was placed on a long bench by the wall with a kid on either side of me, Lucy, a girl of about seven who looked nothing at all like her mother, and the second-youngest, a curly child whose sex I couldn't guess at and didn't like to ask, but who kept staring suspiciously at me, although he/she felt pally enough to leave a sticky dummy on my plate and wordlessly to offer me each tiny fistful of ketchup-reddened fish finger before stuffing it messily into its mouth.

'That's enough, Frances,' Ellen gently admonished the kid. 'You eat yours and Frank will eat his, okay?'

Francis? Well, how about that! She had actually named a kid after me, even if it was only subconsciously. The *irony* of it, I reflected philosophically. I reached down to the kid with a suddenly avuncular feeling and mussed the hair about a bit. 'So, Francis,' I said brightly, 'and what age would you be, then?' The kid said nothing, just suspended chewing and leaned the head out of my reach. I turned to Ellen. 'What age is he?'

'He's a she, Frank. Frances with an e. We called her after

Laurence's mother. She's almost three.' The two older kids were laughing like drains; it was obviously the funniest thing they'd heard so far in their young lives.

'Oh! What a pretty child.' I staged a pathetic recovery, feeling thoroughly foolish. The two bigger kids kept on giggling.

I tried my best to strike up a conversation with the children, asking them about school (only two attended), what ages they were (nearly seven, four and a half, almost three and ten months next Tuesday), but our interests and life experiences were miles apart and the small talk with the small ones soon petered out. Probably, if I'd had brothers and sisters, we'd have got along famously, but there'd been only me. And Dave.

When lunch was over and the kids had been tidied away – two ordered outside to play, the younger two to their beds – Ellen made coffee and sat down opposite me with a smile. I remembered her well enough to know that she was dying to get down to business and was forcing herself, with some difficulty, to go through the motions of pretending that this really was a social call. She tried small talk for a while but the only thing we had in common, apart from our abruptly truncated affair, was Dave and, as he'd been dead for half a year now, she soon ran out of steam. To fill a particularly awkward silence I asked her again who had told her about Claire, but she still wouldn't tell me; she claimed to have forgotten. But, like I said, I remembered her well enough to know that this was unlikely.

And I didn't help her to get to the meat. I found that I still resented what I considered the unnecessarily callous way in which she had given me the push and felt that she hadn't put up nearly enough of a fight for our relationship. Nor could I work out my reaction to her children – I was finding it hard to accept that none of them would ever see me as anything other than just some man who had called at the house. That is, if they remembered me at all, which was so highly unlikely as to be almost an impossibility. I thought that Ellen might at least have made some distinction between me and a casual, no-account visitor, in the same way that she might bestow eternal significance upon some undistinguished and anonymous building by pointing it out to them as where she had gone to school. As it was, she hadn't even introduced me to them or them to me, much less told them that I was a very dear friend of hers from long, long before they were born.

I was also annoyed with myself that, at a mere word from her, I'd lied to PJ Slattery. If Ellen and her husband had given their allegiance to another practice, then she really had no right to come back, bold as brass, looking for help. The analogy between the way she was abusing the Slatterys and the way she had abused me was too close to ignore. So, to hell with her – I wasn't going to help her with her treachery. In fact, I was debating leaving when she began. 'Frank . . . Could you work out what should be the average number of veterinary visits per year, for a set-up like this?'

'Phew! You don't want much, Ellen, do you? May I ask why?'

She launched into a description of the running of the stud farm, so detailed that it soon became clear that she was the one who ran it. She outlined their programmes for routine health matters such as worming and vaccination, their breeding programme, the numbers of veterinary attendances required for infertility problems, ultrasound scanning and everything else, without once hesitating or having to refer to diaries or files. 'So,' she wound up, 'what do you reckon would be a reasonable number of calls to look after a place this size? And cost. Apart, that is, from drugs and medicines – they're pretty much standard prices in all practices. I've checked.'

I thought for a minute, then hazarded a rough guess.

Ellen looked both surprised and triumphant. 'Yeah? That's the kind of figure I'd expect, too. That's almost exactly what it used to be, but it's more than doubled since I changed to Crowther.'

My ears pricked up. 'Is that a local practice?' I pretended to know nothing of the man.

'Val Crowther's practice is over in Breenstown, a bit far

away, I know, but he's certainly the up-and-coming practice around here. He seems to be taking on more staff every month; he's building all these super facilities, buying the latest equipment. It's costing him a fortune but, as he says, if he provides the best service, then the clients will automatically follow.' Somehow I got the impression that her heart wasn't in this eulogy, that she was trying to convince herself that Crowther was indeed the best.

'And is it working out like that for him?' I asked, thinking that there wasn't a whole lot wrong with the Slatterys' facilities – or expertise either, for that matter.

'I imagine so, although he's been moaning for years about how slowly it's happening.'

'For years?' But Ellen had only changed to him the previous year. 'You mean he canvassed you while you were still clients of the Slatterys?'

'Oh, canvassing is too strong a word. Let's say he'd been mentioning it to Laurence on and off for years, half joking, I think. Patience is not one of Val's stronger points.'

'Hang on, Ellen. Back up. Did Crowther actually call at the farm here to do this . . . half-joking touting for business?'

'No, of course not. We'd meet at parties; we'd go to dinner at the Crowthers' or they'd come to us – whatever – and that'd be the sort of occasion when the topic would come up. He didn't confine his overtures to Laurence; he'd mention it to the table in general, as I say, half in joke, if most of the guests were local. Those who didn't have horses or cattle would surely have dogs, cats or budgies. Everybody took it with a pinch of salt; knowing how pushy Val is, we all treated it as a kind of joke. Take us, for instance. We'd been perfectly happy with the Slatterys' service; it wasn't until we nearly lost our best stallion that we finally did change. Between them, PJ and Mike Stone nearly killed him.'

'How come? They seem like a pretty competent outfit to me.'

It transpired that the animal that PJ had described to me, the one that had developed the massive phlebitis and necrotic cellulitis over the jugular vein, had belonged to the Ollins.

'So Laurence and PJ had a bit of a shouting match and we called in Val to repair the damage. He found heavy contamination in the wound so, reluctantly, he came to the conclusion that the Slatterys had, on at least one occasion, used a non-sterile needle.'

'That sounds most unlikely to me. I work there. Their standards are very high.'

'They've obviously tightened up their act now, when it's too late.'

'I'm not really in a position to argue, but I'd say you're wrong there, Ellen. So what about the horse? How bad was he?'

'The skin was falling off his neck when we called Val in. And some muscle also.'

'Literally "falling"?'

'Literally, Frank. It stank and was disgusting to look at.'

'Were there abscesses also? You know, ones which hadn't broken open?'

'No. I used to wash it out every day. I'd have seen ripe abscesses if they'd been there.'

'Then Crowther took his sample, the one that showed contamination, from the open wound?'

'I told you, the skin and muscle were falling off the neck.'

'And he just rolled a swab around on the surface of the wound?'

'Yes. I was there, holding the horse. I'm the hands-on person around here. Laurence has a business in Dublin. He's never at home during the day.'

'I see. Did you also hold the stallion for PJ Slattery while he was injecting him?'

'Every time. For either PJ or Mike Stone – whichever turned up. It was a ten-day course.'

'I don't suppose you saw whether they took a new needle straight from its wrapper every time?' For the second time I found myself going through the same list of questions again. Significant or what? The first time, Melia's cow, I had dealt with a nameless, faceless saboteur; this time there were no blank spaces. Surely it couldn't be this simple?

'I never noticed, Frank. I don't like injections – even watching them gives me the willies.'

Another Patsy Melia, I thought ruefully. Did nobody observe anything any more? 'Well, Ellen, I'm not going to make any judgements, but if the wound was already open when that sample was taken, then there's no way that anyone could conclude that the Slatterys had used a dirty needle. Those bacteria could have come from anywhere, flies, dust, the air – anywhere.'

'Val said that they were a certain type of germ associated with poor hygiene and asepsis.'

This was rubbish. 'Did he, now? He didn't leave you the lab report, by any chance?'

'No.'

'The horse survived?'

'Oh, yes. He's fine now. Apart from that unfortunate scar on his neck, he's a beauty; not a blemish on him. Do you want to see him?'

'No need, Ellen. I'm sure your description is accurate.'

She looked disappointed that I wasn't showing more enthusiasm. 'I reckon that disfigurement has halved his sale value.'

'Were you thinking of selling him?'

'No. He's strictly for breeding.'

'Well, he can perform at his best still, despite the scarred neck.'

'I know.'

'Did you think of going to court?'

'Val talked us out of it. He said it could ruin the Slatterys' practice and that would be an awful price to pay for a moment's lack of concentration or carelessness.'

'Well, good old Val,' I said drily. 'Bully for him.'

We never actually got down to specifics of why Ellen had sought my 'advice' in the first place. She told me that they were having a pretty bad season; several of their best mares had stubbornly refused to become pregnant; one of their stallions had developed a mysterious fertility problem;

bookings for the following season were down; they were headed for their first ever financial loss.

'What can I say, Ellen? The infertility problems are all specific cases and, if Crowther and his experts haven't been able to work them out, then I don't think I have a chance in hell.'

Again she looked disappointed, almost reproachful, as though I'd let her down. 'Oh,' she said. 'I see . . .' as if she had expected more of me.

For the first time ever I became annoyed with Ellen. 'Jesus, Ellen! I'm sitting at your table, drinking coffee. I have never seen the animals involved, or even the farm. I have no access to test results or case histories, and you expect me to wave my magic wand and solve the whole thing right now. I'm very flattered by your blind confidence in my veterinary abilities, but also very puzzled, because the last time we met I was a mere fourth-year student.'

I was as shocked by this outburst as she was – especially the last, personal bit. It had slipped out, unbidden and unexpected.

'I'm sorry, Frank,' she said after a moment. 'I'm truly sorry.'

I rubbed my palm several times across my brow, horrified by my unbidden eruption. At last I regained enough control to speak. It came out in a wavery voice. 'No, I'm the one who should apologise. I don't know why I suddenly got angry. All I meant to say was that you could appreciate how impossible it would be, from an ethical standpoint, for me to help with your health problems. You'd have to change back to the Slatterys again before we could even begin to look into it, and to ask Crowther to pass us on all the relevant records. Which, I assume, is out of the question?'

Again came the little touch of fear in her eyes. 'Totally, I'm afraid.'

I was going to ask her what she was afraid of, but my immature petulance had shattered whatever fragile atmosphere there had been. That had left me with very little option but to take my leave. Anyway, I had work to do.

So had Ellen. There was a heavy shower outside and the two children who had been sent out to play, with orders not to come back indoors until their mother said they could, had pointedly taken up station across from the kitchen, under the grudging semi-shelter of a narrow garage eaves, and were standing, staring balefully at us through the rain-spotted glass.

With further apologies, graciously waved aside, I took my leave. Ellen said, as one does, that I'd have to come and have a meal some evening when Laurence was home early and I lied, as one does, that I'd love to and drove off, furious with myself.

God, but I hoped that Ellen hadn't misconstrued my vicious words as the petulance of a jilted lover consumed by jealousy, when in fact the angry retort had been prompted mainly by my anger at the unreasonable expectations of someone who had long since given up all rights to any claims whatsoever upon me.

9

I lay, aching and trembling in a soaked tangle of bed sheets, now shivering and clammy with cold, next second aflame, perspiring until I thought I'd pass out. I barely had the strength to rise and refill the water jug that Bob, my flatmate, had filled for me before leaving for home. Since mid-morning he'd been showing increasing signs of unease every time he looked into the bedroom at me and, as his train time crept closer, his concern grew. He began glancing in on me every ten or fifteen minutes, giving me worried looks, offering to call a doctor, an ambulance, to get me pills . . . But I assured him it was only a flu, a twenty-four-hour bug. I'd be okay.

I'd taken part in a punishing cross-country race the week before; I hadn't trained properly and had even then been feeling a bit flu-ey. Sheer bloody-mindedness had made me finish, when sheer common sense ought to have made me stop halfway. Or, even better, stay at home. That was all. If he didn't get going soon he'd miss his train. Coming in one last time with a fresh pitcher of water, clinking with ice, he said he'd contact Dave – get him to look in on me. I waved that away, too, because, at that point, I really believed that it was just a passing bug. The rest of that afternoon and evening went by without me being conscious of any of it.

Weaving deliriously between sleep, unconsciousness and wakefulness, I became aware of a cool damp cloth on my brow, in the angles of my nose and eyes, along my shoulders and down my neck and chest; in the background, a soft, long-lost, much-loved voice whispered my name over and over. My eyelids fluttered slowly open and, against the light from the kitchen behind her, I knew at once that it was Ellen. I had thought about her and dreamed about her daily and nightly for months now until finally, I had dreamt her back with me. This day, so full of pain and aching and sweating, these solitary, semi-conscious hours of ague and fevered imaginings were suddenly transformed, as though she had thrown the Christmas lights switch in a shivering, darkened city.

I rolled painfully but urgently on to my back and tried to lift a leaden arm, to raise a hand to her face, but had she not taken it and put it to her cheek it would have fallen back on to the drenched sheets. I began to tell her how I knew she'd be back, how we belonged together, but she stopped me with a gentle 'sh' and a cool wet cloth on my mumbling, parched lips. She placed two gentle fingers on my eyelids and, murmuring to me repeatedly to try to get some sleep, that she'd stay a while, closed them down. In my new febrile–euphoric state, the symbolism of the act escaped me – it was how one shut off the unsettling stare of a dead man. I made her promise not to leave me again and, in reply, she shushed me rhythmically, her hand stroking my clammy brow keeping time with her soft, slow, wordless utterings.

I slept fitfully, but with a reassurance which had deserted me months before, along with Ellen. Every time I awoke I could see her, my Ellen, sitting at the table in the kitchen, my kitchen. She seemed to be writing, but looking up at me every few seconds, watching over me.

I had no idea of the passage of time but, what felt like hours later, I felt her sponging me down yet again. I became aware of her nearness and awoke to find her bending over me, reaching across me to wipe my extended forearm. I became instantly aware of her breasts touching my shoulder, my ear, moving gently against me as she rubbed and swabbed my wrist with an ice-filled flannel. Turning my head slowly, I kissed her nipple and immediately became so aroused that it was almost painful. I saw her pause a moment, then she sat down slowly on the bed. 'I thought you were supposed to be sick. "Dying" I was told.'

'I am dying,' I mumbled, with an effort at a smile, which cracked my lower lip painfully and started it bleeding. 'Part of me's gone stiff already . . .'

'So I'd noticed . . .' she said drily. She pushed the damp hair back off my forehead and rubbed my stubbled cheek with the back of her fingers. 'Uh-huh.' She shook her head. 'Forget it Frank . . . It would not be a wise move.'

'Who's talking about being wise?' I croaked, my hand reaching for her breast. She caught it, held it, but did not push it away. 'Surely you can't deny a dying man his last request?' I pushed against her gently with my hand and she didn't make much of a struggle to repel me.

'You're incorrigible, Frank, d'you know that?'

'Encourageable? So encourage me then . . .'

'Still playing word games, I see.'

'Please, Ellen. Please. Now . . .' I pushed my hand again and this time reached her breast.

Too feeble to initiate any further action, I just lay there, my bloodshot eyes looking up at her, telling her how much I'd missed her, how I wanted her. For what seemed an age, she sat looking down at me with a sombre, deep expression, then, with a strange smile and a bemused shaking of her lovely head, she helped me open the buttons of her shirt and pull the cups of her bra up to reveal the perfect breasts which I'd remembered with such total clarity that I'd been almost able to feel them physically in my hands, against my face, between my lips . . . Suddenly, no longer considering, she stood and turned, leaning forward towards my face so that I was being nuzzled gently by the soft, scented warmth of her bosom. With her right hand and forearm she supported my head and neck, drawing my mouth towards her hardening nipples. Her left hand stroked my chest, my shoulders, my arms, my belly and finally closed slowly around my erection. She began a rhythmic stroking, at first easy and gentle, but becoming more and more wild as the minutes melted away until at last we were both in a heart-thumping, panting frenzy and I was about to climax. At the last possible moment, my face already contorting and my back beginning to arch in ecstasy, she stopped and squeezed tightly, sealing me off. Dimly I was aware of her moving across me. She was no longer in control of herself. Eyes closed, head back, lips and mouth slightly parted, she was panting in quick shallow breaths as she scrambled over me, drew the crotch of her panties aside and, gasping in anticipation, eased herself down on to me. A few frenetic moments later we cried out together, went abruptly still for the space of a few heartbeats, then collapsed as one in a spent heap.

I drifted off into oblivion almost at once, lying snuggled up to Ellen. I awoke again in a few seconds when I felt her move.

'You okay?' I asked the back of her head as she slid out from under my arm.

'I'm getting up, Frank, before I catch your dreaded lurgy. I must be stark, raving mad, but at least I saved you from death by instalments. The advancing rigor seems to have vanished.' I tried to smile but it immediately became a deep, painful breath. 'Don't you dare cough all over me!' Ellen warned, leaning away from me, laughing.

I was beginning to drift off again, eyelids rolling inexorably down over eyeballs which felt as though they were covered in fine grit. Ellen was receding into the blur, along with everything else, as I slipped once more towards sleep. 'That was great . . .' I murmured, beginning to tumble.

'Not bad for a dying man,' was the last thing I heard her say.

I struggled awake once during that long night, but only became lucid enough to totter to the kitchen for a drink and the bathroom to make room for it. Staggering back to bed, I vaguely registered, on top of the fridge, propped against a large jar of pickled eggs, an envelope with my name on it. Beside it, even more mysteriously, was the old garnet-eyed snake ring which my grandmother had given me when I was about twelve so that I could give it to the girl with whom I fell in love. Now, too sick, weak and exhausted to do anything other than wobble my dizzy way back to my bed, I looked owlishly at the ring for a brief moment, kept going, and collapsed back into the sweaty and soggy sheets. Ellen herself I hadn't seen anywhere; perhaps she had gone home to her flat – she'd need to change her clothes, wouldn't she? She'd be back tomorrow, first thing.

But she wasn't. I began to worry when, by noon, there was no sign of her. Nor was there any sign of the letter or granny's garnet-eyed snake ring. In fact, the only sign that last night had not been anything other than one long fevered dream was my stained bed sheets, but even they proved nothing beyond the fact that, at some time during the night, I had ejaculated. Hardly surprising, given the vividness of the surrounding details.

There was the noise of a key in the door and I felt a surge of hope that it might be Ellen returning, but it was only Dave, carrying groceries.

'I was in earlier,' he said, 'but you were asleep. Howya feelin', kiddo?'

'Lousy. I'm feeling lousy, Dave. Ah, don't,' I moaned as he went to draw the curtains, but he did it anyway.

'Holy hell, Frank!' he exclaimed, seeing me properly for the first time. 'I'm getting an ambulance for you. I'll be back in a tick.'

I spent the next eight days in hospital undergoing intense treatment for acute undulant fever, the human form of brucellosis. By the time I was discharged, I'd fully accepted that The Night that Ellen Had Returned to Me had been nothing more than the confused imaginings of a febrile and delirious brain.

Paradoxically and pathetically, I was relieved that it had been a dream because if Ellen had really left the snake ring then all hope was lost. As long as she kept that, she'd think of me every time she wore it. Or even just saw it in her jewellery box.

And so I continued to hope for months and more months, hardly noticing when they turned into years . . .

I dreamt that dream again in Monksford, the night that Ellen and I crossed paths again. Without the wet part. In the morning, I was shaken.

10

PJ was struggling. Despite my near verbatim report of Ellen's damning story, he was still trying to defend the theory that Crowther was not their tormentor: Crowther didn't *need* to resort to such tricks because, at the rate the practice was going downhill, he would soon take over anyway.

'Crowther is the *reason* the practice is going downhill!' I tried to keep the exasperation out of my voice. 'He's not waiting for it to happen; he's *making* it happen.'

'But why then would he have advised the Ollins *not* to sue?' The tone was petulant, the question a last-ditch effort.

'Because, PJ, the only, quote, evidence, unquote, was his malicious "dirty-needle" diagnosis, and he knew the case would be thrown out if that was all it was based on and he'd end up looking a proper dickhead. He knew he couldn't get away with it – no doubt the first thing your lawyer would ask about would be the nature of the wound from which the sample had been taken. There would be no way to lie because Mrs Ollin knew that the samples had come from an open wound.

'So why should he risk court? Would you? Court would be disastrous for Crowther. First off, like I said, he'd look ridiculous trying to back his unbackable "expert opinion". Second, he'd be forced out into the open, his hostility to your practice made public, and consequently you'd have the opportunity to fight back. By hanging you the way he has been, with sabotage, shadowy rumours, innuendo and whispers, you haven't had a chance to defend your good names – you didn't know who your enemy was, so you couldn't fight him. Shit, PJ, up until the cock-up with Fizzikle and Patsy Melia's cow the other day you couldn't be sure that you even *had* an enemy.'

He drew a weary sigh, removed his glasses, and massaged his eyes and the bridge of his nose. 'I suppose Ellen Ollin wouldn't repeat what she told you to the Ethics Committee?'

'You could always ask her.'

'I don't think so. Her husband and I had quite a row – pushing and shoving, although no actual blows.'

I shook my head. 'Crowther must have been thrilled skinny at *that* little fracas. Well, *I'll* ask her then – after all, fair is fair.' Although I was beginning to think that perhaps there wasn't a lot fair about Ellen any more. She wasn't being fair when she breezed into the Slatterys' office even though she no longer considered them fit to do her work and, now that I'd heard about the row between her husband and PJ, I thought her action not only unfair but positively inexcusable. If she'd felt (unfairly) that she just had to contact me, despite our past history – an unfairness in itself, I still felt – then common decency ought to have made her use the telephone.

'The Ollins must have been one of your bigger clients?' I remarked ruefully.

'Yes. But then all these so-called "mistakes" seem to happen only with our bigger clients, the Ollins, Patsy Melia, Frank O'Malley . . . He was the one who had the two ketosis cases.'

'Convenient, or what?' I snorted cynically. 'All those big clients, PJ, they've all been deliberately targeted. And, of course, when the smaller clients hear of the big ones changing, they reckon there's something going on that they don't know about and follow suit . . .'

At that point Mrs PJ phoned to remind him that they were due at a grandchild's birthday party and he left, professing to be dreading it. Understandably, he wasn't in the humour for silly hats, balloons and pinning the tail on the donkey.

I met Laurence Ollin later that same evening. Or rather, saw him.

I was in the newsagents, having a free read of the magazines, when I heard the lady behind the counter say: 'That's two pounds forty-seven change, Mr Ollin. Thank you.' I changed my position quickly to catch a look at the slim, well-dressed man who was headed for the glass door. I could only see his back, but, as he reached the exit, another man, entering, paused and said: 'Evening, Laurence.' Ollin returned the greeting and, as they exchanged further pleasantries, each of them continued to move slowly on in his intended direction, while at the same time maintaining eye contact with the other. The result was that the friend ended up inside the shop, looking out, while Ollin executed a slow pirouette on the pavement until he was facing back inwards again. The orange late-evening sunlight slanted on to a strong face with a broad forehead, a chiselled wedge of nose and a generously wide mouth. A central peninsula of steel-grey hair, sparse at the apex, fought a futile rearguard action against the advancing baldness that had already outflanked it on both sides. Sunglasses hid his eyes which, for some reason, I had the strongest feeling were blue. The pleasantries over, Ollin headed for his car, a bottle-green 7 series BMW. I watched him smile and wave to someone further along the street, open the car door, throw his papers on to the back seat, then sit in and drive off.

His image appeared before me many times that evening, and I studied the disembodied hologram of the man who had smashed what I had thought were the unbreakable bonds which had once bound Ellen Hendricks and me to each other. I tried to look at him from a woman's point of view but I couldn't see anything special – he was neither remarkably tall, dark, nor handsome; nor was he built like a Greek god, at least not so as you'd notice. Then I decided that I really had no idea what attracted particular women to particular men, so I gave up.

Next time I thought of him I wondered, if it actually had come to blows between Ollin and PJ, who would have won? I was unaccountably happy when I decided that despite the differences in age, height and reach, PJ would have dropped Ollin in round one.

It wasn't until I was turning in for the night that I suddenly realised why I felt – why I *knew* – that the eyes behind the sunglasses were blue: I knew because I had met Laurence Ollin before.

I lay awake for ages but couldn't remember where we'd met. In the dark and silence of my room, my freshly exhumed paranoia soon took over. Did I remember him from *college*? Jesus, had Ellen been seeing him all along, two-timing me *from the very start*! God, I must have been a damn fool! Everybody would have known, except stupid, retard, cuckold, me. Then logic came to the rescue: did I remember Ollin with a full head of hair and, if so, what colour had it been? I had no idea. Had it been worn long, short, crew, Afro or Rasta? I couldn't guess. And clothes? What style clothes? Snappy or slob? Not an idea. My only recollection of him was as a balding and greying man, much the same as the man I'd seen at the newsagents. At last I felt reassured that I had met Laurence Ollin only recently, probably within the last year. Mind you, I still wouldn't have taken a bet on it.

Friday lunchtime, the call I'd been expecting (and dreading) for some days now duly arrived. Ellen, in her brightest tones, rang to invite me to dinner that same evening. For a moment I thought of declining on the grounds that she hadn't given me enough notice but, realising that I would merely be postponing the inevitable, I accepted with well-feigned eagerness.

There were several reasons why I was not exactly looking forward to the fixture: first off, I didn't relish the thought of meeting her husband and seeing (or imagining I saw) in his eyes the knowledge of all the intimacies which Ellen and I had once shared before he came along, or, a million times more mortifyingly, the pathetic débâcles I'd gone through afterwards. I was still convinced that he'd been a fascinated bystander, peeking and eavesdropping on all my forlorn efforts to win her back.

Ellen had mentioned a small, quiet dinner party, so for some odd reason I assumed that the 'party' was going to consist of just me and the Ollins, and I had a most unpleasant flash of my brain being clinically picked clean by Ellen (the prize) about the tribulations of her business, while her husband (the victor) sat silently by, observing me (the vanquished), reliving his triumph and getting off on some macho high. But then came the relieving news: there would be several guests and she listed off a bunch of names and professions which meant nothing to me but sounded like page one of *Who's Who in Monksford*.

Another worry was that I didn't have any idea how Ellen had interpreted my outburst at our previous meeting and what her attitude to me would now be – she had sounded relaxed on the phone, but how would it be face to face?

After I'd hung up I wondered if, in fact, dinner party or not, Ellen in her single-mindedness mightn't still try to corner me, while Laurence kept the other guests at bay? Perhaps the Ollins of this world hunted in pairs.

Eve was the only one in the office when I rushed through to replenish my supplies from the store. It was Barbara's afternoon off. I called 'Hi, Eve' as I went, but, as usual, got no reply. I'd given up being annoyed at her coldness, mainly because she treated everyone, except Barbara, the same way. For Eve was the epitome of formality – she insisted on calling me Mr Samson, although I'd suggested on a few occasions that she should lighten up and try a 'Frank' every so often; each time, she had silently replied with a glare of knowing scorn – a cynical, Frank-today-unspeakable-orgies-tomorrow look. When I asked JJ what her problem was, he said she'd been like that as long as he'd known her, which was for ever since she was his cousin; she had never once been known to call any man, staff member or client by his first name and, ridiculously, called even him and PJ, Mr Slattery and Mr Slattery respectively – no Cousin JJ or Uncle PJ for Eve. By contrast, she never shut up chatting with Barbara.

'She called you Mr Slattery *when you were kids*?' They were much of an age.

'Don't be stupid!' JJ laughed. 'But it started the day I came home with the degree. Frightened the livin' shit out of me, it did. I gave up trying to talk her out of it. Don't pay her any attention, Frank. She's a bit odd but she's not the worst. She used to stand in once in a while, or come in when we were extra busy and, as she happened to be . . . eh, between jobs . . . as they say, when Brenda and Michael got married, she stood in for Brenda while they went on honeymoon. But because Brenda managed to get herself pregnant during those two weeks and became incredibly sick, Eve is still here, still standing in . . .' His tone was apologetic, although what he might be apologising for I wasn't sure.

It was hardly his fault that he had an odd cousin, the female equivalent of a misogynist, I thought, until the day I glimpsed on the inside of her locker door her pin-up gallery of Tom Cruise, Paul Newman, Elvis and Brad Pitt, plus a whole collection of sepia-tinted jeans ads models. Eve was into beautiful men, internationally recognised hunks. Actually she was probably more into bodies, as some of the jeans guys had been chopped off at the neck while a few of the others had their faces draped in such sultry shadowing that their features were all but indiscernible. Maybe it was just that Eve had very, very high standards and that all the males she came across in the line of duty in Monksford were so far below par that they didn't even warrant a friendly nod and a first name now and then.

Now, however, the reticent one gave tongue as I hurried back through the office, making for the back door and my round of late afternoon calls. 'Phone, Mr Samson.'

I could have done without the delay – I had things to do

before the evening's ordeal by dinner party closed in over my head. I hesitated for just a second in exasperation.

Eve held the phone towards me. 'For *you*, Mr Samson,' she explained heavily as if I were the town thicko. 'Personal.'

To show that she had now done all that could be done, she placed the phone on the counter and turned her head away to scrutinise the call book. As I pushed the box of medicines on to the reception counter and set down my medicine bag, I was thinking that there wasn't much 'personal' about Eve.

'Hello?' I said without much enthusiasm, expecting the cloud of Ellen and hoping for the silver lining of a cancellation or an indefinite delay. What I got was a sunburst – Claire. '*Hey, gorgeous*! Where are you?' I exclaimed, suddenly animated. Eve's plump hand, which had been writing something on a page, froze into immediate stillness, like a small animal which has just sniffed danger. Or food.

'The airport. Just landed. I managed to get a cancellation on an earlier flight.'

'Great! When are you planning on coming down?'

'Well, as I've just saved myself seven hours, why not this evening? I've had it up to here with cities. What's the weather like?'

'Pretty miserable. In fact, lousy.'

'You've sweet-talked me into it. D'you need anything from town?'

'Not that I can think of.'

'Okay, then, love. I'll stop by the flat for a shower and throw some things in a bag and I should be there about seven thirty.'

'Hallelujah.'

She laughed. 'See you then.'

''Bye,' I said. 'Oh! And Claire?'

'Yes?'

'Drive carefully, won't you.'

'Of course,' she said after a short pause, wondering why I'd said something I'd never said to her before.

There'd been a horrible accident on the Dublin motorway a couple of miles outside town the previous week and the whole area was still in shock. Two brothers, in their early thirties, with their wives (twin sisters) and their children, had been wiped out when one brother's car had blown a front tyre on a corner, rolled and scythed, upside down, through the central strip, right into the path of, incredibly, the other brother. Six of the nine people involved had been killed outright; one – one of the wives – had died the next morning and the two remaining survivors – the youngest child from each family, who had been strapped into baby seats – were on life support systems but were not expected to make it. Half the townspeople had lost family and the whole community was in shock. Even strangers like me were affected.

To make things immeasurably worse, it was the seventh wedding anniversary for both couples – the wives, being identical twins, had, of course, made sure of a double wedding. The effect on the town was amazing, although in retrospect it was almost predictable: cars were shunned as if they were a malevolent alien life form; the streets were deserted; petrol pump attendants were regarded as not much better than collaborators. People passing through, who might have already forgotten that this was where the tragedy had happened and were consequently pushing the speed limit as far as they did in any town, were shocked to find themselves running a gauntlet of enraged pedestrians all making hostile gestures at them. Nobody drove unless it was essential and the Dublin train was packed every day with people who needed to travel to the capital, but for the moment were shunning the murderous motor car. Many of these seemed to feel guilty about attending to business while the mourning period was still very much in operation. People who had to be on the roads, vets, doctors, etc., were just about tolerated.

I suddenly realised that I hadn't told Claire about the dinner party and I was about to call her back when I thought I ought first to check it with Ellen; perhaps she couldn't cater for one extra. 'Do you have the number for Laurel House Stud Farm, please,' I asked Eve.

Looking through a local directory, she took the phone

from me, dialled, waited a moment, then handed me back the receiver. 'Mrs Ollin on the line.'

I explained the position to Ellen, who, I thought, sounded momentarily unsure, like she hadn't prepared herself for this. 'So if it's going to upset your seating plans or numbers, we'll give it a miss tonight. There's always another time.'

Ellen, recovering her composure (if indeed she'd ever lost it), assured me that Claire would be most welcome and that she was looking forward with great interest to meeting her. I thanked her, told her we might be a little late as Claire would want to freshen up after her journey and expressed the hope that it wasn't going to be a very fancy do, because Claire might not have her finest finery with her. She assured me that, in the circumstances, Claire could come as she pleased.

Pointedly passing the receiver back to Eve, I picked up my accoutrements and began to resume my journey towards the yard. Then the thought struck me that Ellen hadn't actually said that it *wasn't* a fancy party, which could mean, à la the old Ellen, that Claire would be more than welcome and not to worry about the fuss of long and elaborate preparation. On the other hand, if Ellen was being her recent devious self, maybe she *wanted* Claire to come in T-shirt and jeans, to a party where all the others would be dressed up to the nines and possibly higher, so that Claire might be embarrassed (which *I* knew she wouldn't be) . . . Still and all . . . The sudden expression of lively interest, which had replaced Eve's customary ennui, made me decide to move upstairs to the flat, away from her flapping ears. I called Claire on her mobile and advised her to pack something suitable for a party, something on the ravishingly stunning side. Just in case . . .

That evening, with Claire's magnificent auburn hair swept up at the back, her recently topped-up tan and her long yellow sheath-dress, we almost silenced the babble of conversation when we entered the room. When I say we, I mean, of course, she. My pale-blue shirt and red tie with its not-quite-circular, multicoloured spots, topped off with the dark suit I'd bought for Dave's funeral, might have cut a reasonable dash in ordinary circumstances, but standing beside Claire, I was the Invisible Man. The other guests, as I had suspected, were taking the party seriously and had dressed accordingly.

I couldn't see Laurence Ollin, but Ellen, looking quite spectacular herself, swept briskly across the room to welcome us. In the few moments we had before she whisked us out into the crowd for introductions she never once gave an inkling to Claire that she and I had once had a serious relationship, or had even known each other in the past. I could feel her tension because she had no idea whether Claire already knew or not. (As it happened, she didn't. But that wasn't because I had kept it from her – by the time I met Claire, all the heartbreak was over, all the wounds healed. And besides, there had been many girlfriends in between.) I was half hoping that Ellen might surreptitiously ask me if Claire was aware of our previous relationship, so that I could hurtfully reply that, as I myself had forgotten all about it, how could Claire possibly know? But she didn't and, even if she had, I knew that I would not have answered so.

At one point, however, while Claire was trading small talk with a large woman dressed like a duchess at the opera, Ellen whispered to me: 'And there was I worrying myself *sick* that I'd broken your heart for ever! Best thing that ever happened to you, Samson, that we broke up. She's only gorgeous.'

'But of course she is. You know me – nothing but the fairest and finest in the land.'

Ellen gave me a long side glance from her blue-green eyes, followed by an enigmatic smile, an acknowledgement of deep secrets still shared, still remembered, still kept. Things that only she and I, out of all humanity, knew. Then the moment broke. 'Thanks for the boost, Frank.' She laughed. 'But I reckon this one's in a class of her own.'

I joined in the fun. 'Well, let's see now. We've had the evening gown bit, now let's go to the swimwear round . . .'

'Don't be smart, Frank. Claire's got six years on me . . .'

'Three and a bit, actually . . .'

'And she hasn't had four children in rapid succession . . .'
Suddenly it wasn't fun any more.

At the other side of the spacious room, Laurence appeared from another door and headed slowly for a small knot of men, leafing through a large book as he went. It looked as if he'd gone to fetch the book to illustrate a point or settle a friendly argument. Before Ellen could catch his attention, his eyes were drawn to the slim, firm, yellow column that was Claire and, excusing himself, he turned the book over to the group and came straight towards us. I'd been right about the eyes; they were remarkably blue – Paul Newman eyes, I thought, remembering the dowdy Eve's hunks gallery. Seeing them up close brought me to the verge of knowing where we'd met, but not quite. Ellen made the introductions and we shook hands.

I said how pleased I was to meet him, but: 'We've met before, I believe? At least, I've seen you before.' Good, suave opening gambit, I thought. Strong, solid voice, firm grip. Not a sign of nerves. Touch of class there, Frankie.

'Yes.' He smiled. 'At the newsagents, the other evening.'

Aw bollocks, I thought. He'd caught me peeking from behind the fuckin' chocolates. 'True,' I said, recovering pretty niftily, 'but the reason I was looking then was because I felt we'd *already* met. *Before* that, if you see what I mean. I was trying to place where, exactly.'

I felt I was now mumbling semi-coherently, babbling almost, although in reality I probably wasn't. It's just that I've never been great with small talk and trivia, and this particular introduction was more fraught than probably any other I had ever undergone, or could even imagine.

'I wouldn't expect you to remember. It was not a happy time for you. We met, very briefly, at your cousin Dave's funeral.'

'Of course!' Suddenly I had total recall of our short meeting outside the church: the blue-eyed face radiating sympathy, the mouth a grim line, his left hand being brought into play to cover the initial firm handshake and convert it into the classic funereal three-hander, the sincere mumble, then the quick dash through the chilling downpour to his car and the vanishing out of there as quickly as possible. I'd wondered at the time who he might be – not family for sure, as his funeral technique had been one grade below the Silent Hug, which would have been the minimum expected of a kinsman. I'd marked him down for something political and now I even remembered thinking uncharitably that Dave's funeral was probably his third of the day and that his rapid departure was because he still had another three to attend. 'Did you know Dave well?'

'Oh, yes. He was a good friend of ours for years. What a sad business.' He tut-tutted sympathetically, shook his head slowly, then swung the blue-eyed charm on to Claire.

'Was it Dave who told you about Claire?' I mumbled to Ellen.

She nodded.

'Then for God's sake why make such a mystery of it? Why didn't you just tell me that you and he had continued to see . . . to bump into each other?'

'I thought you must have known. And when it became clear that Dave hadn't told you, I decided that I shouldn't either.'

'Thanks a lot.' I wondered why Dave had never mentioned Ellen's name to me. Probably his sensitivity had made him silent; he was the only one who knew how distraught I really was. Ellen caught the eye of one of the guests and briskly led me off to be introduced. As I followed, I wondered why I always thought the best of Dave, no matter what; why I always bestowed on him an almost saintlike nobility of purpose. The guy was a crook, a dealer in drugs and misery, and the reason he had never mentioned Ellen to me probably had nothing whatever to do with tact or sensitivity. It was, in all likelihood, just that he didn't want me blubbering and slobbering all over his shoulder and trying to involve him in elaborate but doomed plots to win her back.

It was about eleven when Val Crowther arrived. We'd

finished a good dinner and returned to the sitting room where the atmosphere was one of settling in for a couple of hours of conviviality. Some opera – *La Bohème* according to Claire, who knows about these things – was playing softly in the background and, at any given moment, at least one guest would have withdrawn from the general conversation to hum or whistle along, I assume just so that all the other guests would know that he or she was cultured.

Val Crowther put an end to all that. He hadn't been invited but, judging from the rumpus in the hall, was hell bent on getting in. He was audibly drunk. The argument got louder as it neared the door, which suddenly burst open. Crowther, followed by an angry Laurence Ollin, stormed into the room.

My colleague was a thin, spare man in his mid to late forties, with greying hair that was thin in front but long and curly (and a bit greasy) behind. He had a jutting, belligerent jaw, deep-set dark eyes and a very red face – whether this was his usual colour, or due to blood pressure, a heart condition, embarrassment, or drink I had no idea, but somehow I doubted it was embarrassment. He was dressed in working clothes, as if he was on his way home from a late call.

Nobody seemed to know what to do and Crowther just stood there, nodding at people he recognised and mumbling their names. 'Jesus, Laurence,' he said suddenly, his eyes continuing to roam the room, 'are you not even going to *offer* me a drink?' Laurence looked as if he was considering throwing him out physically, but then stormed across to the drinks cabinet where he put about 2cc of gin into a tumbler and filled it to the brim with tonic.

Ellen had moved to Crowther's side, as though on guard, but she was obviously at a loss as to what to do next. The look of fear was back in her eyes and, this time, stayed. When Crowther's sweeping gaze came to me, his eyes widened and stopped their wandering.

Laurence arrived with his drink and shook his elbow.

'You'd better drink this, Val, and leave. Whatever it is that's bothering you, we can talk about it tomorrow.'

Crowther ignored his reluctant host but, turning his head slightly towards Ellen, while at the same time keeping his eyes fastened on mine, said: 'I've told you, haven't I, a hundred times, that if you need veterinary help, day or night, you call on me? Haven't I?' he insisted and won a meek nod from Ellen. 'Then what's he . . .'

Laurence stepped in with admirable civility. 'Listen, Val. This is a dinner party. If we had needed veterinary help we would have called you, okay? Now sit down, like a good man, and have your drink.'

Crowther continued to stare at me for most of the next twenty minutes until Laurence managed to get rid of him, but he had already shattered the party atmosphere and people began to look at their watches almost as soon as he'd left.

Outside, the night had turned foul. We'd arrived at the Ollins' in warm evening sunshine and emerged to squalls of cold rain and wind gusts striking at us without warning from out of the dark. The whole sky seemed to be on the move: huge formations of dark storm heads rushing urgently eastwards, shedding torn shreds behind them, allowing the three-quarter moon and the stars only the most fleeting of appearances. Collars turned up, the men rushed off to fetch their cars, returning to park tight by the covered porch so that their ladies could step straight in.

There were no protracted goodbyes and, within twenty-five minutes, Claire and I turned into the yard behind the practice. The rain had not yet reached Monksford, although it was hard on our heels.

In the sweep of my headlights I saw that the top half of the door of Fizzikle's box was open. Almost fully recovered now, he was due to go home in the morning and I thought I ought to make his last night with us a comfortable one. I gave Claire the key to the house, then dashed through the strengthening, soughing wind, across the yard to the loose boxes. All around me, I could hear the groans and rattles of the yard – a drainpipe squeaked at its junction with the gutter; a wheelbarrow propped against the gable of the stable block collapsed with a crash just after I'd passed it, making me jump feet into the air. I unhooked the top door of the stable, began to push it to, then stopped, suddenly struck by a feeling of emptiness from within. Fearing that the horse had been stolen, I flicked on the light.

My relief when I saw him lying on the straw was very short-lived.

Because Fizzikle was as dead as a brick.

All three Slatterys arrived in one car; even Joe had been roused from his slumbers for this one. The old man stayed in the car but took sporadic part in the conversation through his open window. Considerate and thoughtful, JJ had turned and parked so that his grandfather's window was to leeward. A moment later Michael Stone came to a crunching halt beside us, a stream of curses spouting from his window, only to be borne instantly away on the storm. And still the rain hadn't arrived.

Claire came up behind us, unheard in the strong wind, and I could see PJ jump to the instant conclusion that I'd been using the venerable family flat as a kind of lust pit of casual depravity. I introduced her and explained who she was, and that she already knew all that I knew. (I'd brought her up to date as we changed out of our party clothes while we waited for the partners to arrive.) Reckoning that I had failed to dispel PJ's doubts, I went on: 'Claire is part of the deal. She was as much involved as I was in those cases which impressed you so much.' After brief handshakes, we moved off towards the stable. Joe, winding up his window, wisely elected to stay in the car. At this point the wind was gusting strongly enough to knock him down.

The smell of death had already begun to seep up from the floor, like marsh gas at the dying of a frosty evening. Michael Stone mumbled more curses and oaths but neither PJ nor JJ said a word. I looked around me at the grim faces of men who had had more than enough, then turned my eyes back down to the dead horse on the floor. A twinge of guilt hovered around me – I'd been off living it up at Ellen's dinner party while poor Fizzikle was being murdered mere yards from my windows. Having saved him once, I felt as though I'd accepted lifetime responsibility for his well-being and security. Short lifetime.

I'd decided not to mention Crowther's drunken antics of a mere hour ago – it didn't actually prove anything and, if we were going to investigate this with cool heads, then it was better not to mention that name just now. Also, I felt that the fact that I'd been fraternising with the Ollins, those recognised allies of the now-hated Crowther, might not go down at all well. As it turned out, there was no need for me to mention Crowther.

'That does it,' said JJ grimly. 'Proof or no proof, I'm going to name that bastard to the cops. If we let him away with this one we might as well just *give* him the goddam practice. Serve it up to him on a plate, with parsley sauce.'

There had been much discussion in the past few days about how to get hard proof that Crowther was the saboteur. Now that the partners accepted that their 'bad luck' was due to sabotage, tensions had eased considerably and they were beginning to take constructive action as a united team under attack from outside. As Crowther could not be charged with anything, not even a breach of ethics, on the circumstantial evidence and hearsay we had to go on, the search was on for something more tangible.

PJ had had a word with some 'high-up' people he knew in the police, but had heard nothing back yet.

Michael had requested a phone tap on Crowther's phone from a cousin of his, a sergeant in the Special Branch, on the grounds that someone must be telephoning Crowther to tip him off about our calls, but his cousin had politely and firmly refused. I suggested to him that his cousin might compromise by getting the itemised past phone records for our office, just to see if in fact calls had been made from here to Crowther's, but the cousin had also declined on this front.

Although it would have been nice to be able to go back over the year's calls, I wasn't too worried by his refusal, as I was pretty sure the office was secure. At the outset it had seemed to be a classic 'inside job' but when I looked through the suspects they didn't add up. Apart from Michael Stone and Barbara, they were all close family and so, I reckoned, above suspicion. As for Michael and Barbara, he was a partner while she had been working for the practice for years and clucked over the place like a mother hen. And so I had begun to look further afield, at the local busybodies and gossips.

In any small town or rural community there are always people who seem to know everybody's business almost as soon as it happens and it was not too far-fetched an idea that a few of these were at work, passing on their news to Crowther. Admittedly, if such people were his only source then he probably wasn't getting information on more than a handful of calls but, despite this, the theory held together quite nicely.

Prime clients, the category the Slatterys seemed to be losing most, would be the local bigshots, just the class of people to come under the closest scrutiny from these busybodies. Also they would be more likely to have staff, indoors and out – on the land or in the yards – who would be rich sources of inside titbits. A few local gossips on his payroll and there wouldn't be much going on in the houses of the local well-offs that Crowther didn't get to hear about fairly promptly.

And that, as far as I was concerned, had provided an acceptable explanation for how Crowther was coming by his information.

For my part, I'd had another long chat with Patsy Melia, who denied any direct approaches by Crowther. The way he stressed 'direct' made me ask him about indirect ones and he admitted that he'd had a few of those all right. A cousin of his and his best friend both swore by Crowther and, over a few pints, when stock was being discussed, were wont to advise him to change vets. When I asked if they had ever actually bad-mouthed the Slatterys, he said no, not as such, just by implication.

'Was that window open, Frank, when you found him?' JJ pointed at a rectangle of glass slats high on the back wall; there was a lever lower down which opened and closed the louvred panes.

'I didn't touch a thing, JJ, except the horse, so it must have been, I suppose. Why?'

'Strange,' he said quietly. 'It was closed this evening when I last saw him. I closed it myself because the forecast was bad. And, what's more, I closed both halves of the door, too.'

'But you didn't lock them, did you?' PJ said and I thought to myself: what a time to pick a fight.

JJ, already overwrought by thc death of his patient, took several prudent breaths, then said tightly: 'Those doors haven't been locked since two or three days after the red blister and you know it. On those few warm nights last week, the top door wasn't even *closed*, never mind locked.'

I cut in hurriedly, 'Assuming that the horse has been killed, why would the killer want to open the stable window and door, and leave them open?'

'So that the wind could blow through? To get rid of some smell?' Michael Stone suggested. 'Maybe the rotten fucker used chloroform. Excuse the flowery language, miss.'

At the mention of 'chloroform' we all began sniffing the air, wrinkling and scrunching up our noses like rabbits on heat.

'He'd want plenty of ventilation for chloroform, all right – so that he didn't do *himself* in as well as the horse,' JJ said. 'Pity the bastard didn't!'

'I'm sure he'd have had a chloroform mask,' PJ replied. 'He never seems short of the proper veterinary equipment, does he?'

Michael Stone fetched a powerful torch from his car so that we could all have a closer look at the dead horse. A full post-mortem wasn't an option as none of us was a pathologist, nor could we claim to be either independent or unbiased. And, as this could all turn out very nasty, with insurance claims and whatnot, it was essential to do the right thing from the very outset.

There were no marks anywhere that we could see. We checked carefully all along the possible intravenous sites for small puncture wounds or tiny blobs of blood but saw nothing; then we turned him over and repeated the minute search on the other side. Still zero. The only clue as to the cause of death was the dark-blue cyanosis of the mucous membranes of the eyes, lips, gums and tongue. That signified death from oxygen starvation, but meant little, as it could have arisen from natural causes.

JJ, whose case it was, went to phone the late Fizzikle's owner, Phil Jones, who arrived, dishevelled and distraught, a bare twenty minutes later. Fortunately, he had been to see the horse earlier in the evening, so he knew that it had been in the best of health. They'd had Fizzikle out to check the hock and he'd been sound at the walk and almost sound at the trot, and Phil had been right pleased with him. He was obviously upset that his horse was dead, but he didn't try to blame anyone; in fact, he said, erroneously assuming that the dead animal had been discovered during routine rounds, he was most impressed that we did an inspection of the yard at midnight. There was a long pause while everybody waited to see if someone else wanted to put him straight, but it soon passed the point where anyone could, without branding the others a pack of colluding, lying curs. And so the Slattery practice would have yet another false rumour doing the rounds in the morning, only this time favourable. So what? They were due a break.

Back in the office, Claire said goodnight and went off to bed.

I waited and waited for Jones to leave but too much had happened that night and they were all in for the long haul. At last, I excused myself and, hoping that Claire hadn't fallen asleep, headed upstairs. She hadn't – we hadn't seen each other in over three weeks.

'What's a chloroform mask?' Claire asked drowsily, ages later.

I fought my way back through the heavy curtains of sleep. 'A chloroform mask?' I mumbled. Claire, with uncannily bad timing, was always doing this and I knew she wouldn't be fobbed off with a promise to tell her in the morning. 'Well . . .' I began with sleep-thickened tongue, 'it's shaped like a flowerpot but it's made from a type of canvas . . .' I drifted off again, rocking gently away on a stream of dimming consciousness . . .

'Type of canvas,' Claire murmured with a tiny shake of her hand, just enough to recall me. 'Go on . . .'

'Aw . . .' I used a supreme effort to awaken myself fully for the few seconds it would take to finish the description. 'The wide end is open and is wide enough to slip up along the horse's nose. It has a long strap at one side and a buckle at the other. The strap goes behind the ears and across the poll, and is then buckled to keep it there. The bottom or narrow end is also open but has a zipper that can close it. Okay?'

'How do you use it?' she whispered, miles, possibly whole worlds, away.

'We don't nowadays – it's pretty stone age stuff. But when it was used, the mask was fitted on like I said, and a wad of cotton wool soaked in chloroform was put in at the bottom end and the zipper closed. The level of anaesthesia was controlled by removing and reinserting the cotton wool as required. Are you with me so far?'

But she wasn't. Claire was fast asleep, her gentle breaths wafting rhythmically across my chest. I lay awake for the next hour, in an agony of gravel-eyed exhaustion, with nothing to occupy me other than hating her.

I called Ellen early to thank her for the dinner party and ended up spending whole minutes trying to reassure her that Val Crowther's 'unfortunate intrusion' – as she put it – had not spoiled the whole evening. 'Detracted from, yes; spoiled, no,' I said comfortingly, wishing yet again that I could ask her why she was so scared of the man; of his very name, even. Trying to tack a zigzag course towards this, I asked her if she had any idea how Crowther could have known I was at the party, but she seemed to think that he had just gatecrashed and lost the rag when he saw me there.

'That can't be, Ellen. I never saw the man before in my life and I doubt he's ever seen me. How could he have known me from Adam? Are you sure you didn't tell him I was on the guest list?'

'Sure, Frank. I haven't spoken to him for weeks.'

'Does he often get drunk and gatecrash parties – yours or anyone else's?'

'If he does, then I've never heard of it. He certainly never did that in my house before. I've already spoken to some of the others this morning and it came as a total surprise to them too. He's not a heavy drinker, never has been. I don't think I've ever seen Val even *tipsy*.'

I digested this. If being drunk was out of character for him, then what had caused him to go on a binge before he gatecrashed the party? And *why* had he gatecrashed the party? If he'd a few too many, why not just go home? The only answer that made sense was because the party and his uncharacteristic binge were connected and, as I seemed to have been the sole focus of his attention as he stood, weaving and bleary-eyed, in the embarrassed room, it was more than fair to conclude that I was also the reason for the binge.

That in itself was interesting: had he learned that I was here in Monksford in a double capacity? Or was he one of the colleagues PJ had spoken of, one of those who viewed me as 'Frank Samson, Veterinary Surgeon and Famously Effective Busybody and Amateur Sleuth'? If he was and he had a guilty conscience, then my presence could very well upset him to the point that he'd go on a bender, and then come and stare at me . . . Which meant that he must have known I'd be at the party. That was the *really* interesting question – how did he know I'd be there?

'Do they all know him? The other guests?'

'Oh, yes. Everybody around these parts knows everybody else.'

'Maybe one of them told him I'd been invited.'

'No, because none of them knew you were coming.'

This pussyfooting with Ellen was getting me nowhere. I decided to go for it and to hell with the consequences. 'Listen, Ellen, when we arrived back last night I did a quick round of the yard and I found one of our patients dead.' I paused to let that sink in, but when there was no comment from the other end continued: 'There was no excuse in the world for this horse to have died – it had fully recovered from a minor hock injury and was supposed to be going home this morning. Now I'm not even *suggesting* that Crowther had anything to do with this, but I want you to know that, last week, in fact on my very first day here, two men tried, in the dead of night, to put a red blister on the same damaged hock. If I hadn't surprised them, the horse would have been a write-off by morning because its hock would have been burned beyond repair, do you understand me, Ellen?'

'I don't see . . .'

'You don't even *want* to see. Let me ask you this, Ellen. Do you think Val Crowther is a stupid man and/or a lousy vet?'

'Frank, I don't think that this . . .'

'Just answer the question, Ellen. Yes or no?' I said tersely down the line. 'I mean, Jesus, it's simple enough.'

'I'm not sure I like . . .'

'Ellen, I'm trying to eliminate people as suspects. Now, please, can you just answer me yes or no? After all, you did choose him as your vet last year, so I have to assume that you consider him to be a good vet and not stupid, right? Please, Ellen?'

'Well . . . Yes.'

'Good. I agree. But then answer me this: he's not stupid and he's a good vet, so how come, when he took the samples from your stallion's neck, he took them from an open, contaminated wound, a wound which had flies rambling about on it with their filthy feet, a wound which had dust and dirt blowing on to it and then concluded that the infection had been caused by a dirty needle? Ellen, a first-year vet student, even a particularly obtuse one, would have known better than that. So to what do we attribute this experienced and good and non-stupid vet's regrettable lapse? There aren't many choices, Ellen: we've ruled out stupidity and ignorance, so, in my book, that leaves just an unfortunate momentary lapse of concentration or deliberate malice. Am I wrong?'

'You're browbeating me, Frank. I can't think straight.'

'Sorry. Maybe I am. But can you please tell me where I've gone wrong in my reasoning?'

There was a long silence. I thought she'd left the phone off the hook and just walked away from it, from me and my angry persistence. 'Ellen?'

'Yes, I'm here.'

'You okay?'

'Yes.'

'Do you want me to call you back or something? Would you prefer to call me?'

'No, Frank. What's the point? Yes, I do think, now, that Val was acting out of malice. But I swear that I didn't realise it before. I never thought of the open wound . . .'

'No reason why you *should* have. It's not your field. It's forgivable for you, but not for Crowther.' I tried to reassure her that it was not her fault before moving on to the next part. 'How do you feel, Ellen, about undoing some of the damage Crowther has done to the Slatterys? Would you be willing to give a statement to the Ethics Committee of the Veterinary Council that he's been canvassing, even jokingly, for years?'

'Frank, I can't. Just take it from me and please don't ask me to. I just can't.'

'Why not, Ellen? Fair is fair.' When she didn't answer I went on, probing as gently as I could, 'Has Crowther got some power over you? Is that it? Is that why you always get that frightened look about you when his name comes up? I know you say I'm imagining it but I know I'm not and you know perfectly well that I'm not.'

There was a long hesitation, like before, and I thought she might answer, but then she said in a scared and unsure voice, which was almost wavering: 'You must have been mistaken, Frank. Oh, God, there goes the baby, got to rush. 'Bye.' And she hung up. I hadn't heard any baby cries in the background.

Claire and I did all the work that day. The partners were fully tied up with the pathologist and the police. When we returned to base for lunch, the police came upstairs moments behind us and spent some fifteen minutes questioning me. Had I noticed any cars 'lurking' nearby at any time last evening or night? Their theory was that the premises were being watched constantly by the same intruders I'd interrupted on my first night and as soon as those two knew the coast was clear, namely when they saw Claire and me drive out last evening, then . . .

'You mean, they came in and polished off the job?'

'Yes, sir. That's the idea.'

'It's possible, I suppose, but I doubt they've been watching the place all the time.' And I told them about two other nights I'd been out – to Michael Stone's house for dinner, and to one of the clients who had invited me and JJ to his daughter's engagement party.

'I see, sir. So you reckon that maybe they just got lucky? Dropped by on the off chance?'

'No. I didn't say that at all. Perhaps someone knew I'd be away for most of last night?'

That kept the conversation going for a while. Who had invited me? Who knew I was going? Who had been at the party? Had either of us noticed anyone slipping out soon after we'd arrived, or making a call on a mobile phone or the Ollins' house phone? How long had we been away from the surgery? Would that, in my expert opinion, be long enough for someone to gather together the gear needed to kill the horse, the chloroform, mask, etc.? Oh, yes, indeed it would.

Could I think of any other profession or line of work, apart from a vet, that is, who would have such gear to hand? No, I couldn't. Only a vet or a person working in a veterinary practice. Could I think of any vet who might do this? This was my chance to mumble something about Crowther, but as I had no proof I answered 'no'. As this kind of thing, horse murder, had never been heard of before in this area, did I know if any new vet, apart, that is, from myself, had come into the locality recently? No. Could I offer any reason as to why the first attack on the horse had been merely to injure him, whereas the second had been honest to God, no beating about the bush, in your face murder? That was puzzling me too, but so far I'd been unable to think of an explanation other than that if the blister had worked, Fizzikle would have had to be put down anyhow, so in that sense the first attack could be said to have also been murderous in intent. The police talked this over between them but seemed to think that it was far too convoluted and dismissed it.

They changed the stream of their questions. How come I'd noticed the top door open, as it had been open many nights since the first incident? Why had I decided to close it? Because the night was turning filthy. Could I describe the two people I'd interrupted on the first occasion? No, not in any detail, I'd been too far away. That is the occasion on which it was decided that calling the police would be a waste of time? The last sentence was said very pointedly and carried the suggestion that if we *had* called in the experts, then this present disaster would not have happened; it was all our own fault. I hoped he hadn't passed that opinion on to anyone, especially to Phil Jones.

Soon after the cops left, JJ trotted up the stairs, shouting: 'Yoo-hoo, you two! Are you decent?'

'JJ of the one-track mind,' I said, opening the door. 'What's happening?'

'The pathologist has left – he reckons some chloroform was used, although not enough to kill him. He thinks the horse was heavily sedated first and then suffocated by putting a plastic bag over his head. Poor bastard.'

'Christ!' said Claire. 'What kind of animal would do a thing like that?'

This was the first opportunity I'd had to put the partners abreast of Crowther's behaviour at the party. 'Where are your father and Michael?'

'Downstairs.'

'Ask them if they want a cup of coffee. I've got something to tell them.'

'What is it?'

'It's about Crowther. Ask them to come up. Then the one telling can do for all.'

Later that afternoon I happened upon a strange conversation.

I'd replenished my drugs supplies from the store, checked the call book, said goodbye to Eve and Barbara – they'd have closed up shop by the time I got back – and was heading for the Land Rover, when I suddenly realised I'd forgotten to ask Eve if a client I'd seen that morning had called back with news, good or bad, of his very sick prize Jersey bull.

Eve was not at the counter but I could see her through the slightly ajar door of the inner office; as I approached it, I heard her say in a loud, adamant whisper: '. . . getting too risky. If we don't cool it for a while, we'll be caught for sure. I think she's getting suspicious. Can't talk now. I'll ring you later. Seven on the dot, as usual, but I'm warning you, as far as I'm concerned, it's over for now.' The phone went down with a crash.

I gave a loud cough and rapped. Eve swung round in horror, her rather plain face blushing scarlet, her whole demeanour the picture of guilt.

'Sorry to interrupt,' I said. 'Any message about John Downey's bull?'

She didn't know where to look but eventually stumbled out a 'no, no message'. I left her to it and went off, wondering what the surly Eve was up to. Who was the 'she' who was getting suspicious? A girlfriend? A wife? Was the prudish Eve having an affair with a married man? It certainly seemed like it. I mean, what about the seven o'clock *on the dot*? With affairs, I could see that half the battle would be knowing when it was safe to phone and sticking to it. There'd be nothing worse than taking potluck, getting connected to the cuckolded spouse and then hanging up – a real giveaway, that. Eve? The demon temptress? The passionate mistress? I couldn't see it. Somehow it just didn't ring true.

But the obvious alternative explanation – that Eve could be the spy and Barbara the unnamed 'she' of the conversation – passed me by a mile. I had jumped to the not unreasonable conclusion that I'd overheard a fraught moment in a dodgy love affair.

Besides, I didn't have an open mind at that point: I had already come to my conclusions, and the local gossips and busybodies had been elected chief suspects.

Dummkopf.

12

The local weekly came out, as it always did, on Wednesday about noon, and this time, a mere five days after he'd stormed the Ollins' party, Val Crowther was all over the front page. Unfortunately, this was not for reasons the Slatterys would have liked; quite the opposite, in fact. For Crowther was a real-life, genuine hero, the toast of the county.

Mind you, it was no scoop for the provincial paper. The news was two days old by the time the paper had been put to bed. The national dailies had carried it on the Tuesday and so had the other media. The Slatterys' arch enemy had been interviewed from his hospital bed on Monday's 9 p.m. TV news and the clip had run on the main bulletins on Tuesday. Crowther had come across as a man awash to the eyeballs in humility, humanity and a seemingly limitless propensity for self-sacrifice. Seeing the horse murderer, all bruised, bandaged and sanctimonious, with the infrequent (almost, but not quite suppressed) grimace of agony was enough to make me want to throw up. Still, I had to admit that Crowther, in this instance anyway, had done the business . . .

What had happened was this: on the Monday afternoon, he had been driving his Mercedes through one of the leafy streets of his home town, Breenstown, when suddenly, without warning, three children on bicycles hurtled directly into his path from out of a side road. Witnesses later swore that, had it not been for Crowther's instant reactions, he would have ploughed through the three children and nobody was in any doubt but that the youngsters would have been killed stone dead. Coming, as it did, so soon after the recent horrific slaughter of the two families on the Dublin motorway, this near miss took on an added, almost supernatural, significance and Crowther was promoted by local opinion from being merely a very good driver (and a self-sacrificing one, it had to be conceded) into what amounted to little less than an Instrument of God.

All the elements were present. The three children were two sisters and their brother. They were cycling home from school when, at the top of the steep hill which swept down to, and through, the near-fatal crossroads, the brakes on the youngest girl's bicycle failed. In panic, the elder sister and the boy, who was aged between the two girls, sprinted after her, hoping to catch her and stop her before the junction. But everything went wrong: they caught her at the actual junction itself, at which point they were going too fast to stop. So, in a single bunch, they shot through the crossroads. Crowther, on seeing this appalling apparition materialise mere feet in front of him and realising that his brakes could not stop him in time managed, with superb coolness and consummate skill, to wrestle his Mercedes on to a small traffic island which had a cherry tree in its centre, and that stopped him dead in his tracks, inches from where the terrified children were streaking past. Shards of the Mercedes's broken headlight glass were later found in the woollen weave of the younger girl's scarf. That was how close it had been.

The pictures and interviews took up almost a whole page and there was a neat biography of Crowther: where he was born, his education, the various places he'd worked in before coming to Breenstown, his family details ... It all read uncomfortably like an obituary. The piece went on to point out that he had been a reasonably successful rally driver in his earlier years, which explained the rather puzzling opening sentence of the main article: '*Breenstown vet, Valentine Crowther, drove the race of his life last Monday afternoon.*'

There was an accompanying picture of Crowther leaning against a sports car, but it certainly hadn't been taken in the rallying days of his youth – he looked almost the same as he had at the Ollins' the other night, except that he was smiling broadly in the photograph, not scowling. Fair play to the man, I thought as I turned the page. Credit where credit was due.

In a bottom corner of page four I came upon the ominous headline: TOP LOCAL CHASER DIES AT VETS' SURGERY, but the article was accurate and concise, and stated clearly that the horse had been at the vets' for several days and had made a full recovery by the time the 'incident' took place; the death was being treated as foul play; Gardai were investigating.

I was on my way to bed when I was struck by a sudden thought, which sent me back searching for the paper. Turning to the picture of Crowther and the sports car, I looked more closely at it, then took it directly under the table light and studied it again. Under the brighter light the grainy picture became clear. Crowther was on the left, arms folded across his chest, buttocks against the side of the car's bonnet, which swept away in a graceful curve the perfection of which was spoiled only by the silvered figurine of a springing jaguar which was, unfortunately, headless.

I seemed doomed to sleepless nights in Monksford. I'd been roused on my very first night by Fizzikle's attackers, the red blister brigade; next had come half a night of worry as I tried to place Ellen's husband and when I'd first met him; then there'd been the night that Fizzikle had been killed – hours in the office with the partners and Phil Jones, followed by athletic, long overdue lovemaking and, finally, a small lecture on the use of the chloroform mask . . .

Now, here I was again, wondering if the Jaguar in the picture and Dave's Jag were the same. Was there some connection between Crowther and Dave? Was it even the same car? Dave's had been blue, but the picture in the paper was in black and white, so that was of little use. Anyway, even if they were the same colour, it proved nothing – the car could have been resprayed. Perhaps Dave had bought the car from Crowther or vice versa? But that wouldn't prove a connection between them either. The sale could have gone through an ad in the paper, a dealer, an auction, or some other form of middleman. In fact, I concluded, there was no reason why either man should know the other. It could be a simple case of two different cars, with nothing but the coincidence of a decapitated Jaguar emblem in common. Still, it bothered me enough to keep me awake into the small hours.

And anyway, so what if they had known each other? They had mutual friends, or at least acquaintances, in the Ollins. I'd ask Ellen next time I saw her. I thumped the pillow into shape, determined to put all such thoughts and queries aside. I needed the sleep and besides, knowing whether or not Dave had sold the car to Crowther or Crowther had sold it to Dave would be about as much use to me as a matchboxful of navel fluff.

Another thing they shared, I thought, sinking into late sleep, was their shady characters. Perhaps one had *stolen* the car from the other?

I ran into her in the supermarket while I was buying the makings for a meagre and unwholesome lunch. She was alone. 'Having a solo day out?' I said, coming up to her as she subjected a marmalade pot to brow-furrowing scrutiny.

'Hey, Frank!' she said, smiling. 'What are you doing here?' She put the marmalade into her trolley.

'Oh, nothing exciting. Just shopping for my lunch. These places always confuse me. I can never find anything. I look at the shelves as I go, but my eyes don't see a thing – they just kind of glaze over, you know? I've just spent ten minutes looking for sardines and found that I'd already passed them twice. I'll tell you where they are if you tell me where to find black peppercorns.'

Ellen laughed. 'There, you ninny. Right behind you.'

'Well, I'll be . . . ! I've passed here twice as well. Funny meeting you here, Ellen. I was just about to phone you, as soon as I got home. First thing – phone Ellen.'

'Yeah?' Sceptical glance.

'Yeah. I see your local friendly vet has become the people's choice. Man just needs to die to become a fuckin' saint. St Peter, no doubt, already looking into the minor details – you know, halo size, preferred style in wings, harp tuned to A minor or G flat . . .' Seeing her expression change from smile to grim, I held up my palms. 'Sorry. Out of order. Actually, I've got to admit he's one hell of a driver and one hell of a cool customer under pressure. These two outstanding qualities apart, he's an outstanding asshole. What kind of Mercedes was it?' I rushed on hurriedly as I saw her turn grim again. I was surprised that she seemed to be on the side of Crowther, a man whom she obviously feared so much – perhaps she was related to the three lucky kids. Or just knew them. 'Something fancy, I imagine?'

'Undoubtedly. He's into cars, is Val.'

'So I saw. The picture in the paper had him perched on some kind of sexy Jag. Did you see it?'

'Didn't everybody?'

'What kind of Jag was it? Apart from sexy. Do you remember it?'

'No. Sure it was a Jag? I thought Val stuck to German cars, Mercs, BMs, Porsches . . .'

'Well, this one was definitely a Jag. It had the Jag emblem on the front, although it had lost its head. Ever see him in that?'

'No, but then I wouldn't, would I? We're not exactly inseparable buddies, as you seem to think.'

'I never thought anything of the kind, Ellen. Do you know why I was going to phone you?'

'Do I want to know?' she asked wearily, annoyed at herself for not sticking to monosyllabic answers.

'Probably not. Look. Can we sit and have a coffee?' When she hesitated I said: 'You can walk out whenever you want. I'm not going to turn violent, y'know.'

'Okay, then.' She sighed. 'I suppose a cup of coffee isn't going to harm either of us.'

I could have done with less of the resignation, I thought,

as I followed her through the arch of the plastic-vine-draped pergola that marked the cafeteria area. But at least she knew what was coming and hadn't refused to sit with me. That was something. Progress.

When I drove into the yard an hour later there was a squad car parked tight up to the back gate. For one chilly moment I thought there'd been another sabotage attempt. This could have been a very unfortunate development, especially for me, as the man whom I had all but accused of being the saboteur was at present reclining in comfort in his hero's hospital bed – basking, more like, as his injuries were now known to be slight. Thank God. Still, before I pushed through the door, I'd reminded myself that there *had* been two intruders that first night, neither of whom, as far as I could recall, had resembled Crowther's shape very closely. That pair had had more meat on them.

But the police had merely brought a copy of the pathologist's report: the expert had ended up concluding that his speculation of a few days ago had been correct – the horse had been given sufficient chloroform to knock him down and the job then finished quickly by placing a heavy-duty plastic bag tightly over the head. Quite how he had worked that out I had no idea, but that was why he was an expert and I wasn't. Apparently the plastic bag was a not uncommon method of killing horses that didn't quite live up to expectations and allowing the disappointed owners to claim the insurance money. Very few of the unfortunate animals, I imagined, would have had the comfort of an anaesthetic before being hooded with the lethal bag. Probably, most were DIY jobs. Fizzikle would never know how honoured he'd been – having a fully qualified vet to murder him.

We held a short discussion but there wasn't much to talk about and soon the police left. PJ put the report into a box file containing all the other paperwork on the dead horse, plus several sealed plastic evidence bags of short brown neck hairs and long, coarse, black mane hairs. These were being kept against the unlikely day that a suspicious chloroform mask or piece of clothing, tack or rope turned up.

On my afternoon rounds I went over, again and again, the strange exchange I'd had with Ellen in the coffee shop.

First we'd sat for a surreal twenty minutes while I tried to start several conversations and she just sat opposite me, staring silently at the table, brow furrowed, looking like she was thinking hard. Following the relatively fluid banter of our encounter between the laden shelves of the supermarket, she seemed to have gone totally into a shell and, on the few occasions when she'd actually responded to my opening gambits, she'd done so with brief, almost grunt words. Otherwise she'd said hardly anything apart, that is, from asking me to fetch more and more coffee.

When I brought our third cappuccinos she raised her face towards me and asked me what, precisely, I wished to know.

'About what?'

'Val Crowther.'

'Are you serious?'

'Well, if I *don't* tell you, I know you won't let it be. You'll just go and ask somebody else, won't you? Then someone else and someone after that, until the whole damned country is abuzz with it. I know you, Frank. You mind everyone's business but your own.'

I thought this unduly harsh. I was willing to admit to having a probing mind, a nose for sniffing out something wrong, especially if the wronged one happened to be a friend. I told her this but received only a shrug and a snort in reply.

Having offered to tell me about Crowther, I thought that was it, that Ellen had decided to tell all, but she hadn't, and there followed a strange pattern of question and answer that reminded me of something I had once read about how an inside source in the Watergate investigation had insisted on passing information to Bob Woodward and Carl Bernstein. Like their source, Ellen would only respond to questions which required just yes or no answers; she would then answer 'no' when the answer actually was 'no' and refuse to answer at all if the response was a 'yes'. It was all terribly tortuous and, when I finally stumbled upon the formula, I had no idea what purpose it served her.

It worked like this:

Me: 'You're afraid of Crowther, aren't you?' No reply (= yes).

Me: 'Has he threatened you?' No reply (= yes).

Me: 'Physically?'

Ellen: 'No.'

Me: 'So what's he doing, then? Blackmailing you?' No reply (= yes).

Me: 'For money?'

Ellen: 'No.'

Me: 'So what does he want if not money?' She looked at me reprovingly. Yes or no questions only, please.

Me (groping): 'For . . . for . . . *sex*?'

Ellen: 'No!' Withering scorn.

Me: 'Sorry. Well, then, eh . . . For your *business*?' No reply (= yes).

Me: 'Ah! I see. Can you tell me what he's got on you?' This drew a pursing of her lips and a shrug, which I took to mean maybe. I waited some more but she didn't say no.

Me: 'Have you done something wrong?'

Ellen: 'No.' But this time there was a bit of equivocation in it.

Me: 'Something bad?'

Ellen: 'No.' Another dodgy one.

Me: 'Illegal?'

Ellen: 'No.'

Me: 'Then what's the big deal? Tell me about it.'

Ellen: 'No.'

Me: 'Have you told Laurence about it?'

Ellen: 'No.' This 'no' was accompanied by a scornful, almost amused snort. At first I thought she was indicating that Laurence was an insensitive, heartless bastard who wouldn't be any help at all, but then it struck me that it might just have been the very idea of telling her *husband* that was so ludicrous. Therefore my next question:

Me: 'Ellen. Are you having an affair?' That would explain why she had scoffed at the idea of turning to Laurence for sympathy and understanding. Nor would an affair have been illegal.

Ellen: 'No.'

Me: 'Have you had an affair that Crowther knows about? Is that it?'

Ellen: 'No.'

Neither of these two 'nos' was delivered with anything like conviction. 'Ellen,' I said, 'I'm not playing any more. If you want to tell me the whole story, fine. If you don't, then that's fine, too.'

She hesitated for a few seconds, carefully swallowed some tepid coffee, which by now had grown a thin raft of skin, dabbed fastidiously at the corners of her mouth, then started off in a gush, as if, at last, she was relieved to be able to talk about it. 'Crowther suspects, and he's right, that I'd like to change from him to another vet. He knows I'm not happy with his services, or his enormous fees, but he says he can't let me change or others might follow. I didn't have an affair, at least not like you mean, but he says he'll tell Laurence I did. He says the stud farm is a high-profile, grade-one client and that's why he can't let me change to another practice.'

'But if he can't back up his charge, then what's the problem? He might just as well tell Laurence that you've committed . . . genocide! Talk is cheap.'

'It's not that simple, Frank. There may not have been any fire, but there's been a fair deal of smoke about. Stupidly, I've been perhaps . . . a bit too friendly with a man we knew, although I swear it didn't become . . . sexual. Oh, it could have, but . . . it hasn't. Didn't! It's over now.'

'How do you feel about that? About it being over.'

'It should never have started. It's just that Laurence is always so busy that I rarely see him and . . . and . . . I suppose the devil finds work for idle hands . . .'

'Are you in love with this other guy?'

'Hell, no. I may have been infatuated at the time. And flattered. He's very dishy, Frank, and usually goes for much younger women.' She shook her head as if awaking. 'Why am I saying all this? That's enough about him. More than enough.'

'And Crowther got to know about the affair?'

'It was *not* an affair. An ... a ... friendship. Well, he knew I was meeting this ... eh ...'

'Dish?' I suggested helpfully.

'... friend ... occasionally for lunch, or whatever ...'

'Laurence didn't know?'

'No, of course not.'

'So you may have been unwise. What's the big deal? If nothing happened, nothing happened. Surely Laurence would believe you before Crowther? His wife's word against his vet's word. I mean, he'd at *least* give you the benefit of the doubt, wouldn't he?'

Ellen had developed a glazed stare and seemed totally lost for words. Christ, I thought, this can't have been her first time. That's why she couldn't take the chance on Crowther telling her husband. Ellen was a serial adulteress ... I felt almost angry, as though she had been cheating on me ... Perhaps she had, all those years ago, although I couldn't quite figure out where she would have found the time as we had been together almost constantly in those days.

She said nothing for a long time, then swallowed hard and began to speak, slowly, unsurely, as if she herself wasn't entirely sure of the events of her near affair. 'Actually, Frank, Laurence did know ...'

'Hey! Hang on there,' I protested. 'You just told me he didn't. What the hell's going on, Ellen? Are you bullshitting me?'

'No, Frank, I'm not. Some of Laurence's friends were beginning to remark on the fact that I seemed to be seeing a lot of this man and he wanted it to stop at once. Oh, I kicked up a bit – I had to, didn't I, or it would be tantamount to admitting guilt – and told him that the fact that his friends knew proved that it was all above board; if there'd been anything . . . untoward . . . going on, we'd have made certain that *nobody* saw us, neither *his* friends nor anybody else's either. He didn't argue – Laurence never does; it's infuriating. He just told me, po-faced, that I was belittling my own intelligence and letting myself down badly by using such a naive line of argument, which depended completely on the *ludicrous* premise that every single one of my "meetings" with this man, without exception, had been observed from start to finish. He said that the relationship, innocent or not, was bothering him, that he had no intention of hiring detectives to establish its precise nature and that the next step was up to me. He said marriage had to be built on trust; it was not a court of law where someone was presumed innocent until proven guilty beyond all reasonable doubt before action could be taken. It was supposed to be a secure, happy, trusting and comfortable relationship. It could come under severe pressure from ill health, financial pressures etc., but where these were not a factor and the threat came from within, what was the point? The usual lecture, you know.'

I shrugged, suddenly glad that my relationship with this woman had fallen through. I wondered if Ellen had had to receive this pep talk often, why she'd called it the 'usual' lecture. 'But if Laurence already knows . . . what can Crowther tell him?'

No answer.

'There's *more*?'

She thought for some time again. I assumed she was weighing up the pros and cons of telling me. 'Well . . . When I promised to stop seeing this man, I told Laurence all the places I'd met him or been with him, you know, making a clean breast of it all . . .'

'But?' I prompted after a pause, knowing what was coming.

'Well, there was one place I *didn't* mention because it looked too damned suspicious and I knew he'd never believe it was innocent. I suppose, to be totally honest, it wasn't really innocent either. Only by default.'

She'd been looking into her coffee cup during most of this

136

but now she darted a glance at my eyes to see how I was taking it – as if it mattered to me. Her eyes dropped again after bouncing off my neutral stare. 'I'd been to stay for a few days with Kathy [Ellen's elder sister, whom I'd totally forgotten about until now] and I'd agreed to meet my "friend" on the way back. It's only a three-hour drive from Kathy's, as you know, and it's no problem to do it in one go, but . . . jeez, Frank, you must think I'm *awful* . . . well, eh, I decided to . . . eh . . . break my journey. I told Laurence I'd be back about lunchtime next day, that I'd be leaving Kathy's after breakfast. In fact, I left Kathy's about six in the evening. I'd arranged to meet my . . . friend . . . for dinner at eight thirty and I'd fully intended spending the night with him. It was to be a surprise – I'd been refusing him for so long and I knew he wanted me so badly. Men always do. The first few times. Anyway, I was quite late getting to the rendezvous – you remember my lousy sense of direction? – and he was pretty drunk when I got there.' She gave an ironic laugh of self-deprecation. 'We slept together all right, but sleeping was all we did. So, my honour remained unbesmirched, even if only accidentally. And now you know as much as I do and I can't really think why I've told you.' The last few sentences were delivered in a relieved gush and, having finished, Ellen was breathing hard as if she'd just come through an enormous ordeal, which, I supposed, she had.

'When was this?'

'Oh. Last year. Just before I changed from the Slatterys to Crowther. Obviously, eh? And now I don't want to talk about it any more, okay? I've told you all there is to know and I bloody well expect you to keep it to yourself, Frank. Okay? It's strictly confidential and if I didn't know how infuriatingly persistent you can be I'd never have mentioned it. I didn't sleep with the guy and I won't. I decided that night that there was some kind of divine intervention at work, that it was not meant to be. I don't meet him much any more; he's around, but we don't meet on our own. He's phoned once or twice but I give him short shrift. He claims he's still hoping for another chance, says he'll never drink again, just in case I change my mind – he doesn't want to miss it a second time. There won't *be* a second time.'

'He's *still* trying to seduce you?'

'You find that strange, Frank? Am I that undesirable?'

'You know that's not what I mean, Ellen. I just reckon that after being rebuffed a year ago he might have got the message by now and given you up as a lost cause.'

'Maybe he just finds me adorable?' Ellen fluttered her eyelashes in an exaggerated Betty Boop way.

I refused to react. 'So. Crowther finds out about this overnight meeting, right?'

'Don't ask me how, but yes, he knew. Within a week, he rang to ask me if I could recommend this particular hotel. He said he'd heard that the bed in room number so-and-so – I've even forgotten which room, now – was particularly comfortable. A few weeks later he asked me to change from the Slatterys and, when I said I couldn't think of a valid reason to do so, a reason that Laurence would believe, he laughed and said I should wait a few more days.'

'The infected jugular?'

'I assume so. He knew that PJ Slattery had just finished treating the stallion, although I don't know how he could have known it. *I* certainly didn't tell him; if you have a sick animal on a stud farm, especially a stallion, then you keep very, very quiet about it. When I challenged Val, he denied point blank that he'd had any part in causing the neck to . . . rot. I was furious at the damage to the horse and I'm still certain that somehow he caused it. Like he promised, it happened in his "few more days". Spot on. If I'd been able to prove it was him, I'd have killed him. Would it have been possible for him to do that, Frank?'

'Easy peasy. Any irritant substance injected into or under the skin would cause it.'

'The bastard!'

'Ellen. Would you swear to what you've told me, under oath?'

But Ellen was thinking more of her own hide than of taking revenge on Crowther, despoiler of her stallion, ruiner of the Slatterys' practice. 'Swear?' She looked at me as if I was mad. '*Swear*? I'd *deny* every word of it. Laurence would never believe in my innocence. And nor should he. Jeez! He'd throw me out. It really was no thanks to me that nothing happened. Virtue in the absence of opportunity is no virtue at all, or words to that effect. *The Vicar of Wakefield*, I think. I can't remember any of that stuff any more.'

I knew there was no point in pressing her further. There wasn't much more to tell – her 'friend's' name, although it would hardly mean anything to me. 'Do I know this guy?'

'Busybody snoop! Even if you did, I wouldn't tell you.'

'Makes no odds, Ellen. I think you're just steeped in luck to have a bloke like Laurence. Nine out of ten men would not have taken it as lightly as he seems to have. If I were you, I'd be wary of pushing my luck any further. The man's a saint. A saint or a pushover.'

'He's no pushover, Frank. I got hell for months. We went nowhere, turned down almost all invitations and had no parties. That party you and Claire came to was just the second or third since . . .'

As we walked out of the supermarket, I remembered to ask her if Crowther and Dave had known each other. She told me that they had, from way back.

'Way back when?'

'College days, Frank. College days.'

'*College*?' Crowther was much too old to have been at college with us.

'*We* were at college – Crowther wasn't. Dave didn't hang about much with students, if you remember. Apart from you and me, most of his friends were older guys.'

Thinking back, it was true. Even then, doing the course he never finished, Dave had been a bit of a mystery man, probably already sniffing about on the edges of the easy pickings.

'Did you know Crowther in those days?'

'I met him once, for about twenty minutes. That's all.'

'With Dave?'

'With Dave. Why?'

'No why, I suppose. I never met him at all – never even heard of him.'

As I watched her walk to her car, I couldn't help but feel that there was a sprightliness in her step, as if a huge burden had been lifted from her shoulders. I flattered myself into believing that I was the one who had soothed her troubled mind.

Dummkopf, Frank. Again.

13

The late news on Saturday night carried the story of a kidnapping in County Tipperary.

A millionaire property developer had been abducted from his isolated country estate, presumably by the three men who had been seen earlier in the evening in a 'suspiciously parked' dark-blue van in a wooded area close to the victim's house. A van of the same or similar type had been seen speeding away from his gates at about 9.20 p.m. and this timing had been corroborated by two transatlantic phone calls made by the victim's partner, some twelve minutes apart.

The first had been answered and the 'victim' had sounded perfectly normal and untroubled. But the crucial second call, the deal clincher which he'd been eagerly awaiting, had gone unanswered. Getting more and more worried, the partner in New York had tried three or four times, the last time at 9.05 p.m. and, when there was still no answer, suspected that there was something wrong – a heart attack, he'd thought – and phoned the emergency services. Knowing that his colleague was alone – his wife and family being on holiday – he had been particularly alarmed and the 999s had responded with alacrity, a police car and an ambulance being dispatched within minutes.

They had found the hall door wide open. In the study, on the desk by the telephone, a cotton wool wad lay, still reeking of chloroform. The swivel chair beside the desk had been knocked over. There were no further details at the moment, but more were promised as they became available. Before the newscaster went on to the next item, a picture of a van identical to the suspect one was flashed on the screen and all owners of such vehicles – in view of the fact that this was the weekend and their vans might be parked up until Monday morning – were asked to check at once that their transport had not been stolen from yards, lock-up garages etc.

Sunday morning it was all over. The kidnap had ended ignominiously turning into one of those great heroic failures where you almost feel sorry for the sinners. The left front tyre had blown out some nine miles from the house, its wall slashed open by a sharp rock which had fallen into the road from one of the dry-stone granite walls which lined the minor road the kidnappers had chosen as their getaway route.

In the eighteen hours since they'd stolen the vehicle, the gang had serviced and tuned the engine thoroughly, but they hadn't thought of anything as mundane as a puncture, and now all three of them were grunting and sweating on the side of a dark, deserted country road trying to shift wheel nuts which seemed to have been welded into place. The cross brace which they had found in the back of the van, along with the jack and the spare wheel, was proving totally unequal to the task and there was a danger that the hexagonal nut heads would become rounded, in which case they'd *never* be shifted, bar with a cold chisel. The atmosphere was one of barely suppressed panic. The whole plan depended on them being able to get to their *brilliant* hidey-hole before anybody realised that their millionaire meal ticket was even missing. Now a passing motorist could destroy their meticulous planning, a farmer driving carefully home from the pub or some such – there was hardly likely to be much else stirring on this lonely road in the dark hours. Which was why they'd chosen it in the first place. And if they couldn't get the wheel changed, where were they going to find another vehicle? None of them wanted to face *that* question.

The man in the back was also wondering about this. Now almost fully recovered from his short sleep, he'd been aroused when two of his captors had begun rummaging, cursing and swearing, in the spare-wheel well at his feet. By the time they'd found what they wanted he was sufficiently in control of his senses to feign continuing unconsciousness when one of the men shone a weak torch on his face and pinched his leg. Satisfied that he was still out for the count, and too preoccupied with their urgent predicament to think straight, the men had carted the spare wheel and tool kit round to the front and let the rear door of the van just bang to. It hadn't even closed, let alone locked. When he knew that all three kidnappers were occupied with the wheel-changing, the captive took his tiny, slim mobile phone from his inside pocket and he, too, dialled 999. He spoke to the police in a firm whisper, reporting both his situation and location. Outside, the battle to get the nuts free was in full swing.

One of the gang was doing his best to keep the wheel brace jammed as far in and as straight as possible on the nut to prevent it from shearing. A second had a death grip on one of the cross bars, ready to jerk up on it at the same split second that the third brought down, with all his might, a large rock on the opposite arm of the cross. The plan was to crack the nut free by the sudden sharp torque of the large rock and simultaneous upward jerk.

A good plan. In daylight. It being pitch dark, however – apart from the useless light from the small torch – the two gang members attached to the wheel brace were, understandably, nervous. This was the first nut and, with five more to go, they reckoned that if one of them didn't get his hand smashed right now, first go off, then it was just a matter of time. The captive lay and listened to the commotion outside.

'Don't worry,' a voice said reassuringly. 'I'll be careful.' There was a grunt and a sudden loud bang. The man in the back felt it jolt through him. 'Did she move?' asked the same voice.

'No,' said another.

'Fuck,' replied the first. 'I'll give her another tap.' 'Tap', a euphemism designed to comfort the other two, seemingly meant 'thunderous blow with this large and knobbly rock'. The procedure was repeated and this time there was relieved jubilation. The nut broke loose in its thread and was unscrewed.

The next nut took two goes also, the second of which was attended by howls of agony, curses and loud recriminations.

'*Aargh! Ya blind fucker, Liam! Ya nearly took me fuckin' hand off! Ah . . . Jaysus!*'

The brace had spun off into the night, making a ringing noise as it hit the granite wall. The subsequent search through the profuse and thorny roadside vegetation delayed progress somewhat, the injured party moaning and cursing throughout. When the brace was recovered, the injured one refused to hold it any more, despite the flattering assertions of the others that he was the strongest, the best able to keep the socket firmly on the nut. The captive in the back was wondering why the brace holder didn't wrap something round his hands when, eventually, one of the gang suggested it.

'Tell you what, Ted. Take off your jumper and wrap it round your hands, why don't you?'

'Yeh,' agreed the other, the one with the stone, the one called Liam. 'Only do it fast. It'll be the fuckin' dawn soon.' It was still only 9.45 p.m. Obviously Liam was inclined to exaggerate.

By the time they attacked the last nut, the captive was sitting on a damp rock in a field some hundred yards away from the stranded van, talking, out loud now, to the converging police cars, guiding them in. He watched the three men finish changing the wheel, heard Liam tell the others to leave the punctured wheel and the tool kit where they lay and get the fuck out of there. He watched all three pile into the van without even checking the rear door and he laughed out loud when he saw them shoot off with a squeal of rubber, heading away into the night and their chance to make tomorrow the biggest payday of their lives. He also knew that less than a mile along the road, just short of the first turning, there was this huge roadblock . . .

The 'victim' was back in his house before 10.30 p.m., where he righted his office chair and immediately resumed his phoning. All he was interested in was whether or not the US deal had gone through.

Simultaneous searches of the would-be kidnappers' homes and premises were carried out just after dawn next morning and, among other things, the police found a large Winchester bottle three-quarters full of chloroform – Veterinary Grade. This had been found in the garden shed of Liam McMurrow, the leader of the trio, a hitherto petty criminal well known to the Gardai. The kidnap had been a step up for him, an effort to get into some serious money. Despite the fact that his fingerprints were all over the bottle, McMurrow at first professed to have no clue as to how it came to be there. He had, he claimed, never seen it before. A while later he changed his story: he suddenly remembered that, many years ago, a vet had left it behind.

Which vet?

He couldn't remember, it was so long ago.

He was at a further loss to explain how a bottle of chloroform which, according to the label, had been manufactured just sixteen months before, could have been left in his garden shed many, many years ago, way back in the shadowy mists of time, when you and I were young, Maggie. Eventually he 'came clean' and admitted that he had stolen the bottle from a vet's car.

Why?

Just on the off chance that it might come in handy, like, ahem.

Which vet?

He didn't know.

Where?

He couldn't remember.

When?

He couldn't be sure.

Come in handy for what?

Well . . . you never knew, did you . . . You just never knew . . .

McMurrow's telephone diary, when it was examined, showed an entry for 'Vet', but, curiously, this was on the 'C' page. This deplorable illiteracy was not as bad as it first seemed because, when the number was dialled, it turned out to be that of 'C' for Crowther.

Why did he have the phone number of a vet who lived over eighty miles away?

He had known Crowther for years – ever since Crowther had worked, as a young vet, in his home town, Kyleglas. They had been fairly friendly then and he had kept the number just because he might be up Crowther's country one day and might like to call and say hi. Maybe sink a pint if it was evening.

Had they been very friendly?

No, not really.

Did they meet often?

He hadn't seen or heard from the man in twenty years, since he'd left the town.

But he still kept his number, right?

Right.

With all the changes in telephone numbers and area codes in the intervening years, he still managed to have the most recent telephone number of a man with whom he was not that friendly and whom he had not seen for almost twenty years?

Correct, yes. That was correct.

Despite having no contact during that time?

Yes. Well, ahem, actually, no actually. He'd been going through the telephone directory a few months back, looking for another number, a different one entirely, and he just happened to spot Crowther's name and that sparked off the memory and he jotted it down, like.

But Crowther lived in a different directory area and there wasn't a directory for that area in his house . . .

So?

So how could he have seen Crowther's name when he'd been looking up another number in a directory which didn't cover Crowther's area?

Who said anything about him being in his house? This was in a phone box, man, with lots of directories.

Where was the phone box?

He couldn't remember – he had a very bad memory.

Did he always carry his home telephone diary with him, that fragile plastic thing with the buttons that popped up the required page?

Always, he would never leave home without it.

Then why had he not had it with him last night when he'd been arrested at the roadblock? Why had it been left by the telephone in the hallway of his house?

He'd decided to leave it last night for the first time ever, because he had no phone calls to make.

Whose number had he been looking up, on or near the page with Crowther's number?

Ah, now there they had him; for the life of him, he was fucked if he could remember.

I came by these minutiae in a roundabout way. One of the kidnappers, Teddy Wright, had not been seen in the country for years and was generally thought to have either gone abroad permanently, or to have been murdered and well hidden. He had been and – now that he had turned up alive and well, except for a smashed hand – was still wanted for questioning in connection with a Dublin jewellery shop robbery, which was supposed to have been masterminded by Dave. I learned this from Inspector Curley, who came back into my life at this point to see if I had ever seen Wright with Dave or if he looked in any way at all like anyone I had ever seen in Dave's company. He didn't have to send mugshots as the pictures in the paper were better than anything they had on file, which had all been taken years ago, anyway, and a man could change.

Regrettably, I was unable to help but we got to talking on the phone and he it was who gave me all the background information on the cocked-up kidnap. The stuff about the chloroform and the vet didn't come out in one long spiel as I've recorded it – it was more a case of one thing leading to another.

I asked him eagerly if Dave mightn't have been chloro-formed before his killers had injected him with the lethal dose of heroin, but he dismissed the idea. He was probably right: they'd have had to hold him down to gas him and that would have left marks; also, if the veterinary pathologist had been able to detect chloroform in the corpse of Fizzikle, no doubt the human one would also have been able to spot it in Dave's tissues.

It was Curley who mentioned Crowther. He wondered if I might know him, seeing as how we were in the same profession and I must, at this stage, know most of the vets in the country? I gave him a non-committal affirmative.

He told me that Crowther could offer no explanation about why McMurrow should have his telephone number but, when reminded of the early friendship, said he vaguely remembered him. But he hadn't seen the man in years and he knew nothing about any chloroform. He had never handed out chloroform to anyone in his life and he never carried it in his car, except to, and back from, a specific job. It was too dangerous to carry on spec. If one had a slight accident and the bottle broke, one could be dead in seconds. So no, he'd have known if any had been stolen from him and none had. Curley didn't wonder that Crowther didn't recollect McMurrow – after the shock he'd had with those three kids, it was a wonder he remembered his own name, he was one hell of a driver, eh?

Then he asked me what I thought: did I think Crowther could have been the supplier of the chloroform? I said he should make up his own mind. That made him pause and then he said: 'I see.'

We were back to Ellen's game of the other day – if you don't actually say 'no', then it's a positive.

When Curley got off the phone, I sat down with my usual scrap of paper, like I always do when things begin to turn complicated.

1 Dave and Crowther. Two crooks. Connected, at least socially, through the Ollins and presumably others in that circle. Also connected by the Jag?

2 McMurrow and Wright. Two crooks. Connected by the botched-up kidnap.

3 McMurrow and Crowther. Connected via the telephone number and, most probably, the chloroform.

4 Wright and Dave. Possible (probable) connection through a jewellery store heist.

5 Chloroform connected to Fizzikle's death. Crowther? McMurrow? The killer(s)?

I called Curley back and asked him to lean hard on all three kidnappers for alibis for the night that the horse had been killed. He himself wasn't actually involved in the kidnap investigation, he explained, his only interest being the sudden reappearance of Teddy Wright but, if I could explain exactly why I wanted this information, he could ask the officer in charge to do him a favour. At that point I had to tell him all, although I held back on Ellen's indiscretions.

In the evening I went out for a drink. The journey to the pub took nearly two hours of hard driving, but that was because it was in Kyleglas. It took me less on the way back as I didn't go astray so often.

Straddling a small river, McMurrow's home town was not much bigger than a village. It had only four pubs. The first had just a few old men sitting silent and immobile behind pints, watching highlights of a hurling match on TV. The ancient barman in the stained apron glanced at me from his perch on a stool at the far end of the room, but didn't make a move towards the counter, obviously knowing I wasn't going to stay. The sign painted on the window read D. Carter, Lounge, in fancy old-fashioned script.

HIGHBALLS (hoho), number two on my walkabout, was the favourite of the younger set, complete with jukebox, and I drew puzzled looks from its clientele when I shoved my ancient head round the door.

The third was more of a lounge bar with pretensions to poshness both in its plush decor and its waiter service; most of its patrons seemed to be couples who had dressed up for their Sunday night out and sat in groups around tables with other similar couples. This would be a poor second choice, I reckoned, if Kyleglas turned out not to have a 'real' pub, but number four was it, the real thing.

The majority of the drinkers were men of an age too old for the jukebox and too young for the departure lounge across the street. Many of them looked like they took their drinking seriously. I found a rare space at the bar, sat and ordered a pint of Guinness. Here, too, the hurling highlights were on TV and many were watching, shouting and cheering as though they were actually at the match. With the end of the sports programme came the news and a hush descended as the bar awaited the item on the local desperado. But it didn't come. Liam McMurrow was history already.

It wasn't hard to pick up information on McMurrow. The whole bar was talking about him and I had my choice of conversations to listen in on. On one side of my fairly central position the lads were reminiscing about the wildness of his youth, several of them, it seemed, having been involved in one or more of his wild escapades; on my other side the discussion was more concerned with 'Liameen's' bleak future and what would happen to his hardware shop and cattle-jobbing business. Before long the two conversations fused and I found myself sitting in the middle of a general discussion. Liam had been an irresponsible tearaway who had progressed from high-spirited boyhood prankster to feckless adolescent to reckless teenager, at which point he had left the town for a few years. He had to, as he had sired several children by several local girls, and more farther afield in surrounding towns and parishes. When he came back he had evidently done well for himself financially and had bought a small farm, and begun to buy and sell cattle. But he hadn't become any more responsible and soon there were several girls again blaming brief encounters with him for their rapidly expanding bellies. According to one admiring crony, if Liam came upon an unexpected chance of 'a bit of duty free' and didn't happen to have any 'rubbers' with him, he'd tell the girl he'd had a vasectomy. That caused general laughter, although I noticed that several men just looked rheumily into their pints and took synchronised draughts. The laughers also noticed the divided reaction and their mirth ceased abruptly, to be replaced by coughs and sniffs.

Sunday night was early closing and I sat there as the crowd began to thin out. Soon there were only me and a few diehards scattered along the long bar. I'd been courting Paddy, barman and owner, since my arrival and we were now on first-name terms. I moved to a seat across the bar from the sink while he was clearing up, washing glasses and emptying the slops into a bucket for a couple of pigs he was fattening out back in the yard.

'Are ye from the newspapers, Frank?' he asked me.

'No. What makes you ask that?'

'I just thought you might be. You've been nursin' that pint for the past hour and a half so you're obviously not thirsty. You're not a cop?'

'No.' I laughed. 'Do I have to be something official?'

'I suppose not,' Paddy allowed, although he didn't believe a word of it. 'What line are you in, then?'

'A vet, Paddy. I'm a vet.'

'Oh? Not from around here, though?'

'No. I was passing through and I felt like a pint. Then the conversation was lively so I stayed. I'm in no rush. No one waiting at home for me.'

'Not a family man, then?' Paddy probed.

'No. Yourself?'

'Never got around to it.'

'What about our friend Liam? Has he a family?'

'Indeed he has. A wife and six kiddies.'

'Plus another dozen roaming the countryside, according to the lads.'

'Well . . . He certainly caused enough heartache in his time. It was an awful shameful thing for a family in those days if a young one got herself pregnant. A few went across the pond and put their mortal souls in danger by having an abortion, but most of them were sent off to "homes" to have the baby and then had them adopted, so I don't know how many young McMurrows would actually be roaming the countryside, as you put it, under a different name. At least not around these parts.

'And then, later on, after he came back, he was still screwin' everything he could get his hands on, but without issue, as they say. At least as far as I know. In fact, they began to say there was something wrong with Liam, that he had picked up some dose while he was away. The word was that he put at least four girls up the pole in the year he came back and not one of them but didn't have a miscarriage. Some say he might have had brucellosis. You're a vet. What'd you think yourself?'

'Like you said, Paddy, I'm a vet, not a doctor. Did his wife have many miscarriages?'

'I doubt it. Six kids in about eight years. Youngest isn't school age yet.'

'Well, if he did have some dose, then it seems to have cleared up.' I finished my pint and handed him the glass. 'I met a vet once who worked here in Kyleglas for a while – at least I think it was here . . . or was it Kylemore?'

'What was his name?'

'Crowther.'

'Not *Val* Crowther?' Paddy paused in his energetic wiping of the bar top.

'I think that was it. Val. Yeah, Val. Do you remember him?'

'Aye,' he snorted, 'I do. Well. He wasn't here very long but I remember him all right. A good few around here will remember him. Skinny guy?'

'Yep. That's him.'

'A bad bastard he was. He didn't last too long.'

'Jeez, I thought he was a nice type of a man. What did he do on ye here?'

'What *didn't* he do, you mean! In fact, it's funny you should mention him tonight because himself and Liam were

152

mates – well, more like partners in crime, I suppose. Liam used to buy cattle a lot in those days; it was just after he turned up again in the town and he had visions of becoming a big buyer. The word was that himself and Crowther were in cahoots. Crowther would go and see a sick animal, maybe with nothin' wrong with it more than a toothache, but he'd tell the farmer it had a very bad heart or cancer or a brain tumour or something and to get rid of it as soon as he could before it died on him. Then Liam'd just happen to turn up, out of the blue, morya, buy the beast for half nothing and sell it for the full whack. Himself and Crowther would split the profit fifty-fifty. Well that's what was said, anyway.'

'Talk, Paddy,' I said dismissively. 'That could be all talk.' I was goading him into relating further incidents, as if he needed goading.

'Well, you could be right there, but a cousin of mine took a ewe in to Crowther because she was having trouble lambing. He left her in the surgery because Crowther was out on his rounds. He collected her that evening, herself and her two lambs and a fine big bill for a Caesarean operation. A couple of days after, the same ewe got her horns stuck in sheep wire and broke her neck. In the struggle, the stitches in her side opened up and my cousin swears that those skin stitches were the only ones in her. There was no cut at all in her belly underneath the skin. Crowther had just cut the skin, stitched it up again and charged a fortune for an operation he didn't do. That happened to a lot of people but, after my cousin spread the word, there was a sudden steep drop in the number of Caesareans I can tell you.'

'But if that's true, Paddy, Crowther would've been struck off. Did your cousin not report it?'

'Arra no! By that time Crowther had such a bad name that he was doin' no business anyway. He'd doomed himself without any help from anyone. When he came here first there was an old vet here, a Mr Finlay, did ye ever hear of him? He's dead this past ten year.'

'No.' I shook my head. 'Can't say that I did.'

'Well, Crowther thought he could muscle in on the old

man, him being the young buck and all. But Finlay took on an assistant himself and soon, every time Crowther told a farmer his animal was going to die and he should get rid of it quick, at any price – just like I told you, right? – the farmer would call Finlay's and the assistant would come out and fix up the animal. He made a right fool of Crowther, although I don't know if he ever realised it; you see, the farmers would never tell him that Crowther had already been. Vets don't like to hear that they're being called in as second choice – there's no need to tell you that, I'm sure – and they're a canny, private bunch around here, the farmers.'

'They're the same everywhere, Paddy, not just around here.'

'I suppose you're right. Anyway, be that as it may, Crowther left soon afterwards. Good riddance. Then, with the competition gone, Mr Finlay let young Slattery go – that was the lad's name, if I remember correctly – and everything returned to normal.'

'*Slattery*? Are you sure it was Slattery?'

'Aye. Slattery. The same name as the paper shop people, although they weren't related.'

'Do you remember his first name?' Maybe this could be the reason for Crowther's special attention to the Monksford practice.

He stopped wiping the counter and thought for a moment, then shook his head. 'No.'

' "PJ" doesn't ring a bell?'

'Naw. I'm not even sure I ever heard it – he was only here a couple of months. Why? Is it important?'

'No. It's just that I know a Slattery too.'

'Small world, aye? Someone said they saw Crowther on the telly a few days back, something about a car crash?'

I told Paddy about Crowther's recent heroism and Paddy reckoned that maybe he had turned over a new leaf, that there was good in all of us, that God had put us all here for a purpose. I didn't bother to put him straight on his new-leaf theory, but wished him goodnight and headed out into a dismal, drizzly night.

On the trip back I reviewed my various bits of information on Crowther. He seemed to create instant suspicion wherever he went, but everything about him was hearsay. Paddy the barman had provided authentic-sounding anecdotes but could they be proved? McMurrow and his chloroform bottle and Crowther's phone number formed a highly suspect coincidence, but who could say for certain that it was anything more than that? Perhaps McMurrow himself might, after a few days in a cell, especially if the law made a deal with him.

Ellen's word could damn Crowther as a blackmailer, but she had left me under no illusions about her willingness to stand up and be counted. I could whistle for that. I smacked the steering wheel in frustration – there was no way in the world that Crowther wasn't guilty, but knowing it and proving it were two separate matters.

And besides, there were still some unsatisfactory loose ends lying about. For instance, I couldn't imagine how Crowther had been able to prevent PJ's two ketosis cases from improving. Unless he knew of some substance which could produce ketosis when injected, or could inhibit dexamethasone from curing it, I was baffled. I'd have to do a bit of reading up on the subject.

I decided not to say much to the Slatterys or Michael about my trip; after all, it was largely a private matter, to look for a more solid link between Crowther and Dave than the mere social acquaintanceship I'd been told of by the Ollins, or the common link to a Jag with a decapitated emblem. I would of course give them their long sought-after motive for Crowther's singling them out for personal attention, which ought to cut down dramatically on the amount of bewildered head-scratching in the practice. The mood had already begun to pick up – they were still no closer to being able to prove anything criminal against Crowther but they expected a break in the onslaught, now that he would be out of commission for a while. He was due to be discharged from hospital next day but would have to rest for at least another week.

I assumed that the police would now be investigating the Crowther–McMurrow link and wondered briefly if I should pass on to Curley the harvest from my journey to Kyleglas. I decided not to bother as it was all ancient history by now, merely hearsay, and didn't amount to much anyway. Besides, Curley was interested only in Dave and Wright, not McMurrow and Crowther.

14

'Fancy a pub lunch, Frank?' JJ, looking pleased with himself, caught me halfway up the stairs to the flat. 'I'm buying,' he called up, as if that made any odds.

'Well, in that case', I said, coming back down, 'you're on. What's the big occasion?'

'Oh, nothing. It's Monday.'

Mondays you got a good lunch down at Pearson's. Not too many people there and some nice cold cuts left over from the Sunday Carvery – pheasant, venison, guinea-fowl and the like. Pearson's was indisputably Monksford's classiest pub. It had been there for years but its young owner, who had inherited it just in time from his reactionary old father, had developed it to keep pace with the neat, flourishing industrial 'parks' which had grown up around the town, lured to this area of once low employment by special incentives, tax breaks and grants. It had become the eating and meeting place for the hundreds of executives who ran these parks, and was also the unanimous choice of Monksford's upwardly mobile and professionals.

'Lead on,' I said.

I followed JJ's hard-driven car, trying to recall the names of all the vets I'd met since I'd graduated and finding it impossible. Faces floated briefly before me, but I couldn't attach names to all and I now understood why, when I'd asked him earlier, PJ could clearly recall Finlay and Kyleglas, while Crowther's name rang no bell at all. He couldn't remember ever having heard of the man until he'd opened the practice in Breenstown some years before.

The exotic cold cuts seemed to have got lost along the way and we sat behind platefuls of burgers and chips, and half-pints of Harp, watching the comings and goings of the few neophyte tycoons and moguls of tomorrow – despite Pearson's and a few decent golf courses nearby, Monksford was very much a mere rung on the way up the corporate ladder. Or down. Depending on your age.

JJ took a bite from his burger and mumbled to me: 'I was thinking of taking the girlfriend to Spain for a couple of weeks – she's got some time off and things aren't too busy here at the moment. As you know.'

'Hopefully they'll pick up now, with Crowther out of action.'

'Well, even if they do, Miriam will soon be back on duty.'

'Ah! The Family Practice. It must be great, JJ, to be able to take off on a whim whenever you like.'

'It's about the only advantage to being in a family practice. Believe me, Frank.'

'Does Michael, being non-family, not get a bit fed up?'

'He's family, too, by marriage. Brenda and my mother are some sort of cousins.'

'Hey! Full house! Miriam and Eve. They're not sisters are they?'

'They're not even related. Eve is my father's niece. Miriam is my mother's. You'll like Miriam. She's great – a real live wire.'

'What does Eve call her? Mrs Whatever-her-name-is?'

'No.' He laughed at the thought. 'That's for men only. Miriam is Miriam. I wish Eve would lighten up and be more like her. There was another big row the other day.'

'Between you and your old man?'

'No. Between Eve and him. For once, I'm on his side. Because she's family, Eve reckons that she, and not Barbara, should be practice manager. But to be honest, if it weren't for the fact that she *is* family, Eve wouldn't be here at all – you know yourself how sullen she is and she's not the world's brightest either. You can imagine what the old man thinks of her – I mean, he doesn't even give credit where it's due, never mind make allowances.' He swigged from his glass, swallowed, and emitted a long, satisfied sigh and a burp. 'Oops! Beg pardon, yer honour. Cousin Eve's only here because of her mother, Dad's elder sister. Most of the time he's barely civil to her.'

'Maybe that's why she calls you both Mr Slattery. Your father doesn't treat her like family so she's not going to treat him like family either. Maybe she's just making a point.'

'Maybe. But then, she treats all men the same way, family or not.'

'I don't know.' I shrugged and thought that Eve didn't treat *all* men quite so coldly – what about the bloke on the phone that day I'd overheard her?

Later, attending to my few afternoon calls, I fell to thinking that JJ's news about Eve should make me reappraise my original conclusion that Crowther's intelligence was coming through local watchdogs and not from within the Slattery practice. If Eve felt that she was only grudgingly accepted as part of the family, then she might, understandably, be resentful. Her stubborn insistence on calling her uncle and first cousin 'Mr Slattery' suggested that she herself had already erected barriers against the family, at least the PJ–JJ branch of it. But, I wondered, did her disaffection stop at that? Could her disgruntlement have slipped from passive into active? Could she, in fact, be giving her allegiance to someone else? Crowther, for instance? Did her 'exclusion' from the family proper provide a motive for treachery? Mightn't she see it as merely teaching them a lesson they deserved, as chickens coming home to roost?

As for opportunity, Eve, being receptionist, would know what calls were in even before the vets did. All Crowther needed to do was give her a list of the special clients he was interested in and wait for her reports on this select target band of prime clients.

I began to concentrate hard on Eve, trying to see how she

might have fitted in as the mole. For starters, she tied in beautifully with the onset of the practice's trouble – she'd arrived about a year ago to stand in for Brenda Stone who had gone off on honeymoon and stayed on when Brenda had become pregnant immediately. That was precisely when the 'troubles' had begun, about a year ago. I was off to a flying start. But would she provide answers for other inconsistencies which had arisen?

She certainly answered the question of why Crowther had left the Slatterys alone for his first four years in the area – he'd simply had no way of finding out what was going on in their practice. Not until Eve had joined the strength.

And what about the vet who had sabotaged Patsy Melia's cow and had been cocky enough to plant an empty xylazine bottle, an action which I had at first considered almost suicidally stupid? With Eve on the inside, it wasn't stupid at all. There was no way that the label details would have been different from those in the Slatterys' stocks. Eve would have checked. More likely still, she'd actually have supplied the empty bottle . . .

And of course, having herself put me through to Ellen, she knew I was going to the Ollins for dinner that night and that Fizzikle would be unwatched and thus a sitting duck for a second shot at nobbling him . . . In fact, she was the only one in the practice who knew . . .

Over the next hour or so I gradually tied little details to each other and found nothing to preclude Eve from being the spy – except one persistently thorny problem. How could she, or Crowther, or *anyone* for that matter, have prevented Frank O'Malley's two ketosis cows from getting better?

Apart from this one imponderable question, the more I thought about Eve, the more sure I became that she was the spy. The phone call I'd overheard was not her telling a lover that he'd have to cool it; it was probably her whispering urgently to Crowther that she was afraid she'd be found out and that Barbara – the unnamed 'she' of the call – might be getting suspicious. By that time Eve had every reason to be afraid – there was open talk in the office of Crowther's involvement, talk that was becoming less speculative and more firm with every hour that passed.

So far, so good, but how was I going to prove it was Eve? How would I even *test* it?

High on a hillside, I sat in my Land Rover, watching and waiting. I was now in my fourth hour of staring fixedly at a gate far below me and my eyes were hurting. I'd finished the crosswords I'd brought with me hours ago, smiling at one clue: '*Damaged uterus requiring a stitch*?' The answer was '*Suture*' and I'd chortled aloud as I'd filled in the letters – in the circumstances it was a particularly apt clue. But that had been the only bright spot for over an hour until, in the middle of a huge yawn, it suddenly came to me how it could have been possible for O'Malley's ketotic cows to have remained uncured, despite JJ's best efforts. And again, it tied Eve in nicely.

Ironically, it was the strict security routine in force at the practice that had made it all really rather simple. In the previous year or so the vets' cars had been broken into several times, presumably by druggies looking for syringes, needles or whatever. In response, the practice had made it a strict rule that, apart from the vet on emergency call, all cars had to be emptied every evening, their contents being locked in the secure and well-alarmed storeroom. The key to this was kept in the receptionist's drawer with a tag reading 'Loose box No 7' on it, again to fool would-be raiders. There were only six loose boxes.

If Crowther had been informed of the call to Frank O'Malley's cows *before* PJ picked up his bag for his morning rounds – the office opened at 7.30 a.m., the vets usually arrived at about 8 a.m – he could have instructed Eve to go through PJ's bag, find any dexamethasone bottles and replace the clear medicine inside with plain ordinary water. A large syringe could draw out the contents in one go and the same syringe would inject water back in, and PJ, thinking he was using the real thing, would have been injecting mere water into his ketotic patients.

Simple substitution, a bit tortuous, but perfectly feasible. It all depended on whether the call had come in before 8 a.m. and whether the farmer had reported, *specifically*, that his cows were ketotic. I made a note to try to find that call in last year's book. If it checked out, then the seemingly impossible was, in fact, as easy as ABC.

As the dismal day decayed into its depressing evening, and chilling shadow seeped up the hill towards me, I was finding it more and more difficult to focus on the tiny, distant gate. I'd soon have to move – another half-hour and the gate would dissolve and retreat into the gloom. It was no longer just psychologically cold, and both my little fingers were turning white and clammy. In the absence of gloves, I slid my hands in under my buttocks. The Land Rover was being buffeted by a rising wind, shuddering now and then under testing gusts, physically shivering, like me. Vicious little draughts traversed the cab as if none of the doors fitted or the floor were full of rust holes. I'd never noticed these draughts before. I looked out at blackthorn hedges being whipped through short arcs on their sturdy stems and spiky rushes beaten flat by the rising evening wind. Even with the windows closed tight and the radio on, I could hear the mournful moanings of the wind as it was sliced by telephone lines, taut as cheese wire. The only relief from the boredom that had returned almost immediately after the brainwave about Eve was provided by the infrequent traffic which passed the gate. Too far off to give details like make, registration plate or number of occupants, I'd been record-ing, since I'd arrived, each vehicle as it passed, noting things like type – car, tractor, truck – colour, which direction it had been going, east or west, driving fast or slow. I wasn't quite sure just why I was doing this, other than that it might possibly come in handy – I had no idea how – and that it gave me something to do. As I also counted the vehicles, I knew that thirty-four had passed the gate in the three hours and forty-six minutes I'd spent perched atop my lonely eyrie.

My mind kept wandering back to Eve. Could it really be her? Against her own flesh and blood? She was a strange one, no doubt — not *very* strange, mind you, not exactly weird, but still . . . Ah, well, we would soon know. My mind veered off again. Counting infrequent cars can only keep you riveted for so long; it makes trainspotting look like abseiling down frozen waterfalls, without the rope . . .

If Eve was an enigma, then she wasn't the only one. I'd only seen Ellen once since her 'confession' and I'd expected to receive the wide, carefree smile of someone who is profoundly relieved to have got a troublesome load off her chest; in fact, what I'd seen was a wary, anxious look, like I'd expect from someone who was wondering if they'd been found out yet, which made me think that Ellen might not have told me everything. With anybody else I might have dismissed the suspicion as being all in my mind, but I knew Ellen far too well.

There was something not quite right about her story, I was sure of it. But I couldn't figure out what it might be, or even why. After all, she'd been the one to volunteer it — nobody had forced her. True, I might have been needling her a bit, but she could have told me to get stuffed, that it was none of my business.

I thought over the inconsistencies: first she'd told me, emphatically if I remembered correctly, that Laurence hadn't known about the 'near affair', then, seconds later, that he had. I mean, what kind of rubbish was that? Inaccuracies about small things like times or dates were understandable, but in an important matter like whether or not the injured spouse knew? Pull the other leg, Ellen. I mean, come *on*!

And what about those long pauses, the twenty minutes' silence before she even *began* her story, just staring at the table while I fetched coffee after coffee? What the hell had that been in aid of? If it hadn't been so damning of herself, the whole tale might have been fabricated, the initial lengthy silence needed actually to compose the basic story, the other, shorter pauses occasioned by her trying to carry out running repairs when some of the hastily assembled 'facts' didn't quite dovetail or produce the desired result . . . But who the hell would want to make up a story like that about themselves? Much less tell it. And the hunted look in her eyes? Surely, if she was unloading . . .

A dark-coloured car appeared from the west and drove past the gate, slowing right down as it passed. It was the first one to have done that . . .

Surely, if she was unloading something that had been preying on her mind, there should have been some relief or at least some look of a positive emotion in her eyes? But I knew I wasn't mistaken – Ellen had looked troubled throughout, hunted. That was, I supposed, only natural, to be expected, given the content of her story, but it didn't have to be for that reason alone. Maybe the hunted look was really anxiety that she'd contradict herself or let something slip, some detail she was holding back . . .

I sat bolt upright. A dark coloured car was approaching slowly, more like cautiously, from the east. It slowed almost to a stop as it approached the gate, then its brake lights flared as it stopped right at the gate for perhaps twenty seconds before resuming its journey. Pulse beginning to speed up, I waited, staring at the place where it had gone out of sight, knowing it'd be back. I picked up my mobile phone, pushed the numbers for Patsy Melia's and held my finger over the 'SEND' button. Suddenly the wind and the cold and the hours of waiting were forgotten. The trap was about to snap shut.

Within minutes the car returned. I watched it drive to the gate and stop. The passenger door opened and a man I didn't recognise got out. Immediately, the car drove away and, in the gloom, I could just make out that the man was carrying a case, for all the world like a vet's bag. He seemed to tug at the padlock for a moment, then he began to climb the gate. I hit 'SEND' and seconds later, after half a ring, was answered by Patsy Melia.

'He's on his way, Patsy. Just gone over the gate.'

'Is it Crowther himself?'

'No.' We hadn't expected that it would be; after all, he was just out of hospital. 'I don't recognise him. Give him ten minutes to get stuck in. I'll be with you by then.'

I turned the key and switched on the heater. There was no danger that the man, whom I could see intermittently through gaps in the hedge, could hear me as he headed for Patsy's sheds, the same sheds I'd gone to the afternoon I'd called to see his aborted cow. I watched him lay his vet's bag behind a small bush and disappear around the back of the farm buildings; next time I managed to pick him up he was back at the bush, where he retrieved the bag and walked towards the sheds again. He must have done the whole round, checking for signs of life.

This time he opened the door to the first shed and, discovering the decoy cow, entered and pulled the door to behind him. I put the Land Rover into second and let her roll down the hill.

So it *was* cousin Eve. I wondered how the family was going to take that. Would they publicly denounce her? Or would they 'forgive' her, finding it more palatable to ignore her treachery than face exposure to the town's chattering classes. I wondered if I might already have gone further than they would have liked. Maybe I should have just reported my suspicions and left the decision up to the others. Perhaps I ought to have taken at least JJ into my confidence.

After Pearson's, which was when the penny had begun to drop, I'd done my few calls, then headed for Patsy Melia's house. I'd briefly considered approaching Phil Jones, owner of the late Fizzikle, but dropped the idea in favour of Patsy, whom I already knew and who had expressed a dislike and distrust of Crowther. Either man made an equally attractive 'prime' client for Crowther: Phil Jones had a reasonably affluent racing yard while Patsy was one of the biggest beef farmers around. Both were obviously high on his hit list – they'd both been the targets of recent sabotage, Jones twice. But when it came to the actual baiting of the trap there was no doubt that Patsy's farm was far more suitable. To be specific, his outlying farm. All Jones's animals were housed in his yard, with grooms and others liable to pop up here and there all over the place.

It had taken me some time to come up with what I considered the type of call which would attract Crowther, a call that would give him (or one of his accomplices) an ideal opportunity for a little undetectable sabotage. Eventually, from a shortlist of three, I chose a prolapse of the uterus, a not uncommon, potentially serious, but rarely fatal condition of cows in the forty-eight hours post-calving. And Patsy had cows by the ton.

Of course, the call would be a fake call, but evidence that a cow had suffered a prolapse of the uterus could be simply and very convincingly faked. Any vet in the world who saw a cow with a newborn calf at her side and a large transfixing suture across her vulva would immediately assume that the cow had prolapsed her womb shortly after the calf had been expelled. The stitch was to discourage further straining or, if the worst happened and the cow tried to force the uterus out again, at least retain the organ inside her so that it didn't come through again to the outside and the contamination and injury that awaited it there.

Despite the stitch, sometimes a cow would push and push with such power and persistence that the retaining stitch would be forced through the flesh until it actually fell to the floor and the womb could prolapse again. A re-prolapse shouldn't really happen if the organ has been repositioned correctly in the first place and, on the rare occasions when it does, the vet will almost invariably be blamed for not having done the job properly the first time. An absolutely tailor-made gift-horse for Crowther.

Patsy had taken a little convincing, baulking slightly at a full mock-up. He had a fresh-calved cow all right, several of them, in fact, but he wasn't sure about allowing me to stitch her vulva across just to make it *look* fully authentic. Ethically I might have been on dodgy grounds but I fixed it with my conscience, convincing myself that my proposed gratuitous surgical interference was for the greater good.

Secretly, the poetic justice of it appealed to me, but I didn't tell Patsy that. All those years ago, when he was just setting out on his life of trickery in Kyleglas, Crowther had

used false sutures to suggest surgeries he hadn't done; now I
was going to put an end to that career by using false sutures
to suggest a surgery *I* hadn't done.

Patsy came round – he had seen enough uterine prolapses
in his life to know that the transfixing suture never did any
harm and rarely even caused discomfort. So we drove his
cow into the crush, I injected a local anaesthetic epidurally
between the vertebrae at the top of the tail, waited a couple of
minutes and then stitched her. She didn't feel a thing. We
transferred her into the shed beside the crush and tied her up
with hay and water under her head in the manger. The
newborn calf was given the freedom of the shed, clocking in
for a feed from her mother whenever she wished. Then I'd
left.

I was pottering in the office when Patsy phoned at 3.15, as
per arrangement. Eve took the call and wrote it in the book.
When she hung up, she told me about the emergency,
impressing upon me that the cow was at the outlying farm
and that Mr Melia would be waiting for me there with
enough help to do the job. I said I'd go right away and put
my initials by the call – I didn't want any of the others going
there, which was why I had to make sure to be in the office at
the appointed time. I half considered trying to sneak back on
some pretext to see if Eve was on the phone, but thought
better of it – a vet en route to a prolapse should really not be
shuffling about the premises.

I drove to Patsy's house and we sat and talked beef-cows
for an hour – we knew that nobody would turn up until I'd
have had ample time to finish the job and leave. In fact,
they'd probably give it a couple of hours or three, allowing
for Patsy to come back several times to check on his cow. We
both reckoned that the onset of night would be when they'd
come and we'd been spot on. Still, we didn't want to take any
chances, which was why, for the guts of four hours, Patsy
had been sitting in his hayshed with his mobile phone while I
had been on lookout duty from my chilly perch high on the
hill.

I pulled in some distance short of the gate, opened another

gate into another field and drove in. I didn't want my vehicle to be seen and possibly recognised if the dark car should come cruising back again. Anxious now to get to the shed, I quickly climbed the wall between the fields; I didn't want to arrive too late or too early but it was hard to judge an exact time. I assumed that the man with the bag would by now have given the cow another epidural and would be waiting for it to work so that he could forcibly tear my stitches through the vulval labia. Then he would reach into the cow, pull the whole uterus back out again, steal away into the night and leave Patsy to find his cow tomorrow, possibly dead (especially if he were to nick a few arteries here and there), and draw his conclusions. Another botched-up job by the Slattery practice.

We didn't intend him even to get started but, if he did get his hand into the cow, he'd have the surprise of his life to find that the uterus was involuting nicely and was now less than one tenth of its pregnant size and could not be pulled out.

Patsy saw me coming and emerged from the hayshed to meet me. Wordlessly we tiptoed towards the cowshed and paused at the door. We listened for a moment, heard a voice say, 'Now hold steady for a minute, atta good old girl,' then burst in through the door.

15

The timing couldn't have been better, not even if we'd had a closed-circuit TV camera in the shed. Frozen into temporary petrification by our sudden entry, the intruder stood behind the cow, one foot up against her hind quarters, about to push himself back into the sling of rope that went around his back and was attached at the front to a chain which vanished into the cow's vagina. Once he took up the slack, he'd place his second foot against the cow's buttock and exert considerable force – this was a technique often adopted by a person on his own, faced with the need to pull a large calf from its mother, the ends of the ropes (or chains) being attached to the calf's legs. In this case the cow had already calved – there was nothing in there to attach the chain to, except of course the two transverse 'legs' of the large, square, doubly transfixing mattress suture I'd put in some five hours ago.

The flash of my camera broke the spell.

'What's wrong with Patsy Melia's cow?' enquired Patsy Melia mildly, totally confusing the stunned young man who probably assumed that one of us was Patsy Melia. 'Can we help at all?'

I popped off another flashbulb at him, this time catching him with his mouth wide open.

He made a brave effort at a bluff. 'Eh. Em. The cow . . . She prolapsed her uterus. No . . . eh . . . help needed, though. Thanks. I've just finished. Thanks again, though.' And he stepped out of the rope sling. He was visibly trembling. The possibility that we might just be a couple of inquisitive neighbours might at first have given him some tiny hope, but the sudden introduction of the camera would have killed it stone dead. He knew he was for it. I pressed the zoom button, close-focused on the chain vanishing into the cow's innards and took another photograph.

'You'd find it much easier to remove that suture if you used scissors,' I said, kicking the last stool of hope from under him. 'I always use scissors, or a scalpel blade, sometimes, now that I think of it . . .'

'I don't believe we've been introduced?' Patsy carried on the charade of civility, moving towards the crumpled man. 'What's your name?' When there was no immediate answer, Patsy asked again and this time there was no effort at civility.

'Robbins. Tony Robbins.'

I was surprised that he'd given his name so readily. Maybe he knew that we'd find it out in no time anyway, and was hoping to pass off this distinctly odd and awkward situation as some sort of little misunderstanding. On the other hand, maybe it was a false name – how did I know? After all, there's no law which says you *have* to use John Smith.

'You're a vet, of course?' Patsy's eyes bored into his.

'Yes.'

'Working for?'

'Mister Crowther, Breenstown.'

'And what brings you here, Tony? Slatterys of Monksford do my work. All of it.'

'I was sent to see to a cow with a prolapse. By . . . eh . . . the office.'

'Which you did. Right?'

There was no reply.

'You're a hell of a man, Tony, to be able to put back a womb without water or soap or a couple of helpers to hold it up in the air for you – those wombs weigh a ton, Tony, don't they? If you don't have them held up, sure they just keep flopping out again. Stick back a bit and it's dragged out by its own weight again before you can grab another handful. And

lookit! Not a drop of blood on you, the floor, the cow . . .
Gifted, Tony, is what you are. What would you say, Frank?'

'Oh, definitely. A rare and priceless talent. You should see
the mess I make, Tony.'

Patsy came back in. 'Oh, I have seen it, Frank. Yes
indeed-i-o, I have! The place looks more like a slaughter-
house after you've finished the job. Takes me a whole *week* to
clean up after you. How come, Tony, you knew to come
directly to this rented outfarm? Why didn't you go to my
house first?'

'I was told the cow was at an outfarm.'

'But how did you know where the outfarm was? That's the
ques—No!' He held up a restraining palm. 'Don't tell me. Of
course! You knew because you were here a while back,
weren't you? Giving another cow something to make her
abort . . .'

'I swear I've never been here before in my life. I was given
directions.'

'I see. That's a pretty efficient practice Mr Crowther runs
there, Tony. Why can't your lot be more like that, Frank? By
the way, Tony, where's your car? I never saw a vet before
that didn't have a car.'

'Listen, Tony,' I broke in. 'Before you go any further you
ought to know that this here is Mr Patsy Melia, the owner of
this cow, and I'm Frank Samson of Slattery and Partners,
Mr Melia's vets. So I'd stop the bullshit if I were you. I
placed that suture in the cow this afternoon and I know
exactly what you were doing. You were going to force the
stitch through, then reach in and pull out the uterus, and
leave it dangling, weren't you? There's no other possible
explanation.'

'The uterus had re-prolapsed . . . and . . .'

'Tony, Tony, Tony . . . Would you ever just shut up and
listen! The uterus hadn't prolapsed in the *first* place. All I did
was put a suture in a healthy, fresh-calved cow. The call was
a set-up, that suture just window dressing. In plain English,
you've been had, Tony.'

Taking a pair of scissors from my pocket, I went to the

back of the cow. 'Would you mind holding the tail to the side, Tony. Your hands are already dirty,' I explained when he hesitated. When he had deflected the tail, which was hanging totally flaccid because of the epidural anaesthetic, I cut the stitch and removed it. 'See? Much easier this way, don't you think?' When the stitch came out, the chain fell from the vulva, clinking, link by link, into the gutter. At its end was a stainless-steel eye hook, one of the more drastic-looking obstetrical instruments used by vets. Stretching out the chain, I placed the hook alongside the cut stitch on the floor and photographed them, both from a distance and then close up. Once again, I wasn't quite sure why I was doing this, probably on the off chance that it might, some day, come in handy. In reality, it probably wouldn't.

'What time is your driver coming back for you, Tony?' I asked, snapping the lens cover shut and tucking the camera back into my anorak pocket. 'Handy things, these little cameras.' I patted my pocket.

'Eh . . . driver?'

I snorted in affected mirth. 'Here we go again, aye? The driver who let you off at the gate after he'd made a few passes to check it out. You don't, I hope, still think we just *happened* to stumble upon you. I told you: the whole thing has been a set-up from the start. We were close by, watching every move. So what time will the car be back?' But Tony wasn't budging on that one. 'Okay, then,' I said after a minute. 'Have it your own way. It's no trouble to us either way. Patsy, why don't you take a stroll to the road right now? The car will be along any moment because Tony here should just about be finishing his dirty work by now. Just take the number. I'll stay here with Tony. Have a chat. Don't forget to bolt the door from the outside in case he tries to make a run for it.'

I spent the few minutes that Patsy was away trying to convince Tony Robbins that he might just possibly save his skin if he exposed all Crowther's underhanded work, but that it would have to be all, not just edited highlights. The absence of Patsy's six and a half foot wild-man bulk seemed to have unfrozen his brain and he came up with an almost plausible explanation in an impressively short time.

'Look,' he said, 'I don't know what's going on here. I was passed this call, then driven here because I didn't know where it was and came to check the cow. When I saw her all stitched up I thought the client might have done a DIY job so I thought I should check her before leaving, see that he had actually replaced the uterus properly, you know? And that's all I know. If you guys were playing some pissing-about game, that's your privilege, although it has wasted a lot of my time.'

'Nice one, Tony. You'd have me worried if you had *cut* the stitch. But it won't work because I know what your plan was.'

'So now you can read my mind, huh? You can tell what I was thinking, what my intentions were? Madame Zsa-zsa the mind-reader, huh?'

'There's no other explanation for having a calving hook around that suture and the rope around your back . . .'

'Whoa, there! Whoa! That's your word against mine.'

'And Patsy's. And the camera.' I tapped my pocket.

'The camera shows nothing that can incriminate me. A calving chain going into the vagina? So what? That's where they're supposed to go, isn't it? A chain and hook lying on a concrete floor beside a piece of fancy string? Gimme a break, man! I want to see a lawyer. You two are trying to frame me. You call me out here to this rigged set-up and then try to frame me. Which of you sent in the bogus call? You or the one-eyed giant? It's a fucking set-up, asshole, and I'm not going to take it lying down. You've picked the wrong patsy for this. Just wait until my lawyer gets on your ass.'

'Why would either of us want to set you up? Before now, I wasn't even aware of your existence and I'm sure the same thing goes for Mr Melia.'

'Not me, man. You weren't after me. But the whole world knows how the Slatterys feel about Unc—Mr Crowther's success . . .'

'Uncle Val? Hey, hey! So he's your uncle, is he?'

Tony Robbins looked annoyed. It was his one slip-up in an otherwise very cool performance.

Uncle Val would have been dead proud of him.

Patsy came back. The car had passed by, slowing and flashing its beams twice as it approached the gate, then speeding on again. He had taken the number and read it out to us. Tony's expression didn't change.

'Did he see you?' I asked.

'Naw. I was on the other side of the road. He was focused on the gate.'

'Could you see him?'

'Not really. It's a bit too dark now. But he wasn't a skinny little shit like Crowther.'

'Please, Patsy. Please! A bit of respect. *S'il vous plait*! It's *Uncle* Val . . .'

'Is it now, bejasus? Is that a fact?'

'Can I see you outside for a moment, Patsy?'

We held a rapid war council. I had to admit that Tony Robbins's smooth story – and worse, his smooth demeanour – had me slightly worried. I had no idea what a smart lawyer could do with the situation, involving as it did entrapment, that word I had heard so often in connection with villains squirming away from their just deserts. A smart young vet hadn't done too badly and him under mighty pressure. Imagine what a seasoned, case-hardened lawyer could do with it.

Neither Patsy nor I had actually thought much beyond checking out whether or not Eve was Crowther's mole and, having accomplished this, neither of us had much of a clue as to what we should do now. The main complication was the driver who would soon be passing back and forth ever more anxiously; it couldn't be long before he came to the conclusion that something had gone badly amiss and sped off to raise the alarm. At that point, tracks would be hurriedly covered and my main worry was that Eve would get the tip-off to say absolutely nothing, a tactic at which she already excelled. It was vital to get to her before she was tipped off.

We decided that Patsy should stay with Tony until the police arrived and that I would leave at once to find Eve. We moved out of earshot of the shed and called the local Garda station. Patsy gave them the number of the dark car and asked them to hold the driver for questioning; it shouldn't be any trouble to nab him as the car was patrolling the same stretch of road, over and back, and a squad car coming from either end would snare him. He told the cops only that he had caught a man trying to kill one of his cows which, although blunt, was actually true.

On my way back to Monksford I phoned JJ and asked him where Eve lived. He jokingly advised me to stick with Claire – she was more my type, more *anybody*'s type for that matter. I laughed dutifully and said I wanted to drop off her make-up bag which she'd left in the bathroom at the office; maybe she had a heavy date and needed the paint.

Fifteen minutes later, praying that the warning call had not yet come, I pulled up outside Eve's flat and rang the bell.

'Who is it?'

'It's Frank Samson, Eve. I need some . . . advice.'

'Advice?' She sounded genuinely puzzled. 'From me?'

'Yes.' So they hadn't yet got through to her. Thank God for that.

'About what, Mr Samson?'

'I don't want to discuss it over the intercom. It's private. May I come in?'

'Well . . .'

'Or can you come out here? It makes no difference.' It was actually better if she came out – get her away from her phone.

'Eh . . . Well, eh, okay. I'll come down there. My flat's in a state.'

Not half as much of a state as you're going to be in, my girl, I thought. 'Thanks,' I said.

I thought she had changed her mind, it took her so long. She was wearing make-up and she did look as though she might be going out. 'Sorry to bother you,' I said. 'Going out?'

'No. No. I'm not. Em . . . What advice were you referring to, Mr Samson?'

'Ah. A very delicate situation has arisen, Eve. Very delicate. I need to know what to do about . . . Tony Robbins . . .'

Beneath the blusher, Eve's face drained of blood and her jaw dropped. She reached behind her for the door frame and sagged back against it, shaking. Her rounded mouth made unformed 'Wha . . . wha . . .' noises. 'What . . . what . . . about him?' she eventually managed.

'You tell me,' I said, acting dumb.

Thinking that maybe it wasn't as bad as she had first thought, Eve pulled herself together somewhat. 'Well . . . we've been going out for some time now . . .'

'A year or so, right? Since shortly after you took over for Brenda?'

'Well, what of it? I know my uncle wouldn't agree . . . but he can't tell me who I may or may not see. It's a free country.'

Romeo and Juliet all over again, I thought. 'Granted, Eve. But I'm not talking about romance. I'm talking about having met Tony Robbins this evening. Can you guess where, Eve?'

'No.'

'Oh, come on. You know where because you sent him there. He was trying to kill one of Patsy Melia's cows. He told us that you had phoned the call through, that you've been doing it for ages.'

Half sitting, half fainting, Eve folded down on to the doorstep with a thump.

Trembling and coughing nervously, Eve waited at the door of Joe Slattery's flat. I stood beside her, making sure she carried out to the letter, what she'd agreed. I'd offered her a choice: she could talk to the police, to her Uncle PJ, her cousin JJ, Michael Stone, Miriam, or to her grandpa Joe. She'd opted at once for Joe. Good choice, I reckoned. He was her best chance, perhaps her only chance of surviving within the family. I didn't think any of the others would have shown her much mercy.

Although she had wanted to take her own car, I'd insisted on driving her there – just in case her memory needed any help, or she forgot where he lived or the purpose of her visit. She'd shivered convulsively all the way over in the Land Rover and not a word had passed between us on the journey. I almost had to drag her physically from the passenger seat and I propelled her firmly by the elbow up the short path to the old man's door. I rang the bell and she wailed 'Oh Jesus!' softly as its peal sounded. When the slap-slap slipper footsteps became audible behind the door, she bowed her head and pressed her hands to her brow.

'Eve, child, what's the matter?' Joe exclaimed anxiously, when he opened the door and switched on the light in the little porch. Then he saw me and his eyes hardened as he jumped to the wrong conclusion. 'What's the matter, sweetheart?' He turned his attention back to the wretched girl who was now leaning against his chest and sobbing uncontrollably. 'Come in, love. Come in and tell me.' He didn't actually include me in the invitation but he left the door open so I followed. Eve was now in near hysterics. He asked her many times what the matter was and eventually turned to me. 'Perhaps you know what this is about, young man? Maybe you can explain why the poor girl is in this sorry state?' Suddenly I was young man, not Frank.

'Actually, sir, I can. Regrettably, I can.'

I told my story and watched the old man disintegrate further with each bludgeoning piece of evidence. Pathetically, he kept glancing towards the distraught Eve, willing her to tell him that none of it was true, but she just sobbed and moaned and, hugging herself, rocked back and forth in the armchair on which she had perched when we entered. At last I put a comforting hand on his thin, shaking shoulder, said how very, very sorry I was to have been the one to bring such great sadness into his home, advised him to call Eve's mother over and left. There didn't seem to be much else I could do. I'd already done enough.

Back at the surgery, not able to concentrate on anything, the image of Joe Slattery's ravaged features and tear-rimmed old eyes filling my mind, I took down last year's call book and, starting at the back, began desultorily turning pages. Eventually I came across the Frank O'Malley call. It had been the first on the morning of 3 October, clocked in at 7.35. And it clearly stated that the call was for two cows with ketosis.

Bingo, I thought, but with no feeling of elation.

Eve didn't turn up for work next day. Nor did anybody mention her, either her absence or her name. Barbara moved between her own office and Reception as if there never had been a receptionist.

There was a sense of shock around the office and I was not at all comfortable – I felt as if I had done something very wrong. Oh, it was fine that I'd finally nailed Crowther, his practice manager and his nephew, but not quite so fine that I'd also found his spy, that I'd peeled the scab off the Slattery clan and exposed to the whole town the maggot that was causing the rot.

Returning JJ's lunch of the day before and hoping to re-establish communications with the practice, I invited him to Pearson's, but even the usually garrulous JJ was reticent today.

Tony Robbins and the driver of the car, George Kilroy, had spent much of the night being questioned at the local Garda station, but had been released in the morning on personal sureties. Kilroy was the practice manager and a long-time business associate of Crowther's. Crowther himself was said to have gone away for a recuperating holiday and was not expected to be in touch for some time – nobody knew where he had gone, maybe abroad. The word was that he had left for his holiday the night before at about 9.30. It had obviously been a spur-of-the-moment decision because he'd been seen by several people in Breenstown during the evening, latish, and he hadn't mentioned a holiday to any of them.

JJ knew Tony Robbins from college, although not well – all students know most of the students in the years above them and practically none in the classes behind; Robbins had been three years ahead of JJ. He'd had no idea that Robbins and Crowther were related. The thing JJ remembered most about him was that he was an avid womaniser who would regale his friends (and anyone else who happened to be in the common room) with graphic descriptions of the previous night's debauches.

In fact, he had a trade mark phrase which never failed to bring the house down: a girl would have great knockers, fantastic buns and legs up to her armpits, just like any other self-proclaimed Lothario would describe, but only Tony Robbins would describe her as being five-four, five-six or whatever, *long*. He never used the terms 'tall' or 'in height' because, as he would explain to his voyeuristic audience, women never remained vertical for long when he was around, so he could only remember them lying down – which was all that counted, right? He had also invented a grading system – more like a degrading system, JJ said – for the 'bad chicks' he sometimes picked up when he was drunk and therefore not to be blamed. There were four grades: The Dog; The Double Dog; The Super Double Dog; and, finally, The Rat. JJ couldn't remember the definitions for the first three, but a Rat was a chick so awful that she made you want to gnaw your arm off at the shoulder rather than risk waking her as you made your escape in the morning. Tony Robbins had also claimed to have invented what he called the 'Rodeo' position. This, as far as JJ recalled, was just an ordinary missionary position, except that, at some time during the proceedings, you began to call the girl by another woman's name and then tried to stay on board for more than six seconds . . .

Most of the female vet students had hated Tony Robbins. 'They obviously had more sense than our stupid little hotpants Eve.'

I shrugged wryly. 'What'll happen to her?'

'Who knows? Gramps Joe pretty much calls the shots. He's still head of the family, and of the practice too for that matter, and he seems to be for forgiving her. Dad'll top her, or himself, if she comes back to the office.'

'Surely she wouldn't have the nerve . . .'

'Eve? Not half, she wouldn't. Don't you believe it, Frank! She's got a skin like a bloody rhino. There's going to be some kind of family meeting about it. I'm sure Miriam will want to give her another chance, too – she's more soft-hearted than ever since she had the baby.'

'What about Michael?'

'He'll go along with whatever Brenda says. Brenda is Eve's godmother. I never knew that until today.'

'And how about you, JJ? Which way will you go?'

'Don't know, Frank. I genuinely don't know. I'm too upset at the moment to think straight. Right now I feel like beating her to a pulp with a lump hammer. But last night I wanted to kill her slowly, piece by rotten piece, with a blunt knife, so it looks like I'm softening too. The way I'm going, in another few days I'll probably want to have the stupid little slut back and give her a huge fucking rise.'

'Blood is thicker than water, aye?'

'And Eve is thicker than both. What would you do, Frank?'

'Leave me out of it.' I grinned. 'I don't have a vote. Why did she do it, JJ? Love?'

'Who knows? Maybe, but I'd say it was also for the money. Crowther would pay big bucks for the inside info that Eve could supply. Really big bucks. I sometimes wondered how she was doing so well for herself – sexy flat, good clothes, nice car . . . At one time,' he snorted, 'I wondered if she wasn't on the game . . . Or at least had an old sugar daddy stashed away somewhere.'

I got a hammering a few nights later on. It was an ambush, in the yard, and I was taken totally by surprise.

I didn't recognise the attacker who suddenly materialised

out of the dark as I was about to step down from the Land
Rover, glad to be home after a late evening call. The first I
knew was when the door was slammed hard against me as I
was half in and half out. My knee was jammed painfully and
I yowled. Then rough hands seized me, pulling me out and
swinging me about in a rough circle by the back of my collar
until my squashed knee gave way and I collapsed, sprawling,
to the ground. At once, a large weight flopped on top of me
and began to flail at me with fists, legs, knees and elbows.
The ferocity of the attack took me aback and, before I had
time to get myself organised, I had a bloodied nose and a
pummelled groin.

I began to hit back, but I was already miles behind on
points. My assailant was everywhere. He was large and soft,
and smothered me like dough, and the few punches I did
manage to swing at him just sank in, their force dissipated
among the huge wads of fat, long before they could make
contact with anything hurtable. He felt like a Sumo wrestler
and he smelled like a Sumo wrestler who had recently been
on the hoy – on the few occasions on which we were face to
face, I felt as if I was standing outside the open door of a
busy pub late on a Saturday night.

His sheer soggy bulk was smothering my attempted
defensive movements and I was beginning to worry seriously, when I found myself unexpectedly with one arm free
and looking at the back of a thick, bulbous neck composed of
several horizontal pillows of flab, peppered spikily with
greying stubble. At once I shot my free hand over his head
and on to his sweating, straining forehead, where I paused
momentarily, my hand sticking, tenacious as an octopus, to
the sweaty brow. I located the bridge of his nose with my
middle finger, then, making hooks of my index and ring
fingers jabbed them into his eyes and pulled them up under
his eyelids. Instantly he froze, immobilised, and gave out a
loud moan. This manoeuvre has the exact same effect on
large obstreperous cattle, although it is not a practice which
would meet with the approval of most vets, never mind the
RSPCA.

Still, in extreme circumstances . . . 'Leave off, you bastard, or I'll gouge your fucking eyes out,' I panted. I was fighting seriously for breath because I was on the bottom.

'Aw. Aw. Aw.' He made little regular groans of pain and fear, sobering suddenly. The flabby body went still, the head rigid.

'Are you going to stop?' I upped the pressure the tiniest bit. 'Are you?'

'Argh. Yes. Jesus, me eyes! Argh. Yes, yes, ah yes!'

'Okay. I'll count to three and ease off a bit. Then you roll off me. If you even think of double-crossing me I'll fucking well blind you for life, okay?'

'I won't! I swear! Argh.'

I slackened my claw grip slightly and he instantly began to edge away. As soon as his weight had shifted enough to let me wriggle free I let go and rolled rapidly away. But all the fight had gone out of him and I began to take stock of my own wounds.

We sat side by side on the ground, him moaning and rubbing his eyes, me massaging my knee and gingerly checking the private bits. 'Who sent you?' I panted after a while, assuming it was Crowther.

'Nobody sent me, ye miserable lyin' shite! You cost Evie her job and her good name, you slimy bastard, tellin' her Tony had spilled the beans on her when he hadn't said a word. You lying turd! You miserable asshole, you useless fucking wanker . . .'

'Aw, shut your dirty mouth, you fat bastard, or I'll give you another goin' over. Who the fuck do you think you are? Her father?'

'Too right, I am. You fooled the poor lass into confessing. You prick! *Entrapment*, that is.'

'Entrap—? What are you, a fuckin' lawyer or something? You know . . . I don't believe I'm hearing this. You're accusing me of pulling a fast one on your daughter, when she's been pulling fast ones for the past year on her own family?'

'PJ? Mr Fuckin' High and Mighty PJ Slattery? Esquire? Some family that pooftah shite is! Miserable sod.'

'Well, what about the rest of them? By the way, do you want me to put some drops in your eyes? It'll do them the world of good . . .' I was feeling guilty as hell at his obvious agony – not that he had deserved the Queensberry rules or anything, but eye-gouging was even outside the Geneva goddam Convention . . .

We continued our bellicose conversation as we stumbled into the surgery to dress our wounds. Then I made Eve's father drink strong black coffee for an hour before driving him home.

At 1.45 a.m. I deposited him and his streaming red eyes outside the door of his very modest little terraced house, declining his invitation to come in for a moment to meet the wife. I looked at him in amazed disbelief. The very *idea* of it! I thought I'd sobered him up, but evidently I hadn't. Or maybe he was just naturally crazy.

Jeez, but I'd be glad to get out of this mad place, come Friday evening.

16

In the days following Eve's exposure the practice developed an atmosphere more suited to a hospice for the dying. PJ and JJ drifted in and out like zombies, going through the slow motions, trying to come to grips with the family treason. To make matters worse, PJ had decreed that he and JJ would do all the work. He claimed that they needed, for their peace of mind, to be kept fully occupied, but both Michael and Barbara reckoned the real reason was that they were trying to put spin on the truth, give the clients a tailored version of the family scandal which, like a river in spate, had flooded over the area the very same night that I had escorted the sobbing Eve to her grandfather's door. Presumably they didn't trust either Michael or me to propagate the official family line with sufficient enthusiasm or conviction. Anyway, for whatever reason, there was almost nothing to do and I was bored.

Claire had been recalled to Dublin and was now back in Algeria, where there'd been yet further inhuman massacres. Slaughtering for God (the God of Peace, Love and Justice, that is) had been the main justification for the most unbelievably savage wars and butchery in all places and throughout all ages. I wondered how it was that so many people, some of them intelligent and otherwise open-minded, could still cling to the belief that their particular brand of religion was the one and only correct one and that all others – in other words the vast majority of the world's population

– were wrong. To me, organised religion seemed like the most dangerous concept on earth, with more viciously butchered, beheaded and dismembered corpses to be laid at its bigoted door than could be attributed to any other single human cause.

Eve and her mother had gone away 'for a rest'. This left her father free to lurk around near the surgery. He didn't attack me again but the fleeting bonhomie of the early morning I'd driven him home had clearly evaporated with the hangover and I was getting thoroughly fed up of seeing his fat, sullen face staring hatred at me whenever I came into or left the surgery yard. He also seemed to materialise like a genie if my Land Rover was parked anywhere within a five-mile radius of Monksford for more than ten consecutive minutes. I'd been counting the days to departure; but whenever I encountered him I began to count in hours.

All three generations of Slatterys, Michael had told me, had blamed the no-good part of Eve on a few bad genes from her father and I was sure that he'd been left under no illusions about this; they had never, he said, accepted him as being good enough to become a member of the clan. There is nowhere more snobbish than a small provincial town.

'Maybe she heard them talking like that about her father?' I speculated as I sat across from my giant hairy colleague in Pearson's and rotated an optimistic fork in my spaghetti bolognese. 'That would explain a lot – if she loves her old man, which she probably does.'

I gave the fork one more twirl and, thinking that at last I'd got the hang of it, raised the spaghetti-entwined implement towards my mouth. As soon as it became airborne, the fat white strings uncoiled and slithered back on to the plate. 'Bollocks,' I said with feeling and picked up the dessert spoon. Spaghetti was fine, I liked it, but was it really worth the hassle?

Across from me, like some enormous Vernesque shark of the deep sampling a small life raft, Michael bit the second of his three large hamburgers in half, grunted and nodded. 'Do you know', he asked, when he'd swallowed, 'why those ketotic cows didn't recover? The ones PJ attended at Frank O'Malley's?'

'Eve substituted the dexamethasone with water?'

He paused, with the third burger on its way to its two-step demise. 'Normal saline, actually, but just how the hell did you know that? She only owned up to it in a letter that arrived this morning.'

'Sure I'd worked that out even before I turned her in. I don't see how it could have happened any other way. The call was on the third of October last year. Look it up.'

'Jeez, Frank. Yer a quare one. What kind of a head is that you have on you at all?'

I smiled at him enigmatically, a kind of Mona Lisa one. 'Any news of Crowther?'

'No. Still on "recuperation leave". He'd be as well to stay on leave, the same man. I still can't figure how that nephew of his is free and working away as if nothing had happened.'

As this was to be my last full day in Monksford, I went up to say goodbye to Johnny the barman and gave him a good tip. He'd looked after me well.

The man who'd been responsible for getting me to Monksford in the first place was also the man who made me stay longer than I'd either planned to or wanted to.

Joe Slattery was found dead in his bed at 7 a.m. on Friday, the same time that I'd begun, in his one-time apartment, to gather my effects together in one place for packing later, looking forward to getting away from this vaguely uncomfortable family practice with its uneasy undercurrents between father and son.

When, during the chaos of that morning, PJ asked me to stay on for another week I didn't have the heart to say no. To be honest, it couldn't have come at a worse time for me because Curley had informed me, just the day before, that he had at last finished with Dave's personal papers and he wanted me to run my cousinly eye over them, see if I could spot anything odd or out of place from my perspective.

Eager to have Dave's case put back into his 'Open' file, I had earmarked the next week for the task. So I compromised.

I told PJ that of course I'd stay and phoned Curley to ask if he could send Dave's effects on to Monksford. He could, no bother, and they arrived, all three boxes of them, some six hours later. I just put them in the flat upstairs, having no time at that moment for anything other than trying to sort out the chaos downstairs where the number of townspeople calling in to sympathise and offer condolences outweighed the professional callers by about twenty to one. Barbara held the counter, I covered the yard and surgery, while Michael did the farm visits.

Because of their recent troubles, the family had insisted on Joe being autopsied every which way, but the verdict stubbornly refused to change: death from natural causes.

So the Slatterys buried their patriarch grudgingly, resentfully, hinting that if Crowther hadn't actually done him to death personally with his own bare hands, then his recent illegal antics had done it: all the despair of his faltering practice, the worry and, finally, the heartbreak of discovering that his own flesh and blood had been corrupted by money and a flashy gigolo to conspire in the destruction of her family.

They probably were right at that certainly my visit with the distraught Eve had not done Joe a lot of good and he had looked ten years older by the time I took my leave, leaving him alone with his traitor of a granddaughter, trying to salvage what he could from the ruins of his lifetime's work.

Maybe Old Joe had been unable to face the devastation and nature, in an unguarded moment of uncharacteristic generosity, had just allowed him to turn off all the vital switches and call it a day, a life.

It was a huge funeral. I saw Laurence and Ellen there, but they had the decency to keep to the outer fringes and not to shuffle past in the long crocodile of hand-shaking sympathisers. Eve was there too, right in the middle of the line with the family; she wept uncontrollably, inconsolably, racked with great shuddering sobs, probably feeling guilty as all hell. But nobody shunned her. In fact, she spent most of the time standing between her mother and PJ, all three of them comforting one another, hugging and consoling. Tellingly, JJ's fiancée-to-be was there beside him in the front, dressed and veiled in black, seemingly more part of the family, which she hadn't yet even joined, than Eve's father who'd been 'an associate member' for twenty-eight years or so, but had never quite made it on to the first team. He was out there somewhere, lost among the general crowd, an outcast still, even at such a hugely important family event.

The workload shifted completely with the discovery of the cold remains of Joe. Now Michael and I did everything and it was the two remaining Slatterys who were sidelined. Consequently, I had little time for studying the contents of Curley's boxes during the day and had to wait until night-time to get a good run at them.

Before tackling the cheques and accounts, which might yield something, I went through three large envelopes of photographs but, after the initial shock of seeing Dave so vibrant and alive, I soon got bored. Although I scrutinised each one with the utmost care, I saw very little of interest to me. I had a vague recollection of having met one or two of the girls who appeared on his arm at various dinner dances and parties, but that was all. No Crowther, no Ellen, no Jag with a decapitated statuette on the front.

Some of the photos were crumpled and creased, some of the older ones ulcerated from chemical damage, probably from being stuck together face to face – many showed signs of having had to be prised apart. Obviously they had all been chucked in a drawer, willy-nilly, and none of them had held any great significance for Dave, not even a rather good shot of his parents, smiling to camera in the grounds of their home, which was one of the most battered photos of them all.

There were several featuring Dave and me together, and I took those out and kept them. Shit, we really did look alike! I stopped for coffee, remembering, as the kettle boiled, the occasions on which they'd been taken and felt sad.

With much less enthusiasm I turned to the dry accounts and stuff. Curley's people – it wouldn't have been Dave – had stapled everything into tidy piles. All bank statements were in chronological order, ditto for phone, electricity and other bills relating to his apartment, and this made the job easier. I discovered that Dave had accounts with four different banks, all current accounts, all in the black to the tune of £400–700. There was no sign of big money there.

Cheque stubs were filled in meticulously in his handwriting and there were no surprise cheques. The highest to an unknown person (as opposed to a services bill) was £312.76 to a Felix R. Norton and it was marked as 'Various'. To me it had the look of a trip to a hardware or an electrical store with something big, like a new VCR thrown in. But even if I was wrong and Felix R. was a dodgy one – a drug supplier or some such – I couldn't see anybody buying £312.76 worth of cocaine or crack or grass. For some reason I also thought it unlikely that there'd be a drug dealer (or fence or pimp), called Felix R. Norton and a crooked Felix R. who took cheques in payment for his crooked services was almost unthinkable. I didn't know who Felix R. was but I assumed that Curley had already taken note of the transaction and checked it out. A name like that, there could only be one in the phone book.

There were bills, receipted and unreceipted, from a number of 'respectable' establishments. I made a note to ask Curley if the unreceipted ones had since been paid and, if not, how we should go about paying them. The largest outstanding bill was for £92 plus change, the smallest for £31 exactly. There were five others in between.

As I went on through the boxes, I wondered just what exactly Curley expected me to find. The details were as bland as could be. Perhaps he had already removed the hot stuff. All seemed to be in order, much the same as I'd have left my affairs if I'd been the one to go. Except that I only dealt with one bank.

It took another two nights of work before I came to the last category, a large sheaf of letters, both personal and junk. There were elaborate brochures from top-class hotel chains, seductive free offers to buy all types of magazines, glossy inducement mail from companies offering financial and investment expertise, shiny circulars to those with more than enough disposable income. I wondered why Curley hadn't dumped them – perhaps he wanted to show the contrast between the plush, lavish hotels and the relatively small bank accounts. I shrugged and passed on.

I found several invitations to opening nights at various art galleries and I wondered about these: I made a note to ask Curley if Dave's apartment had housed substantial works of art; I had never noticed signs that he might be interested in the arts and so thought it puzzling that so many galleries should have had his name on their automatic invitation list. Unless, of course, my late cousin had been more of a celebrity socialite than I realised and had been invited to add extra glamour to the event . . . Or to supply the cocaine.

At the other end of the spectrum were postcards going back years. Not one of them held any suspicious messages – well, postcards wouldn't, would they? They came from most of the countries of Europe, a few from the US and a few less from Australia and New Zealand. I myself had sent two of them – wish you were here messages – one from France, the other from Malta. I was surprised to see that both carried almost identical messages, word for word, although they'd been sent more than three years apart. Thinking what a truly boring and unimaginative old fart I was, I pressed on with the task in hand. I checked all the postcards for drawing-pin holes, but found none, so they hadn't been pinned up. There were cards going back six years whose colours were as vivid and jolly as the day they'd been sent. Clearly they'd been well protected from light; again, probably thrown into the jumble of a drawer.

The handwritten letters I left until last – probably because of an early-inculcated reluctance to read other people's private letters. There were at least forty, possibly fifty.

Again, there were two which I had sent, one of these shortly after the last birthday we'd ever share, thanking him for the Hi-Fi. The other just informed him I'd been passing the nursing home where his father was and had called to see him. It said I was sorry I couldn't drum up even one hopeful thing to say about Uncle Clem, but I hoped that maybe he somehow realised that I had called.

Another nostalgic coffee break.

I looked at the names of the senders of all the letters and recognised very few.

There were about six, spanning some three years, from the Hartes. These were mostly informing Dave of various problems with the house – two broken slates, a leak behind the bath in the master bedroom bathroom which, according to the plumber, was only symptomatic of clapped-out piping all through the house and asking if they should look for quotations . . . Totally innocuous stuff. I glanced through the equally unriveting contents of all the other letters whose signatories I recognised and, finally, bored into somnolence, called it a night.

Next night, settled with coffee and Grieg for the long haul, I started on the last of the letters, the ones from those who were complete strangers to me. There were thirty-two in all, some single-pagers, some tomes, but with an average of about four pages. The hands ranged from copperplate clear to near-illegible scrawl and I decided to tackle the easy-to-read ones first.

The first letter to raise an eyebrow was a three-pager from a woman called Cecily, which I came upon within the first twenty minutes. The contents were not really suspicious in themselves, apart from one short piece which would have passed me by were it not for the date: Cecily's letter had been dated 15 May of the year I'd graduated and in it, among a whole lot of very personal and descriptive stuff, she expressed regret that Dave had to be abroad for a whole fortnight and she couldn't celebrate his birthday with him. She was, she claimed, itching (underlined), to have him back again by the twenty-third. And so on . . .

The thing was, Dave and I had celebrated our joint birthday, 18 May, together that year, as we always did and I had a very clear recollection of that particular evening. We'd eaten in Lamb Doyle's in Sandyford, at a window table overlooking the lights of the city. Dave had insisted on paying the whole bill, claiming that his conscience wouldn't permit him to take money from a poor student, but that next year, and every year afterwards, when I was a super-rich, multimillionaire vet, I could pay.

So Dave *hadn't* been abroad, at least on the evening of the eighteenth. I made a note for Curley, just in case there might be some significance in the little deception. Maybe there wasn't. Perhaps Dave had just needed a rest from the gagging Cecily before his heart gave out. Or his back.

There was another, shorter letter from Cecily dated 25 May in which she expressed herself devastated that Dave's business was going to keep him away for yet another week. She thought she might go mad with the frustration of waiting. Just hearing his voice on the phone made her break out in a sweat. 'Sweat' was heavily underlined and had half a line of exclamation marks after it. She swore that she wouldn't put a foot outside the door until he was back and, although she had really been looking forward to the Masked Ball, she was not now going to attend.

She went on to explain that Audrey looked incredible in her Cleopatra costume and gave Dave a detailed description with quite a skilful line sketch on a separate page.

And then came the bombshell which sent a sudden shudder through me and started my heart racing. For Cecily had written that she hoped Dave wouldn't be angry, but she had offered to lend 'The Ring' to Audrey for the night, as it was so 'quintessentially Cleopatra', but Audrey had refused it saying that the little red eyes staring at her gave her the willies and she'd be expecting all night to feel its venomous fangs sinking into her finger. And anyway she had a hidden plastic snake which she would, at the right moment, clasp to her bosom – not that Audrey had the greatest of bosoms for clasping snakes to, or anything else 'snaky' for that matter, and wasn't Dave the lucky 'STIFF!!!!' that in their family, she, Cecily, had got the tits, while Audrey had drawn the short straw of the long Pinocchio nose?

Halfway through this passage I suddenly lost the ability to read. My mind absconded and bolted off on its own, abandoning the rest of the letter to my eyes only, so that the words were at once readable and indecipherable. I needed whole seconds to discipline my thoughts back to Cecily's letter and deal both with the points she made and their implications.

A ring with red eyes and fangs could only be a snake ring.

Cecily had asked Dave if he minded her giving it to Audrey, so it had to have been a gift from him.

But perhaps Dave had managed to find *another* snake ring?

Even as I suggested it I knew it wouldn't be that. He could have bought (or stolen) any kind of ring and there was no need for him to look for a snake ring. He'd have no specific interest in snake rings in general – except for that one, mine.

Although he'd never said so, I'd always felt that he'd not been too happy when our grandmother, shortly before she died, had given the ring to me, to give to the girl with whom I fell in love.

I'd blushed furiously when she said this as I hadn't yet left the girl-hating stage. Dave had given me endless stick, calling me a cissy, but he'd also been a little jealous   not of the ring, but of Grandma's treating me as though I were special.

We both knew, by that age, that she, and only she, seemed to consider it significant that I'd been born nearly seven hours before Dave. In her mind it was more like seven years and she always treated me as the senior member of the next generation. Perhaps it wasn't the seven hours thing – maybe it was just that I was always that much more sensible than madcap Dave.

My mother has another theory: she reckons that Grandma favoured me because my mother, her daughter, had barely been aware of my passage into the world whereas Dave had nearly killed his mother, her other daughter and, again according to my ever-cruising mother, her favourite.

Whatever the truth of it, it was a fact that Aunt Heather had never been robust when I knew her and that she'd died early. Anyway, there was no denying the fact that Grandma did tend to favour me and I'd had a family heirloom bestowed upon me while Dave had been fobbed off with a tenner. At the time, I'd gladly have swapped. Fortunately Granny had died long before the ring had been passed on. In Grandma's world, falling in love was synonymous with marriage, so the ring was guaranteed to move on through the clan, from generation to generation. But things had changed and love was now a very two-sided thing.

I'd done my part by not giving the ring to Ellen until I'd been sure that we were a lifetime couple. The rest is history, as they say – it hadn't turned out that way and it now looked as though the ring would become an Ollin heirloom . . . assuming that Ellen still had it, which I very much doubted.

But how could Dave have come by it? Surely Ellen, aware of its significance to me, would never have given it to him? If Ellen had decided she no longer wanted it, she'd have given it back to me, somehow . . .

. . . Slowly, my dream of her visit to me on that long-ago night of illness began to emerge from the dark and hidden places in my head, and flesh itself out. I remembered the cool sponge, the gentle soothing voice, the fevered lovemaking and, later on, the letter and the ring on top of the fridge . . .

Well, what if I *hadn't* been dreaming? Suppose the ring and envelope really *had* been on the fridge? But then why hadn't they still been there next morning? Piece by piece, details stepped out of the shadows: I visualised Dave coming in with an armful of groceries the following morning and telling me he'd been in earlier but that I'd been asleep . . .

What if Dave, on his earlier visit, had found the ring and letter and, seeing that the letter hadn't been opened, assumed that I hadn't left my sickbed all night and therefore was totally unaware of their existence? And if the letter had said that Ellen was returning the ring because it was finally over between us and that we could never ever meet again, wouldn't he feel absolutely safe in taking the ring? If Ellen and I were never going to meet or communicate again, how would I ever know that she'd returned it, or how would she know that I'd never received it?

Trying, yet again, to give Dave the benefit of the doubt, I wondered briefly if he hadn't been trying to protect me from yet more bottomless troughs of depression when he'd taken the ring. But it didn't wash because, if that had been the case, wouldn't he have kept it for me until I had fully recovered from losing Ellen and then given it back? Instead, he'd promptly given it away to some girlfriend.

I checked the date on Cecily's letter and remembered the approximate date of my 'dream', mid-February. There were just three short months between them. And I had no way of knowing how long Cecily had had the ring before she wrote the letter. Perhaps he'd given it to her the same day he'd taken it from me. The more I thought about it, the more it looked as though he'd pocketed the ring because it might be worth something, or because it might come in handy for seducing some woman, or perhaps it was his way of avenging himself on Grandma. And me?

Ellen's precious letter he'd have torn into ticker-tape because it was the only evidence that the ring had been returned.

The miserable sod! All he had to do was ask me for it . . . He knew that.

My anger abating into sadness, I went back through the photographs, pausing only for shots of Dave with women, hoping each time to find one of them wearing a snake ring that would be similar to, but unquestionably not, Ellen's. I went through them a second time, but finally drew a blank.

I felt emotionally drained and I went to make some coffee. As I waited for the kettle to boil, I reflected on the fact that, inadvertently, *very* inadvertently, Dave might in fact have done me a huge favour. The fact that Ellen *hadn't* returned the ring had been the only tiny light of hope in the utter blackness of my despair during all the long months of my mourning her. Had I realised, during that first year of my desolation, that she had in fact snuffed out that tiny candle, I couldn't think, now, what might have become of me . . .

I forced myself back to the desk to read the other letters but they were harmless, of no interest to anyone and, by 11.45 p.m., I'd finished.

That night I added yet another almost sleepless one to the long list of almost sleepless nights in Monksford.

If the letter and ring part of that 'dream' was true, then what about the rest of it?

17

I called Ellen at 8.20 next morning. I knew that Laurence left for work at 8 a.m. sharp, but I forced myself to wait until I actually saw his car pass the surgery and brake at the top of our tributary road, awaiting his turn to slot into the growing flow of traffic. The tragedy of the family deaths had not been forgotten, but the cars were back now, as thick as ever.

The peeping made me feel dirty, but I needed to be sure that he actually had left the house before making my phone call. Matters were delicate enough as they were: I wasn't sure how I was going to broach the topic of the ring with Ellen, but I'd have been totally stumped if I'd got through to Laurence – it'd be hard to explain to a man just why I, an old boyfriend, was phoning his wife at 8 a.m. Telling him that it was about a ring I'd once given her to prove my undying love would not have impressed him. At all.

Ellen answered with a distracted 'Hello?' and, when I said it was me, stated tersely that she was extremely busy with the children and what could she do for me. I apologised for the bad timing and asked if she'd be shopping today, that I needed to see her urgently. 'How about the supermarket cafeteria again?'

'There's nothing more to tell, Frank . . .'

'It's not about Crowther, Ellen. If I could just . . .'

She cut me off abruptly as a child began to wail in the background. 'Eleven thirty, Frank. I'll be there at eleven thirty.' Then, without waiting for a reply or goodbye, she hung up.

Although I was more than five minutes early Ellen, in regulation Barbour jacket and Hermès scarf, was already seated, an almost empty coffee cup in front of her, a crumpled Mars bar wrapper in the ashtray. She had chosen the same small table we'd sat at before. Last time we'd met at lunchtime and it had been the only vacant one but today the place was empty. As I approached, I wondered what had led her back to this miserable little table. It was crowded, even for two, and jammed uncomfortably up against a plastic pseudo-Doric column which was lit from within by a pukey, pink-orange, tinned-salmon glow. No wonder there'd been no takers last time – who could eat lunch with one elbow being jammed tight to the ribcage by a plastic column?

She looked up from her quartered newspaper, some annoyance still lingering on her beautiful face. 'My word, but you just don't give up, do you?'

'That's not right, Ellen . . . You *know* I do. Eventually.' I was alluding to years ago, living in the past this morning.

Ellen either didn't, or chose not to, notice. 'So tell me. What's today's big flap?' she said.

'In a minute,' I said. 'I need a coffee.'

'That bad, huh?'

'I just need a coffee. Shall I get you another?'

'Why not? I've got news for you too.'

'Yeah?' I nodded at the crumpled wrapper. 'Another Mars?'

'Not guilty. It was there when I arrived.'

Which, I thought as I headed for the counter, made her choice of that table even more puzzling. All the others were perfectly clean, yet she had to pick the only one with leftovers still on it.

I placed the cappuccino in front of her and said: 'So what's *your* news?'

She sipped coffee, grimaced at the awful taste and began. She had it 'on the best authority' that Val Crowther was coming back the next day. Tony Robbins had agreed, for an 'enormous consideration' to take 'sole and full blame' for all misdeeds which had, or might yet, come to light. The story would be that Robbins was suffering from a rare nervous condition and had been for a year or so, totally unsuspected by anyone, friend or family . . .

'Well, balls to that!' I interrupted indignantly.

'. . . and it was this "affliction" which had made him single-handedly try to win over all the major farms in the area to his uncle's practice.'

'Excuse me, but haw bloody haw! You mean all the major farms who just happened to be Slattery clients. A fairly selective nervous condition, wouldn't you say?'

Ellen shrugged, impatient at my second interruption. Take it or leave it, it was no skin off her nose. 'I'm just telling you what I heard, Frank. I thought you'd like to know. And you'll find out about it soon enough anyway. You always do. Frank the Fanatical Ferret. You just don't give up, do you?'

I'd already answered that. I was a bit disappointed at the grudging way in which she'd given me this piece of hot news – almost as if she was doing an unpleasant but unavoidable duty. Having told me the whole story of Crowther and the hold he had over her, I expected her now to be fully on the side of the angels and actively trying to nail him. Or at least look a little less glum that he was getting his come-uppance.

'So Crowther gets to remain in practice, with his reputation reasonably intact . . .'

'Exactly. And Tony is to be sent abroad immediately (with *his* reputation in shreds) on Voluntary Overseas work. It is hoped that by the time he returns, all the fuss will have blown over. As, of course, will his nervous breakdown.'

'They must be *nuts* if they expect that to work.'

'Why shouldn't it work? If they move Tony quickly enough, he'll be gone before there's an investigation, and these charity organisations are always desperate for trained and willing personnel and won't look too deeply into the proverbial gift-horse's mouth. With regard to the nervous condition and its cure, they've got Al— a ... an eminent psychiatrist who'll see to that.'

'Who's that?' I asked.

'Eh ... I don't know ... I forget the name.'

'Makes no odds. How sure are you about all this, Ellen? It's pretty sensational stuff to be doing the rounds already. Before it even happens, like?'

'It's hardly "doing the rounds", as you put it. But it does come from close to the source. You know Yvonne Fuller? She lives in that gorgeous house on the river, just as you cross the bridge in Monksford? Oh, how silly of me. Of course you know her. You sat beside her at our dinner party.'

I remembered. Yvonne, a young and slim seventy plus, with the most beautiful, drop–dead, violet eyes, had relished giving me the private lowdown on half the guests. Although totally charming, she was the very last person I could think of who should have access to top secret stuff. 'I remember.'

'Yvonne's niece is married to Ronnie O'Neill, one of the partners at Crowther's. He knew nothing about what was going on and he's mad as hell. Livid! Talking of suing Crowther.'

I shook my head. 'Tony Robbins as a lone maverick? I just can't see it, Ellen. The arse'll fall right out of it once Eve starts answering questions. She'll implicate them all. For one thing, she's crazy about Robbins and, unless Crowther tells her that it's all a plan, which he won't, she'll think that everyone is trying to dump on her boyfriend and I can't see her standing for that. Also, if she ever wants to be received back into her own family, she'll take no chances on telling further lies for the opposition.'

I shut up at once. What the hell was I thinking, shooting my mouth off? Better not to mention the Slattery practice at all. For all I knew Ellen, for whatever reasons, might yet be on Crowther's side; after all, he still had the secret meeting at the hotel to hold over her.

Loose Lips Sink Ships, Frank. Partner-Ships.

A sudden thought struck me, a thought which could explain much – like Crowther's inside information on the hotel, room number, Ellen's lack of satisfaction at the turn of events which would see Robbins heading off on the missionary trails for the foreseeable future: 'Christ, Ellen! Don't tell me your dishy toyboy was Tony Robbins!'

'Toyboy?' She looked genuinely puzzled. 'What are you talking about, Frank?'

'The "friend" you were seeing on your indiscreet near affair?'

'Oh, that? . . . No. Not him.' There was no blush, no body language to suggest she was lying; she just looked vague, as if she'd forgotten that whole business already, as though it no longer had a place in her mind or even her memory. Once again, it was almost as if it had never even taken place.

And that was all Ellen's news. 'So what's your big flap today, Frank? Why the dawn phone call?'

'Sorry about that. I know it was really early, but it was urgent.'

'What was urgent?'

That put me firmly on the spot. I decided to come straight out with it, no preamble. 'You know Granny's snake ring . . . ?'

She looked confused at first, then her expression, for a brief millisecond, became soft, then turned briefly to worried, before becoming businesslike again. 'Those were the days, eh? Funny thing, but I thought of it only the other night at the dinner party. I noticed that Claire wasn't wearing it. Don't tell me you'd given it to someone else before her, someone who refused to return it? Or does your gorgeous lady only deign to wear it on extra-special occasions?'

Her answer was so all-encompassing that I suddenly had no need of all the downstream questions I'd prepared. Ellen had returned the ring. It had not been a dream.

Now convinced that nothing about that night had been a dream, I felt an irresistible compulsion to hear the truth from Ellen's own lips. Given the time that had passed, it made absolutely no difference, but I just couldn't bear to let it be. 'Ellen, when you came to see me the night I was sick, when you returned the ring, I think things might have got a little

out of hand, or rather' (little laugh) 'vice versa, *into* hand . . .'
I added laddishly, more from embarrassment than anything
else.

She froze for an instant, then, with a suddenly shaking
hand, lowered her coffee cup back on to its saucer. 'Please,
Frank . . .' she said very quietly, with a tremor.

Caught completely off guard by her reaction, I did a rapid
U-turn: 'Well . . . For what it's worth at this stage, I'm
sorry.'

'Just leave it, okay?' Dropping her eyes, she reached for
the Mars paper and began to fiddle nervously with it.

'I got carried away.'

'Fine, Frank. So did I. Now can you please just leave it?'
The waxed wrapper fairly flew through her agitated fingers.

'You see, I thought you'd come back for good and that was
why . . . Then, when you didn't turn up the next day, or the
day after and every day after that I became convinced that it
had all been one long dream . . .'

'Oh, *Jesus*, Frank! Will you please, for God's sake, just
leave it be!' She threw the paper down angrily and I thought
she was going to cry.

I couldn't imagine why she was taking it all so big. Then
she was suddenly staring at me, a puzzled expression
wrinkling her brow. 'But how could you possibly have
thought I'd come back? I explained everything in the letter.
It took me half the *night* to write it, dammit! It was as clear as
day.'

'I saw the letter on top of the fridge, beside the ring, but
next morning they'd both vanished. I never read the letter,
Ellen. What did it say?'

'*Vanished*?'

'Yes, vanished. What did the letter say, Ellen?'

'How do you mean what did it say? What do you think it
said? It just said goodbye, is what it said. Vanished? The ring
and the letter? *Just like that*?'

'You had to sit up half the night just to write "goodbye"?'

'Oh, I suppose I wrote it a hundred different ways. And I
suppose I apologised in a thousand different ways for our

split-up and I probably said in a *million* different ways that we could never see each other again . . . How could they have vanished, Frank? Things don't just . . . *vanish*.'

There was silence for a while, during which Ellen fidgeted, seemingly distraught, and I tried to think why the memory of that night seemed to be so distressful for her. It certainly wasn't the fact of the letter and ring vanishing – she'd begun shaking well before that topic had come up. It clearly had to do with our brief, passionate lovemaking, but why? It wasn't as though we were strangers, or that it had never happened before. And she had certainly had no second thoughts or regrets that night. Perhaps it was the fact that she had been unfaithful to her fiancé or, worse still, husband? Surely she hadn't been married at the time? I thought I ought to check, although I didn't want to ask her straight out.

'You know, it's funny how completely I lost all track of you,' I said, tacking up to the subject. 'I mean, you had Dave to tell you the odd snippet about me – not that it mattered to you, of course, but little things like Claire's name . . . But as far as I was concerned, you might as well have vanished off the face of the earth. I mean, I don't even know when you got married?'

'The year after we split up, Frank.'

'Oh? I'd had the impression that it was even earlier than that.'

'Actually, you might have heard that because originally we were to marry in December, but then Laurence was promoted and had to go to New York for three months' training at the beginning of the year, so we postponed it until the end of April, a month after he came back . . . God, I feel so *awful* about the ring. I know what it meant at the time, to both of us.' A thought came to her and she put her hand on my arm. 'Oh, Jesus, Frank, I hope I locked the flat door as I left.'

'I'm sure you did. Look, Ellen, please don't worry about it.' April. So she hadn't been married – I remembered being in the hospital all through mid-February and hoping for a

Valentine card from her, even if it was only one of those comic ones. It had never come.

I was finding it extremely hard to believe that this totally out-of-character upset could be the result of a long-past infidelity.

Ellen had always been a joyous lover, certainly not inhibited. Technically, she had been free at the time, so why the big scene now, years later? If she could narrate to me without any expression of guilt, as she had at this very table a week or so ago, a lengthy near affair at a time when she was very definitely not free to conduct such a relationship, how could she be so affected by a single one-night stand with her old lover, years and years ago? It made no sense at all.

'Tell me, Ellen. How did you know where to find me that night? You'd never been to that flat. And *why* did you come on that particular night?'

Now that we were moving away from the *intimate* details of her long-ago night visit she became less agitated. 'Dave. Dave is the answer to both questions. I ran into him and a crowd of his pals at a pub in town. I asked about you, as I always did, and he told me that your flatmate had contacted him to say that you were on your own in the flat, very ill, and as Dave didn't seem to be making much of a move to check on you I said I would. He gave me the address and told me where to find the key. To be honest, Frank, I'd been wanting to see you anyway, for ages, to give you back the ring. I wanted to return it to you personally . . .'

So much, I thought, for Dave, the constant, selfless guardian of my peace of mind, the ever-altruistic deflector of bad news . . . If Dave had such a keen interest in my well-being, then how come he hadn't even bothered to come to check on me when my worried flatmate had asked him to? 'You realise, don't you, that returning the ring would have killed me at that particular time?'

'Rubbish! You have the resilience of an ox . . . but I didn't want to trust it to anyone else. I wanted to put it in your hand and tell you that I hoped one day you'd find somebody more worthy to wear it.'

'Ox or no ox, it would have killed me. I'm telling you.'

'Flatterer!'

I gave up. 'Do you remember any of the pals Dave was with that night? Was he with a woman?'

'I'm not quite sure if he'd made the kill, but he was certainly stalking one. A busty blonde, name of Celia or Clarissa or something like that. I used to know her sister Audrey. She did First Arts with me but dropped out before the exams – probably just wanted to dabble in student life for a while and after all, Daddy had pots and pots of loolah.'

'Might her name have been Cecily?'

'Cecily! That was it. Cecily Curtis. There were three of them, commonly known as the Alphabet Sisters, ABC – Audrey, Beatrice and Cecily.'

'QED,' I said, getting in on the acronyms myself.

Ellen made her excuses at this point and left. She was still looking a bit shaken, although not as bad as she had been.

On my way back to the surgery I wondered if I should tell the partners about Crowther's plan (according to Ellen), but there was nobody around when I got there so that took care of that decision.

I suddenly remembered that Yvonne Fuller had in fact invited me to call and take tea with her some time and, although it was the kind of vague invitation that's not really meant to be taken up, I decided to surprise her. I fetched the local phone directory and, moments later, had a date with a delighted-sounding Yvonne for four o'clock.

Yvonne had me thinking that seventy mightn't be a bad age to be. Apart from those incredible violet eyes and wide, ready smile, she had good skin, a trim, athletic figure, a feline walk and seriously good clothes sense. Yvonne Fuller dressed to be admired. I wondered if she had put on those clothes this morning or only after I'd phoned. I didn't know and couldn't find out, but somehow I reckoned she dressed well every day. A house like hers would have driven a sloppy, casual dresser mad.

The room was large, light and airy, done in muted yellows

and creams, with the odd shock of a modern painting in striking primary colours and strict geometrical shapes. Double doors in the end wall led out to a long garden, which ran all the way to the river. The furniture looked antique to me, but I'm not a great judge. There was far too much of it for my taste, too many small, fiddly pieces. A thing that struck me as odd almost at once was that, despite her beauty, there was not one photograph of Yvonne in the whole room, either on her own or with others – I'd been surreptitiously casting about to see what she'd looked like in her earlier decades. Nor were there several photos of any man: husband, lover, whatever. The one man who did appear twice was obviously of an earlier generation, probably her father.

I presented Yvonne with the best box of liqueur chocolates that Monksford's one and only delicatessen could supply and she made delighted noises, professing them to be her favourite. And the violet eyes sparkled as she smiled. If I'd been older, she'd have had me rolling over to have my tummy tickled. Or if she'd been younger and I weren't already spoken for, I'd have been trying to roll her over and tickle hers.

There was no need for me to lead in to my subject. Yvonne, as soon as we had dispensed with the very pleasant pleasantries and were seated in two matching linen-covered chairs with a precious-looking tea service between us, began the conversation, much as a chairman might have called a meeting to order. 'Well! That was an abrupt end which Crowther put to Ellen's little soirée the other evening, wasn't it?'

'Yes, indeed. A pity. It was very enjoyable up to then.'

'Crowther! Awful little man. He has the table manners of a seagull. I won't have him here. Pushy, too, you know. Still, we have to forgive Ellen the odd unpleasantness – her parties are invariably so enjoyable. Never an iffy meal, an unsuitable wine, or dull company. I don't know how she keeps it up, especially with the new baby. She hasn't had the easiest of times with that baby, you know. It seems to be allergic to everything, poor mite.'

Spot the deliberate mistake, I thought to myself. 'They do those rather grand parties often?' I asked. Ellen had distinctly told me the opposite.

'A couple a month I would have guessed. It's not just for the sake of parties, you know – nobody can afford to do that these days. Laurence does a lot of business locally. Many of our fellow guests last evening would have been clients. He's in investment advice or something like that. I'm afraid it's all a bit beyond me.'

As I was still convinced that there was something odd about Ellen's story, I took advantage of the early opportunity to cross-check. 'But didn't Ellen tell me that they'd taken a long break from parties last year? Or am I mistaken?'

If Yvonne thought my question abrupt, she gave no such indication. 'Break?' she said, looking slightly puzzled. 'I certainly don't remember any break and I go to them all. They know I sometimes get lonely here and they're very sweet. Laurence calls me Aunt Yvonne, although I'm not really his aunt. I'm his mother's best friend and have been for ever. I can't remember any noticeable break in the parties. You must have been mistaken. You're probably mixing her up with someone else.'

So much for Ellen and her first or second party of the year since her 'affair', I thought. She'd lied to me. But why? And had it all been a lie, or just some of it? I turned back to my hostess. She was so open and unsuspecting that I reckoned I could test just one more little step. 'I knew Ellen at college, you know.'

'I didn't know that. Did you know her well?' The violet eyes lit up and widened; the teacup and saucer were placed back on the tray. Her whole attention was going to be needed for this one.

Sorry to disappoint you, Yvonne, I thought. 'Not really. We hung around for a while with the same crowd. I hadn't seen nor heard from her since then, until I came to Monksford. I'm delighted to see that she's so happy and settled. They seem to be the perfect couple, herself and Laurence.'

'Oh, they're having their problems. We all do, I dare say.'

Ah, Here it comes! I thought. 'Really? I'm sorry to hear that.'

'Yes. Their stud farm seems to have taken a dive. I'm not sure of the details and there wouldn't be any point in my telling them to a vet anyway. Oh, yes. And Laurence and PJ Slattery had a most unseemly brawl last year about one of their stallions and they changed vets.'

Which brought us back full circle. 'Oh, that!' I said, trying to get the conversation back on track again. 'Those kinds of problems are nothing. As long as there's harmony in the home, as long as there are no inner tensions in a marriage, then all other troubles are minor. Everything in perspective. That's what I always say.'

It didn't work. It sparked no response in Yvonne, not even a glance of surmise. 'And which vet did they then get? Crowther!' she said, her lip almost curling in contempt. 'Silly girl, Ellen. He's not a good person. As you have now so ably demonstrated. Come,' she said, rising lithely from her chair. 'It's a beautiful afternoon. Let me show you my garden before the midges wake up.'

We strolled towards the river, with me getting a lesson in botany as we went. Right on the bank, Yvonne settled on an old park bench, its wrought iron lovingly painted, its timber strips varnished to a high old shine, and patted the seat beside her. I sat. The unruffled water slid, black and metallic, from beneath the twin arches of the limestone bridge up to the right, picked up the cloud shapes and colours of the September sky as it turned through an almost right angle around the end of the garden, then continued on towards another, smaller bridge some two hundred yards downstream. Willows at the end of the lawn trailed languid fingers in the flow, glassy and night-dark beneath their shade.

'I was delighted when you phoned today.' Yvonne wanted to talk about Crowther's sudden downfall. I didn't mind: I didn't think I could get much more mileage out of Ellen – not without creating suspicion, anyway. 'You seem to be the one common factor in all the accounts I've heard so far – you as their nemesis. But you never know what to believe, do you, and I wanted to hear it from the horse's mouth, if you'll excuse the analogy. I'm told you laid an evilly crafty trap for Crowther and came up with his nephew. However did you come to suspect them?'

For the next half-hour I told her and answered her questions, mostly honestly. During that time Yvonne seemed to turn into my greatest fan. At one point, during what had now become an informative discussion, Yvonne mentioned the name of the psychiatrist who was going to see Tony Robbins 'all night'. It was Albert Conroy, a name which I instantly recognised.

I expressed shock that the eminent doctor would become involved in such underhand matters and Yvonne explained that Crowther and Conroy had been friends for years.

Why was I not surprised?

I took my leave, promising to call by again soon.

En route back to the surgery I thought about the psychiatrist. He had become a kind of guru in the past few years and was always being interviewed on TV, radio and in the press. Every time there was a kidnapping, hijacking, or hostage-taking anywhere in the world, Albert Conroy would be there on the screen, in his trade mark studied but expensive scruffiness, holding forth on the state of mind of the victims, perpetrators, negotiators, survivors, relatives and friends, and telling all of Ireland what the Peruvian soldiers surrounding the Japanese embassy ought to do next. Why us? I had, in that particular instance, wondered. Tell the Peruvians. Tell the Japanese.

I reckoned, myself, that he was a bullshit artist. Anyone who never says 'I don't know' just has to be.

Then I wondered why Ellen, having started the famous name, should suddenly stop and claim not to remember. It was like someone, when alluding to a famous politician, saying: 'Marg—' and then claiming not to be able to remember the '—aret Thatcher' part. Ellen hadn't forgotten

– she'd just decided she didn't want to say the name. Perhaps she was, or had been, a patient of Conroy's and, in direct contrast to what's commonly believed of female patients and their shrinks, actually hated the man.

18

'Eve is a week late,' Michael said. We were scrubbing up for a Caesarean section on a small Jersey heifer which had precociously gone in calf to an early-maturing bull calf no older than herself. Our patient couldn't have been more than about fifteen months old and her calf, although it would have been small in a grown cow, had no chance of coming through the tiny pelvis which, like the rest of the mother-to-be, had had its normal growth stunted by having a healthy, demanding foetus competing from within for nourishment. The owner should have separated his calves earlier.

'Late for what?' I asked, pulling on a green gown and turning my back to Michael to have the tapes tied. There were no gowns for normal-sized people; they were either Slattery-small or Stone-huge and I opted for one of Michael's. I might be walking on the hem but at least I could move my arms freely.

'You know? Her period. She was at the house last night, talking to Brenda for hours. Brenda is her godmother . . .'

'So I hear . . .'

'Eve is worried sick that she's pregnant.'

'Well Halle-bloody-lujah.' I sighed resignedly. 'That's all we need – the evil Crowther seed polluting the purity of the Slattery clan. PJ will personally stone her to death in the town square.'

'Brenda reckons she's not pregnant. She claims it's

probably just because all the recent fuss has upset her hormones.'

'Maybe. And there again . . .'

'That's what I said. Anyway, they've gone off to town today to have it checked out one way or the other . . . Do you want to do this lady or will I?'

'I don't mind, Michael. It's up to you. She's your case.'

'You do it then, Frank. She's too low for me. She'd do my back in.'

'Okay. But then you have to buy lunch.' It was to be another Pearson's day. Brenda and Eve wouldn't be back until evening and Michael didn't like going home to an empty house – it made him feel lonely, he claimed.

We had decided to operate with the heifer standing, tied along the wall of the theatre. Michael would have had to sit on the floor to get down low enough.

She'd already been sedated, prepped in the lower left flank area, draped in sterile green from shoulder to tail, and given local anaesthetic in an inverted L block, the longer vertical leg of which ran up her body wall forward of and parallel to the proposed incision site. The shorter, horizontal leg ran from the top of the vertical leg a few inches back towards the tail and above where I would start my incision. The anaesthetic had been infiltrated into the skin and all the muscle layers beneath. The heifer stood peacefully, chewing the sweet hay we'd given her, ignoring us as we wheeled the instrument trolley with its gently rattling contents to her side.

I pulled on gloves, fitted a scalpel blade on to its handle, pricked down my incision line with a needle to make sure the local anaesthetic had taken effect, then sliced the skin in one smooth stroke. Cutting through the individual muscle layers took little more than a minute; in such a young animal there were no large bleeders, no severed blood vessels haemorrhaging strongly enough to require ligaturing, tying off. Arriving at the glistening peritoneum, I picked it up carefully with a forceps, made a tiny nick in the resulting 'tent', through which I introduced a larger forceps. The purpose of this was to enable me to elevate the peritoneum, to lift it well clear of the abdominal organs so that I didn't inadvertently nick one of them with my scalpel as I opened a ten-inch-long incision in it. Clear yellowish peritoneal fluid splashed out round my boots as I reached into the floor of the abdomen and located, slightly towards the rear, the pregnant uterus. The calf's hind legs were clearly palpable inside. The rumen, which occupies almost the whole left abdominal area of cattle and other ruminants, bulged obstructively into the incision and Michael repelled it gently but firmly towards the 'head' end of the heifer, allowing me to lift and exteriorise the uterus from the rear. I did this by firmly grasping the leg through the wall of the organ and carefully drawing the uterus up to the incision in the body wall until it filled it.

Once the uterus occupied the incision site, Michael could release the rumen and turn his attention to holding the uterus steady for me while I made another smooth slice through its wall and laid bare the calf's yellow-brown hoof and fetlock within the thin transparent covering of the foetal membranes. I made a small nick in this 'bag', then reached in to grasp the tiny limb at the fetlock. Holding this clear, I took its fellow and, drawing both legs out, handed them to Michael. Before beginning the pull which would deliver the calf, I checked to see that the incision I'd made in the womb was long enough to allow the calf through without causing a tear; I decided to lengthen it by an inch or so, just to be on the safe side, then gave Michael the okay. Twenty seconds later the wet and steaming bull calf was snorting on the ground under his young mother's head. Doped by the sedation, she looked quizzically at him for a moment, then went back to chewing her hay.

While Michael had been pulling the calf, I'd held on tightly to the uterus and I didn't let go until he returned, gloves changed. If I hadn't held it, the opened organ would have slipped back into the abdomen, discharging foetal fluids, and possible infection, inside. Once Michael had a firm grip on the cut edges, I removed whatever of the placenta came away easily, then spent five minutes suturing the uterus closed. Swabbing the neatly closed suture line clean of a few stringy blood clots and dribbling antibiotic along its length, I replaced the uterus in its proper position. Next I stitched up the peritoneum, then each of the abdominal muscle layers individually and, finally, closed the skin incision with large metal staples. About thirty minutes from first cut to last staple. Average. We stripped off our gowns and gloves and, while Michael went to call the yardman, I gave the cow (as she had now become) antibiotic cover. She'd have more injections for the next few days, staples out in a week.

We instructed Georgie, the yardman, to keep an eye on her, to discourage her from lying down if he could and, as soon as she was steady on her feet, to walk her and her calf to the box which he had prepared while the surgery was in progress. 'Slowly!' Michael warned with a menacing growl, as if Georgie hadn't done this a hundred times over the years.

Late in the afternoon, on my way in from my rounds, I was wondering about the result of Eve's pregnancy test and the implications of a positive result, when I suddenly found myself thinking about Ellen with a startling clarity, and all at once I knew how to check her story about her near affair, the story which I'd begun to doubt more and more.

When the practice closed down for the evening and everyone had left, I took down last year's call book again from its high shelf in the accounts room and carried it upstairs to the flat. I sat at the kitchen table and began to flick through the pages.

The first thing that struck me was the numbers of calls; there were at least twice as many as this year and I could see the true extent of the impact of Crowther's malicious campaign. I flicked towards the back of the book and from about September on there was a steady decrease in call numbers each day. By end of year the numbers were down drastically. Year's end was a quiet time in any practice but last year's December figures were still better than the paltry numbers which had become the disastrous norm for this year. And it was only September . . . No wonder morale was bad.

But that was not what I was looking for – I already knew all that. I returned to January and began to scan down the names for each day. At that time the Ollins' name appeared with some frequency; it increased during the stud season, as it would and, by August was tailing off again.

In August also, the handwriting in the call book changed abruptly. One day it was someone's whose writing I didn't recognise (presumably Brenda Stone's) and the next day it was Eve's. Exactly one week later, Michael Stone's initials no longer appeared beside calls and didn't reappear for another three weeks. It was all there in black and white, Brenda taking a week off before the wedding, Eve taking over, then Michael working up to the day before the wedding – a Friday, that'd be right – then vanishing for three weeks on honeymoon. So I could now pinpoint when Eve had taken over and I wondered if Crowther had turned her before or after that had happened; probably after, I reckoned, because he couldn't have known that she'd be taking over from Brenda or that she would become permanent because of Brenda Stone's early pregnancy. But I wasn't looking for any of this either.

What I needed to find was when Ellen had changed over to Crowther. I pressed on, turning pages. In early November I found the series of calls to the stallion, the one whose neck had subsequently begun to rot away and, after that, no further mention of the Ollins. It was at this point, presumably, that PJ and Laurence had had their fight, and Ellen had changed over to Crowther. So, according to her story, Ellen had had her dalliance at the hotel within the previous month. I closed the book and went slowly back downstairs to replace it on the shelves, trying to figure out just why Ellen had spun me such an elaborate yarn of mistruths.

I ploughed through a ruminative and barely tasted supper, during which I came no nearer to figuring why Ellen should have told me such a whopper. I finally forced myself to give up and turned my attention to the letter which had been delivered by hand to the surgery in the afternoon by the local squad car. It was from Curley.

He opened by thanking me for all the hard work I'd put in on Dave's papers. Some of my observations had turned out to be very important: the fact that Dave and I had met on our birthday, the year of my graduation, had put paid nicely to his alibi for a large payroll robbery, which had been carried out two days earlier – a 'friend' had sworn that Dave had been on board his yacht with him all through that fortnight, cruising the Scottish Isles, and that neither he nor Dave had ever left the boat for more than two consecutive hours. The yacht had indeed been there – there were ample records in harbour masters' logs etc. – but if Dave had been dining with me at Lamb Doyle's on the evening of 18 May, then clearly he couldn't have been aboard the yacht in Skye. It felt very strange, dropping Dave right in it, and I wondered if I'd have been as honest and co-operative if he were still alive?

With regard to my other remarks and concerns, Curley assured me that all 'provable' outstanding bills would be settled – Dave's solicitor was handling all that sort of thing – that there had not been any significant works of art in Dave's apartment – so it didn't seem that he had been a collector and therefore his presence on the mailing lists of all those galleries would seem to have been purely social – and finally that all the cheques I had been unable to recognise or account for had been traced, except for one, a cheque for £75 made out to A.C., which probably would never be traced as it had not been presented.

I remembered the cheque stub, but dug it out again for another look. It had been written the day before Dave died, the second of three on that day. The first was made out to 'The Firm', a health club I sometimes used when I was in town and of which I was a 'provincial' member. It was in the amount of £300 and this was for 'qr'tly m'ship'. The last cheque was to Gaynor Bros for £27.30. I looked them up in the directory and found that they were an off-licence in Baggot Street, about three miles from The Firm, which was in Leinster Road, in Rathmines. I glanced through the cheque stubs for his other three banks but none of them showed any recent transactions.

So who was A.C.? And why hadn't A.C. cashed the cheque? Was A.C. a friend who couldn't bring him- or herself to cash it once they had learned that Dave was dead? Or was A.C. an enemy, a mortal enemy, who didn't want to cash the cheque because it might tie him or her into a meeting with Dave mere hours before his murder? Having gone through all the cheque stubs again for all the banks, trolling for another A.C., or a full name with those initials, I gave up. There was probably nothing mysterious at all about it – maybe someone had just lost the cheque. It happened . . . in my case, only too frequently, usually laundered and churned to death in the washing machine.

Although I couldn't now figure out the A.C. cheque, I couldn't help feeling that if I actually went to Dublin for a day I might at least be able to narrow down the field of search for A.C. At the moment it wasn't a field at all – it was open, limitless steppe.

Ah, yes. I definitely needed a day in Dublin.

19

If I were to look closely into the matter I'd probably find that, by a factor of ten, I am the undisputed, all-comers, all-eras, all-weights, both bare-knuckle and rules, Monksford Open Insomniac Champion. Such were the mindless thoughts that struggled leadenly through the fudgy morass in my head at 7.30 next morning when, in Pavlovian response to the shrilling of my alarm clock, I dragged my mutinous body in front of the bathroom mirror and delicately cracked open two painfully swollen piggy-red eyes, only to snap them to again in recoil. Liberal application of cold water all about the face, head and neck brought me somewhat back towards the land of the living, but it took a full-on ice-cold shower to drill away the comatose cocoon that enclosed me in its deadening wraps and blast me fully awake. My head throbbed as I towelled myself dry and dressed, and my tongue felt as if it had sprouted some foul and deadly lichen overnight.

As I'd thrashed through the hours when I should have been sleeping, my mind hopped randomly from subject to subject, trying to deduce further than I'd managed so far the significance, if any, of Dave's cheque, his theft of my ring – not to mention Ellen's letter – and so on, back again to Ellen and her magnificently detailed but totally untrue story of near infidelity. I longed for night's return and the hope of some solid sleep, as I hauled myself down to the office and wished everyone good morning.

The Slatterys were beginning to recover from their double shock, both surviving generations beginning to make brief but lengthening appearances in the office. They rarely came in together and Michael thought this strange – 'I wouldn't mind, Frank, if Joe had left a widow who needed constant company in the first days' – and opined that what PJ and JJ required at this point was more work, not less.

The calls burden had increased considerably even at this early stage and the word was out that Crowther's clients were deserting him in droves. It was generally felt that, had he not been the one who had single-handedly and selflessly saved the lives of those three schoolkids, he'd have been wiped out overnight. It was ironic, Michael pronounced, that in view of the fact that nothing had yet been proven against him, Crowther seemed headed for rapid bankruptcy, solely because of rumours. 'Hoist with his own whatchamacallit, Frank?'

'I don't know, Michael.'

'Poetic justice.' He settled for the compromise.

Later on, PJ called me into his office. Despite the fact that he, JJ and Miriam were now back in harness, PJ wanted me to stay on. Again. My first reaction was to say no as I reckoned, not without a modicum of contempt, that the only reason PJ desired my continued presence was in case there was any follow-up dirty work, like revenge, by Crowther or his henchmen.

But I prudently delayed before answering: in my business, word of mouth is the number one goodwill spreader and I had the feeling that if I were to decline, no matter how tactfully or however good my reasons, then that would be what he would most remember me for. Despite his magnanimous assurance, on the day we'd agreed on the *real* reason for my employment, that I could pull out whenever I wanted to, I could just see PJ telling other vets at future meetings and conferences, should my name arise, that I was all right, but a bit of a clock-watcher, not one for going that all-important extra mile, the type who would pull out just when he was needed most. I might have been wronging the man, but I didn't think so. I'd met others like him before, control freaks who found great difficulty with 'no' answers. Accepting them, that is.

But that wasn't the only reason which made me oblige PJ; in this case there were other factors to make it the best plan.

I was fully aware of the probability that I would be by far the most likely target for Crowther's vengeful wrath and it probably didn't matter where in Ireland I was, for he could easily find me. At least, here in Monksford, I'd be on my guard and surrounded by people – the gigantic Michael Stone sprang immediately to mind – who knew the enemy and his minions, and who would be doughty allies if Crowther did try anything on. I'd be safer in the citadel, even if it was under attack.

But the main reason for agreeing to stay was my feeling that Dave and Crowther had too many 'meeting points' in their crooked lives to be mere happenstance. I wanted to learn more if I could and Monksford seemed by far the most logical place for this. Despite his treachery, I didn't want Dave's death to remain a mystery for ever.

'Just for a few more days, Frank,' PJ wheedled. 'If you could see your way at all. Miriam is on light duty only, helping Barbara around the office as . . . eh . . . we're a bit short-staffed in that department at the moment . . .' He wouldn't mention Eve by name.

I wondered if he'd heard of her pregnancy scare, which had turned out, mercifully, to be negative. Brenda's diagnosis of stress-confused hormones had been correct.

So I agreed, although I told him I'd have to check it through with my diary, make a few calls and the like. Adjustments, he understood? He did. I saw no reason not to make him sweat a little. I could not warm to this man and I wanted him to get the message that, if there were any other thing at all on my books, the teeniest most insignificant task ever, then I'd be gone. However, I told him, a day up in town was inescapable, maybe even two.

'Of course. Not today, I hope?'

'It'll keep. How long do you think you'll need me? I don't

want to push you, PJ, but I need to know when to start accepting bookings again.'

'Em . . . End of next week? Can you handle that?'

'I think so.' I picked up the desk calendar. 'I always finish on the Friday evening, after surgery, so what we're talking here is the evening of Friday next week, okay?'

We shook hands on it and I left the office.

Michael was standing by the counter, talking with Miriam and Barbara, as I went out towards the yard. 'It's *petard*, Frank. Petard,' he shouted after me. I waved a hand in acknowledgement as I continued on my way.

Although I had forced myself not to telephone Ellen that morning, I still contrived to find myself driving in the immediate vicinity of the supermarket at 11.30, which seemed to be her usual shopping time. I spotted her car, parked as far away as I could and, trundling a nearby abandoned trolley ahead of me, entered. I feigned surprise when, during an exhaustive search for oxblood self-shining shoe polish, I happened to run into her. 'Ellen!' I said, eyes wide. I was not looking forward to this.

'Hello, Frank,' she returned in a voice such as the Ancient Mariner might have used to greet the arrival of yet another albatross. 'Busily shopping for lunch again, I see.'

'Got to keep the inner man going, you know.' I grinned before I noticed her glancing at my collection of steel wool pads, a small screwdriver set, a packet of plastic tea-towel hooks with gummy backs, a toilet brush and holder, a book of logic puzzles and a vacuum-packed tin of mixed nuts which would make a noise like a gunshot when I cracked the metal-foil seal inside. Nonchalantly, I added a packet of chocolate biscuits, which happened to be the nearest edible item. 'But I was just thinking of having a coffee break. Fancy a speedy cappuccino?'

'Not today, Frank. I'm late already. But thanks all the same. See you around.' With a small wave, she pushed her laden trolley off towards the checkouts.

Foiled and frustrated, I headed for the coffee shop

anyway: I didn't really want coffee, but I could hardly walk out of the store empty-handed before Ellen left and she'd probably be ten minutes at the very least at the checkout. I abandoned my trolley where it stood – the supermarket had enough scullions to put all the stuff back.

I bought a newspaper, a beef sandwich and a pot of strong tea, and headed for the seating area; just to be perverse, I chose the mean little table by the Doric column and, as I neared it, I still couldn't figure out what had attracted Ellen to it on that second occasion.

'Mind if I join you?' Ellen said, plonking down a coffee cup on the table. I hadn't seen her approach, my head being buried, as usual, in the crossword puzzle.

'Sure,' I said, half rising. 'No problem. But I thought you were in a big hurry?'

'I have a flat tyre, dammit,' she said. 'I was hoping you'd help me change it.'

'Of course. You want to do it now?'

'No hurry now, Frank.' The rush, she explained, had been to collect Frances from playschool, but the puncture had put paid to that. She'd rung one of the other mothers who was going to take her home and feed her, the little mite.

'Well, is there anything else you have to do? You sure you don't want me to change it right now? It'll only take a minute.'

'No, Frank, honestly. I had a hair appointment for later, but I've rescheduled it for tomorrow morning at eleven. In fact, it suits me better like that.'

Having put her busy life to rights, Ellen said she would now like to sit and chill out for a few minutes, if that was okay by me? I assured her that it was. She sipped from her cup, her nose wrinkling with distaste. 'I've had one of these already this morning. I don't know what brand they're using now, but the coffee's gone to hell over the last few days. I meant to complain.'

'Can I get you something else then? It doesn't have to be coffee.'

'No, thanks. I'll just sit a minute while you finish yours,

help you with the crossword. How come you're sitting at this crappy little table? There are lots more.'

Dang! Now I looked like a weirdo. 'Well . . . Em . . . Yes, but the others are four-seaters and there is, was, only one of me. Do you want to move? Now that there's two of us.'

'No. It's fine.' She eyed the paper. 'Give us a clue.' Ellen was no mean crossword solver herself.

'Okay. Fourteen down, six letters. "Get a fix, about two." Second letter "E" which is a big help. Not.'

'Repair. "Re", about. "Pair" is two. Repair is "fix". Write it in.'

We fiddled with the crossword for a few minutes, both of us marking time.

It was Ellen who brought it up first. 'Sorry I blew up at you the other day, Frank. I was going to ring you, but I thought I'd see you around. You must think I'm an awful person . . .'

'No, I don't.'

'Don't tell me you approve of . . . my scarlet woman conduct. What's got into you, Frank. You used to believe in Loyalty Above All.' She made it sound like a motto. She was mocking me. Having lied to me like a good thing, she was now *mocking me*. I wasn't hurt or anything; after all, it didn't matter to me any more. All it did was make it a bit easier for me to slap her down.

Not quite sure which disloyalty she was referring to – (a) her betrayal of me with Laurence, the new love of her life, (b) her betrayal of Laurence, the fiancé, with me in my sickbed, or (c) the pretend almost betrayal of Laurence, the husband, with the dishy-looking, make-believe would-be stud – I said: 'I still do believe in loyalty, Ellen. The reason I'm not giving you disapproving glares is because I didn't fall for your story. I *nearly* believed you, mind, but not quite. You should write fiction professionally.'

She went pale immediately and stared at me, trying to pretend she didn't know what I was talking about. 'I . . . I don't understand, Frank. What do you mean? Why do you say that?' She was beginning to look agitated, the first sparks of panic already showing in her wide eyes.

'Calm down, Ellen. Calm down. Okay? Just listen a minute.'

'But it's true . . .'

'No, it isn't. It can't be. First of all you had me running up and down for coffee for half an hour – I couldn't understand what the big silence was all about, but now I know . . .'

'What?'

'You were busy concocting a big story for me, that's what.'

'And just why should I do that?'

'I don't know. Maybe you were fed up of me asking you about Crowther all the time and you just wanted to stop me from rootling around any more, to get me off your back. Like you said, I'm Frank the Fanatical Ferret. So you made up this great yarn about being blackmailed because you'd had a few "innocent" lunch dates with the Dishy One.

'That might have worked, Ellen, if we'd left it at that; but I screwed up your fine story by asking an awkward question: why, if the lunches *were* so innocent, didn't you just ignore Crowther and *let* him tell Laurence? To hell with Crowther! Your husband would surely take your word against Crowther's, any day.

'You saw at once that I was correct, that there was a basic flaw in your story – that, realistically speaking, you could hardly be in *serious* trouble with Laurence for just being a bit foolish and unwise, and that the tiny "crime" you had "confessed to" hardly constituted enough grounds for even the most desperate or optimistic of blackmailers. You realised that you had to come up with something much spicier than a few foolish but basically pretty harmless lunch dates, something to make your little story worthy of being an instrument of blackmail.

'And so you had another pause and, this time, invented a secret tryst that not even the most gullible or forgiving of husbands could accept – the supposed overnight rendezvous in the hotel. I'll bet you here and now, Ellen, that there never was such a meeting.'

Ellen's head stayed down, like she'd been knocked out.

'I don't know why you bothered with the he-was-drunk-so-nothing-happened bit. I assume you were trying to have your cake and eat it. Maybe you didn't want to look too bad, too wanton. So you went for the near miss, not the full head-on collision.

'Whatever the reason, there never was such a meeting. Or if there was, then you, Ellen, have reached levels of depravity which I cannot, in the depths of my being, believe you to be capable of.'

Ellen looked up and stared at me dumbstruck. But, I noticed, she didn't deny anything.

'You want to hear how I *know* it's all a lie? Aye?' When her expression didn't change I said with a quietness bordering on compassion: 'What the hell, I'm going to tell you anyway.

'Last year's call book in the practice shows that you had the problem with your stallion in early November, correct? And your name doesn't appear after that, so – according to your story and backed up by the call book – it was some time around the middle of November that you changed to Val Crowther. But that change took place only because – according to your story – Crowther had a hold on you over this illicit hotel meeting which – again, according to your story – had taken place a matter of weeks before, let's say, for argument's sake, mid to late October. Are those dates correct, Ellen? Not precisely, but near enough?'

I glared at her until she nodded.

'Right, then,' I said. 'You agree, broadly, with those dates?'

She nodded again, looking sick, maybe by now realising what was coming.

'Now let's look at some more dates. Your youngest child, I think you told me, was ten months old in the middle of this month, September. Correct? Which means he was born in mid-November last year, correct? But you've just agreed with me that your stallion was under treatment in early November last year – and I've seen the dates on the book anyway – so, if your secret hotel session with the Dishy One took place a matter of a few weeks before the stallion went bad, then that puts it at, say, mid-October. Which means that when you went to this hotel to meet your "lover" you were eight months pregnant. I suppose it's not impossible, but . . . dammit, Ellen . . . I mean . . . Come on!'

Ellen had buried her face in her hands and her shoulders were heaving. I was talking to the top of her head. I glanced quickly around but nobody seemed to be looking our way. 'There's no other way, Ellen,' I said gently. 'Is that the way it was or did you invent the whole story?' When she didn't answer, didn't even acknowledge, I murmured, 'I'll get us some more coffee.'

When I returned to the table she'd gone. I headed for the car park at the back but she wasn't there. Her car was, but she wasn't. Then, remembering the puncture, I rushed around to the street and was just in time to see her getting into a taxi.

Late that evening I worked it all out. Well, at least, a Hollywood TV series about lawyers worked it all out. Flicking through the channels, I'd caught the single word 'entrapment' and, in view of my recent snaring of Tony Robbins and his accusation of entrapment, I sat back to watch how the case unfolded. In fact, there was hardly anything about entrapment. Most of the drama centred around plea-bargaining, a process by which someone facing serious charges like murder can offer to plead guilty to a lesser charge with a guaranteed more lenient sentence. And to hell with the facts. So the perpetrator, his defence counsel and the prosecutor – and maybe even the judge, for all I know – get into a huddle and concoct a sanitised (buzzword for false) version of events, add on a happy ending, well a *relatively* happy ending compared with the electric chair, and this goes into the public record as the truth, the whole truth and nothing but the truth.

Blind Justice with twenty-twenty vision when it comes to keeping the case lists rolling; Blind Justice, standing on a plinth carrying a motto, in Latin or Greek of course, Time is Money. *Tempus Argentum Est*, or some such, carrying in one hand a gold Rolex stopwatch instead of balance scales and in the other, instead of a retributive sword, a teacher's cane.

These were the sentiments being eloquently expressed by one impossibly handsome and idealistic young lawyer on the screen. Whether plea-bargaining was right or wrong, moral or not was immaterial to me – all I knew was that plea-bargaining was exactly what Ellen had been doing when she made up her superficially seamless tale of infidelity. She had done it because, as she herself had said, she thought I'd keep ferreting around until I discovered the real truth. She had concocted something 'bad' enough to explain, with some degree of credibility, Crowther's grip on her, which at the same time might stop me from digging into the matter and getting at the *real* truth. In other words, Ellen was pleading guilty to a lesser charge.

So what the hell was the *real* charge?

In the end, it didn't really take much brainstorming to work that out.

At first, she had only shown signs of agitation when Crowther's name was mentioned, but these had been minor compared with the distress she'd evinced when I mentioned the night she had come to call on me and we'd ended up making love. That was what had really upset her so it had to be connected with that act, that night. I couldn't believe that she could still be so distressed so many years later, so it had to be something more than the act itself – some consequence of it. And the most serious consequence of unprotected lovemaking in those pre-AIDS days that I could think of was pregnancy.

For a moment I forgot all about Ellen. My thoughts were suddenly filled with wondrous images and magical pictures of fatherhood, and I felt as though I'd never be the same again, not now, not ever. Then a shouting match in the courtroom on the TV jerked me back to reality.

It suddenly seemed very naive of me not to have considered pregnancy before this, but it had never even crossed my mind because, all during our relationship, Ellen had been taking the pill and pregnancy was a thing we'd never even thought of. In my subconscious I must have assumed, if indeed it had entered my head at all, that she was still on it, now that she was with Laurence. But Laurence had gone away for three months and maybe she had decided to take advantage of his absence to give her system a rest from the daily hormone dose. That made sense – doctors recommend it.

And then, halfway through her temporary celibacy, she had called to give me back the snake ring and, for whatever reason – nostalgia, pity, loneliness or just plain old horniness – lost her head, forgot the danger and ended up in bed with me. Maybe she'd been emotionally overcome, faced with saying her final for ever goodbye to her ill-used and star-crossed devotee. Maybe this, maybe that . . . It wasn't even of academic interest at this stage.

So, if Ellen had conceived that night, then where was the baby? Our baby? Had she had a miscarriage? I ruled that out instantly – she couldn't possibly be so upset after all this time; after all, a miscarriage, although undoubtedly trauma-tising, was nobody's fault, an act of God.

Her distress carried real guilt and, for a pro-lifer like Ellen used to be – and presumably still was – that pointed to one thing only: an abortion. It was the sole explanation that could account for all that grief and guilt.

And Ellen had been vehemently pro-life. I remembered her dealing so confidently, albeit hypothetically, with all possible 'termination scenarios' during numerous debates and seminars at college. She'd had pat, infallible answers for the 'what-if-you-were-raped' question and the conundrum about abortion to save the life of the mother. She knew how to rubbish the thorny matter of terminating the 'known-to-be-malformed' foetus. She had given the most closely argued advice in numerous college and youth magazine articles and other publications; she had been indefatigable in distributing pro-life literature both on and off campus, doing long hours of voluntary work in contraception clinics, advice bureaux, student services centres ... Abortion being illegal in the Republic of Ireland, there were no clinics to picket, but if there had been Ellen would have been there every spare hour of every day. At that stage she'd had all the answers.

I thought through the almost inevitable dilemmas which pregnancy would have given rise to and I could see, at every turn, how she'd had no choice, how she'd been funnelled down a well-trodden path, worn by the desperate steps of many before her, forced to take what, for Ellen, would be that last, unthinkable, unforgivable step.

For a start she'd realise that if she wanted to keep the baby she'd have to say goodbye to Laurence and their golden future. If he'd only just left or was due back in a week or so, she might have debated trying to pretend the baby was his, although I doubt she'd have considered that. She probably wouldn't have thought of it. But even if she had, the timing was all wrong. Laurence had left in early January, Ellen had conceived in mid-February and Laurence had returned at the end of March. It had happened right slap bang in the middle.

The way I saw it, that had left her with just three choices:

She could have tried to reason with Laurence in the hope that he would forgive her and press ahead with their plans anyway. But that was fairy-tale stuff – a rare few saint-men might have agreed, but I didn't think Laurence would be one of them.

Or she could have broken off with Laurence and come back to me, the natural father of her child. That obviously had not been an option for her. She'd never even contacted me, never told me she was carrying my child and I was starting to have very mixed feelings about that.

Or she could have remained a single mother.

And that was about it, really.

Frankly, I would have bet all the shirts I had that she'd have taken the third option: remained a single mother. Perhaps I didn't know her as well as I thought I did.

But Ellen had taken the fourth choice, the unspeakable

one, given her beliefs. It must have been hell for her, like cutting out her own heart.

Frightened and alone, Ellen would have made her anguished, tortured choice and, having once done so, would have gone ahead and done what was necessary. She would have made an appointment with a clinic in Britain, presented herself at the correct time and on the correct date, then returned home, devastated, riven with guilt and self-loathing, to throw herself into the planning of her wedding with rigidly imposed joy and gusto. Anything less than a perfect display of the hope, optimism and enthusiasm expected of a bride-to-be would be spotted at once by her soon-to-be in-laws.

Christ, I thought, in the dark of the night when she was alone she must have suffered agonies.

I had no idea how, or even if, I should try to talk to Ellen about this. What right did I have to stir all that up again? I sat and brooded for a long time and eventually, before turning in for another night of fractured sleep, wrote her a letter. It was probably the most gentle and sensitive letter I've ever written in my life, full of compassion, support, understanding, well-wishing; it was an offer to help but only if requested and there wasn't a judgemental word in it. I had to write it because I couldn't possibly phone her again and, if I were just to meet her 'by happenstance' in the supermarket one more time she'd surely scream the place down demanding Security. I couldn't blame her, really.

The day she'd spuriously invited me to lunch so that she could pick my brains, Ellen Ollin née Hendricks had made the biggest mistake of her life.

Next morning at 11.05 I drove past the hairdresser that Barbara had told me was the best in town. Ellen's car was parked some way along the street, so she'd already gone in. Hoping that it wasn't one of these open-plan places where the street door gives on to the whole shop floor, I entered. The only person in sight was a magnificently coiffed and made-up lady at a small maroon leatherette reception desk this side of a dividing screen. Muzak played softly in the background and I hoped that the saccharine strains of this, plus the hum of hairdryers on the other side of the flimsy screen, would drown out my voice.

'By any chance, would there be a . . .' I turned the neatly typed (and well-sealed) envelope towards me to read off the name . . . 'Mrs Ellen Ollin here?'

'Yes, Mrs Ollin is here.'

'I was asked to deliver this letter to her and I was on my way to her house, but a lady I asked directions of told me she'd just seen her come in here. Can you give her this, please.'

'Of course. Who shall I say . . .'

'Just give her the letter, thanks. I was told there's no need to wait for a reply.'

And I scarpered, hoping that I hadn't overdone the mysterious-stranger bit. Too late I realised it was quite possible that in a small town like Monksford, the lady beneath the hair and behind the paint might have known exactly who I was, despite her asking for my name. In which case the rumours would really get going. But what the hell. I couldn't have taken a chance on posting that letter. It had to go direct to Ellen only.

'How did you find out?' The tears were coursing freely now. I passed her a handful of not very absorbent tissues from a dispenser which had appeared on the grotty little table by the plastic Doric column. We were back here again, this time at Ellen's urgent request. I'd suggested that we meet somewhere more private, or at least at a different public venue, because people would soon begin to notice and talk, but she'd insisted and I hadn't had the heart to go against her.

'Process of elimination, really,' I said and went on to map it out for her. I didn't mention the TV show. 'Is that what Crowther has on you, Ellen? Is he saying he'll tell Laurence that while he was in America his bride-to-be became pregnant by another man and . . . em . . . got rid of the baby?'

I could see her edging towards hysteria. With great difficulty she stopped herself and began in a barely controlled shaky voice: 'Frank. You remember how I used to feel about . . . what I did?'

I nodded.

'Well, then you must know how my action has affected me. Sometimes I think that it's slowly killing me. I bury myself in breeding horses, throwing parties. I've got four great children but I can never think of them without thinking of the one I don't have, the one I killed off myself . . .'

'Ellen, Ellen!' I said urgently. 'Stop torturing yourself. You've got to get a grip on life. You've got a husband and family to look after. You've got your life to lead . . .'

'Which is more than you can say for my dead child . . .' I felt like correcting her. It was '*our* dead child'. But the floodgates had opened. One or two of the nearer people noticed and I hoped they didn't recognise Ellen. Or me.

Ellen seemed suddenly aware of their glances and composed herself at once. 'I'm sorry, Frank. I thought you deserved an explanation for my odd behaviour the other day. After all, it's not as if you hadn't been involved. Perhaps I should have told you at the time, but I panicked. You probably don't want to hear this, but I loved Laurence so much that the thought of losing him was just not an option. When I say that I loved him even more than I loved you, Frank, you'll realise the intensity of my feeling for him. Because I did love you, Frank. An awful lot.'

'I loved you too, Ellen. An awful lot as well. Maybe even an awfuller lot.'

'I know.' She smiled wanly at my effort to lighten the atmosphere. 'So now, I'm glad you know. Relieved. It may even ease my guilt a little.'

'I hope so, Ellen. I really do.'

'God, I hope so, too. Now that you know, Frank, I'm going to ask you, to *beg* you, to implore and beseech you, on the love we once had for each other, never to mention it to me again. Ever!' Through the tear trails came a brief but unmistakable smile of trust. She was telling me that she knew she was safe with good ol' Frank.

What could I say? I said: 'Just one more question and you're on. Is that what Crowther had on you?'

'Yes. But don't ask me how he knew.'

Which would have been my next question.

20

It could have been a good evening and I had started out with great hopes for it. Not only were Claire and I returning the Ollins' hospitality, but I was demonstrating to anyone who might be interested that Claire and I were a team, an item, as they say.

I especially wanted Laurence to know, in case someone had told him that his wife and I had been seen, not once, but several times, quaffing coffee in the local supermarket caff, like old buddies, except that, a few days back, I'd had her sobbing hysterically.

I was beginning to wonder if Laurence knew anything at all of his wife's previous involvement with me – he had certainly never given any indication to me that he was aware of it. Maybe Ellen had never told him. I didn't know and I sure as hell wasn't going to ask.

Ellen wrecked the evening, all on her own. She had already had a head start when we met up in the bar of the Dark Horse, the best restaurant by far within twenty miles of Monksford, and she had carried on drinking purposefully while we waited for our table and during the meal. By pud time she was, frankly, pissed.

I had never seen her drunk, not even as a student, and I was not impressed. Judging by the grim expression on Laurence's face, he hadn't seen it very often either. I was relieved when she became too drunk to talk because, up until then, I was dreading her announcing to the table, and the restaurant in general, that she had had an abortion while Laurence was in New York, because I had made her pregnant.

Loose Lips Sink Ships. Relation-Ships.

Because of Ellen's pickled condition, conversation never really developed. Many, many topics arose in rapid succession, but each was chopped off prematurely by Ellen's daft and slurred comments, perhaps on a subject that had had its twenty seconds of glory way back during the soup.

At one point Dave's name came up, brought up by Laurence. He commented on how *eerie* it was to sit here in this softly lit restaurant and feel that he was looking at *Dave*, that's how incredibly alike we were. 'You could actually *be* Dave,' he said, whatever that meant.

Ellen mumbled that Dave was dead but whether this was just on a point of general information or to take issue with the last speaker's statement by pointing out a possibly hitherto overlooked but nevertheless significant difference between Dave's present state and mine I couldn't tell. Ignoring her, Laurence asked if there had been any further developments in the investigation into his death and I told him no, but that as far as I knew, the police were still working on it. Not very enthusiastically, mind you.

'You know,' Laurence went on, 'I read all the stories at the time and, after the initial shock, I began to feel that it was very unfair that Dave had been branded a common criminal without any saving graces. Because, you know, Frank – I don't need to tell you – Dave had a good side, too.

'I'm a member of the local Rotary Club and, last year, I met Dave at some function or other – nothing to do with the Rotarians – and he asked me if I knew of any charitable organisations or NGOs which dealt with deprived children in the Third World. He said he might be able to arrange some shipments of milk powder, rehydration solutions, water purification tablets, medicines and the like, if not absolutely free, then certainly for a fraction of what they were paying now. I gave him our secretary's number and I don't know what happened after that. *Mea culpa* – I ought to have followed it up. But the point is, at least he was *trying*, at least he had a social conscience, which is a lot more than you can say for many of the entrepreneurs of today.'

Despite the fact that Dave was in my bad books as he had never been before, I was genuinely moved. 'You don't know how much that means to me, Laurence,' I said. 'I've had nothing but negative crap since the day he died. I keep telling Curley – Curley's the cop in charge – that Dave was not all bad, but he just won't listen to me. As far as he's concerned, Dave was just a jerk who was too lazy to get a job and turned to the soft option.'

'A job? But Dave *had* a job. He was managing some company or other – at least that's what he told me. I asked him how he intended to supply the stuff he was offering so cheaply and he told me he ran a small pharmaceuticals suppliers on behalf of some overseas foundation which had a strong philanthropic bias. He thought it might be some kind of tax dodge, but he didn't care as long as the money went to where it was most needed.'

'I knew nothing about any of this,' I said, my heart lifting even further. Dave was the same old Dave after all. Okay, so he'd gone off the rails, a tad seriously in places, but basically, behind it all, he was the same old good-hearted, generous guy I knew, a kind of international Robin Hood . . . 'Do you know which company it was?' I asked eagerly, intending to get a few glowing references to present to that miserable, cynical bastard, Curley of Nottingham.

He thought a moment, then shook his head, bent back to his dessert and the grim evening ground on.

Some time later, during yet another hiatus in the conversation, Laurence suddenly said: 'Medineeds. That was it. That was the company – Medineeds. Not a very catchy or memorable name. As I think I've just demonstrated,' he added with the first attempt at humour from anyone all evening.

I laughed in recognition of his effort. Me? I'd never heard of Medineeds and I'm in that business. Or maybe I had, but, like Laurence, just couldn't remember.

As soon as I could decently do so I called for the bill and we trooped out into a night of fine mist, which hung golden orbs of aura on the car park lights like the most delicate of Christmas-tree decorations, and settled instantly in a dew on our hair, coat shoulders and faces. We said our goodbyes and made the usual pacts that we just must do it again some time soon. Like hell, I thought, unless Ellen gave a written guarantee to stay sober.

Ye gods! What a nightmare.

Claire and I took the long way home, the scenic route which, on a night when the moon was blanked off by low cloud and a soft drizzle, would have been daft, except we weren't interested in scenery. We just wanted fresh air and a chance to walk in a silent place, where we *knew* the unseeable vista about us was beautiful.

We walked for some minutes, breathing in cool, damp, clean air, unwinding after our fraught evening of host- and hostessing, congratulating ourselves on our brilliant decision to take a walk, even in the drizzle. Claire remarked that the fine cool aerosol of tiny rain droplets was adding to the pleasure. She was snuggled into her working anorak, which was always in the back of the Land Rover, and marching along sturdily in her farm boots. She must have looked ridiculous in her little peach silk number under the farm gear, but I couldn't see.

I had not donned any overcoat and probably looked even more ridiculous in rapidly dampening light clothes, but it felt appropriate, somehow, because I was doing penance – I was sure that tonight's dismal performance by Ellen was a direct consequence of my prying into history she was trying so desperately to forget, or at least to come to terms with.

We turned back when Claire began to sniff; the fog was getting to her lungs, she said.

Back in the Land Rover, without premeditation or warning signs, we were suddenly making love, urgently, uncomfortably and awkwardly, sprawled undignifiedly across, draped over and at times slipping down beside the front seats. Disengaging afterwards became a kind of Chinese puzzle involving limbs shackled at the ankles or knees or elbows by incompletely removed clothing and lingerie, and the more tangled we became in steering wheels, gear levers and various other metallic projections, the more hilarious it became. At one point, almost helpless with laughter, I thought I was in big trouble when a seat belt seemed to develop a malevolent life of its own and commenced purposeful efforts to strangle me.

On our way home, with Claire leaning sleepily against me, she suddenly asked, 'What's the Ollins' address, Frank? What do they call their farm?'

'Laurel House Stud Farm. Why?'

'I thought that's what it was.'

'So?'

'I just wondered. You know?'

'Know what?'

'The way some people call their houses makey-up names, by jamming bits of their own names together – like there's a house near my parents' called "Perita" and we always wondered as kids if that was the name of a place in Italy or somewhere until, years later, we found out that the names of the couple were Percy and Anita. I just wondered if Laurel House mightn't be made up of the Laur of Laurence and the El of Ellen. That's all.'

I laughed. 'I don't know, love. But I can ring in the morning and find out.'

Some minutes later, as we waited for the recently appointed nightwatchman to open the gate into the yard, Claire said, with a worried frown: 'If Benny married Anna, what should they call their new house, Frank?'

'Eh ... Benanna House?' And we both burst into laughter. That was the start of a game we still play. And love. Like kids.

We kissed goodnight, and I buried my head in my pillow and was almost instantly asleep. The all too common, gentle but persistent shake of the shoulder came moments later.

'Wha, wha ...' I grunted.

'How about Rupert and Barbara, Frank?'

'Who's Rupert and Barbara?' I'd totally lost the plot.

'The couple who live in Rubarb Villa, of course!' And the bed started shaking with her laughter. I smiled and sank back towards sleep again.

In a moment, there came yet another shake. 'Frank? If Conor married Dominique?'

'Ah, Jays, woman,' I grumbled. 'Would you ever leave me alone.'

'Oooo! Excuse me. Old peevish grumpy ass,' said the beautiful Claire in mock protest, but after a quick nibble on my shoulder she left me alone. Which was the main thing.

I was up and gone before Claire awoke and by the time I got back to the flat she had left. At the end of her four-day break she had to get back to town, even though she wasn't scheduled to go abroad for the next few days. She'd rung me on the mobile to say goodbye but she'd also left a note to inform me that she hadn't forgotten about looking up Medineeds, as she'd promised, and wondering if I could suggest a house name for her cousin, Nicholas and his wife, Ursula? They were as strait-laced and po-faced a pair of tax accountants as you could ever meet. I decided to order a twee plaque with 'Nichurs House' written on it in flowery script and, on April Fool's Day next year, fix it to their gatepost while they were at work.

A little after midday Ellen rang. (Laurence had already done so and thanked us for a great evening. He made not one single reference to Ellen's insobriety and talked plural all the time. We enjoyed . . . It was such a pleasure for us . . . We hadn't been for ages . . . We'd forgotten how good . . . Next time it'll be our treat . . . I was beginning to like the man.) Ellen suspected that she had been out of order at some stage of the evening but wasn't sure . . . ? I disclaimed all knowledge of any such lapse. When she suggested that perhaps she might have had a little too much to drink, I rejoined with a surprised 'Yeah?' as if that were news to me. To steer her off the topic I asked her if she had any idea how I might contact Cecily Curtis of the Alphabet Sisters. I said I wanted to see if this old girlfriend had any really good photographs of Dave and, if she had, then ask her for copies. As I was going up to town next day, I'd appreciate it if she could do it fairly promptly. Ellen said she knew somebody who still kept contact with Audrey, Cecily's sister, and she would see what she could do. An hour later she rang back with the posh address and telephone number of mother-of-three, Mrs Cecily Lamb. I began to feel old – Ellen, this Cecily woman, most of my erstwhile classmates, most of the friends of my youth, all married and breeding away, and here was me still, not only acting, but also thinking, like a teenager. I thanked Ellen for her help and hung up: all I wanted from Mrs Lamb was to see if she still had Grandma's snake ring and, if so, if I could buy it back.

Later, meeting PJ coming out of his office, I reminded him that I was taking tomorrow off to go to Dublin. As I had told him.

He frowned. 'You're on duty tonight, Frank, aren't you?'

'Yes.' I began to prickle all over – just what the hell had that to do with the price of turnips?

'Well, I'll take the night duty so you get going now, as soon as you like.'

Which just goes to show how wrong you can be.

21

Late that same evening I found out just how wrong Laurence
Ollin could be, too. Claire had done a quick preliminary
check on Medineeds International plc, as its full name was,
or had been, only to find it had folded and vanished almost
overnight. 'And guess when that happened, hey? At the exact
same time that Dave was murdered.'

I raised my eyebrows at that. 'Did you find out who owns
it?'

'It's one of these holding company things, with layer upon
layer of other companies blanketing the final owners. I talked
to the people over in the Business Section today and they
had a record of it, but knew very little other than that
Medineeds had done a moonlight flit. They tell me it's not
the first nor the last time that has happened in the business
world, but what makes the Medineeds vanishing trick
different from most others was that the company actually
paid off all its debts in the final days before it folded its tent
and snuck off. Because Medineeds owed nobody untold
millions, its sudden disappearance created little stir in the
business world.'

'So why vanish, then?'

'That's what the people in Business couldn't figure. And
by the way, nobody had ever heard of Dave being involved.
Now that, they said, would have been an exciting lead at the
time.'

I wondered if Curley knew anything about Medineeds.

By 10.30 next morning I found out that Curley had never heard of Medineeds International plc either. What's more, he expressed extreme doubts that Dave had been running the company, or any other company for that matter. He based this conviction on the fact that Dave had been shadowed and trailed for the last five months of his life so, if he had been running a company – actively running a company, that is – then it was almost a mathematical impossibility that this fact would not have been noticed and noted. He wound up with, 'No, Mr Samson. The only company your late cousin was involved in was bad company' and was so pleased with this witticism that he stopped briefly to admire it, then repeated it in a savouring manner. I had the feeling that, come lunch hour, the phrase would be whizzing around the staff canteen, earning sycophantic chuckles and fulsome chortles from the rank and file.

But I had to concede that Curley could be right – after all, Laurence had been talking about more than a year ago. However, didn't Curley agree that it was highly coincidental that this company should have done a runner at the exact time of Dave's death? Especially as there didn't seem to be any reason for it? Curley shrugged, conceding that it was an interesting point, but at the same time I could see the shutters coming down behind his eyes. He wasn't going to drop everything and go speeding off to check out a company which had done nothing more illegal than discharge all its debts and then leave without telling anybody. And he wasn't about to waste valuable time either on the by now stone-cold trail of a long-dead gangster.

'Well, how about that A.C. cheque, then? Did you try to see why that hadn't been cashed?'

'Yes,' he replied with exaggerated weariness. 'We sent it to the deceased's nearest surviving relative to see if he could throw any light on it or suggest who or what A.C. might stand for, but you couldn't. So there. We're not about to comb the land for businesses and people whose initials are A.C. If the cheque had been made out to a Z.Q., then maybe, but A.C.? Not a chance. Forget it.'

Curley was in one of his moods. I couldn't really blame him for his impatient sarcasm – during the short time I'd been sitting across from him there'd been an almost constant chain of phone calls, people coming in and out with papers for his attention, for his signature . . . When next he had a spare second I rose, held out my hand and said to him: 'You need a holiday or you'll end up being able to ask Dave, corpse to corpse, who it was that killed him.'

'Sorry about this,' he said, reaching for the importunate phone with his left hand. 'Well, if I do have that opportunity I'll get back to you next Hallowe'en at midnight, okay?' He smiled as he let go my hand. I was about to come back with something spirited about having the Ouija board set up and ready, but he had already turned his eyes away from me and was giving the phone his full attention. 'Hello? Yes. Speaking . . .' I just walked out.

The Firm was in the second echelon of Dublin's fitness and health clubs. The name, as all the employees were instructed to explain, had nothing to do with a cool in-name for the mafia; nor did it have anything to do with business – as like being a synonym for company, concern, or suchlike – nor was it meant to appeal to lawyers who felt like being part of a John Grisham 'firm'. It simply was The Firm as opposed to The Flabby. It struck me that if it was so subtle that it had to be explained, then they should have called it something else altogether like, for instance, Muscles. Shortish, perhaps, on subtlety but at least everyone knew where they stood.

The Firm had most of the facilities which the top clubs had, except for residential quarters where serious seekers of eternal youth could clock themselves in for weekends of healthy pampering. I had joined some years before on Dave's recommendation and had kept up my annual membership. I found myself using it less and less often of late, but I still knew all the staff, both administrative and technical. Dave and I had shared the same trainer, a fine specimen and walking advertisement for the club, called Nils. Nils had a purple birthmark on the left side of his face and neck, from cheekbone to collar bone, and I often wondered if the reason he kept himself in such tiptop shape wasn't to offset this slight and superficial blemish on an otherwise perfect physique. Clearly, I never asked. Nor did I ask him where he'd got the name. Was he of Scandinavian stock and, if so, why did he speak with such a broad Dublin accent?

'Hey, Mr Samson!' He spotted me lurking in the doorway and came across, hand outstretched, large smile. 'Long time no see. Where ya bin, man?' The broad Dublin accent had became tinged with a soupçon of Brooklyn.

'I've been busy, Nils. Jeez, you look good.'

Without thinking, Nils did something which reduced slightly his overall size but made him lumpy all over. An uninitiated observer could have been forgiven for thinking he might have been trying to pass a small but bothersome parcel of wind or something. He held the body clench for a moment, then relaxed, releasing the briefly stopped breath while hanging on to the smile. 'Listen, Mr Samson . . . I was real sorry about Mr Ryder. Sorry I couldn't get to the funeral . . .'

'Yeah, Nils. It was a shock. And him in the best of shape at the time . . .'

'Jeez, man, that's what bugs me the most. I had him goin' great. He was in here the day before . . . or that same day, maybe. What time did it happen?'

'Small hours of the morning. Well, after midnight.'

'Yeah? Well, then it was the day before. We did a big work-out and afterwards we talked about stepping up the pressure even further for the ah, the ah, future . . . He seemed in pretty good form. I mean, like, man, he seemed – normal.'

'What time did he leave, do you remember?' At this, Nils looked at me oddly. This was more than just reminiscing. Nostalgia with pointed questions. I saw him realising for the first time that I didn't have a kitbag with me and figuring out that I wasn't here for one of my increasingly infrequent bursts of activity. 'I'm only trying to find out about his last hours, Nils. As you know, we were cousins.'

'Man, I thought you were *brothers* until I saw the different surnames.' He shrugged. 'I'd say it was about fourish, not much later. I had a four p.m. client and he was already doing warm-ups when Mr Ryder left.'

'Left you or left the building?'

'Left me. I didn't see him leave the building.'

'When he left you, had he already showered and dressed?'

'No. Like I said, he'd just finished his workout and we were talking about upping the . . .'

'What about your client? How come you were still with Dave while your four o'clock man was already on the floor?'

'He's not a regular and he's no spring chicken. He needed a long warm-up, man, like, I'm talkin' hey, most of his hour. He didn't mind; he could get along with it. I was keeping a good eye on him. Just like I'm doing now with that gentleman in the fetching mauve tracksuit over there.' He raised a hand in salute and the mauve-suited one answered with a similar wave. I couldn't see how he had spotted Nils's wave as he had his back to us. Mirrors, I supposed. There were enough of them around anyway – 360° narcissism.

'I suppose Dave didn't mention where he was going after he left here?' This was a real shot in the dark: why should Dave have told Nils where he was going?

'The doctor's,' Nils said immediately.

'The *doctor*'s?'

'Yep. He said he had a doctor's appointment at four thirty.'

'You remember that?'

'Clear as day. Like I said, we were discussing his new regime but he interrupted me – he said he was sorry, but he had a four thirty doctor's appointment and he'd have to get back to me about the new routine during the week.'

'You sure he said doctor? Not dentist?'

'You're wondering why he was going to a doctor, right? Just after a heavy workout, which he breezed through, without hardly sweating, correct?'

'Correct.'

'And why, if he'd been sick earlier in the day, he hadn't

just called in and cancelled the session, aye? That's what you're asking yourself, right?'

'Right.'

'It bamboozled me, too. "Go figure," I said to myself. I mean the guy was almost as fit as me and I haven't been to a doctor since I had my polio drop-on-the-sugar-lump. Touch wood,' he said, rapping the door frame with, presumably, incredibly fit knuckles. I waited for more but there wasn't any.

'He didn't mention a name? Or address?'

'Nah.' Nils shook his head. 'Sorry, man. No names. He just said he had an appointment.' He appraised me professionally. 'You doin' any gym work, Mr Samson? Looks like the spare tyre is ahead on points at this stage. You need to call in to see us more often.'

'Time, Nils. Time is the problem.' I pinched the incipient midriff roll with a rueful expression. This was purely for Nils's benefit because I couldn't have cared less, at least not at the moment. I had other things on my mind.

As I eased the Land Rover out into the lunchtime traffic, the pips for the one o'clock news came over the radio and, as is my custom, I checked the dashboard clock. Spot on.

Driving along, I got to thinking that a doctor's appointment after such a vigorous workout didn't have to be so strange after all. I mean, Dave could have been going to a dermatologist to see about a rash or a mole; or to a plastic surgeon to see about a nose job; or to a physician for a full medical (after a workout) for insurance purposes. You didn't actually have to be *sick* to go to a doctor. Maybe he needed a tetanus jab. Although £75 for a tetanus jab would be a little on the pricey side.

But I was jumping to conclusions; there was nothing whatever to say that the A.C. cheque had been made out to the doctor. In fact, it probably wasn't – if I'd written a cheque for a doctor, I'd have instinctively written 'Doc' or 'Dr' or, in this case, 'Dr C' on the stub. Dave might have made many stops that afternoon and, realistically, the A.C.

cheque could have been for any of them. It might even, I suddenly thought, have been made out to Audrey Curtis, the first of the Alphabet Sisters. I'd have to check it out with Cecily when we met.

I passed Gaynor's off-licence and noted the time on the dash clock – 13.17. The driving part of the journey had taken seventeen minutes and there hadn't been any delays or hold-ups. I decided to accept seventeen minutes as a reasonable average time for the trip between The Firm and Gaynor's. The first parking space I found was almost half a mile further on and I walked back along a crowded pavement with seemingly everyone hurrying in the other direction. They all appeared to have worried, preoccupied expressions on their faces, as if there were a bomb scare up ahead.

The shop itself was quiet and it was easy to believe that it had, as the gold leaf sign on the door claimed, been 'Estd. 1875'. It seemed not to have changed since then and was filled with the hushed, almost reverential air of a library. It was empty, except for a figure observing me politely from behind the counter. He looked like a butler, although never having met a man of that profession I only had a casting director's idea of what they looked like. Ignoring the self-proclaimed 'superior' wines in racks on all sides, I approached him and introduced myself. I asked him if he was Mr Gaynor and he replied that he was the *present* Mr Gaynor.

Dave had been a regular customer and he had known him well. A most unfortunate incident. Yes indeed, he remembered well the last time Mr Ryder had been in, the evening before . . . the . . . unfortunate incident. A butler with limited powers of expression.

He himself had served him. Could he remember the approximate time of Dave's visit? Roughly 5.10. He knew this because he always went for his tea at 5.30, when his son, the *young* Mr Gaynor, relieved him for an hour and Mr Ryder had come in some twenty minutes before that, perhaps a little more, but hardly thirty minutes before. Was there any particular reason why he remembered Dave's visit so well? After all, it had happened a long time ago now. Had there been anything odd or memorable about that particular occasion? Nothing sir, except that he had read, the very next day, how Mr Ryder had been found dead and he'd been surprised. Surprised? *Very* limited powers of expression.

Having established that Dave had made no mention of where he'd come from or what his next destination was to be, I asked the present Mr Gaynor if he had noticed anything strange about him?

'Strange, sir?'

I gave him some hints: had he been (noticeably) agitated, reflective, depressed-looking, thoughtful, pensive, worried-looking, excited, or in any way at odds with his usual, normal self.

The present Mr Gaynor hadn't noticed.

I bought a couple of bottles of what I was told had been Dave's favourite wine, just for nostalgia's sake, and left. Not much info there.

Except the time. If Dave had a doctor's appointment at 4.30 and was in the august presence of the present Mr Gaynor by 5.10, latest, then he had probably come straight from the doctor's. He could hardly have had time to fit in yet another call – as it was, the visit to the surgery would seem to have been uncommonly brief. In these circumstances the A.C. cheque, sandwiched as it was between the other two, had probably been made out to the doctor after all. Devil's advocating just for the hell of it, I threw in an objection to my reasoning: could Dave not have posted off the cheque to someone he owed money to? In theory, yes, but in practice, hardly. As I'd already figured, there just wouldn't have been time. And so I decided to settle for the hypothesis that A.C. and the doctor were one and the same.

So why hadn't the doctor lodged it? Indeed, why (more probably) hadn't the secretary or receptionist lodged it with the rest of the takings. I couldn't imagine a doctor being so upset about the death of a patient that he/she couldn't bear to cash an ante-mortem cheque. There couldn't even be vague guilt feelings in this case, as Dave had not died because of slipshod medical advice or care; he'd been murdered. Or OD-ed if you wanted to accept Curley's less troublesome theory.

And what kind of physician would be charging £75 per consultation? Maybe all of them, I suddenly thought. Maybe that was the minimum fee now for a surgery visit. What did I know? For I, like Nils, hadn't been near a doctor since childhood. I looked around for some wood to touch for luck, and almost ran into the car in front of me.

Paying more attention, now, to the traffic stream of which I formed an integral but inattentive part, I suspended deep thinking on Dave and the doctor. The only other real thought I had on the subject was that the £75 might have been in respect of a course of treatment he'd undergone, payment for a series of visits already completed. I wondered if Dave had kept an appointments diary – busy man like him.

I hooked up with Claire for a quick sandwich. The idea, when we'd parted this morning, had been that she would come with me for the afternoon and we would do the 'further investigations' together. However, she was too tied up and there wasn't even time to update her on the morning's developments before she rushed off out again, clutching her half-eaten sandwich.

I called Curley about the diary. I was lucky to get through first go off, but unlucky in my quest. No appointments diary had been found among Dave's effects.

I waited until I was out of the noisy sandwich bar and in the Land Rover before making my next call. With the number Ellen had given me propped on the dashboard, I pushed the buttons on my cellphone and cleared my throat to produce the most respectable voice I could. 'Mrs Lamb?' I sang brightly when the phone was picked up.

But it was not Mrs Lamb – it was the housekeeper and Mrs Lamb was having a lie-down.

'Oh. When's a good time to get her?' More brightness, this time trying to impress the housekeeper.

'Who is this, please?'

'My name is Frank Samson. Actually, Mrs Lamb doesn't know me.'

'I see. Can I give her a message?'

'Well, I need to talk to her, just for a few minutes.'

'Hold on, please. I'll see if she's awake.'

'Wait!' I shouted.

'Yes?'

'Sorry for shouting like that – I thought you'd gone. Please tell her that I'm Dave Ryder's cousin and that I'd like to call at her convenience to talk briefly with her. It shouldn't take more than ten or fifteen minutes max.'

'I'll tell her – if she's awake. I'm not going to wake her.'

'Of course not.' You crabby old battleaxe!

In a few minutes she was back. Mrs Lamb, presumably awake, had said she could see me any time between 4.30 and 6 this afternoon. Did I have the address?

With time to kill I searched for, and eventually found, the derelict premises from which Medineeds had carried on its business before bolting. It was a tiny office in a small cul-de-sac not far from the canal and I wondered what sort of business could be carried out from here. It was no bigger than a small launderette, but I knew I was at the right place because I could just about read the name Medineeds International plc on a dust-covered notice which had fallen to the floor, presumably from the relatively clear rectangle of window-pane through which I was peering. The rest of the plate-glass window was almost totally opaque.

A stout peroxide blonde, long overdue another go at the bottle, appeared at a door a few houses down and watched me cup my hands to the filthy glass for another look. 'There's nothing in there to see, son. Not even a chair.'

'Hello,' I said, moving towards her. She was wearing a dangerously stretched floral nylon housecoat. 'Has it been closed for long?'

'Months. They came in a van and carted all the stuff away. Three trips, it took. To empty it.'

'Who's "they"?'

'I don't know. Never saw them before.'

'What kind of van?'

'A white one. Just a big delivery van. Like you see all over.'

'Nothing written on the side? Like the name of a van rental company or any other company?'

'If there was, I don't remember. Are you the cops?'

'No. Not exactly. I'm an investigator,' I lied, although technically speaking it was, at least at that moment, the truth. I *was* investigating. Well, more like mooching about, really, but I couldn't very well tell her I was a moocher.

'Yeah?'

'Yeah.'

'I seen loads of them on TV but I never met a real one. Kept busy, are you?'

'Run off me feet most of the time. Do you know anyone who used to work here?'

'Aye. Charlie McMahon.'

'Do you know where I can find him?'

'No need, love. He should be here any minute.'

'How come?'

'I phoned him as soon as I saw you. I thought you were the chap who used to be in and out. From the back you look the same. Even from the front there's a strong likeness.'

'So I've been told. But that guy, the one who looked like me – he's been dead for months. What made you think I could be him?'

'I knew one of them was dead – just didn't know which. There was another one who used to come, too. But neither of them ever came more than once every couple of weeks.'

'But there were loads of photographs of the one who died, the one who looked like me. All over the papers and TV . . .'

'I never read the papers and I only watch the soaps on the telly. Everything else on the box is rubbish. Ah, here comes Charlie now.'

Charlie coasted an elderly Honda 250cc to a halt beside us and, staring at me, removed his helmet.

'Sorry, Char,' said the woman. 'It's not him. False alarm.'

'That's all right, Kate. But this one looks like Dave, Kate, the one that died. So how could it have been Dave?'

I was glad that Charlie, too, was unimpressed with Kate's conclusions.

'I know, Charlie. But you see, I wasn't sure which o' them had died. It coulda been the other one.'

He turned to me and put out his hand. 'Charlie McMahon,' he said.

'Frank Samson. I'm pleased to meet you. You got here in a flash, Charlie.'

'I'm owed redundancy money and I'd like to sue for unfair dismissal. I know me rights and where's a man o' my age supposed to get another job, aye?'

'I'm sorry about all that Charlie, but I don't think I can help.'

'Have ye nothin' to do with this place, then? You must be Dave's brother.'

'Cousin, Charlie, his cousin. I had no idea that this place even existed until a couple of days ago.'

'He's a private eye, Char. Like Magnum PI.'

'Oh!' said Charlie, clearly impressed.

'Can you tell me what you did here, Charlie, what your work was?'

Charlie did, in a rambling way, from which it was clear that he didn't really know what he did. All he did, he said, was work the computer. But he had no computer skills whatever and couldn't tell me what he was doing. He had been shown a series of movements; he knew how to move the mouse and he spoke with some reverence of 'double-clicking' as if it were a rare ability. 'Real fast, with one finger. DA-DA! Like that. It takes a while to get the hang of it. DA-DA!'

Mind you, I'm no computer hotshot either, but it sounded to me as though he would download certain incoming data on to floppy disks, which he would then place in a wall safe, the only thing that the company had left behind, wide open and empty. He had never opened a floppy to see what was on it; he didn't even know what I was talking about because he told me that the floppies he used couldn't be opened, not without damaging them like, 'cause they were all of a piece, no screws nor tabs – nothin'! Charlie was the eunuch in the harem, the illiterate, deaf-mute servant in the inner, secret sanctums of power.

'What happened to the floppies, Charlie – the ones you put in the wall safe?'

'They'd be gone the next time I looked. When they'd phone me to tell me what time I was to switch on the computer, they'd give me the new combination for the safe at the same time. It was always different.'

'You mentioned that there were two men, Dave and . . . Do you know the name of the other one?'

'Sure I do. Val.'

Talk about keeping the best wine until last! 'Val what, Charlie?'

'Haven't a clue. They never introduced themselves at all. I just picked up the Dave and the Val bits by hearing them talk, call one another. Just like you now know this lady's name, I'll bet?'

'Kate,' I said.

'See?'

Charlie had a key and we spent a long time in the small dingy office, searching for any tiny scrap of an invoice or a letter which might have thrown some light on whatever activity went on here, but there was nothing at all. Apart from the open wall safe and the notice on the floor, the place had been swept bare. There might have been fingerprints and I decided I'd mention the possibility to Curley later on, but I knew he wouldn't do anything, apart from giving me a bollocking for poking about where I had no business to be, so I decided that maybe I wouldn't tell him after all.

I asked Charlie to describe Val and it was Crowther to a T. I took both my companions' phone numbers and, promising Charlie that I'd have a go at getting him his redundancy money, left to ponder over this latest link-up.

And this one connected Crowther to Dave right at the time of Dave's death.

The question now was: had Dave been murdered because

Medineeds had closed down or had Medineeds been closed down because Dave had been murdered? Or had both acts merely been parts of some wider scenario? And what, if anything, did Crowther have to do with it?

And finally, how come the Business Section boys of the *Daily Instructor* were even aware of the close-down of such a seemingly tiny, one-employee operation?

22

Cecily Lamb kept me waiting for almost ten minutes. As I walked through her front gate and up along her twenty-metre pathway, I caught a curtain flicker at an upstairs window, and glimpsed a face, a fleeting, thirty-something female face as it drew quickly back into the shadow of the room. Trying to look as if I hadn't noticed her, I continued to the front door of the opulent, creeper-clad, detached des res in the heart of Dublin's stockbroker belt. I'd arrived at exactly five o'clock, thinking it better to put in an appearance nearer the middle of the time she had indicated. Too early and she might have felt I was rushing her; too late could signal that I didn't give a damn one way or another. And above all, I wanted her to be in a good mood, favourably disposed to me.

I needed just two things from Mrs Cecily Lamb: irrefutable proof that it was Dave who had stolen the ring and, for some odd reason – whether it was connected to Ellen or Grandma or even to Claire, I knew not – to try to get it back. Maybe I felt I owed it to Grandma or perhaps I had some idea that if I did manage to retrieve it it would lessen Dave's 'crime'. The whole bloody world was at it, me included. Plea-bargaining a grand larceny rap down to the far lesser charge of 'temporary borrowing without informing the borrowee'.

The housekeeper, who actually *was* a grumpy old wagon, left me in a room where three small blonde girls were glued to cartoons on the TV. I wondered if they, too, had been named A, B and C. I sat through a couple of Popeye shows and could have altered colour and shape, developed many new heads, and changed both the location and quantity of my limbs several times over, without the little blondes being aware of a thing.

When Cecily arrived she was done up to the last, as if she were off to the ball. She looked steadily at me as she approached, then gave me a cool hand. 'Mr Samson, I presume?' She laughed quickly, nervously. 'You look more like his *brother*. It's uncanny. I'd recognise you anywhere.'

She'd featured in at least three of Dave's photographs with women, the ones I'd searched so assiduously for a sign of Ellen's ring. 'I'd recognise you too. You haven't changed a bit.' In fact she had and I wouldn't have recognised her at all, anywhere, not even if she'd been carrying enlarged copies of the photographs.

This puzzled her. She furrowed an already slightly furrowed brow as we crossed the hall towards a more formal sitting room. 'Have we met before, then?'

'No.' I laughed politely and semi-heartily at her erroneous conclusion. 'Ha, ha, ha.' Like that. I wanted to keep her as sweet as I could. 'No, we haven't . . .'

'I didn't think so. I'm sure I'd have remembered. So how . . . ?'

'I recognise you from your photographs.' Not to mention – I remembered her steamy letters to Dave – the tits.

'Which photographs?' She indicated an armchair.

'The ones Dave had. He had lots of photographs of you. Lots,' I repeated and hoped I hadn't overdone it.

'Ah, Dave,' she said, with a melodramatic sigh. 'He was a wild one all right.'

We talked wall to wall Dave for a while, his life, his death, but the trawl didn't come up with anything even vaguely useful.

I asked her about their friends. She mentioned some of hers but said she'd hardly known any of Dave's, because they liked being alone. Reading between the lines, and interpreting the looks and the body language, I reckoned that she and Dave seemed to have spent most of their time together horizontal.

She'd been abroad, she said, when he had died. Otherwise she'd have been at the funeral. *She* would have been; her husband wouldn't. I gathered, as I was clearly meant to, that Dave had not been Mr Lamb's favourite person. The reason for this was pointedly not stated: I could draw my own conclusions. Leftover jealousy from before they were married, or what? Mrs Lamb's change of tone when she mentioned her husband gave out signals as blatant as distress flares, that she was lacking excitement and adventure in her now sedentary suburban life. I had the feeling that Dave had either been the actual high point of her life himself, or had happened to her at the zenith of her time.

Eventually I gave up on the idea of finding any groundbreaking clues about his death and worked the conversation around to the snake ring. I asked her if she still had it, explained that it was, although of little value, a kind of family heirloom with long and deep significance for 'our people' and told her that if she'd consider selling it I'd be willing to give her a fair price for it – plus more. I was thinking of becoming engaged myself in the future and I would very much like to be able to give it to the woman I loved . . . 'Not as the actual engagement ring, of course,' I assured her quickly, making an instant course correction when I saw the look of horrified disbelief steal into the corners of her eyes. Clearly, heirloom or not, old snake-eyes would not pass for an engagement ring.

'You're not married either, then?'

'No.'

'How come two sexy hunks like you and Dave managed to escape capture for so long?' Was she beginning to flirt seriously? Shit, I hoped not. Then, remembering her throbbingly lusty letters, I thought that probably she was. I shrugged, but couldn't think of a reply. 'Too busy playing the field,' she said. 'That's why. Breaking hearts all over the place, lovin' them and leavin' them. You don't have to look innocent, Mr Samson. I know you guys. Remember? Inside and out!'

Instinctively, my thighs clenched.

The housekeeper brought in tea and biscuits just as Cecily was telling me that if I lived up to my surname half as well as Dave Ryder had to his ('and I'm not talking horses here') then I must be as strong as an ox. The intrusion saved me having to answer, although I already had decided on nothing more than a pleasant and slightly puzzled grin.

I wondered, as the tray was unloaded and its contents placed in their 'proper' positions on the low table between us, if Cecily was some sort of nymphomaniac who accosted men in general or if it was just because I reminded her so much of her late demon lover. I gave her the benefit of the doubt.

'How ever did you find me?' she asked, pouring.

'A woman I know used to know your sister, Audrey . . .'

'Oh?' She inclined the teapot spout slightly towards the vertical. 'Who's that, then?'

'Ellen Hendricks.'

'Ah, yes.' She resumed pouring. 'Ellen. I remember her. I didn't know her well, though. As you said, she was Audrey's friend. Audrey is older than I am. Then there's Beatrice, then me. A, B and C, me. They used to call us the Alphabet Sisters.'

I laughed heartily. 'The Alphabet Sisters! I like it! Cle-*ver*! You must be very close.'

'No more than ordinary sisters. It's not like we were identical triplets or something.'

'Still. I bet you all live within a few miles of each other?' I reckoned that I wouldn't get a more natural lead-in to ask about Dave's A.C. cheque.

'No. Beatrice is an architect and lives in London – she's not married, she's a career woman, she says – and Audrey and her husband own several hotels in California. He's of Polish extraction and has an unpronounceable surname beginning with Z-C-W- or some such and she rarely comes home, maybe once every two years. We're going out to stay with them this Christmas. "Wel–come to the Ho–tel Ca–lif–ornia,"' she sang and laughed.

'Did your sisters know Dave?' I asked, grinning back.

'I think Audrey might have met him once, years ago, but Beatrice would have been off at college or else travelling the world.'

Strike Audrey as the payee. The cheque stub would have read A. ZCW . . . not A.C. Back to the doctor.

'By the way, how is Ellen now?'

That pulled me up sharpish. '*Now*? What do you mean, now? Has she been ill?'

Suddenly she looked worried. She put a hand up to her mouth. 'God! *She*'s not your wife-to-be, is she?'

'Ellen has been married for years. She's Mrs Ollin now.'

'Phew! That's a relief. I thought that you . . . I'm always putting my foot in it . . . Has she got children?'

'Four. All under the age of seven or thereabouts.'

'Ah, that's good. So much for her worrying herself to death, then. Audrey told me, oh, years ago, that Ellen Hendricks was almost a basket case . . .'

'*Yeah*? She seems to be a perfectly ordinary, well-adjusted, pleasant woman now. Was something the matter with her?' I hadn't come to investigate Ellen, but Cecily had brought it up and I was only being mannerly, making polite conversation. It would have been unforgivably rude of me to cut my hostess dead. Or so I told myself.

'Well, I don't know for *sure* but when a woman who holds the rigid views on the sanctity of the life of the unborn foetus that Ellen Hendricks did suddenly starts panicking that she'll never be able to have children, two and two would suggest . . .' She stopped, perhaps deciding she'd said enough, or maybe searching for a euphemism.

'A quick trip to the UK, you mean?' I offered, supplying one.

'The UK? What for? There are lots of clinics in town. Not openly trading, you understand, but . . .'

'That may be true of now,' I cut in, 'but didn't you say that Ellen was worried about this years ago?'

'Not *that* many years. *You*'re talking the dark ages. Where've you been? Nearly everybody knew who to go to if they got themselves into trouble. And if you didn't know, all you had to do was ask. And I'm not talking back-street hags with filthy knitting needles either. There were lots of doctors doing it, especially the younger ones, the ones who were hungry for money, impatient to catch up. You'd be surprised at some of the present pillars of the medical profession who, in their earlier years, kept themselves swathed in Armani mohair by doing illegal abortions for Dublin's finest.'

She shook her head, as if she herself found it hard to believe. 'Do you want to see the snake ring?' she asked suddenly.

'I'd love to, if it's not too much trouble.' I sprang up because she had.

'No trouble,' she said and left the room. I watched her go, musing that if she'd tried walking out crabwise they'd have had to widen the door.

Christ, what a mess! No wonder Crowther had found out about the abortion. I hadn't been ten minutes talking to this total stranger and she had told me. And Ellen thought it was a secret. Hah! They were probably still discussing it on the buses and in pubs and up and down the length of cold, shuffling queues all over Dublin. I didn't know whether I should tell her when I got back to Monksford or not. I wondered if Laurence also knew. Probably not, I thought, because if he did, then Crowther would have had no hold over Ellen.

When Cecily returned, wearing the ring, I longed to ask her if there were any theories about who might have got Ellen pregnant, but decided it was too chancy – the subject had passed and to reopen it would in itself invite unwholesome speculation.

I was surprised, when I took the ring from her hand, that it had lost all its magic for me. Perhaps it had become too closely associated with the negative parts of my life – Ellen's leaving me and, in the very recent past, the traumatic discovery that Dave had stolen it.

But I had come to get it back, if possible, and I still felt I ought to try, even if it was only for the sake of Grandma's memory. So I oohed and ahed over it, and tried to develop a look like a mystic, eyes half focused like an old Sioux chief making his last visit to the sacred burial grounds of his tribe, communing with unknown and countless generations of forebears, letting the plasma of the universe and of my clan flow and surge through me, and feeling a right twit. Through my slitted eyes I could see Cecily of the incredible knockers watching me, taking it all in and, when eventually I shook my head out of its trance and stretched the ring out to her, she said: 'No. You keep it. It obviously means so much to you . . .'

'Oh, no, I couldn't. I mean Dave gave it to you . . .'

'I've got other ways to remember Dave . . .' She firmly placed the ring in my palm and folded my fingers over it. 'Now, take it.'

'Aw . . . hell! I feel awful . . . Well I insist on paying for it.'

'Look, just take it. Knowing it's back where it belongs is enough for me.'

And that was how Grandma's snake ring came back into the family.

It was already developing a tragic history. One grandson gives it to the woman he loves, only for him to suffer great misfortune and unhappiness when she gives him the boot and leaves his young life in touch-and-go ruins.

Then, later, she returns the heirloom, which is immediately stolen by another grandson who gives it to a woman he loves (?) – or at least wants to shag – but he is subsequently murdered.

Then the first grandson, the one to whom the curse was originally passed, relocates it and gets it back from his murdered cousin's ex-lover, who has herself been punished by marrying a cruel husband . . . It didn't take much imagination: 'The Curse of the Mummy's Tomb', 'The

Curse of the Grandmummy's Ring' . . . You can see how these things get off the ground . . .

I was wondering if Grandma had given it first to her son, Edward, who had been killed, water-skiing, a few months after his wedding, when Cecily Lamb glanced at the ornamental mantel clock and asked me to leave. Her husband was due home and, because of my uncanny resemblance to Dave, whom he hated, even still, after his death, she feared that my presence in the house would be enough to put him in bad form for weeks, which would end up being a pain in the ass for her, not to mention Deirdre, Ethel and Francine, their three alphabetical blonde daughters.

As I drove away, waving vigorously to the figure in the doorway, I wondered why, as I'd passed her by at the hall door, she'd had tears in her eyes. They couldn't have been for me, so were they for Dave, or for her rapidly receding youth? I felt incredible sorry for her at that moment.

Ages and ages later I met Cecily at some party or other. The pity I'd felt for her flared up again, almost as a reflex, and I immediately went across the room to her. I'm soft, both in the heart and in the head, because Cecily was a transformed woman.

Within minutes she told me she thought that ring had been the ugliest piece of chicken-shit jewellery she had ever seen, that she had never, ever, worn it and that she'd kept meaning to throw it out, but hadn't got around to it and couldn't believe her luck when I turned up, actually looking for the damned thing. She, she admitted with a great laugh which wobbled her upper slopes alarmingly, had been ham acting and had felt all along that I had been, too. She slitted her eyes and did a good imitation of my ancient Sioux chief impression and we both folded up with laughter. I thought Cecily might have trouble straightening up again, being on the top-heavy side and, with a lewd wink, said so, which only doubled us up even more.

As we'd both been a bit tiddly and in a confessional mood, I told her, with much nudging and winking, that I'd read her letters to Dave. Many times. I said she had a real future as a writer of soft porn and she told me that those early letters to Dave were mild by comparison. 'Actions speak louder than words, you know. Any day. Or any night, even. Or . . . just any time!' She said if I wanted to read a really horny-porny letter, then she'd write me a special one – provided, of course, she could find some heat-resistant paper (more folding up with hilarity and knee-slapping) – and we could meet and discuss it later. I think I waggled my eyebrows in reply, but she couldn't have known what it meant, because I myself didn't. Anyway, the letter never arrived. Perhaps she's still writing it. Or maybe it just keeps spontaneously combusting.

Back on the streets again, I wondered where I should go from here.

What, for instance, should I do with the information about Medineeds, Crowther and Dave? After all, as far as anyone knew, there was nothing illegal about the company, although I'd long since stopped believing that it was a charitable organisation dedicated to the supply of cheap food and medicines to the starving and ailing masses. Once I knew Crowther was involved and heard Charlie McMahon's vague description of his 'computer job', it was obvious that there was something fishy about it – honest businesses are just not run like that.

I re-reconsidered my earlier reconsideration but it still didn't seem worthwhile approaching Curley – I knew his attitude only too well. His priorities were not mine and vice versa. I thought of going to see him but changed my mind and instead, dropped the ring off at a jeweller's for cleaning. Driving away, I hoped that none of Dave's old gang would rob the joint until I had it back. Now that would *really* get the legend going.

Back at the flat, I topped a beer and sat, thinking hard, trying to figure how I was going to work out who A.C. was. I thought the timing through again, this time jotting down notes, as it was far too complex to keep track of mentally.

Dave leaves Nils at 4. Allow another ten minutes for him to shower, change and pay his bill – if he hadn't already attended to that on the way in – and that would put him exiting the building at, say, 4.10 at the *absolute* earliest – one hour exactly before he turned up at Gaynor's.

From that sixty minutes, I now had to deduct seventeen minutes of driving time, which left me with forty-three minutes.

Another time adjustment would have to be made for parking and retrieving his car. I decided to give him really close-by parking everywhere – a mere four minutes for each episode, which was really generous in that part of the city. So – assuming, of course, that he hadn't been able to walk to the doctor's at either end – that meant he had to retrieve his car when he left The Firm, park and retrieve it at the doctor's and park it at Gaynor's – four four-minute jobs, another sixteen minutes gone.

That left me with twenty-seven minutes at the doctor's, but *only* if the surgery was actually *on the direct route* between The Firm and Gaynor's.

I thought of what would happen at the doctor's – a short sit in the waiting room, then actually going in to see him, then coming out and paying the bill with the cheque – again assuming that the doctor actually was A.C., which I'd already accepted as being the case. So I gave Dave four minutes in the waiting room – or having his details taken or whatever – and four minutes afterwards to get his bill, write his cheque etc. and that meant that I had to deduct another eight minutes from my running total of twenty-seven. Which left me with nineteen minutes actually with the doctor.

That was reasonable. In fact, I would have thought that ten minutes might have been more like an average, or even less, as he wasn't actually sick.

I decided at this point that I might have been slightly optimistic in my timings and deducted another five minutes as a correction factor. I now had fourteen minutes' consultation time. I reminded myself again that this only applied if the doctor's visit required no deviation from the direct route.

If Dave had had to deviate from that route, then, allowing a mere five minutes' consultation, he had, at most, nine minutes of extra driving time and, as he had to get back on his main route again, that meant that, at the very most, the doctor could be four and a half minutes' driving off Dave's direct pathway from The Firm to the off-licence.

That narrowed things down a fair bit. Apart from indicating the general area of the surgery, it also meant that Dave just wouldn't have had the time to make another unsuspected visit to someone else (an A.C.?). He wouldn't even have had the time to write a cheque and post it off to a faraway A.C. Therefore A.C. almost had to be the doctor.

I went to the desk and fetched back an *A to Z* of Dublin. I located the spot on which The Firm stood, then pinpointed the booze shop. Both were within the main city area, the part that nearly everyone who had spent any time at all in Dublin would know well. These became my two fixed points and I drew a figure which resembled a boomerang-shaped sausage enclosing both premises, one in either rounded end. The bend in the sausage was necessitated by the bend in the main way between the two premises; the width of the sausage was supposed to represent a four-and-a-half-minute drive to left and right of the main thoroughfare.

Having now defined my search area, I fetched another beer and the Yellow Pages, and ran my finger down the list of doctors to the Cs. There were almost thirty Cs but only seven with an A in their initials and of these, only two were within my area. I jotted down their addresses and phone numbers, and put an asterisk against Cronin, Alfred, P. Not that I had any reason to suspect Alfred P. in particular, but the other one was Clancy, Rosalyn A., Specialist in Gynaecology and Obstetrics. If I had to place a bet, it would not be on Rosalyn A.

Then I noticed that what I had been reading through was a list of GPs – don't ask me how Rosalyn A. had strayed in –

which meant that I'd missed out on specialists. Fitzwilliam Square, Dublin's answer to Harley Street, was in my area and that would be packed with all kinds of doctors. I turned to the index at the back of the Yellow Pages and made a list of all the medical specialities plus the pages on which they could be found. I made a complete list, not ruling out even the unlikely ones – anaesthetists, geriatricians, gynaecologists and paediatricians – and began my search anew. Ten minutes later I had added a dermatologist named Anita J. Cartwright, a neurologist by the name of Allard W. Costain and an orthopaedic surgeon who had broken with tradition by being, and remaining, plain old Alf Carr. A moment later and already beginning to think of how I might eliminate the A.C.s one by one, I hit paydirt. For Albert Conroy, darling of the TV talk shows, the one who was going to see Crowther's nephew 'all right', the one whose name Ellen couldn't bring herself to utter, was listed under psychiatrists. In Fitzwilliam Square. Where else?

I sat back, breathed 'Well how 'bout that then, laddie!' and wondered why, like Rome, all roads led eventually to Val Crowther. Then, being a methodical plodder, I sat forward again and completed my run through the assorted healers of Dublin's fair city. Albert was the last A.C. in any of the remaining specialities. No wonder Dave had written A.C. – they'd been part of the same clique, fellow satellites in orbit around Val Crowther.

Massaging my temples and closing my eyes, I tried to recall all I'd heard about the psychiatrist. It didn't amount to much – Conroy and Crowther had been friends for years (this intelligence courtesy of Yvonne Fuller) and Dave and Crowther had also been friends for years ('from college days,' according to Ellen). Which almost certainly meant that Dave and Conroy had been friends all that time too.

Straight after that came the memory of just a few hours ago when Cecily Lamb had mentioned that many of Dublin's leading medicos had done abortions on the side in their younger days. Many might have been an exaggeration, but there undoubtedly had been some. Recalling Ellen's reluctance to speak his name, and in view of the fact that Dave and Conroy had most likely known each other at the time that Ellen became pregnant, was it not likely that she had turned to Dave in her hour of need and that he had made arrangements with his pal, Albert Conroy? This was pure hypothesis, circumstantial conjecture at best, but it was a possible scenario. And Val Crowther, being one of the pals, would therefore have known of Ellen's abortion right from the very beginning.

I was trying to formulate other hypotheses and wondering if I ought to ring Cecily back and ask her straight out if Albert Conroy had been one of the doctors she'd hinted at, when Claire phoned and asked me to collect her from the office. Her car had been towed away.

I decided against calling Cecily. The rumours would never stop. And besides, I didn't think I wanted to go through all that heavy seduction stuff again. Even if it was in jest, which I wasn't sure that it was.

23

I obeyed the 'Knock and Enter' sign on the first-floor door
and poked my head into a very comfortable reception room.
You could have dropped a laden metal tea tray on the thick
cream carpet and nobody would hear a thing. Several well-
placed, comfortable armchairs had small tables between
them, each displaying new-looking magazines. Well-
established indoor plants and a large, beautifully lit, limpid,
marine tropical aquarium complemented the gracious and
peaceful space.

Dark oil paintings with sumptuous gold frames hung on
the walls, each illuminated by its own muted strip-light, as
though it was a rare and precious work of art.

To the left, standing guard beside a polished wooden
door, was a polished wooden desk. Behind this sat a perfectly
groomed and coiffed middle-aged lady, regarding me quizzically through a gap between a computer plus its gubbins on
her right and a large vase of fresh flowers on her left. From
outside the closed windows came the polite noises of
Fitzwilliam Square, the purr of expensive cars, the refined
click of real leather soles and heels.

I smiled and stepped towards the desk. 'Good morning.' I
flashed her one of my most winning smiles.

She looked for a moment as though she thought I might
be trying to sell her something, then returned the smile and
the greeting. She was a remarkably handsome woman, an

Yvonne Fuller in the making. 'And how may I help you, sir?' She had obviously given up the salesman idea.

'I've come to pay a bill.'

'A bill?' The handsome brow puckered briefly. 'Are you sure you're in the right place?'

'Oh, yes. Dr Albert Conroy's rooms. One bill, £75.' I produced my wallet and began to leaf out twenties.

'I think there must be some mistake, sir. May I have the name, please?'

'David Ryder.'

This shut her up. She probably began to think I was a brand-new patient with an insane desire to pay my bills before I even incurred them and an equally loony idea that I was David Ryder. Julius Caesar, Napoleon, Jesus Christ she could have handled, no bother – she'd probably had them all through before, many times – but by the look on her face, I was her first David Ryder – apart, that is, from the real one. If she remembered Dave, then our similarity must have been adding to her confusion.

She glanced at the thick door to her left, but the doctor wasn't in. I knew, because I hadn't entered the premises until five minutes after I'd seen him leave. The handsome woman was all on her own.

'Em. Mr Ryder *was* a patient of Mr Conroy's but, I'm afraid he passed away some time ago.'

'I know that. I'm his cousin, Frank Samson. The *bill* is David's.'

'Oh!' Relief washed over her.

'Now do you get it?' And I unleashed another charming smile.

'But I don't think there's an outstanding account . . .'

'There has to be. David wrote a cheque for £75 but it was never cashed. I assume it's been lost. So I've come to pay it. Again. I'll pay cash this time if it's all right with you?'

'Well . . . of course . . . but I really don't think that . . . In fact, I'm almost certain . . .'

'Although maybe you'd prefer another cheque? The way

the world is these days, it's chancy keeping money overnight on the premises. God, I hope you don't do that.'

'Eh. No. No, we don't. Cash, cheque, it makes no odds really because we deposit every evening.'

'Wise move. It must be bad enough having psychiatric drugs and pills and syringes and stuff like that on the premises, without tempting in the burglars as well as the junkies, eh?'

She looked at me in suspicious silence, then opened a drawer in a small filing cabinet. 'I still don't think that Mr Ryder owes us . . . At least his, eh . . . estate . . . eh . . .' Cough, cough.

'Well, my word, but what beautiful flowers!' I exclaimed, moving a few crab-steps to bury my nose in the abundant mixed blooms. From there I had a perfect view of the computer monitor, which at that moment was showing a screen saver of Disney characters. The keyboard lay on the desk in front of her, facing her square on, but the screen was almost at right angles to her. This odd arrangement was dictated more by the space available on the narrow desk than her own choice. Whatever, if she brought up Dave's file – and I didn't see how she could avoid doing so – I'd be able to read it as if I was looking over her shoulder. With an annoyed sigh, she closed the drawer and rolled herself back to the desk where, with the mere touch of the mouse, she eliminated two other mouses – Mickey and Minnie.

Some double-clicking, which would have had Charlie McMahon gasping in dazzled awe, led to the sudden appearance of 'RYDER, David Clement (deceased)' on the screen. There was half a screenful of personal particulars which, I assumed, I already knew – just as well, as these were obviously of no interest to the receptionist, who scrolled briskly through them.

Then a page of columns appeared and went on for another screen and a half. She lingered just long enough for me to read the column headings which, from left to right were: Date, Appointment Time, Session Time, Details, Fee. There were some fifteen entries in all – Dave appeared fifteen times on a psychiatrist's case list! I couldn't figure out whether it was a relief or not to know that he wasn't mad, just bad.

The Dates column showed his first visit to have been almost four years before, the last for 4.30 on the day before he had died. The 'Session Time' column showed ten minutes. The second-last visit had been in April of the previous year and a fee of £75 had been paid.

None of the cheque stubs that Curley had sent me went back that far, which explained why I hadn't been able to locate another A.C. or any other payee with those initials.

The Details column consisted entirely of the word 'Consult' except for a group of four 'Nicotine Addiction/ Hypnosis' one after the other, then back to 'Consult' again.

The Fee column showed a list of different amounts with a tick beside each. There was a heavy line at the bottom of this column. The last figure above the line was £75, ticked paid, and the column beneath, beside the abbreviation, 'Bal. Due' showed just a line across. Dave had indeed paid as he went.

Dave paying struck me as odd; I reckoned his visits to Conroy had not been professional ones – except for the hypnosis/nicotine ones. Maybe he and his friend in crime were just keeping up pretences all the way. He probably had his payments refunded at a later date.

'No account.' The lady shrugged and spread her hands Frenchly.

'But there must be. The last cheque he paid you, for £75, was not lodged.'

She flicked the screen back to life, frowned; she did some more nifty double-clicking and this time summoned up a Lodgements file. Frowning even more deeply, she pulled out a drawer, removed a lodgement book for Allied Irish Banks, discovered that it didn't go far enough back, then rooted around for the correct book and the correct record, and spent a minute studying that, this time frowning up a storm. Then she turned to the previous page and said, 'Ah yes. *Now* I remember . . . I had to make out *two* lodgement slips for that day. The first did indeed contain Mr Ryder's cheque, but then Mr Conroy took it out as he needed some money for that evening. So I cancelled that lodgement slip and made out a second one for £75 less. It's all here. Mr Conroy himself must have lost the cheque, or perhaps the person who cashed it for him did . . .'

'Ah! I see. That would explain it. I never thought of that. Well, in that case I don't feel I owe you this sum any more. I thought you might have lost the cheque, or spilled ink over it or something and then not known where to send a bill for a replacement . . . so . . .' I was running off at the mouth while I tried to deal with the implications of what she had just said.

She began telling me how honest I was, how you didn't expect such honesty in these times, how refreshingly hopeful it was to find that there were still people about with sound moral standards, etc. etc. – all of which gave me further time for thought.

'I suppose there wasn't £75 in *cash* in that lodgement?' I asked.

She'd looked at the docket before she thought that it was none of my business and although she told me, a bit frostily, that she was not at liberty to comment on that, I could see in her eyes that there had been and that she was wondering, as I was, why the doctor hadn't taken the suddenly required £75 in universally acceptable *cash* rather than in the unwieldy form of a cheque.

Through the receptionist I had now established *what* the doctor had done.

The fact that he had neither cashed nor lodged the cheque, although not conclusive proof, was at least a powerful indicator of *why* he had done *what* he'd done.

The fact that he had taken these precautionary steps *before* Dave had been murdered was really going to nail his scrotum to the wall. That ought to be enough for anyone to take action, I thought, with the possible (probable) exception of Inspector Curley, who still considered me an unbalanced and desperate zealot willing to do anything, including fabricating elaborate stories, to find a killer, any killer, to pin Dave's death on.

272

But there was one flaw in my story: Curley would object, reasonably enough, that it would have been pointless for the good doctor to destroy the cheque if Dave had identified him clearly and unambiguously as the payee on the stub. For my evidence to stick, I would have to prove that Albert Conroy actually *knew* that he himself could not be identified from the stub in Dave's chequebook. I knew it had to be so – otherwise, as Curley would object, it would have been pointless, even stupid, for him to have ditched the cheque. So how could I *prove* that he *had* known? Unless I could prove this essential fact it would end up being A.C.'s word against my speculation, a contest I couldn't hope to win – he'd actually been there whereas I was playing mind games almost eight months after the event . . .

I'd already been standing there in silence for nearly a minute, with the receptionist giving me increasingly worried looks, and I was just thinking that I'd better leave and ponder the problem in private somewhere when a tiny spark of inspiration hit me. 'David told me that Mr Conroy was standing beside him as he was writing the cheque. Do you remember that? It was written, I think he said, at this desk?'

After a speculative pause she nodded slowly, watching me really warily now, but reluctant to challenge me because I seemed to know so much, to be merely in search of confirmation, not information. 'Yes . . .' she replied. 'That's correct. But why would your cousin have told you that?'

'Who knows? One last thing. Forgive me – I've wasted enough of your time already – did my cousin seem to be in good or bad form when he was leaving?' She began to look even more uncomfortable. 'It's not that important. But as he and I were so close – I'm even going around trying to pay his *bills*, for God's sakes! – it would be a great relief, a great *personal* relief, for me to know.'

'Well . . . I knew Mr Ryder fairly well, over the years, you know? I'd say he was a little preoccupied, subdued, possibly something bothering him. But then again, this *is* a psychiatrist's office and many people come through here looking preoccupied . . .'

I thought I'd really be pushing it if I asked her to look up Dave's case notes. As it was, I reckoned it was fifty–fifty that she'd mention my visit and questions to her boss. I would, of course, have preferred that she didn't, but if I were to ask her not to, then she'd be *certain* to do so. If I just faded away right now, without another word, perhaps she'd forget.

I bade her good morning and left the office.

'Yes!' I punched the air in elation as I headed down the softly carpeted stairs to street level. Now that I'd refreshed her memory, she'd be a ripe witness when I finally did manage to interest Curley and her testimony would knock all the props from beneath her boss when the hard questions began.

The flash about the cheque being written at her desk wasn't watertight, but I'd been desperate at the time and I reckoned it contained just about sufficient logic to make it a worthwhile risk. Even if I'd been wrong, it wouldn't have been too disastrous. With time now not so pressing I unravelled the almost simultaneous thoughts that had led to it.

First I'd assumed that Dave and Conroy had been alone together in the consulting room, in total privacy, so if Dave had offered to pay at that point Conroy, who certainly did not want the cheque, could easily have put him off. He could have insisted on writing off the bill altogether on grounds of friendship, or the fact that Dave was a special client, or that he'd just become the 10,000th client – any old excuse at all to avoid Dave's cheque. It shouldn't have been hard to convince Dave – most people would be only too pleased to be talked out of writing a £75 cheque. It followed (probably), therefore, that the subject of payment had not arisen until they were no longer alone and that (hopefully) left only two choices – either the receptionist had come into the consulting room (unlikely) or Dave and Conroy had gone out into the waiting room. At this point it had seemed only natural to conclude that Dave had requested his bill.

Conroy would be stuck – with the presumably totally innocent receptionist now a witness, he couldn't object. The receptionist would think it odd and might wonder what was so special about Dave. And when she read of Dave's death in the papers next day, she might remember her employer's strange behaviour . . . and wonder again.

If I was right up to this point, then the cheque almost had to have been written at the receptionist's desk – after all, most people pay their doctors' bills at reception and besides, the desk was the only surface in the waiting room suitable for writing on.

So Conroy had been forced to stand by and watch as Dave opened his chequebook. He'd have looked on glumly while Dave wrote the cheque that would link him to a meeting with Dave hours before his death. Although this in itself would not be a disaster, it would almost inevitably lead to a visit from the police and Conroy, who at the very least had to have known that Dave was a marked man on a very short life expectancy, would clearly have preferred to avoid that.

His spirits must have swooped upwards with joyous relief when he saw Dave write the nondescript initials on the counterfoil, close the chequebook and put it back into his pocket. A.C. Who the hell was A.C.? It could have been *anyone* with those initials and there was nothing whatever to connect him, Dr A.C., with Dave after all. It was as if Dave had never even written the bloody cheque. All he had to do was make sure the cheque itself never reached the bank and he was as good as home and dry. How lucky could one man get? Praise the Lord!

I smiled smugly to myself as I opened the door of the Land Rover, but had cause to smile even more smugly before I'd even put the key in the ignition.

Dave's autopsy had shown no signs whatever of physical or chemical-induced restraint – which was the reason that Curley could stick so adamantly to his theory that the heroin had been self-administered – but nobody had suggested *mental* restraint.

Hypnosis . . .

I still can't figure why exactly I didn't head straight for

Curley's office as soon as I left the fancy waiting room. I suppose that, having been turned down by him so often, I was afraid that he'd just give me the big horse laugh again and show me the door. And this time I'd have left him valuable evidence.

Maybe, on reflection, that was what was worrying me most. I didn't feel I could trust him enough to treat it seriously and I could almost imagine him pretending to go through the motions, just to humour me. I could hear him talking to (the ultra-respectable) Dr Conroy, giving him an apology in advance for the inconvenience about to be caused, but a half-crazy citizen had been trying to link him with the accidental death of his cousin, a junkie and a criminal. The doctor would have replied that of course he knew Ryder, he'd been a patient for years; daft as a brush, nutty as a fruitcake, between you and me, Inspector – this is strictly confidential, doctor–patient y'know, nudge nudge, wink wink – he was also a repressed paedophile, possibly about to become active, maybe *already* active, into SM, hearing voices, mutilating small animals and birds . . . blah, blah, blah. They were both anti-Dave. I decided to hold off until there was nothing for Curley to baulk at, no way he could go on denying Dave a proper investigation. I probably had enough already, I reflected, but it was all over the place, bits of it coming from so many different sources.

I decided to put off any visit to Curley until I could sit down with pen and paper, write everything out, explain how Crowther and Dave were connected, and Dave and Conroy, and Conroy and Crowther, and who could vouch for each of my conclusions, under oath if necessary.

Also, I still had no idea as to why they should have killed him, but I thought that might come out in the thoroughness of an official investigation where questions could be asked openly by experts and answers demanded. My only real aim was to start the official ball rolling. I'd get it all down on paper this evening. Dave had already waited seven months for justice, another night wouldn't kill him.

On my way towards the motorway to the west, I began to

think of Medineeds. Was it not very strange that a company being run secretly by Crowther and Dave, a couple of crooks, had been so conscientious about paying its bills just before it put up the shutters for the last time? Was this touching bout of honesty meant to ensure that none of its creditors or its single employee would be hurt in any way?

I thought not. In fact, I speculated that the reason for such impressive honesty had far more to do with making sure that nobody would have any excuse for digging into the affairs of the company. Pay up and avoid investigation. Like Conroy and the cheque: tear up and avoid questions. But nobody seemed to know anything about the business of Medineeds.

If the Business Section at the *Daily Instructor* didn't know, then nobody did – and they would have pulled out all the stops for Claire. I could figure out no angle on this and reckoned I never would, no matter how long I tried, because my brain, unlike the *Daily Instructor*, doesn't even *have* a Business Section. Still, I thought after a while, just why, in the first place, should the Business Section at the *Daily Instructor* have known anything at all about a company whose office was tiny and shabby, whose only equipment was a computer and a wall safe, and whose sole employee was that computer-illiterate double-clicker, Charlie McMahon?

I rang the *Daily Instructor* and was put through after some delay to the Business Section where I spoke with Edwin Savage, a man I had met once or twice at office parties and the like. He explained that Medineeds bought and sold abroad, and had a large turnover, large enough to spark interest if anything untoward happened, like the sudden closure of its Irish head office. Head Office? That was the company *Head Office*? I interrupted to ask Edwin if he had ever been to what he called the Head Office and when he said no, he hadn't, I told him that figured. He went on, after a short puzzled pause: Medineeds' business was pharmaceuticals, which were forward-bought and then shipped to customers worldwide. Their whole business was bulk orders and they dealt only with bodies like UN projects, governments, major charities and other large NGOs. They were very competitive in every way, price, delivery, quality, reliability and were generally highly thought of in the field. The company itself had not closed down, yet, but there were conflicting reports about its future – some thought it was merely ticking over, fulfilling its last orders and commitments before winding up, while others reported it was still actively seeking business and making pitches for every contract that arose, still going aggressively for every sizeable tender. He had never heard of Dave Ryder being involved until Claire had mentioned it the other day and he had never heard at all of a Val Crowther.

I returned to Monksford at about 2.30 and found the whole staff of the practice assembled in PJ's private office. I'd phoned Barbara from some twenty miles out to see if there were any calls I could do en route. She said that there weren't but that PJ wanted to see me in his office as soon as I got back and when exactly would that be?

Feeling that there was probably a row in the offing, I had psyched myself up for battle and, by the time I drew up in the yard, I was ready to take on a company of marines. I strode into the general office, found nobody there, not even Barbara, and rapped forcefully on PJ's closed door.

'Come in,' he called gruffly and I pushed the door open with more vigour than was required, but considerably less than I wanted to use. I'd felt like not turning the handle at all, just hitting the door beside the lock with the sole of my boot – well, maybe that's an exaggeration, but you know what I mean.

I strode into an outbreak of grins and an immediate, energetic, if slightly discordant chorus of 'For He's a Jolly Good Fellow' from the assembled staff, which took me totally by surprise, and then suddenly everyone was grinning and back-slapping, and pouring champagne and cutting an incredibly gooey cake into incredibly gooey slices. I hadn't a clue what the occasion was but I seemed to be the centre of it.

'What's going on?' I asked Miriam as she handed me a slice of the goo.

'The big Three-Oh,' she said. 'Just listen!'

PJ was on his feet now, calling for calm and lashings of hush, ladies and gentlemen, if you please! I won't give the verbatim version of the speech which, in reality, dragged on for less than five minutes, but rather a digest, in which I was generally lauded. The reason why today was so important was that, for the first time in over eight months there were over thirty calls on the book. The book lay open in the centre of PJ's desk, propped underneath so that it rested at a slant like some great religious tome at a solemn ceremony in the centre of the high altar. In fact, there had been thirty-two calls, but number thirty was marked with my initials and highlighted, nay *illuminated*, in day-glo yellow. That call had been left for me to do and that was all I was to do for the rest of the day, bar showing up at the banquet to be laid on in my honour this evening at – where else? – the Dark Horse. Nothing but the best for our Frank. Seemingly, I was generally regarded by one and all as the saviour of the practice.

I gave a short, simple reply during which, I admit it, I was almost moved to visible emotion, mainly because, although I liked Michael, Miriam and Barbara, I still couldn't warm to either of the Slatterys, especially PJ. I wanted to, but I just couldn't. Mind you, I hid it very well.

And so, for the second time in a week, I found myself standing in the car park of the Dark Horse, replete after a good meal and looking forward to getting to bed. There was no way I was going to tackle Curley's report tonight.

The day must have been more wearying than I'd thought because now I was becoming quite exhausted. As the goodbyes lingered and last jokes were shouted back and forth, I tried to count what drinks I'd had. I knew I'd been careful – since the accident in which the two young families had perished the police were all over the place, breathalysing everyone – but I felt as if I'd been on a major bender. I realised how bad I was when, on turning ninety degrees out of the car park, I dragged my rear wheel over the kerb. I paused briefly but, reckoning I'd pass the breathalyser with flying colours, decided to continue on. It was just exhaustion. A half-hour of steady, slow, careful driving and I'd be tucked up in my bed.

A few hundred yards along another woozy wobble, this time accompanied by a feeling of nausea and a blurring of my vision, made me wonder if I shouldn't stop JJ and his girlfriend, who were still behind me at this point, and cadge a lift, but that option vanished with a merry tooting of the horn as they swept by me in his sporty little Honda and began to open a rapidly widening gap between me and them. I had a sudden feeling I wasn't going to make it back and reached for the headlight flasher to recall them, but my movement was sluggish and, by the time I'd located it, their tail-lights had vanished over the crest of a hill and I found myself alone in the dark landscape of small cross-country roads and narrow country lanes which were the quickest way back to Monksford. I opened my window, hoping that the cold night air and the drizzle might revive me, and concentrated on driving.

I was trying blearily to navigate my way, weaving from side to side, making desperate last-minute course corrections to avoid the hedges and ditches, when a pair of headlights appeared suddenly behind me. I hadn't even noticed them until they were sitting on my tail and I was almost blinded by them. Reaching to turn my rear-view mirror away my concentration, such as it was, lapsed totally and I lost what little control I had. The front wheel suddenly mounted a rock, tearing the steering wheel out of my weakened grip; my head bounced painfully off the roof and I was pitched sideways, slamming the ridge of my eye-socket and my temple against the window post. I felt myself canting slowly over as the Land Rover slid down into a deep ditch, turning almost gracefully on to her side as she went, like the final roll of a sinking ship.

There was no sense of fear, no adrenalin rush, only a great

weariness and a nausea, which would not be denied much longer. Vomit began to creep scaldingly up my throat and I felt one last violent spasm of pain as the whole contents of my stomach splashed over me. The spinning vortex in my brain was the last thing I remembered . . .

24

Waking slowly, wincing with the excruciation in my head, I remembered the crash as the Land Rover hit the bottom of the ditch and began immediately to fill with cold, filthy water with things floating in it. The creeping chill around my legs and waist roused me enough to realise it was coming through the window I had opened to admit reviving cool night air. During those lucid few seconds a torch beam played down on me and, lulled by the knowledge that help was at hand, that at least I wouldn't drown, I surrendered my stupefied wits and passed out.

I had no idea of how long ago that might have been.

A voice came from nearby. 'I think he's waking up, doctor. His eyelids are fluttering.'

'Show me . . . Ah, yes. That's good. Another few minutes . . . Call me.'

There was the sudden sound of people talking and a Dr Carey being called over a PA system in a nasal twang which grated on my ears. These sounds lasted just a few seconds before becoming muted, almost silent again, the door opening and closing, I reckoned. I was exhausted and my mouth tasted foul. The vomit. Yuck! It made me want to puke all over again – but not with this headache . . .

Seconds past, or maybe hours.

'Are you awake? Can you hear me?' The voice said softly close by.

'Yes.' I nodded slightly and even that caused pain. 'Yes. I can hear you. I'm very tired.'

'Take your time. Have another little snooze if you want. There's no hurry.'

As from a great distance, I heard the same twangy voice paging a Dr Bennett. 'I think maybe I've slept enough . . .'

'Whatever. It's up to you.'

I opened my eyes and saw absolutely nothing, not a shape nor a shadow, nor even a faint glow. Nothing. I closed them again to clear them, then fluttered them open tentatively. The darkness was total.

'Ah,' said the voice. 'Welcome back to the world. How do you feel?'

'Fine,' I answered automatically. 'I feel fi—' Wait a minute! If it's totally dark in here, then how does he know my eyes are open? 'How do you know I'm awake?'

'Well, unless you can sleep with your eyes wide open, as far as I'm concerned, you're awake.'

I can't see! I thought in sudden panic. Oh Jesus! I can't see. I stretched a hand out towards the voice and it was immediately taken and held in both hands of . . . my nurse? attendant? what? 'Where am I?' I asked, bewildered, trying to swallow my fountaining fear. 'Why is it all dark?'

'Take it easy. Just calm down. What do you mean "dark"? Can't you see me?'

'No. I can't see anything. Jesus! I can't see anything!'

'Nothing at all? The lights are on. It's bright as day.'

'No,' I wailed. 'It's pitch black. Aw, Jesus! What's happening to me?' I pressed the bulbs of my palms to my eyes and started to rub them, but the nurse grabbed my wrists and pulled them away. 'You mustn't do that. Leave them alone. I'll call the doctor in a minute, but promise me you'll leave your eyes alone. Are they painful?'

I paused for a second to check. 'No. They're not.'

'Look, I'm sure it's purely temporary. That happens, you know. And you have a hell of a concussion there. Two, in fact. Just relax, close your eyes and I'll get the doctor.'

Close my eyes? He must be mad, I thought, staring about with them open as wide as they'd go.

'I really think you'd better close them, protect them from the light.' But I didn't want to and I held my wide-eyed, panicky stare. 'It's up to you,' said my nurse. 'They're your eyes.'

'Oh, God!' I moaned. Despite the dread within me, I thought that was a hell of a callous thing for a nurse to say, even a male nurse.

'Only for your own sake, don't look towards the door when I open it. It's very bright outside in the corridor. Either cover your eyes or close them. I'll be back in a tick.'

He took his hands away from mine, I heard the scrape of a chair as he stood, then four footsteps, then the brief noise of the human traffic from outside as the door opened and closed, but there was not the slightest change in the blackness of my world. I saw nothing.

Panic was erupting in my brain when the noise of the world outside intruded briefly again and the doctor and nurse approached my bed, talking in low tones about concussion. Already my other senses were sharpening to compensate.

The bed sagged as someone sat beside me. 'Frank,' the doctor said gently and with the compassion of one bearing bad news, 'I'm going to touch your head, so don't be alarmed. Lie back on the pillow now, like a good man. Fine, that's it. Here comes my hand, okay.' His voice was noticeably nasal and muffled; I assumed he had a head cold and was wearing a face mask so that his patients wouldn't catch his germs.

'Okay,' I said and immediately felt his fingertips wandering carefully over my head until their gentle exploring encountered the mighty bump right on top. He sucked in breath and said: 'Phew, that's a biggy!' Seeing me wince, he apologised and then said to the nurse: 'Wasn't there another?'

'Yes, doctor. Left brow to left ear.'

The doctor caught my chin, rolled my head gently away

from him and touched the far more painful contusion on my bruised temple. 'Hmhp,' he said and took his hand away. I could hear the click of a ballpoint pen and some scribbling. Then I felt what I guessed was a clipboard being set on the bed beside my leg. 'I'm going to take a look in your eyes now, Frank. Ready?'

His fingers spread the lids of my right eye and I heard what I assumed was the click of a torch. It could have been an ophthalmoscope, although the ophthalmoscopes I use don't make that sort of click when I switch them on. 'Roll your eyeball upwards, please. That's good. Now down . . . Any pain?' I said that there wasn't and he said 'That's good' again, and repeated the procedure on my left eye. He gave a small grunt as he picked up the clipboard and there was the ballpoint click again.

'We'll take blood from you now, Frank, and run some lab work on it. From now on, though, I want you to rest without moving. That's very important. In fact, it's so important that I'm going to give you a shot to make sure you lie absolutely still, you understand?'

'Yes. What do you think is wrong with me, doctor? Is it from the concussion?' I was thinking trauma to, and resulting swelling of, the brain and a DMSO drip, or whatever they used in humans, to reduce it. I was trying not to give even a glancing thought to brain haemorrhage or any of the other appalling possibilities.

'I think so. I hope so. As I said, I want to run these bloods through first. We can't say anything until we see the results of those. Okay?'

'And you'll be able to tell then?'

'Well, I should think so. At least we'll have a much clearer idea of the cause of the problem. But don't you be worrying, now. It'll all probably vanish in a day or two. See you later.'

Vanish? The vanishing had already taken place. The whole fucking world had vanished!

He came back some ten minutes later, gave me a pill to swallow and stuck a needle in my buttock. With a few soothing words, as if he were settling an excitable child down for the night, he went out; again, I heard the twangy, whingy PA voice paging Dr Ibrahim Khan. As consciousness ebbed away, I sensed myself regressing towards my childhood at great speed. The nagging, whining voice of the PA announcer became that of Miss Olive Fox, maid, house-keeper, governess, babysitter and childminder, who had terrorised me for the first nine years of my life. Had I not actually attended her funeral some twelve years ago I would have sworn that Miss Fox was now working as an eighty-plus–year–old PA announcer at . . . At where? I had no idea where I was but, I thought, did it really matter? My suddenly tiny world now existed only within my own immediate surroundings. Like a snail, I carried it with me wherever I went.

I had wild and weird dreams, which oscillated between terror and euphoria, peace and panic, shifting in nanoseconds from one to another without connection or succession. They were peopled by total strangers, some not quite human, and I recognised none of the situations or locations. At times I was right at the centre, taking an integral part; other times I felt as if I were an invisible observer and, although I might be looking the participants straight in their strange eyes, the creature-people in the dream were as unaware of my staring presence as a TV newscaster would be. I thought I awoke several times and opened my eyes to the new dark that encased me, but perhaps this was just part of another dream, or a dream within a dream.

When I awoke I was sweating and cold. I was also still blind. 'Nurse?' I called, not wanting to be alone in the dark.

'Hey, you're back! Good sleep?'

'No. Not really. I dreamt a lot. How long have I been asleep?'

'Nearly seven hours. But don't worry; you need all the rest you can get.'

Seven hours! It didn't feel much more than seven minutes. 'I must have been exhausted. How long did I sleep between the crash and when I woke up the first time.'

'Couple of days.'

'*Two days!*'

'Near enough, anyway.'

I found this extremely hard to believe. I'd been aware, although not with any sharp memory, of at least *some* of what had been going on all the way through. I'd felt myself being pulled out through the passenger door of my ditched Land Rover and hauled up to road level. I'd heard somebody being called 'doctor' and thought how fortunate I was that there was a doctor on the scene so instantly. I'd felt an injection and gradually going deeper, but not before hearing a conversation about getting the Land Rover out of the ditch as soon as possible and I thought I could recall someone called Chris being told to go and get a crane at once. I'd been aware of being loaded into a car and driven, although I had no idea what sort of distance we might have covered before I sensed myself being half led, half dragged into a building. My memory, from the moment they laid me on a bed and began to remove my sodden, filthy clothes, was not quite as detailed, but I'd been aware of comings and goings which gradually, over a period of maybe an hour, had lessened until it had become quiet. I hadn't even needed the loo when I awoke. Maybe I'd peed myself while I slept – after all, if the blow had knocked out my sight centre, then it could just as easily have damaged my pee control centre, too. That is, if there was a pee control centre in the brain. I couldn't remember. Or even a sight centre . . .

'Do you want some water?'

I put a hand to my jaw to run ginger fingers over the cut on the temple, but was immediately struck by something far more interesting – on the palm of my hand no stubble rubbed. This was very surprising. I'd shaved before going out to the Dark Horse but, if that had been two days ago, even one day, then my jaw should have been like sandpaper.

'Sorry, what did you say?'

'Would you like some water?'

'Eh . . . water? Please.'

'Okay. I'll be back in a jiffy.'

Unless they had shaved me? But I doubted that as I could

still feel caked mud on my neck. If they'd wanted to clean me up, surely they'd have washed the muck off my neck before worrying about shaving me. In fact, unless they'd shaved me dry or with an electric razor, the muck would have come off in the water. What sort of hospital would leave a comatose patient dirty for two days?

Miss Fox was calling a Dr Sisley as the door swung open and closed. The name made me think of Cecily Lamb, which brought me back to the real world outside. I began to wonder if the hospital had informed the Slatterys? Or Claire? But perhaps Claire had already left on an assignment. I didn't know what day it now was, but I knew she was due to be off inside a day or two when I'd left town.

Lying prone, without the distraction of sight, there was nothing to do but think and I wondered how come, if I'd been out cold for two days, I hadn't been parched with thirst when I finally came to? I wasn't on a drip when I awoke – I distinctly remembered flailing my arms about in the panic of my realising I couldn't see – so why wasn't I dehydrated and parched? Now I carefully palpated the areas in which drips are usually given – the backs of the hands, forearms, crooks of the elbows – but there was no tell-tale band-aid and no pain, not even when I pressed. Perhaps they'd fed me through a nasogastric tube.

I put a hand to my bumps and immediately wondered why the doctor hadn't already assessed my head injuries during my supposed forty-eight hours of oblivion. It was clear that this doctor was seeing me for the first time. Maybe he was new to the case. Perhaps he'd been off for two days? With his head cold? Maybe he had just come back on duty, or maybe he was a consultant who had been called in.

I tried to start positive thinking about how blind people coped, but a moment later I was back wondering again why the hospital had not taken diagnostic blood samples as soon as I'd been admitted. Even in veterinary practice I'd have done that straight away.

The nurse came back in, this time unaccompanied by the Miss Fox voice, although she started up immediately the door had swung to, calling a Dr Holly or Colley, I couldn't quite tell through the door. I drank the water through a long flexible tube, sucking it up and again wondering why, after a seven-hour sleep, I wasn't really thirsty. Something about this whole set-up didn't gel but I had no intention of asking pointed questions until I had had time to figure it out a bit further.

'No improvement in the sight, then?' my nurse asked.

'None. Has the blood work come back from the lab?'

'The doctor will be in shortly. He'll tell you everything.'

'What's his name, the doctor?' I asked, thinking I'd try a couple of unpointed questions.

'Dr Smith. Jim Smith.'

'I like him. He gives me confidence. Has he been looking after me from the start?'

'Right from the start. You're in safe hands there. He's the best.'

'Neurosurgeon, right?'

This seemed to flummox the nurse. There was a slight pause. 'Don't you worry. He's the best.'

The best what, I almost retorted. Gynaecologist? I smiled, portraying 'Confidence', and hoped that my dead eyes didn't betray the lie behind the smile. So Dr Jim Smith who, according to the nurse, had been looking after me for two days, hadn't seen my bumps before. Interesting. I would have thought that in any normal hospital they would by now have taken X-rays and possibly even done a CAT scan.

'I'm going to shine a torch in your eyes. See if you can tell which eye I'm shining it into.' There was a click and a pause. 'Okay, Frank. Which eye?'

'I have no idea. I can see nothing at all.'

'Nothing?'

'Not a glimmer.' The panic and depression were much less now – I had an overwhelming feeling that my sight would be as good as ever in a short time. I couldn't explain it to myself better than that I just didn't feel blind. I felt that I had been given some substance which could cause temporary blindness, although I had no idea what that substance might be.

'I'll try it with the ceiling light off. For contrast.' He moved the four steps to the door and flicked the wall switch, then came slowly back towards the bed, feeling his way in the sudden dark, bumping into the chair with a loud 'Oops!' and a little laugh – silly me!

I wondered why he didn't use the torch he was about to shine in my eyes, to avoid the furniture, but again said nothing.

We went through the charade of the torchlight in the eyes again – with the same negative results. I had no idea when or even if he shone the light in my eyes. He fumbled his way back to the switch by the door, clicked it on again, said 'Ah, that's better' and came back to the bed. 'Would you like some more water?'

'No, thanks. I'd like to go to sleep again, now. I don't feel too good. I didn't get much rest with those dreams. Did you say the doctor would be in soon?'

'Yes, but that doesn't matter. He'll be around for ages. Get your kip and he can pop in when you feel rested and better. Would you like another pill?'

'No, thanks. I reckon that's what gave me those dreams.'

I heard him go out into the corridor of the hospital that ran without bureaucracy. So far, no one had even asked me my name, let alone all the minute details required by almoners and other interested parties. Apart from myself, only Claire could have furnished them with those and they certainly hadn't got them from her – if Claire knew I was here, she'd have been sitting by my side for as long as it took.

I lay still for many minutes and thought. I was utterly convinced that my blindness was temporary, possibly induced here in this odd hospital for some unfathomable reason which would, if my assumption was correct, soon become clear. But I couldn't help wondering if that comforting certainty wasn't based on my refusal to face the stark horror that the condition might be permanent. Perhaps I was giving unwarranted importance to individual little inconsistencies which my hypersensitive brain was now picking up on and busily moulding into a conspiracy theory? A gruff few words from the nurse, a seemingly suspect remark from the doctor, no red tape . . . Was it not possible that the nurse was just being gruffly friendly, all boys together, the doctor overworked and the hospital being humane in leaving the lousy bookwork until I was feeling better? No, I decided, it wasn't. Because allowing that would lead me straight back to the unthinkable.

All the while I'd been listening intently to the sounds that were coming through the dark to me, deliberately silencing my slow breathing to make sure I could hear everything. There was the constant low background noise of human traffic outside the door, punctuated every minute, or less, by Miss Fox's sound-alike, plaintively but imperiously summoning some doctor or other to different locations. On one occasion Miss Fox called a Dr Smith and I wondered if it was Jim, who had been tending me constantly for two days but wasn't quite sure if I even had a second bump on the noggin. Blind, my foot! I wasn't blind! These guys were playing games with my head.

There was also vague birdsong and the rise and fall of a motorised lawnmower as it moved to and fro about its business. Every so often a car or lorry would sound briefly At least that meant it was daytime. Neither songbirds nor lawnmowers operate much by night. I wondered where the window was, or if these noises were coming through a ventilator grille or such – I hadn't been aware of the garden sounds before, nor the cars and trucks. Perhaps it had just turned dawn.

There was something odd going on.

The doctor had warned me not to move, in case I had a clot on the brain or something but, as I refused to believe that *any* of this was real, I decided to ignore him. I swung my legs on to the floor and sat up.

I waited a moment to see if my head would suddenly explode and, when it didn't, stood up, leaning to keep one hand in contact with the mattress until my legs stopped wobbling. I could feel a coolness down my spine and found that I was dressed in a short hospital robe and nothing else. Tapes tied loosely down the back held the two sides together. The front was all one papery piece.

After a minute or so and two false starts, I cast off from the bed and moved slowly towards where I thought the door to be. I had decided I wanted to phone Claire's parents and also Barbara at the practice, and reckoned that someone out there would dial the numbers for me. When I eventually located the door – quite a distance from where I thought it would be, I found that it was locked.

I was suddenly incredibly happy. The locked door was proof that I was not blind. They feared that I might get my sight back at any moment and walk straight out. There could be no reason in the world for locking up a *genuinely* blind man.

My hand explored the door, inch by inch. There was no knob or handle but what I did find was a smooth Yale-type lock – not, as I'd have expected, the knob which turned it, but the smooth, steel, slotted face that needed the key to open it. The lock had been put on the wrong way round, literally inside out.

It suddenly began to look as if the hospital might be bogus also . . . What normal hospital would have a room in it where you needed a key to get *out*? What the hell was going on? My initial intent had been to pound on the door and shout my head off until somebody came to see what the racket was about. Now I decided against this. Maybe those were also bogus people out there.

I went back to the bed and sat. If everything was bogus then why not my blindness, too? What if I was being kept in a completely dark room and there was nothing wrong with my sight at all? God knows I'd been in enough darkrooms, developing X-rays, although they hadn't been totally dark because of the dim red ceiling light. The thought of the ceiling light got me thinking. The 'nurse' had told me that he'd switched the ceiling light on and off for contrast when he was checking my eyes with the torch, but had he really?

While searching for the door I had encountered a wall switch, for the ceiling light, I assumed. Ceiling light, me barney! I thought. There probably wasn't even a bulb in the socket. And, I suddenly realised, I could test it. As far as I remembered, the 'nurse', having tried me with the ceiling light off, had switched it back on again, in which case it should still be on. I hadn't pressed the switch either way.

Rising quickly, I located the chair I'd felt five minutes before and dragged it into where I judged the centre of the room to be. Climbing on to it, I straightened up very carefully and, when I thought I had my balance, swept the space above me with my arms waving about like a cockroach's antennae. Nothing. I climbed down and moved the chair.

This time I found the light; my right hand banged a lightshade, which immediately began to wobble all around on the limit of its suspending flex. I managed to catch and steady it and, cocksure of my theory, went straight for the bulb I didn't believe to be there. It was and, with a cry of pain and surprise, I snatched my burned fingers away, and fell, rather than climbed down off the chair.

Thoroughly shaken, I dragged the chair back to its original position and sat down heavily on it, sucking my burned fingers and trying to think my way out of this suddenly very scary set-back. I had to fight very hard to superimpose logic upon my rising panic. It was an accepted fact of everyday life that if a light bulb is on, then it is very hot, but it didn't necessarily work the other way round. A very hot object need not give out light. I had to keep that thought fixed to the fore in my head. I thought of many things that didn't give out light, even when hot enough to burn flesh — electric irons, kitchen ranges. Could something like these be shaped like a bulb? Or could a bulb be painted black so that it gave off no light? Could it be enclosed in metal? I supposed so, but who would go to that much trouble? And to what end?

Then it struck me that there might be a bedside lamp and a few seconds of carefully controlled waving located it. Holding the cold bulb, I ran my hand down along the fitting and on to the cord until I came to the switch. I clicked it on and, in a matter of seconds, the bulb became too hot to hold. I switched off again and, when the bulb had cooled a little, removed it from its socket. It came out exactly like an ordinary bulb and the two metal pins of the bayonet-type fitting felt just right. It was, however, the heaviest bulb I had ever encountered. I rubbed the unscorched fingers of my left hand over its smooth surface; it sure felt like a bulb but, when I flicked it with a fingernail, it didn't sound like one. I guessed it was made from metal, not glass, but decided against the acid test of banging it on the metal head rail of the hospital bed – if it shattered, I'd never be able to come up with an excuse. I returned it to the socket and lay back on the bed to think some more.

Seconds later, and still slightly shaken by my brush with the ceiling light bulb, I was up again, setting out warily in search of the source of the birdsong and lawnmower sounds.

Before long – it was after all, as I was discovering, a pretty small room – my hand touched glass, a window, and a brief search revealed its latch. Expecting it to be locked, like the door, I worked the latch and was surprised when it opened out. At once I felt a breeze on my face and net curtains billowing gently against my cheek. The birds sang louder and the lawnmower was noisier.

Had I not already come upon the unnatural light bulb, this throwing open of the window and feeling breeze and hearing sounds would have convinced me that I was indeed blind. But I had learned by now that nothing in this chamber was as it seemed to be and so I set to figuring out just how the trick window worked.

I moved the window slowly in to close it and, just before I pulled it to, I noticed the rural sounds diminishing. I moved it out again an inch or two and the volume increased, but pushing it wide open didn't increase the volume any further. Moving more carefully this time, I drew the window in and found the point at which the volume suddenly diminished. I explored with my free hand and discovered that the window was some three fingers ajar. Putting my ear to the gap, so that my hearing was unimpeded by glass or wood, I slowly eased the window out again and heard when the volume stepped up. I even felt a tiny click as the frame engaged a switch. I repeated this move twice more, with the same results. The sounds from without were recordings, with two volume settings – 'closed' low, and 'open' high. The 'breeze', I assumed, came from a fan or vent somewhere in front of me, although it wasn't within arm's reach.

As I closed the window for the last time I noticed the other missing vital ingredient, smell. A lawnmower had been operating close by for an hour and there wasn't even a whiff of fresh grass clippings?

Back on the bed again, I reviewed my position as best I could. I probably wasn't even in a hospital. The sounds coming through the locked door were most likely recordings. Miss Fox's nagging voice had not ceased – I could still hear her whining away outside – and if, as the 'nurse' had told me, I had slept for seven hours, then Miss Fox must be on inhumanly long shifts . . . Unless, of course, she'd been on break for all the time I'd been asleep.

I upbraided myself for getting pedantic and began to work the head on what exactly was going on.

If I wasn't blind and, thank God, I now knew I wasn't, then the people who moved freely in the artificially darkened world and could actually 'see' things (like when I opened or closed my eyes) had to be using sophisticated night-sight glasses. That was obvious. But what science fiction film set had this room come from? What could its purpose be, apart from scaring the living hell out of anybody who happened to awake and find themselves in here? Perhaps it was a room specifically engineered to produce sensory deprivation and terror, a hundred times more sophisticated than the old way of blindfolding a captive for whole days on end.

I thought hard for a long time, eventually realising that the only reason I wasn't already a gibbering wreck was because of human error. The props had been almost perfect, it was the cast who had cocked up.

Actually, thinking back, it was the 'nurse', specifically,

who had ruined it for them by telling me I'd been out cold for two days when all my physical parameters told me that this couldn't be – the absence of decent beard stubble, my lack of thirst, no sign of needle- or catheter-marks over the veins in my arms . . .

The doctor had compounded their error by acting as though he was seeing me for the first time. Maybe it wasn't his fault – if he'd been unaware of the fact that the nurse had told me I'd been out for two days . . .

But at this point it didn't matter that much. What I wanted to know now was why I was in here.

Was someone going to ask me to confess to something? If so, who? And to what?

Was I being tenderised before being interrogated? By whom? About what?

Was someone trying to drive me mad? Again, who'd want to do that?

Crowther was the obvious one, but why would he want to scare the hell out of me? Kill me, maybe yes, just for revenge. And where would he find such a set-up as this? I gave up on Crowther.

I began to concentrate on the room. It clearly had been carefully designed and constructed: the door with the wrong-way lock, the false window with its false sounds and breezes, the special 'light bulbs'. These existed only to create illusions, to support and reinforce the 'fact' that the occupant – who would almost certainly, sooner or later, explore his cell – was blind.

The only 'innocent' reason for this fiendish room would be if it was part of some way-out extreme form of psychotherapy, like electric shock therapy, aversion therapy, frontal lobotomy, mind-bending drugs etc. And if this was its purpose, then did it belong to the only psychotherapist I'd ever been in any way involved with, Dr Conroy?

And of course, this begged the automatic question: was Dr Jim Smith actually Dr Albert Conroy? I didn't think so because, like most people in the country, I'd have recognised his voice from his frequent TV appearances. But hang on . . .

Dr Jim's voice was very nasal and muffled. Maybe he didn't have a head cold after all. Perhaps he had a clip squeezing his nostrils and a thick mouth mask so that he could talk to me without my recognising his real voice? It fitted so neatly that from this moment on I couldn't think of Dr Jim Smith as anything other than Dr Albert Conroy.

It was quite some time later, when I was actually beginning to nod off, that the volume on the hospital noises tape swelled briefly and died, and I knew I had a visitor. I quickly decided that, for the moment at least, I'd have to play along. 'Who is it?'

It was just the 'nurse'. Just? Florence Nightingale himself in night-vision glasses. 'Hey! You're awake. Any improvement?'

'No. What about the bloods? What did they show?'

'The doctor will be in soon.'

'You told me that an hour ago.'

'Yeah and you said you wanted to sleep. He docs have other patients, you know. But he'll be by, don't you worry. Let's have a look at the eyes.'

I felt his hand on my cheek and this time flinched. He apologised for not having warned me and leaned forward. He came so close that I could smell his nicotine-tainted breath. He leaned back again and stood up. 'Can I get you anything? Water, a cup of tea or coffee?'

'A glass of water would be fine, thank you. If it's not too much trouble?'

'No trouble.'

While he was away I had a sudden idea how I might trap him, find out once and for all if the room was a specially darkened one or not. When he came back I was ready for him. He handed me a tumbler of water which I drained in a go, then said: 'D'you know what I'd really love now?'

'What?'

'A cigarette.'

'Why didn't you ask me before? I didn't know you smoked. Rothmans Blues okay?' I could sense his hand going for his pocket, then freezing. He coughed awkwardly. 'Em. I forgot. Eh ... eh ... Smoking is not allowed.'

It had taken him whole seconds to realise that he couldn't light up my cigarette without lighting up my whole world – the bright flame of a match or lighter and a redly glowing fag tip every time you took a drag. 'Of course,' I replied, acting innocent. 'Hospital.'

To hide his confusion he went off to see if the doctor was ready. I grinned in glee when I heard the door close behind him. I wasn't a smoker, but then he wasn't a nurse and this wasn't a hospital. A real nurse in a real hospital would have reflexly slapped down my unhealthy and antisocial request.

Moments later, before I had even stopped savouring my little triumph, Miss Fox's voice increased and the nurse and doctor arrived back.

The doctor was upbeat, although he laced it with just a tinge of concern. His voice was still nasal and muffled. For my part, I was anxiety personified, pleading with him to do something, *anything*, no matter what it took, to cure me. I could pay anything, go anywhere in the world, I was insured, I'd do whatever he said, but I couldn't face losing my sight ... I couldn't bear the thought, I was desperate ... The charade continued for a while. At last he came up with the next phase of their plan.

The prognosis was, at best, guarded, although there was one small hope. It was an experimental unlicensed drug which had showed very encouraging signs but was still a long way off being given the go-ahead ...

I didn't care. I'd take it. I couldn't just sit here in permanent darkness. How could I get hold of this drug?

Funnily enough, Dr Jim just happened to have been given a single pill to try out, although the hospital authorities knew nothing about it and he swore me to secrecy.

Bugger the hospital authorities! They weren't the ones who'd been struck blind. I'd do anything.

Eventually he produced the pill and a plastic cup of water,

and told me that if I was willing to risk it then I could go ahead, although he would deny ever having given it to me, he hoped I understood why.

God, yes, gimme, gimme!

I swallowed the aspirin-sized pill, reflecting that that was probably exactly what it was, an aspirin. When should I feel a difference? How long would the course be? Would I have to take them all my life? I didn't care.

Dr Jim didn't know – these were brand new, remember? Untested. After some time they both went out, advising me to try to rest, not to get too excited, nor too depressed if there were no results straight off.

But there were.

After maybe half an hour, I became aware of the dimmest, just barely discernible, muddy light suffusing through the room. It seemed to have crept in without my noticing and while I could see absolutely no detail on anything, I could just about make out different shapes. Try as I might, I couldn't make out any source of light – it was simply all about me, the faintest of easing of the blackness. I looked towards the window, expecting to see some extra brightness there, but there wasn't any. The whole room was equally 'illuminated' – 'stained' more like – by dirty brown, almost non-existent faint light. It never got any brighter and, after perhaps ten minutes, faded slowly back to nothingness, leaving me wrapped once more in the cloying, claustrophobic dark. Now I could almost feel the dark, like damp cobwebs, clinging to my skin.

I tried to imagine what my emotional state would be if I actually believed I was blind. Having had that one tiny, tantalising display of returning back, albeit faintly and briefly, to the world I'd thought lost for ever, I'd be willing, desperate, to pay any price for the next pill. I'd heard of people being deliberately turned into heroin addicts so that they could be prevailed upon to give away secrets by threats to withdraw their fix but, in its own way, this would have been worse.

When they came back I played the part. I was agog with

excitement, demanding more pills at once, reporting that I had experienced no side effects at all and that these life-savers should be licensed right now. Dr Jim promised to do his best to get some more but, although I pleaded piteously and pressed him hard, insisted he couldn't get them until next day, if then. Eventually, promising to make some telephone calls, he said he'd come back to me if there was any news.

I settled back on my bed to await his return. I didn't know exactly what was going on but I had the strongest feeling that their magic pill and the little bit of play-acting with the dimmer switch and the faint lighting was the start of the endgame.

And they seemed to be in a hurry. Dr Jim would be back all right and soon.

I was right. It wasn't much more than an hour before he came in.

'*Did you get them?*' I demanded before he could even speak.

'Frank,' he began in a worried voice as if I hadn't spoken.

'What's wrong?' I asked with just the right amount of panic. 'Is something wrong?'

'Well . . . I don't really know what to say. I called my contact about a proper supply of those pills and . . . and he turned me down flat.'

'*What?*'

'I'm sorry, Frank.'

'Why would he do that? Is he afraid because they're not licensed? Is that it?'

'I don't honestly know, Frank. I was shocked. But I called another person I know, a dangerous character, a man who claims to be able to supply anything, anywhere, any time. At a price. I came across him once in the hospital, many years ago. I stitched him up after a very serious stabbing and, well, he thinks I saved his life and, regrettably, he insists on keeping contact with me ever since. So I told him my story and mentioned your plight, and asked him if there was anything he could do. He rang me back just now. He says he can get the stuff within an hour, as much of it as I want, but he has a price, a strange price . . .'

'I'll pay it! I don't care what it is.'

'You may not be able to pay it. He told me that he has a request from another client that he thinks you might be able to help him with.'

'What! What the hell are you talking about? I . . . don't understand.'

'Neither do I. I wrote it down,' said Dr Jim, shuffling in his pocket for, presumably, the paper on which he'd written the 'strange' request. 'Here it is, okay? He says that you had a cousin called Dave Ryder . . . True?'

'Yes, but he's dead. What about him?'

'It seems that your cousin had some important business records at the time he died and that the partner in that business wants them back. For some reason he thinks you may know where they are. Do you?'

I was stunned for a moment and I wasn't acting either. At last I knew why I was being kept here in this never-never land. *'That's his price?'*

'Yes.'

'Oh, *Jesus*! I know nothing at all about Dave or his business. Surely he'll take cash? You can make him see sense. After all, he owes you. *Please*!'

'I already tried that, Frank. He'll take nothing but the disks. Eh, I believe these records were on floppy disks.'

Medineeds. Dave had made duplicate disks. Bingo!

Groaning aloud, I put my head in my hands, portraying 'Despair'. 'This is impossible. I hardly saw the guy – maybe once or twice a year for the past ten years. Why the hell does your contact think I know anything about these records? Does he know I've gone blind already?'

'I've told him, Frank. But he's a hard man.'

'He's a fucking *madman*, that's what the bastard is! I have no idea in the world where Dave's business records might be. Maybe in a bank or a safety deposit box, or his lawyer's or . . . or . . . or . . . *Jesus! – I don't know! I haven't a clue*!' I shouted, distraught, portraying 'Near Hysteria'.

'Try and think. Maybe something will come to you, some place special. You grew up together, I believe.'

Now just how in the world did he know that?

'Yes, but that was a long time ago. Oh . . . Christ! I have no idea about Dave or his fucking business dealings. He was a criminal, a fucking gangster!' I shouted at him. 'Did you know that?'

'I'd heard rumours. Can you remember any secret hiding places you shared when you were kids, anything like that?'

'The only secret hiding place we ever had was in a bucket lowered down an old well shaft that no one ever opened.'

'Where was that?' He sounded eager – nasal, muffled, but eager, definitely eager.

'It's gone now. That field, which Dave's father owned, became a housing estate many years ago. *Think*! We have to get these pills from somewhere! Offer him double the value of the pills. Three times.'

We sat for a while in silence, ostensibly trying to find a way out of 'our' dilemma. I assumed that this period was to let me stew and sweat for a while, see if my memory mightn't suddenly improve.

And I *was* thinking, hard. But not about what Dr Jim thought I was thinking about.

All I was wondering about was why on earth should this 'shady character' who wanted Dave's disks recognise my name and realise that a Frank Samson and a Dave Ryder were cousins? And why would Dr Jim actually mention my name at all; my name could have no bearing whatever on whether or not the drug was available.

Obviously I didn't express these speculations to Dr Jim. I just begged him to have another pleading session with his friend.

'I'll try, Frank, but you must also keep trying. Dave had the disks so he must have put them somewhere. At least, according to this man. Perhaps I'll go and call on him personally. See if I can't soften him. But in the meantime you keep trying to remember anything at all that might help. Have you found a strange key among your cousin's effects, a receipt, anything? I'm afraid this guy means business, that he'll stick to his demands.'

And with that ominous admonition he went out, leaving the world to darkness and to me.

25

Nobody came into my little dark cell over the next hour, if indeed it was an hour. Time, at that stage, had ceased to have any relevance for me.

At one point I went and checked the door, more for the exercise than from any real hope that it might have been left unlocked. It hadn't. I spent several minutes shuffling about the tiny patch of clear floor space before returning to stretch out on the bed and, staring fixedly at the invisible ceiling, think through my predicament. The one sure thing about it, I reckoned, was that it was going to get a lot worse, and soon.

I had no idea how much longer they would go on trying this 'subtle' charade before deciding they might get better results from a more traditional approach, like pulling out my fingernails, filling me with truth serums (which I had no doubt 'Dr Jim' would have access to) or even, taking into account his murderous forte, hypnosis.

An hour ago I would have had no fear of hypnosis or truth serum, as I had absolutely no idea where the disks might be, but this position had suddenly changed and a most untimely burst of inspiration had left me with the uneasy conviction that I knew exactly where they were – an unfortunate case of premature extrapolation, if ever there was one.

The merest droplet of truth serum, the first oscillation of a bright object before my eyes and I would undoubtedly tell all. This worried me very much, not because I felt spiteful and just didn't want Conroy and Crowther to have the disks, but because I realised that, once they had found them, they'd have no further use for me. In fact, without putting a gloss on it, they would then proceed to murder me.

As if that prospect weren't horrifying enough on its own, there was the ever-increasing danger that I myself might help to expedite matters because I was finding it harder and harder to remember to act like a terrified newly blind person. At some point soon they'd have to suspect that they weren't fooling anybody, least of all me. Then the rough stuff would commence.

Taking all these factors into account, I decided that my best bet was to strike first and have a go at the next person to enter the room, an unexpected, pre-emptive strike, my very own little Pearl Harbor. Tora! Tora! Tora!

Having come to my decision, I lay waiting in the dark, psyched up for action and the sooner the better, while I still had the element of surprise. I wasn't expecting Dr Jim – he'd have to keep up the pretence of being off trying to soften up the hard man – but I reckoned that my 'nurse' might look in soon to see if my memory had improved any. I smiled nervously to myself, amused at the thought that, even if my ambush failed, I might be able to wriggle out of the inevitably ensuing mess by claiming a panic attack: 'I was in a *blind* panic, Dr Jim, honest!' Good ol' Frank. Wise-assing to the end.

I was trying to guess if night-sight goggles would be worn like a hood, with the whole head covered, or like a snorkeller's mask, with just a strap, when the door opened. Miss Fox called for Dr Vine and the nurse was in the room. Launching straight away into my plan, I began fluttering my left eyelid, as if there was something in the eye.

'Doc?' I asked anxiously, just to be sure there weren't two of them. No way would I be able to handle two.

'Only me, Frank. Dr Jim won't be back for a while yet. How's things?'

'Just how the fuck do you think they are?' I barked sullenly. 'Some asshole is refusing to give me those pills unless I tell him something I don't know! How would *you* feel?' I stopped. 'Sorry, nurse. I didn't mean to take it out on you, but it's fucking ridiculous ... I mean, how am I supposed to tell the stupid bastard something I don't know myself? Asshole!'

'Don't worry. I'm sure it'll all work out in the end.'

'I hope so. I've been praying harder than I ever prayed in my life. And now, as if things weren't bad enough, my fucking eye has to start acting up. It feels like there's something in it. Can you have a look, please?'

'Sure. Lie back there. Let's see now ... Here come the hands, okay?'

'Okay.' I waited until I could smell the tobacco, and feel the hot breath and both his hands on my face.

'Roll the eyeball down, Fra—' was as far as he got. I shot my hands up between his, knocking them wide apart and made a grab for his face, immediately encountering the goggles which I gripped and ripped upwards until they were free in my right hand.

Now we were both blind and equal.

Except that he was shocked and I wasn't, so I ought to have reacted faster. All I had to do was roll off the bed, away from him, on to the floor in the narrow space between it and the wall, and I'd be safe.

But I didn't even get to start. His reflexes were sharp and, before I could shunt myself out of his range, he threw himself in an ungainly spreadeagle on top of me. I tried to bring a knee up to push him off, but my feet stuck out over the end of the bed and, with nothing for them to push against, it just didn't work. I felt his hand scuttle rapidly up along my arm, like a huge spider, desperately stretching out towards the vital goggles, and I tried to extend my arm further away still. Despite this, he managed to curl his fingers round the dangling strap and began to pull hard. His face was directly above mine now, a matter of a mere inch or two away, and hot, stringy gobs of the saliva of his grunting exertion fell disgustingly on to my cheeks and eyes, and coursed slowly down along the contours of my face, towards my chin and tightly clamped mouth.

Concentrating grimly on the deadly tug of war for the goggles, I was slow to realise that the knee he was sliding up across my thigh was not an effort to edge himself closer to the prize. It took a tiny shift in his position to warn me that his knee was, in fact, on a deliberate, tactical, attacking move against my unprotected groin. I tried to roll my thigh inwards to cover my vulnerability but couldn't quite manage to. Very worried, now, I tore at his face and head with my free hand, desperately trying to steady his evasive twisting; once or twice, my stiffly hooked fingers raked across his eyes, but the lids were screwed tightly closed as if he knew exactly what my talons sought and all the time, inch by inch, his knee crept closer to its target, moving in small jerks as he worked it along.

At one point I sensed that he had slightly elevated his upper body and presumably his head, and I jerked my head up off the pillow with as much force as I could muster. There was a cry of pain from the darkness above me and warm blood drops began to fall on my face. I didn't know exactly where I had head-butted him but it had felt cartilaginous, like his nose. The blow knocked much of the determination out of him and, although he tried gamely to ignore his pain and cling on, over the next seconds I began to work him loose, to prise his starfish grip off me. When at last I managed to grab his pulverised nose between my thumb and forefinger I squeezed it like a soft tomato; he went suddenly still and actually began to climb off me, trying to squirm away to save his ruined nose. His breath was bubbling and he was coughing violently, drowning in his own blood, I reckoned. I held my grip until I was safely crouched on the floor on the other side of the narrow bed, then pushed him away.

With bloody hands I managed to fit the goggles and instantly found myself looking through a murky world of underwater green at my bloodied and disorientated 'nurse' as he twisted and turned, trying to locate me by sound.

He looked shit-scared and rocketed like a pheasant when I

tapped him from behind and hit him a crisp uppercut when he spun round.

'He never saw what hit him, your honour,' I jeered aloud as the nurse picked himself up off the bed.

Then I darted around it until I was behind him again and, bending close to his ear, roared. That sent him ceilingwards once more but I didn't hit him again. He was not a big man and besides, he was blind.

I also thought I was an idiot for talking and then shouting. What if Dr Jim was about? I was suddenly very worried. But, if he was, I reasoned quickly, then surely 'nurse' would have been shouting for help. I felt better.

I saw him edge a hand towards the bedside table as though he could reach it unnoticed by me. Then I realised what he was reaching for, a single Yale-type key on a ring with a leather tag on it. Scooping it up, I strode to the door and opened it.

I peeped quickly through into another completely dark room, this one tiny, without a stick of furniture in it, unless you counted the speaker which was attached high in one corner, pumping out its inane 'hospital noises' tape. There was another door in this tiny room.

I heard the shuffling of the 'nurse' behind me, as he staggered towards the cell door, a hand clasped to his profusely bleeding nose; I waited for him to bump into me, then pushed him violently so that he ended up sprawled back on the bed again. 'Bye-bye, nurse,' I said and closed the door with a bang. The spring lock clicked home with a satisfying sound of finality.

The door from the second room led on to another tiny dark room with yet another door, and I put my ear to this one before pushing on through. The next small room had a sloping ceiling and lots of coat hooks along its highest wall, some of them with nondescript garments hanging from them, but the most important feature of this little chamber was the fact that its exit door had slits of bright light surrounding it. I assumed it was an under-stairs cloakroom and that some sort of hallway lay beyond. This time I listened especially carefully before stepping through.

I found myself standing in the fair-sized silent hall of what seemed to be a deserted house. There wasn't a sound from anywhere, no ticking clock, no radio from a distant room, no vacuum cleaner noise; the silence was almost as absolute as it had been in my cell. Turning to close the under-stairs door, my heart suddenly surged as I recognised, now bathed in the natural light of day, my own clothes. They hung in an untidy jumble from a single coat hook, with shoes and socks placed neatly on the floor beneath them; I'd passed them on the way out but, seeing only green, had not recognised them. Now I noticed a light switch by the door and I snapped it on, bathing the small cloakroom in a warm orange glow. In the corner, almost hidden by a large tweed overcoat, I spied a washbasin which, after my clothes, was about the next most welcome thing I could think of.

Stepping back into the cloakroom and pulling the door in after me, I dropped the blood-spattered hospital robe on the floor. The basin even had a mirror above it and I washed all the nurse's blood off, enjoying the cold water more than a desert animal would a sunset waterhole. Drying myself with the cleaner parts of my discarded robe, I turned to my clothes. My shirt and jacket bore the vivid stains of when I'd vomited in the wet ditch a lifetime ago, while my shoes, socks and trouser legs were still damp from their immersion, but they were a great improvement on the flimsy hospital gown. I checked quickly through my pockets – my mobile phone was missing, taken by my captors or perhaps lost during my inversion and immersion, but my wallet was still in the hip pocket. In the circumstances I'd gladly have swapped the wallet for the mobile.

There was a canvas shoulder-bag hanging on one of the pegs and I placed the night-goggles in that and slung it over my shoulder. I took the tweed overcoat from its hook by the basin and put it on. It didn't fit but at least it hid the stained clothes beneath. Easing the door open again, I pushed back into the profoundly silent hall. Now properly, albeit damply, clothed, I felt instantly and infinitely better, in charge of my destiny, empowered, like Clark Kent emerging from the phone booth.

I took a quick peek through the four doors which opened off the hall – they led to three rooms and a corridor, all unused and dust-draped. There was no sign of a telephone.

The windows by the front door were grimy, the plain net curtains hanging over them grey and moth-eaten. I rubbed a little clear patch in an opaque pane and, seeing nothing untoward, darted out of the front door and into the most gloriously fresh and clean drizzle, dream stuff after where I'd been.

There was a shortish driveway with just enough curve in it to hide the house from the road and the sound of a car passing by outside the closed wooden gates. These were high and solid, and were set into an even higher and more solid limestone wall, topped with broken glass, which ran round the property. I had to climb the gates, which were electrically locked.

I was now loose, out in the country, but I had no idea where I was until a line of three cars passed, all with Kilkenny number plates. Some distance along the road there was a bus shelter, so I made for that and huddled into a corner in case Dr Jim, returning from his bogus quest, should spot me. Not knowing what car he drove meant that I had to hide my face from almost every vehicle that went by in either direction. Luckily I was alone in the shelter, with nobody to observe my sudden stooping to rummage in my bag, every time one approached. I kept the gate of the house under observation until a bus came and I stepped aboard.

'Where to?' asked the driver.

'Next town,' I said.

'Urlingford?'

'Urlingford.' I thrust a fiver at him. 'Which bus stop is this? What number, like?'

'Six four,' he answered, handing me my change, together with a strange look.

The journey lasted nearly half an hour and it took another

ten minutes for me to find the police station. I met with a sceptical reception from the local force, despite the evidence of the night-goggles, but when I started to bandy Curley's name about things improved. Perhaps someone had rung him just to check. If so, then I was lucky that he had told them to co-operate with me, not throw me in a cell.

We helped each other over the high gate and cautiously approached the house. There were eight men altogether, excluding me, dodging from cover to cover, closing in and circling the house. I was ordered to stay by the gate but didn't. After five minutes or so we all met up at the front; nobody had seen a sign of life. The first inkling that anything had changed since my hasty departure came when the sergeant and I approached the front door. I had left it slightly ajar but it was closed now.

'Are you sure it wasn't the wind?' he asked. A freshening breeze had come in from somewhere and was blowing the bushes about.

'Maybe it was.' I shrugged, trying to recall whether the door had moved easily on its hinges or not. 'But I don't think so. Try the knob, see if it's locked.'

'Just a moment. We're *supposed* to knock first.' The sergeant pressed the bell and rapped on the door. 'Anybody home?' We waited a moment, then he repeated the performance, this time louder. 'Nobody at home, it seems, Mr Samson. Ah, well, here goes.'

The door opened, a bit stiffly. 'So it wasn't the wind after all,' he said. He ordered one man to stand outside the front, another round to the back and then sent two others to search the house. He called the men who had stayed outside on the road and told them to ask around the nearest houses to see 'what the score is on this place', then clipped his walkie-talkie back on his belt and told me to lead off for the dungeons.

I led them, with their powerful torches, through the series of small anterooms and finally to the closed door of the inner cell. The hospital noises were still droning eerily on, with

Miss Fox again summoning Dr Ibrahim Khan. She'd gone the full cycle.

'He's in there,' I whispered, pointing my torch at the door and gingerly turning the knob of the spring lock. 'Or at least, he was.'

Urlingford's finest got themselves psychologically and physically ready to overpower the penned-up, blinded and bloodied miscreant.

But he wasn't in there. Obviously Dr Jim had returned, sprung his 'nurse' and they'd cleared out.

'Fuck,' I summed up the situation, deciding against verbalising the thought that, if they had moved a bit quicker, we might have caught them.

The sergeant barked orders to get some lights in here and turn off that fucking tape, and get the lab lads in for blood and fingerprints and stop all that gabble, he couldn't hear himself think. Then he began to fire off questions at me.

'What did the "doctor" look like?'

'Like I told your superintendent, I never saw him. But, as I also told him. I'm pretty certain of his identity.'

'You *think* you're certain.' The station superintendent had not been too keen on my reasoning about Dr Albert Conroy, Celebrity, Star of the Small Screen. Apparently the police often called him in for psychological profiles of murderers and rapists. 'And the "nurse"?'

'About five-seven, eight, clean-shaven, a bit thin on top, skinnyish . . .'

'Colour of hair? Eyes?'

'Green. Colour of hair, green. Colour of eyes, green. Colour of skin, green. Colour of clothes, green. Colour of blood, green. Colour of everything green. Take a look through those.'

But one of the men had already donned the goggles. 'Switch off that torch a second, sergeant, will you. Holy hell! Ye're all green. It's like in *The Silence of the Lambs* when yer man with no dick was chasin' what'll I call her? Josie Foster.'

*

On our way back into town I had a call on the sergeant's mobile. As soon as I'd got an address for the strange house I'd passed it on to Edwin Savage in the Business Section and he now returned my call with the information that the house was owned by a foreign company, presumably as a kind of holiday home for its executives; however, the really interesting thing about this foreign holding company was that it was also one of the multiple layers in the ownership of Medineeds International. 'What's going on, Frank?'

'At the moment I haven't a clue, but I'll let you know if I find anything, okay? Thanks, anyway.'

'Is that a fact, now,' said the sergeant when I told him, even though he hadn't a clue who or what Medineeds might be. He interrupted me to turn to one of his men in the back. 'Finnerty, would you get on your ol' stumbly-mumbly there like a good man and see if anyone has turned up anything on that house.'

Everybody laughed except me and Finnerty – me because I wasn't in on the joke and Finnerty because he was its butt. It transpired that he had gone to quell a noisy party the previous week but had ended up joining in the revelries and, at three in the morning, had had to call in to report that the party-goers were refusing to let him drive the squad car and could someone please come and pick him up. His rescuing fellow officers had found him stumbling along the road, still mumbling his request for a pick-up into his walkie-talkie, and had promptly renamed the instrument Finnerty's stumbly-mumbly. A light-hearted bunch, the Urlingford fuzz.

By the time we reached Urlingford, further reports over the radio informed us that local enquiries had elicited the fact that the house was never visited, that no one local kept an eye on the place, that the postman never delivered mail and that none of the local plumbers, electricians or carpenters had ever been called in. The house was, of course, supposed to be haunted.

*

313

I spent less than an hour in Urlingford, just long enough to buy some clothes, hire a car, take a bath at the sergeant's house and call the practice. I told a worried Barbara that something had come up on the Crowther business, and that I'd see her in the morning and explain my sudden disappearance to the satisfaction of all. Then I headed out of town and turned for Uncle Clem's house, little more than an hour's drive away.

26

Julia Harte opened the door. She took one look at me then, bursting into tears, turned and headed back into the house as fast as her arthritic old knees could carry her. I caught her up in a few steps and put a comforting arm around the thin, heaving shoulders just as James, his face a mask of the terror of the very vulnerable, came rushing from the kitchen. Julia had gone to answer the door mere seconds ago and whatever she'd found had reduced her to tears.

When he recognised me the fear was replaced by worry for his wife and he rushed to support her from the other side. By the time we had navigated Julia back on to her chair in the kitchen, James had managed to calm her down somewhat and he pulled his chair close to hers so that he could keep a comforting arm around her thin shoulders.

I'd interrupted their supper and I sat with them until Julia had recovered – it seemed she had thought I was her beloved David and, judging by the way she kept glancing at me, I reckoned she still wasn't sure. She then wanted to 'make me something' but I insisted that she finish her own rapidly cooling meal and went off to forage for myself in the fridge. Julia nibbled and sniffed, and watched me through damp eyes as I whipped eggs and assembled the makings of an omelette, the parentage of which would be extremely difficult for a taster to judge; nor would an observer, viewing the final runny product, have fared much better – dogs have landed themselves on my examination table for producing substances far less revolting-looking. I could see, from the slow way Julia shook her head, that she was wondering just what, in the name of all that was wonderful, the world was coming to at all at all when a man had to cook his own supper. It wasn't natural . . . It just was not natural.

They sat in silence until I'd finished my meal. Neatly aligning my knife and fork (the best silver ones from the antique canteen, naturally), I dabbed genteelly at my lips and, folding the starched linen napkin which Julia had set out for the young master, said brightly: 'So how've you been? Any news?'

The floodgates opened again and while James was trying to restore some fragile order I was struggling to think up further neutral, bland opening gambits – I couldn't even flatter her by praising the omelette because I'd cooked it myself. When Julia got back to the sniffing stage again we had another go.

Conversation began shakily, everyone trying to avoid the D-word, but outside Dave, Uncle Clem and the house, there wasn't a lot else to talk about and within minutes we'd exhausted our combined stores of small talk.

So Dave it was. We spoke about him for some fifteen minutes, remembering incidents and anecdotes from childhood and, for a while, it was almost as if he were still alive, as if he'd just stepped outside for a moment. It was an uncanny feeling, but felt, I suspected, mainly by me. The Hartes were used to the house with nobody else in it, whereas I could think of very few instances when I'd been here without Dave.

After a while I got down to business: 'Do you remember, James, you telling me at the funeral that you and Julia were so relieved that he'd called to see you just a few days before he was killed?'

'Aye, Francis. Indeed I do. And thank God he did. It was a great comfort to us.'

'I'm sure it was. Can you remember what day that was?' I asked gently. 'Like, was it the day before, or two days, or three . . . ?'

The old man thought hard, straining to recall. 'I'm sorry,' he said finally, 'I can't tell you. All I'm sure of is that it was less than a week. Probably less than four days . . . I'm sorry.'

'Don't apologise, James. That's really helpful. Four days, huh? How was he? Good form? Worried? Nervous? Preoccupied? Agitated?'

'He was the same as ever, Francis. The same as ever.'

'Same old Dave, eh? Did he say where he'd been? Or where he was going?'

'No. But I had the impression that he had come straight down from Dublin.'

'Did he tell you that?'

'No, but he apologised for coming so late and said he'd expected to be much earlier but that the traffic had been very bad, and I figured that Dublin is the nearest traffic to here.'

I smiled at him. 'I see th'oul' loaf is still goin' like a bomb, James. Can you remember what time he got here?'

They answered simultaneously. Julia said eight and James said ten past. They immediately looked at each other, flustered, as if they'd just failed the most important test of their lives and once again I had to reassure them that there was no need to be *that* precise.

'How long did he stay?'

'I don't know, really. We thought he was going to stay the night, but then Julia heard him driving off in the middle of the night . . .'

'Changed his mind, did he?'

'Oh, no. Well, I don't know. I mean, he hadn't actually *said* he was staying or anything . . . We just *thought* he might be, because of the suitcase.'

'What suitcase was that, James?' I asked, understanding why the Hartes had thought it odd that Dave would have brought a suitcase in from the car if he hadn't intended to stay. I knew why, but I wasn't going to tell them.

'It was about so big . . .' James boxed off a cube of air with his gnarled hands. 'And it was made of metal. Aluminium, I'd say.'

'You didn't see what was in it? Did he open it at all?'

'No, not while I was there, he didn't.'

I paused. 'You didn't happen to get a look inside, Julia?' Julia had always had a reputation, if not for being exactly nosy, then certainly for knowing what was going on around her. The Eye on High, Dave and I used to call her. For she was very tall in those days and we were very small.

'No, Francis. I didn't.' She didn't seem to notice my slight emphasis on the 'you'.

I nodded. 'Did he seem worried about this case? You know – take it with him from room to room?'

'He didn't go anywhere. We just sat here in the kitchen and then moved into the sitting room to watch the telly. We used to have the telly in here, but the rest of the house was growing chill from not being used, so we decided to use it a bit more.'

'Very wise. The place looks great. When you went to watch TV, did Dave take the suitcase with him?'

'Eh, em . . . I think so.'

'He did,' said Julia positively.

'I see. Maybe he was afraid that somebody might break into the house while you were all in the other room and steal either the case itself, or something from it.'

'They couldn't have stolen anything out of it because it was locked,' offered the Eye on High. I was tempted to ask her how she knew that, but contented myself with a small inner smile. Maybe she realised she had given her busybody self away because she immediately stood up and decided we could all do with another cup of tea. James, reacting reflexly as he always did, stood and began to clear away the supper dishes.

'Julia,' I said as she set a delicate cup and saucer in front of me, 'do you have any idea what time Dave might have left? You heard him leave, didn't you say?'

'I did, but it was dark and I couldn't see the clock.' She looked worried, as though she really ought to have checked. Julia's 'middle of the night', I thought, could have been any time between eleven and six the next morning.

'It doesn't matter,' I dismissed her worry reassuringly.

And it probably didn't because Dave hadn't been murdered that night. Curley's men had had him under observation on the night he'd been killed; unless, of course, he'd made the round trip during the few hours when his tail had lost him. But no, the Hartes would have remembered clearly if he'd been murdered a few hours after leaving them.

While we drank the watery herbal tea the Hartes preferred, I finished my gentle questioning. Dave had neither made nor received phone calls and, apart from a two-minute trip to the downstairs loo, he had been in their company all the time until they went to bed. He had sat with them, sometimes watching TV, sometimes passing a few remarks, sometimes browsing through a newspaper or magazine from the rack by the coffee table. In other words, I thought, acting like a man waiting patiently for the Hartes to go off to bed and leave him on his own.

There were a few things that they had thought odd at the time, minor things. Dave had said he'd just dropped by to see them, yet he didn't leave when they went to bed as a purely social caller would have. Because he was there, the Hartes had put off their bedtime for as long as they could, until they were both falling asleep in front of the telly. When, finally, they could postpone it no longer, they made their apologies to Dave. Julia had offered to make him some supper, hot milk and buttered Marietta biscuit sandwiches – God, did that menu bring back memories! – which he had politely but firmly declined. James had asked him if he wanted the TV on or off and had actually begun to move towards the set. Dave had said to leave it on, which had surprised James as there was a particularly boring film showing that Dave had been ignoring all along, leafing through magazines instead. When he had suggested that there might be something better on another channel, Dave had told him not to worry, that this was fine. Then he had hugged them both goodnight, given Julia a big smackeroo on both cheeks, promised to call again soon and shooed them off to bed.

'And that was the last time we . . .' Julia broke into tears again.

Not wanting to repeat Dave's tactic of outsitting the elderly couple until they could no longer stay awake, I asked Julia if I could stay the night. This stopped the tears at once and had her off preparing the room, making the bed, laying out towels and generally fussing about. I told her I'd stretch out on the sofa but Julia wouldn't even hear of it.

Sitting on Dave's bed, yawning and exhausted after the exertions of the day, I set the alarm clock, which Julia had thoughtfully provided, for 2.30 and, lying back, turned out the light, plunging the room into total darkness. I had a momentary panic attack when the sight went from my eyes and I had to stop myself from leaping up and switching it on again. Fine thing, I mocked myself, becoming afraid of the dark at your age.

Despite closing my eyes (so that I couldn't actually see the dark, if that makes sense to you) and thinking distracting thoughts of Claire, I was still far too uneasy for sleep. Twenty minutes later I sat up, put the light on again, knocked off the alarm, hauled on my new Urlingford clothes and crept out on to the landing. I listened a moment outside the door of the Hartes' room before continuing on downstairs, keeping in by the wall and avoiding altogether a certain step which, to my total surprise, I still remembered made a loud squeak.

Downstairs I put on a light and headed for Uncle Clem's library–study, an annexe which he'd had built on when Dave and I were children.

Local contractors had done the grunt work, the walls, roof, flooring and windows, but Clem, a self-proclaimed DIY expert, had done most of the 'finer work'. This had included the huge reddish granite chimney breast he had designed himself and the stones for which he had sought in quarries all over the country. David and I had spent many, many days travelling with him in his Mercedes, criss-crossing the land from early morning to the near-midnight dusks of long summer days, the sagging rear end of the Merc leaving sparks on the bumpy roads on the way home, from the weight of granite blocks in the boot. Aunt Heather would give him stick when we got back, both for keeping the boys out all night and for wrecking the car, but I don't think she ever meant it.

When, eventually, all the rocks had been assembled Uncle Clem set about his masterpiece and, block by rugged block, the construction began. He built this huge granite wall, stretching almost from one side of the room to the other and from floor to ceiling. The wall actually stopped about four feet short of the corners on either side and the resultant alcoves were filled with wooden bookshelves. In the centre was an open fireplace and, at various places along the rock face he left little niches for knick-knacks. They were there still, a gnarled piece of petrified bog oak, a rock containing large yellow crystals, an old carriage clock, a brass microscope, a pair of candlesticks, all spotlessly clean. I wondered how the elderly Hartes got at the high ones. I'd have to tell them not to bother – we'd take them down, put them on a table or something, somewhere safe.

But there was another feature of the granite wall – a hidden compartment which Dave had shown me with as much choking excitement as if it were a secret passage leading to the secret hideout of Cap'n Bluebeard, the Cruel Pirate. As kids we used to open it almost daily, not to put anything in or take anything out – it was just a jump-start for our fertile imaginations.

Uncle Clem maintained that the hiding place was necessary because of the increasing number of burglaries, but his wife reckoned that he was just gadget mad and she was probably right.

Apart from me, Dave and his parents, no one knew about the secret chamber. This, I realised, now meant only me and I hoped I remembered how to open it.

As a kid the granite structure had looked to me like the Cliffs of Moher, it was so big; now it wasn't quite as formidable. In fact, as I approached it, I thought it was intrusive rather than impressive – there was far too much of it. My gaze travelled the rough surface towards its left extremity and I tried to pick out which of the great blocks was the one that pivoted. I moved to the alcove on my left.

I removed some twenty books from the third shelf up from the side nearest the chimney breast and felt in at the back until I located a groove cut into the bottom of the shelf above. It was perhaps half an inch deep and the same wide, and it ran along by the back wall for some two feet. Folding my right hand at an awkward angle, I fingered the groove and straight away felt a metal rod with an eye at the end. I put my finger in the eye and gently pulled it backwards. It came with ease and I was momentarily surprised until I smelled the penetrating oil and felt it on my finger. Dave had probably had a hell of a job getting it open. The rod slid along the groove and came clear of its insertion in the side of the chimney breast. This allowed the small granite slab it had been buried in to swivel open on a pivot, again recently oiled.

This wasn't the secret place itself; it merely housed another rod.

Drawing a deep breath, I took hold of this second rod and drew it slowly upwards. When I'd moved it some two inches I heard and felt a tiny click; the slight tension on it vanished altogether and a section of the chimney breast sprang a narrow lip along a staggered joining, like half a swastika, between the stones. Rubbing my damp palms along my thighs, I reached for the secret door, caught the rim with my fingertips and gently coaxed it open.

27

'*Frank*,' Dave's voice said, '*if you're listening to this, then I'm already dead . . .*' Those first shocking words from the car speakers all but had me off the road. Almost reflexly I stabbed the 'STOP' button and pulled over. I needed to steel myself for this, the eerie, creepy sensation of being alone on a dark night in a dark car with the very alive but disembodied voice of a long-dead man. I wondered how long the tape would be.

I had found the aluminium suitcase, not locked now and, with a blend of trepidation and excitement, clicked it open. Inside were some twenty floppy disks with just dates and numbers on their labels, and a single sixty-minute audio cassette tape with 'For Frank Samson Only' written on it in Dave's writing. The 'only' was heavily underlined. There was also a sheaf of documents, all of which seemed to be either stocks and bonds certificates or title deeds to properties, and a green baize bag containing literally hundreds of what I assumed to be uncut diamonds. There were also five keys, on five different keyrings, numbered 1 to 5 on their plastic tags. I took the audio cassette, closed the case and immured it once more.

I was in the car because I hadn't wanted to take even the slightest risk of the tape being overheard – by the Hartes or anyone else. Unable to find headphones for the basic radio-cassette player which stood on the kitchen windowsill, its shiny little telescopic aerial askew, I'd scouted through the other downstairs rooms, but the Hartes were clearly not music buffs and the small red Sony perched above the kitchen sink seemed to be the only thing in the whole house capable of playing a tape.

And so I'd decided to take a drive . . .

Bracing myself, I leaned forward and pushed the 'PLAY' button: '. . . *and, if I'm already dead, then you will no doubt have heard all the things they say about me. Unfortunately, Frank, I have to admit that most of the charges, if not indeed all, will be true. But just for the record, just in case they try to nail me for every unsolved case they have on the books, I might as well make a clean breast of it . . .*'

I listened as Dave recited a litany of crimes until they eventually became meaningless. He had obviously recorded the tape as he was driving and, on several occasions, he broke his mind-numbing narrative to mention places he was passing, places which had some nostalgic significance for one or both of us.

Among the long list, he confessed that his yachting trip to the Scottish Isles had been bogus and that he had, in fact, been '*doing the job they said I was doing*' at the time. He also admitted to the jewellery shop robbery which Curley had been asking about, the one with Teddy Wright, although Dave didn't incriminate him. In fact, throughout the whole tape he never once mentioned anyone else's name, never fingered an accomplice until, that is, he came to the end, the immediate past, the incidents that he feared, correctly as it transpired, might get him killed. The only thing he didn't confess to was the theft of Ellen's letter and the snake ring but, I figured, in such a morass of amorality it was little wonder that this hadn't figured far up on his list of high crimes and misdemeanours. Still. I was his cousin, which surely should have made it a significant wrong? Evidently not.

Then he wound up the crimes list, claiming that it was as much as he could think of offhand.

The next ten minutes were autobiographical: for whatever reason, he began a slightly rambling story about how, almost innocently at first, he became ever more deeply involved until, at this point, he was almost totally immersed, *embedded* (he opted for a stronger word) in a life of crime. I didn't at first see the point of this rambling apologia, but when he ended with a '*May God Forgive Me*' of forceful sincerity, I reckoned he was already thinking of the afterlife. So much for Dave's committed atheism, I thought. Unless he was trying to con God, too – to pull a fast one on the God he didn't believe in – just in case: a spot of fire insurance.

The tape was running on, nearing the end of the first side, before Dave came to what he described as '*This present upheaval*'. At this point he had switched off the tape and then turned it back on again. It was, however, quite some time before he spoke over the noises of his car and the traffic whumping past him on a busy and wet road.

This present upheaval [he began again, then faltered] *in fact, Frank, the whole reason why I'm making this ch . . . tape or testimonial or whatever you want to call it, is to tell you about the disks you'll have found with this cassette. There's no point in you just sticking them into your computer because you won't be able to open them – they're all in code and they're password-protected about ten different ways. I've written one disk for you, the one marked PPP7, which gives you all the information you need to get into the others and convert them into readable form. They won't make happy reading, Frank. You might as well know that before you start.*

Another click marked where he had again switched off and a second one brought him back. There was another longish pause with just traffic noises, before he resumed: '*I don't know where to start, Frank. It's a complicated story. Have you ever heard of a company called Medineeds International? I suppose there's no reason why you should have, but anyway, check it out.*' He went on to give me the company's and Charlie McMahon's addresses, and to tell me that the company had been closed down abruptly the other day.

When I found this out, I became afraid for my life, Frank. You see, my associates, who actually own the company, had neglected to inform me that they were going to do so and the only reason I could see for them to close their lucrative business was that they were afraid it might come under sudden scrutiny from the police. And the most probable reason they feared that was that we, me and them that is, have had a major running argument over the past few days. I'm not telling this very well, Frank. Sorry about that, but it'll all come clear in a moment. The reason it's so jumbled is that there are several different strands running together and they have not yet joined up. Maybe I ought to go back a bit.

Medineeds is owned by two men I've known for many years. I wouldn't exactly call them friends as such, more like associates. Sure we had good times together in the past, but it was like a friendship based on lucrative business schemes — mostly illegal business schemes. We're all rich enough now to go straight and become pillars of society, but this business gets into your blood, Frank, believe me, and I honestly don't think I could give it up now. [He laughed.] I like that. I 'honestly' don't think I can give up crime. Some choice of words, eh? Anyway, I don't mind mentioning their names now because, if you're listening to this tape then as I said, it'll mean that I've been unable to come back and retrieve it, in other words that I'm dead. And my two erstwhile colleagues will be the ones behind my death, so to hell with them — my betrayal of them will be nothing to the way they will have treated me. It's an 'honest' betrayal: it'll only come into effect in the event of their already having betrayed me. So, fuck them. Here goes, two of the biggest gangsters in the country.

You may even know one of them. He's one of your lot, a vet by the name of Val Crowther? He's a psychopath, money mad, power mad, a control freak. I've known him for years. Be careful of him, Frank. Don't go near him — he'd kill you himself or have you killed as quick as he'd sink a pint, and the pint would mean more to him than your life, than anybody's life. He can, to put it mildly, be irrational.

The other one I can talk to. His name is Albert Conroy,

the shrink you often see on TV. He's not as violent as Crowther, or at least I don't think he is. I've known him for years, too. I've worked with both of them on and off but we're not partners. We each like to freelance, so, at any given moment, we'll each be into something different.

For instance, neither of them has any connection whatever with my jewellery shop business and, by the same token, I have no connection with their scams.

Conroy, I know, is doing highly paid research at the moment into what he calls 'psychological interrogation' — mental torture, to you and me. He's been at it for years — it's at least three years since he told me about it one night when he was stoned, maybe four. He develops fiendish contraptions and drug cocktails to induce all kinds of paranoia — don't ask me how it works or even if it works. How all this came about was that he got to know a bloke — I think it was at medical college, because the bloke is a doctor, too — who later became president of . . . [he mentioned one of the smaller countries in West Africa]. *So this tinpot dictator with blood on his hands up to his oxters, being a medical man, decided it would be a better idea to break minds and spirits rather than tear flesh and bone, as the others of his ilk do. He figured that if there were no physical wrecks coming out of his jails and interrogation centres, no photographic evidence of whip marks, burnings, no missing toenails, ears, limbs or genitals, then Amnesty International and others like them would leave him alone and, compared with the others, he'd look like Mother Teresa. And hand in hand with his Mr Nice Guy image would come grants and loans in great profusion from every Aid organisation in the world!*

(I thought of my blind room and understood now, at last, why it existed. I wondered fleetingly whom Conroy used as his human guinea-pigs because his room obviously couldn't work with compliant volunteers who knew what was going on. You couldn't 'pretend' to believe you were *terrified* at the thought that you had been struck blind.)

Anyway, Conroy soon became his dictator buddy's overseas agent for the supply of medicines and medical equipment for that country and, for a while, everything was legit. After a bit, though, the president was going broke – he was building palaces and huge statues of himself, and the budget for medicines was going down and down. But the country needed the same amount of medical supplies so Conroy and the president worked out a deal – Conroy would buy slightly out-of-date drugs which were due for destruction, repackage them and sell them on to his presidential buddy at a reduced rate. So everyone was happy and, in most cases, the drugs still worked. I believe these things lose their potency gradually? You'd know more about that than I would.

Starting from that, Medineeds recruited 'staff' in most of the main European drug companies and was soon getting its hands on vast quantities of recently expired drugs. It was dead easy, easier even than recruiting guys for industrial espionage. All you have to do is mention the word 'merger' – or better still, 'takeover' – to a forty-five-year-old employee and he sees staff cuts, his job being one of them, and realises that he is now almost too old to get another job. He feels betrayed by the company to which he has devoted his working life and scared stiff of a future on the dole. Many of them will take the extra cash and, with all the pharmaceutical firms merging like the clappers these days, Europe is awash with shit-scared, middle-class, middle-aged middle-managers who still have ten years to go on their mortgages and ten years of education for their kids. I could get you fifty of these guys in a morning's work, with as many phone calls. In fact, that was my main job with Medineeds: finding these guys and bending them.

The huge profits came from buying these just-expired drugs for next to nothing and then flogging them on to the dictator's rubber-stamp government at what looked like very fair prices. Of course, the dictator got a sweetener into his own Swiss bank account, too, every time. So nearly everyone was happy – the sick people got reasonably okay medicines, the government looked great, the dictator got his divvy, Medineeds made a fortune, the guys providing the pharmaceuticals made good money and the companies themselves lost nothing, as the stuff was on its way to being incinerated anyway.

But the most important benefit for Medineeds was that their huge illegal profits enabled them to undercut the quotations of other bodies for legitimate tenders from organisations like the UN, NGOs and even countries with properly enforced standards and reasonably straight politicians. Needless to mention, to these we supplied only top-class goods, but at a giveaway price. By pretending to be a philanthropic outfit, Medineeds could explain its low prices – it was not trying to make a profit, while the others were. What the company was really buying was legitimacy and a good name. In the meantime, the trade went on with every corrupt state they could find and that, unfortunately, takes in most of the so-called developing world.

In my line of . . . em . . . work, this would be considered good business and it was easy enough to square it with my conscience: these poor people couldn't afford the cost of the very best medicines, but they could afford to buy sufficient quantities of a slightly lower quality, so it was better than nothing. Like serving them sirloin instead of fillet. Well, not quite, but you know what I mean . . .

It all went along nicely until last week when there was a huge outcry in the media over a batch of children's vaccines which had not been inactivated properly and which, instead of preventing polio, actually caused it. I'm told this is not the first time this happened but that other time was a genuine, if horrible, error. In the present case, which you may remember reading about, hundreds of children in the Caribbean had been infected with live polio virus and WHO authorities expected the final number to be in the thousands. There was a follow-on story about other recent disasters – contaminated baby milk in Africa, which killed hundreds of children before the cause was found, so-called malaria tablets containing only a tiny dose of the active ingredient . . . It was while I was reading this story, Frank, that I began to realise that Medineeds wasn't just supplying slightly out-of-date drugs. I recognised all the countries and organisations as ones that Medineeds had supplied. I recalled sending the polio vaccine to the Caribbean months before, the malaria tablets to India . . . Medineeds, I realised with horror, was to blame for this, this carnage.

Although you may not believe it now, after listening to this tape, I do actually have some principles. They may not be very high but I draw the line at the wholesale murder of thousands of children . . .

I thought about it for a day then, one by one, I contacted the European 'moles' and asked them casually if they had anything for us. Most of them had some out-of-date stuff, but several reported batches of products which, for one reason or another, had been rejected by quality control. I asked them why exactly the goods had been rejected and each of them expressed surprise that I should ask; neither of my colleagues had ever shown an interest in that before.

My two fine specimens of colleagues had been buying this reject stuff without telling me and seemingly had been doing so for ages. Cutely enough, any dangerous or potentially lethal stuff does not go out under the Medineeds name. They use a different name each time and use it only once. And need I say that this stuff that's rejected by quality control goes straight to government contacts in whatever lucky country they happen to be 'helping out'. I'm not sure, but I've got a suspicion that they're now beginning to ship the stuff without any labels at all, certainly to a few countries. [Here he listed four of the world's weakest and most abjectly impoverished nations.] *It goes in bulk to packaging factories owned by guess who? The president, his family and henchmen, and it wouldn't surprise me if it turned out that they know which is the dangerous stuff and deliberately supply it to the few clinics scattered about in rebel areas of their countries. At least, that was what one reporter hinted at.*

And so the argument began. I was furious and told them so. I was livid because they were doing it and I was also livid because they hadn't told me about it. Conroy says he thinks we should probably try to avoid the more seriously contaminated products, but I get the impression that he's only saying what he thinks I want to hear, trying to calm me down.

Crowther, on the other hand, disagrees totally with me: as far as he's concerned, the best that these kids, the few that survive dysentery etc., will ever have to look forward to is famine, civil war, constant ill health and an early death from AIDS, or being butchered by some local warlord who wants to be the big cheese. He was very angry with me the last time we met and as good as told me that if I didn't get back on the job there'd be trouble. With Val Crowther, that means only one thing. Which is why I'm making this tape. Conroy, like I said, is making conciliatory noises but I can tell that he too is worried and I don't trust him a bit. Stands to reason, doesn't it? For all they know, I may suddenly have turned against them and I know far, far too much.

[A self-deriding snort came from the speakers.] *And, I suppose, I didn't really help myself either. Dickhead that I am, I told them that I would have to think about it. You can imagine how that made them feel. Anyway, I've got to see Conroy the day after tomorrow to let him have my decision: I'm the one who asked for the few days' grace. I said I needed time to think it over but what I really wanted was time to make copies of all the disks and generally try to get myself some bargaining power. I'm surprised they gave me time, really – there's so much at stake. I usually deal with Conroy through his office. We hide the business side by pretending I'm a bona fide patient and we do a perfect background. We have, of course, absolute privacy in his consulting room and I pay for my consultations. I assume he keeps a file on me and my supposed psychiatric problems. God only knows what he writes in it.*

At the moment, I think Conroy has Val under control. That's a big assumption, but I think he must have because, left to himself, Crowther wouldn't have given me two minutes' thinking time, never mind two days. Unfortunately, this might soon change. Crowther will be working on Albert, grinding him down, and if he can convince him that I'm liable to spill the beans then Conroy will be every bit as ruthless. The trouble is he'll be much more subtle.

I've got one very serious weak point, Frank, and there's

not much I can do about it. Believe it or not, I'm a sucker for,
above all things, hypnosis. You probably are too – you should
have it checked it out. It could easily run in the family. I
never knew that there were different degrees of receptivity or
whatever the term is, but apparently there are and I, it seems,
am a pushover, a fucking dawdle! I know this because Conroy
actually treated me for giving up smoking. I'd tried to give up
a hundred times on my own but, in the end, I had to ask for
his help. He found he could put me under just like that [I
heard a faint finger-snap in the background]. *We used to*
laugh about it once, but now it's not so funny. It's all very
well me hiding all this stuff in the old man's hidey-hole but if
all they have to do is put me under and ask me where it is . . .

There was a pause of some duration – I thought the tape had
run out. Then he resumed.

To try to protect myself against this . . . mm . . . weakness, I
went to another hypnotist yesterday and had him hypnotise
me and condition me always to answer a question concerning
the location of the disks with the reply: 'They're with my
solicitor.' He tried getting me to answer the question 'Is that
the truth?' with a 'yes', but that didn't always work because it
seems that I respond with a 'yes' no matter how the question is
phrased which, of course, would be a total fuck-up if they
asked me if I was spinning them a yarn. Then we tried to get
me to respond to a second question about the location of the
disks with 'They're in my bank'. But there was no guarantee
that any of this double-cross hypnosis crap was going to work
so I got him to give me tips about how to resist hypnosis
without the hypnotist noticing, and I'm hoping, if it comes to
it, that I'll be able to pretend I've gone under and answer the
questions as if I'm in a trance. I don't know, Frank. I'm
scared. For the first time ever, I'm scared. I think I'm in
serious danger.

'You should have come to me, Dave!' I cried aloud. 'God,

why didn't you at least call me?' I was losing it, talking to a ghost who lived only on a spool of magnetic tape . . .

But of course Dave continued on through my outburst and I had to rewind to see what he had said.

—rious danger. You may be wondering why I just don't deny the existence of any copies at all, but the fucking computer logged it and recorded my own personal password as the one which had been used to open the files. I tried to eliminate the record but I'm afraid my cyber-skills don't stretch to that. I could have smashed the whole fucking system, I suppose, with a sledgehammer, but somehow I don't think that would have saved me. In our game, coincidences don't exist — there's always something behind them. So, Frank, I'm seriously scared right at this moment. I'm not sure if this is the same fear people feel if, say, they are being wheeled into the theatre for a dicey major operation or if there's something else involved. I don't think it's fear for myself because, in this job, if you get involved in any real way there's always some guy who's trying to muscle in on your action, or who's pissed off because you've muscled in on his and, obviously, we can't take each other to court to settle disputes about unprincipled business methods. So what the hell, if there's something big involved, then people will do nearly anything to protect, or promote, their interests. And Medineeds has got to be one of the leading scams in the country today.

But there's another reason why I particularly wouldn't like to get myself killed at this moment. It's stupid, I know, but I've met a woman, Frank, and suddenly I find that all my plans for the future include her. I'm not good at the sloppy stuff unless I'm just making it up so that I can get into some bird's knickers, but with this woman I can't even imagine telling her lies. Apart from anything else, I think she'd see right through me. I've only just met her and I don't think she has a clue how I feel — I'm afraid of scaring her off. I've booked on to a fucking geology field trip that she's leading, for Chrissakes! This time next week, all going well, I'll be perched on some outcrop looking down on Marrakesh, beating the shit out of some innocent rock with a little hammer and watching the Sahara sun set behind Rachel Donaldson. She'll have an aura of gold all around her and she'll hear that my hammer has stopped banging, so she'll turn her head towards me and see me looking at her . . . [He gave a short bark of sad laughter.] *Dream on. My worst nightmare at the moment – apart, that is, from getting myself killed by my buddies – is that Rachel will have brought a steady boyfriend along. Shows how crazy I am that I never even checked this out before I signed up for the chain gang. Anyway, Frank, she has no idea about this, how I feel about her. If the worst comes to the worst, please tell her what I've just said. I don't know if I could give up the evil-doing but I'd certainly be willing to try hard for her sake. At the moment she's a lecturer at UCD – in geology, of course. However, by the time you get to this tape, if you ever do at all, she may be a grandmother and have no idea what or who you're talking about. You'll be a toothless, doddery old fart by then, so she'll probably think you're just loopy, senile. I'll bet, though, that she'll be a beautiful granny, serene and calm and wise.*

There was a long pause before he resumed and I could tell that he had had to impose some discipline on his voice, control the tremor he'd ended with.

The other contents of the case are self-explanatory [he continued brusquely]. *The five keys are all for safety deposit boxes and I've left you the addresses and numbers on the PPP3 disk. Those boxes are full of cash, Frank, a lot of cash. Crime pays, Frank. Big time. It also kills.*

There's another set of copies of the Medineeds disks in my wall safe at home. They don't know about these because I made this lot from the copies, on another machine. As far as my friends are concerned I've only made one copy. The safe is hidden behind the mirror above the basin in the bathroom. Just press in the top two chrome studs and give them a quarter-turn clockwise, then half a turn anti- and another full

*turn to clockwise again. The mirror will then hinge down like
a shelf. The combination for the safe itself is on PPP3. Don't
lose that PPP3 disk whatever you do.*

I wondered if Curley had found the safe. If he had, then it
must have been empty because the Medineeds disks, if he'd
been able to decode them, would have had Crowther and
Conroy off the streets in no time and they were still very
much at large. A more likely scenario was that the safe had
been found by Crowther and Conroy, and opened, because
they'd never have been stupid enough to kill Dave if they
thought there was even a chance that he might have hidden
evidence away which might subsequently be found. They
couldn't act until they had their copies; the computer had
already logged the fact that he had made the copy, but only
one.

The way I saw it they would have hypnotised Dave, got
him to tell them about the safe or, if they already knew of its
existence, maybe just the combination; then, when they'd
found the floppy disks containing the dynamite on Medineeds, decided that Dave was no longer to be trusted and
finished him off, making it look like an accident or suicide.

For six months they'd have thought that they'd obliterated
all traces and then I'd walked into Conroy's rooms, asking
awkward questions about an uncashed cheque. In the
background I was vaguely aware of Dave's continuing words,
but again I had to rewind to make sure that I missed nothing.

*A word of warning, Frank. I'm not sure how straight you are.
I mean I think you're a chronic good guy – if I hadn't
thought that I might have broached the subject of a little
cousinly scheming more than once. Well, just in case you
decide now to make some big money out of Crowther and
Conroy by dangling this tape and the disks in front of them,
plan it down to the last tiny detail. Ask for enough to see you
through in luxury for the rest of your life – they make
literally millions every year from Medineeds alone, so don't be
shy. Set it up through several layers of go-betweens, have a*

new identity ready and then vanish. Puff! Gone! Because, Frank, Crowther for sure and probably Conroy, too, will have you ground into hamburger meat if they ever trace you. It's true what they say: when it comes to that pair you can run but you can't hide.

I can't think of much more to say. It's funny not knowing when, if ever, you'll be listening to this . . . [He gave a little laugh.] *I mean, do I say, I hope that you and Claire will be very happy? Or should that be: are very happy? Or: have been? Or: were? Or: used to be?* [There was another little chuckle at his own predicament.] *Whatever. You know what I mean. Or should I say 'meant' . . . Oh, shit, let's not start that again.*

My solicitor, details on PPP3, has my will, which leaves the lot to you, Frank. Who else is there? Poor old Dad is just about breathing. [Another laugh.] *Jeez! I hope you don't get to read this before I actually am dead or you'll be out to nail me even more enthusiastically than Val and Albert. But I've instructed the solicitor not to inform you until a year after my death, just to let things cool off. And to let the money cool down. Some of it is distinctly hot at present. Say no more. I'm not going to tell you where it came from in case your conscience gets the better of you and you start wanting to give it back. It may even be legitimate. Think of that! From private, totally legal business interests. Hopefully, I'll have time to make another set of copies of the Medineeds disks, which I'll leave with the solicitor. If I do, then you'll receive all this in a year from now, so Rachel will not be a granny and you'll be, I'm sure, the same rock of sense and probity, if that's the word I want.*

Speaking of private business interests, I've already spilled the beans on Albert's sideline, so I don't see why Crowther should be spared — I told you he was an egomaniac, didn't I? The veterinary business is only a cover. Or maybe a hobby. I know he loves it. But Medineeds is where he makes his money. Apart from that, word has it that he's gone into kidnapping in a big way — got a gang together and all that. Maybe he's

*planning to move to Sardinia and he's just getting his eye in
as it were. Or is that Corsica? One of them, anyhow.*

*I've also heard that he's your man if you want a horse
knocked off for the insurance. Mind you, from what I hear,
by the time Val gets his share of the payout there's not an
awful lot left over for the owner. There are guys in this town
who will knock off people for a tenth of what Val charges for
a fuckin' horse.*

Frank? [There was a pause.] *I know I'm just waffling
now, trying to think of something to say, anything to spin out
the contact. I reckon I'm coming near the end of the tape
anyhow — I don't even remember it switching sides* [neither
did I] *but it must be near the end. Jesus, that sounds awful.
The End. It makes me shiver. Anyway, the tape has been
made at last. It's taken me two days to work up the courage to
start it. It's so depressing, like all things to do with your own
death — making a will, buying a plot in the cemetery, only
worse. It's like . . . I don't know . . . like choosing your own
coffin or watching your grave being dug.* [Then came a huge
sigh, of despair, it sounded to me.] *But I'll tell you what,
Frank — it's ten times more difficult to end it, to say goodbye.
Well, hell, how about that! I've just said it, the magic G-
word. It's going to have to do, Frank. Once is enough. I'm
sorry if you feel personally let down by me, but . . ., it's too
late for me to change my ways now. Perhaps if I'm still alive
next month . . . and if Rachel responds to my look at sunset on
the mountains above Marrakesh . . .*

The click noise came again and I assumed that was that. As I
reached over to press 'STOP', the tape sprang briefly into
life again: *'Eh, I love you, kiddo. Okay? Look after yourself . . .
And, Frank? Live your life for both of us, aye?'* The tape
clicked off again.

But not before I could hear that Dave was crying.

So was I.

EPILOGUE

Actually, I wasn't that honest after all, because I immediately set about editing the audio tape with the greatest of care. Ironically, I did it all on the Hi-Fi system that Dave had given me for our last birthday. I made a new tape which omitted all references to the safety deposit boxes, the solicitor and anything else that would lead Curley to Dave's treasure. I left in the bit about Rachel Donaldson: he already knew about her and also it portrayed Dave in a goodish light, talking about giving up crime. How pathetic, I thought.

In all, this took a day and a half – I was extra careful and double-checked every single step – if I'd got anything wrong it could have been disastrous. I spent another day tussling with my conscience. Should I not just turn everything over to Curley and let him and the courts decide how to dispose of it?

I couldn't work out whether I was just fooling myself or whether I genuinely believed my reasoning when I decided to keep all that information private, at least until I asked questions about how the courts might dispose of it. I reckoned that it probably would have little to do with the merits of the individual claims, but lots to do with how high-powered the claimants' lawyers were. And, I reckoned, the lawyers would end up with most of it anyway. I decided I'd rather see myself getting it than those greedy bastards. So I deferred my decision and resolved to say nothing to anybody about it for the moment, not even to Claire.

On Claire's computer I made a new PPP3, transferring from the original only those files needed to get into the Medineeds disks.

Dave's killers must have had some anxious moments after I escaped but, as day replaced day without anybody challenging them, they had probably begun to believe that I had been telling the truth when I'd said I knew nothing of their precious disks. They may have wondered how, precisely, I had landed up in Conroy's rooms asking his receptionist strange and disquieting questions, but there was a vast difference between that and having access to really incriminating stuff.

Three days after I'd escaped I rang Curley and asked if we could meet for lunch.

He was inclined to refuse. 'Is this social or is it about Ryder's death?'

'It's not social,' I answered.

'Well, in that case, I'll take a rain check. I've got enough on my plate right now.'

'I've found Dave's killers and I've got hard proof that they are also mass-murderers.'

He guffawed derisively at that and said, 'Oh yeah? How many people have they killed, then? Ten? Twenty?'

'No. Thousands. I swear. I'm not joking you.'

There was a long pause, but in the end he said okay, maybe we should, after all, do lunch.

While Curley and his people went through the decoded tapes, verifying all the details, I moved to a hotel. I did so on Curley's advice, although I'd been thinking of it myself anyway – sitting at the computer in the apartment, I'd felt distinctly uneasy, listening for furtive footsteps on the stairs, a surreptitious testing of the door handle.

A quick check had shown Curley that neither of the suspects looked like he was getting ready to flee, so it was decided not to arrest them until a thorough checking of the charges made on the tape and disk could be done. After all, arrested suspects could only be held for a certain length of time without being charged, so Curley wanted to have his charges fully ready to go.

The local police were asked to check up on the Dark Horse to see if they could find out just who had given me the knock-out drops the night I'd ended up in the ditch. Curley had been reluctant to take this step in case Crowther got to hear of it, but even in this we got lucky. Fortune had ceased to smile on the owners of Medineeds.

One of the waiters hadn't turned up for work the night after. He'd got himself totally plastered and had attacked the car and house of another man whom he suspected of trying to steal his girlfriend. He'd smashed windows in both car and house before he was arrested, and had slashed the upholstery in the car. When his pockets were checked at the station they found almost £300 in cash. He claimed he had won it playing poker but couldn't remember the names of any of the other players. He was still being held in custody, mainly for his own protection, as the one who owned the car and his brothers were said to be on the watch for him. On hearing this, Curley had immediately instructed the local police to tell the waiter he was going to be charged with robbery as an elderly couple had recently been terrorised and robbed at their isolated farm and, without a proper explanation for his 300 quid, he was suspect number one. In less than an hour they rang back to say that Crowther's business manager, George Kilroy, had shown the waiter a picture of me and given him £400 to slip a small pill into my dessert. As a joke, he explained. The pill was a very strong laxative, he'd claimed. Some sense of humour. £400 for a lousy joke? Pull the other one!

When it finally happened the arrest of Crowther and Conroy came as a complete surprise to everyone, especially them. They were taken simultaneously on the dot of 4 p.m. Crowther was picked up at his surgery in Breenstown while Conroy was stopped on his way to the TV studios. The charge was first-degree murder – Dave's – plus a whole heap more to be worked out later. The country was abuzz that evening.

Within days the news went international. There were arrests in several European countries and, in many Third World countries, whole populations began to see their blood-soaked rulers for what they actually were. The UN held meetings. New safeguards were discussed. It had all passed away out of my hands.

In the days that followed I made several attempts to contact Rachel Donaldson but kept missing her. She seemed to do endless fieldwork. Some months later I tried again, only to be told that she had taken sabbatical leave in order to lecture at the University of Nairobi. I wrote a short note explaining to her that I was merely carrying out Dave's last wishes and hoping that she would not find the enclosed (severely-edited) tape upsetting in any way.

Several weeks later a letter arrived back. It wasn't much longer than the note I'd sent:

Dear Mr Samson,

I thank you for taking the trouble to pass on David's tape. Although I barely knew him, my tears when I heard his voice brought home forcefully to me what I felt for him. I developed a strong and immediate attraction to him, but after just a few hours' conversation I knew there was an evasiveness about him which could have no part in a good and lasting relationship. I said to myself then and I still say it: What a fine man and what a tragic waste.

I remain, yours sincerely,

Rachel Donaldson.

I couldn't have put it better myself.

About a week after the arrests of Crowther and Conroy I met Ellen in Dublin, in Bewleys in Grafton Street. For a change, she had rung me and asked if we could meet for coffee. Seated by the fire, we spoke of the two men at great length. I let her rattle on as she seemed to be trying hard to steel herself to broach an awkward topic and the only awkward topic I could think of was the abortion.

Apart from not wanting to rush her, I had given her my word that I would never again bring up that subject, so I just sat and waited and listened. Eventually, after the third coffee, she managed to find an opening.

When she had found herself pregnant, she had been devastated. But, she asked, hadn't she already told me all this? I nodded and said 'most of it'. Having made up her mind to go ahead with the abortion, she had approached, not Dave, but his friend, Val Crowther. She hadn't wanted to tell Dave in case it ever got back to me.

Crowther had had quite a name at the time, as he had animal drugs – prostaglandins, I assumed – which were said to do the job nicely. (I suddenly remembered his friend, Liam McMurrow whose pregnant lady friends seemed always to have 'fortuitous miscarriages' – so much so, in fact, that local gossip had it that he might have a 'dose' – and I wondered if Crowther had been supplying him at that time.) But Crowther had been unable to help because 'his medicine' didn't work until much later in pregnancy and Ellen could not wait that long as Laurence was due back. And so he had introduced her to his friend, Dr Albert Conroy, who had been only too willing to oblige.

She cried a few times but it seemed to me to be now more from sadness than from the awful guilt which had racked her for so long.

Then she asked me about the snake ring. Had I found it? I said I hadn't.

(As a matter of fact I still haven't gone back to the jewellers to collect it – and I'm not sure that I will).

We talked for almost an hour, until she said she had to go.

I kissed her goodbye on the bustling street in bright sunshine and watched her walk away towards St Stephen's Green until the crowds and the flower-sellers, the poets and the pipers, closed in around her and she was gone.

She hadn't turned to look back, not even once.